To Emma,

SEDUCING HOPE

ADALINE WINTERS

Thank you for your support.

Adaline Winters

For Nanny Carol, who made me believe in magic. I hope I make you proud. But if you're reading this from your perch in heaven, please skip the sex scenes.

C haos.

She was created in anger as a punishment, a weapon of devastation, a sacrifice. She was never meant to survive. She defied the gods to become something more. Darkness himself feared her. Molded from earth, sculpted with water, forged in fire, and cooled by air, she could not die, for she was never born. Life and death knelt before her, as have so many since creation. An eternity of suffering is her destiny, until she will be called upon to surrender.

Chapter One

Natia

A Taurus speaks two things: sarcasm and truth.

Gravity is a medieval torture rack stretching my limbs, and my joints feel ready to dislocate. My arms sway, and my legs are numb.

I blink. My eyelashes flutter several times before I make out the faint beam of moonlight streaming in through the dusty, oblong window at the bottom of a solid concrete room. Odd—windows aren't normally at the bottom of walls. Running water trickles nearby, and the pungent smell of mold with an undertone of feces stings my nostrils.

Something scuttles across the ceiling. My eyes track the tiny shape as it scampers, but soon, it multiplies. Two, four, no, eight… forget it. There are too many to count. Fur brushes against my fingers that still graze the low ceiling. Jerking my hand away, I squeal—it squeals back. Tipping my head to get a closer look at the creatures, I swallow, trying to soothe my sore, dry throat.

"Rats," I mumble, watching their unmistakable long tails whip above my head.

My lazy eyes rove the dim room, and I'm shocked to find that I feel surprisingly… calm. My heart beats in a slow rhythm, and my breathing is deep and even, as if I'm half asleep.

"Natia?" a weak voice croaks.

"Eve?" I slur at my friend and roommate. My throat feels constricted, and my thoughts swirl about in my head. I try to hold on to them, but they're consistently tugged out of my grip as my muddled mind struggles to focus on my surroundings. Where was I before this? I shake my head—what is happening to me? I don't remember drinking.

"Are you hurt?" I ask her.

Soft sobs flutter fearfully from behind me. "I'm okay..." Her voice is trembling. "They jumped us on our way home. They kept going on and on about how weird you are and that the boss 'has to see it.' W-what are they talking about, Nat?"

"I don't know," I mumble. Idly, I worry about Penny, our new kitty, my first pet. Am I really going to fail as a pet owner because I've been kidnapped?

My eyes snap open as the furry balls screech high-pitched, excited noises and scurry away. Rhythmic pounding along with the click-clack of heels signals the approach of several people. I try to move to the corner of the room, but my limbs won't cooperate, and my attempt makes me nauseous.

"I can't see it," an unfamiliar, silken male voice drawls behind me.

"She's shielding." A shrill woman's voice this time. A pair of beaten-up sneakers, pink stiletto heels, and expensive men's shoes come into view as my body sways toward them. I frown as the pink stilettos move closer to me. A sharp pain explodes in my stomach when she pummels her fist into it. I grind my teeth, forcing the scream back down my throat.

"Who are you? Where am I?" I demand the three pairs of shoes lined up in front of me, trying to sound formidable, but the slur negates my efforts. The pair of beat-up sneaks shuffles forward. My

4

scalp stings when he uses my long braid to yank my head to the side, making me hiss. My brain struggles to catch up as the world tilts on its axis.

His round face comes into view. Greasy blond hair obscures flat gray eyes, and his thin lips curl into a smirk. "You're at Four Seasons, sweetheart. Now be a good girl and drop those shields to let my boss see your pretty colors."

Excellent. I've been kidnapped by crazy people, because normal kidnappers wouldn't be enough for Natia Waterford.

He slaps my face. Their footgear flashes past me as the room rotates, first clockwise before reversing its course and settling back to its original position. I reach out to return the slap, but he's been replaced by Expensive Shoes. Staring up, a niggling feeling tells me something isn't right with this scene (apart from being kidnapped). Pinstriped, navy blue, trouser-clad knees shield his feet as he crouches; then a handsome man in his forties with a trimmed beard and intelligent green eyes stares at me.

My gaze rakes over him. "Why are you upside down?"

He chuckles. "I think Bass gave you too much sedative. It'll wear off soon."

I roll my eyes. "Why don't you people give straight answers?"

Warmth envelops my cheek as his large hand cups it. A slow smile spreads across his face. "You really are quite beautiful."

"Still not an answer," I mutter.

"So, Natia Waterford, would you like to tell me what you are?" Expensive Shoes asks.

"Bored, tired, and a little thirsty," I quip. Apparently, my superb sarcasm intensifies in times of extreme duress.

His hand slips from my face to caress my throat. I swallow, and the pressure of his thumb against my windpipe increases.

I give in and confess, "I'm a dancer."

"Hmm… I can imagine." His gaze runs over my body. "But I mean, *what* are you?" His voice loses all vestiges of friendliness.

I dart my gaze around the room again. Some of the rats huddle underneath a chair leaning against the wall, squabbling to get farther away from whatever kind of crazy is happening. For the first time in my life, I wish I was a rodent. My vision blurs as he gives me a brief shake.

"Stop! I don't understand," I tell him.

Pink Stilettos sighs. "Are you human?"

"Of course I'm human. What kind of question is that?"

My synapses spring to life, and connections spark, allowing me to make sense of the world again. Glancing "down," I find my feet attached to hooks. I'm dangling from the ceiling of a room in the sewers with three crazy people—oh yeah, and they think I'm an extra-terrestrial.

Expensive Shoes turns toward the others. "Describe it to me again."

Beat-up Sneaks shuffles about excitedly. "She was glowing."

My hands smack across my mouth to hide an escaped giggle.

"What color?" Expensive Shoes continues, ignoring me.

Oh, this is priceless. I'm a glowing alien.

"Different ones, with a shiny outline," Beat-up Sneaks tells him.

I lose it. Blame it on the stress of being kidnapped, drugged, or hanging upside down for too long, but I lose it. In a futile attempt to control my thunderous laughter, I clutch my aching stomach.

Expensive Shoes frowns at me like I'm insane. "Get the girl."

My chest tightens, and my heart races. Pink Stilettos tip-taps her perfect heels out of sight. Scuffling sounds accompanied by a symphony of pained cries blare behind me. Eve is dragged into view by her hair and thrown at Expensive Shoes's feet. Her pretty hazel eyes are rimmed with red, and pink blotches mar her flawless complexion.

Expensive Shoes catches a tear trickling down Eve's cheek with his thumb and licks it. This guy really freaks me out. He smiles, showing his commercial-worthy teeth. "Drop your shields, Natia."

I focus on Eve, trying to silently reassure her it will be okay. "I don't understand. I don't have any shields."

Expensive Shoes grabs Eve's short dark hair and slams her forehead against the concrete floor without breaking eye contact with me. Eve screams in agony as blood trickles down her face.

"I don't know what you want me to do! I don't understand—"

A thousand diamonds explode across the floor, cutting me off. A gray cylinder the size of a can of beans rolls into the center of the room from the broken window, releasing a dense fog and filling the room in seconds. Maybe the mothership has returned to rescue me? Expensive Shoes mutters curses as he sheds his clothes. I want to close my eyes, but I'm so confused about the impromptu strip that I can only stare. "Aren't you a little old for a starring role in *Magic Mike?*" I mutter.

A terrifying roar vibrates across my skin, raising every last hair on my arms. Clenching my jaw, a primeval urge to stay extremely still takes over. I curse the slight sway of my body, torn between leaving it be and using my hands to steady myself. I shiver, and my breath mists the air as the temperature drops, my shorts and summer halter top offering little protection. Scanning the smog for the source of a sudden steady, rhythmic growling, I risk using my fingers to spin myself around. Hot breath passes over the base of my exposed neck. Ignoring the pain, I grind my short nails into the concrete in an attempt to stop spinning. It's not enough. My eyes remain wide open as I await my fate.

Two sets of solid black orbs hover inches from my face. Blindly, I reach behind me to grasp Eve's hand as she continues to sob quietly.

"Guard her!" Expensive Shoes barks.

A grunt sounds from one of the creatures, blowing a decaying animal odor in my face. I swallow the burning bile boiling its way into my mouth. An extended snout pushes into my hair, earning it a nip to its neck from its twin. It pulls away with a snarl. Both creatures have four sets of sharp black fangs that hang over pale, translucent skin pulled tightly over bone. A familiar pair of sneakers lies underneath one of the beasts' bellies.

My eyes widen. "Beat-up Sneaks?" Large, triangular, pointed ears angled toward the back of its body twitch in response. I glance at the second creature, confirming my suspicions when a pair of pink stilettos sits upright before it. I'm processing the ridiculous notion that two people have turned into unidentifiable canine creatures when blue fire whizzes underneath my dangling head to lodge firmly in one beast's gut. Stunned, my mouth gapes open. What I fail to realize is I'm about to be covered in demon dog, so when he explodes, I get a mouthful of barbequed meat.

I'm still spitting it out when I feel eight sharp points vibrating against my neck as the rhythmic growling begins again. I freeze. Obsidian pupils glare at me in accusation.

The sensation of something otherworldly prickles across my body. An electric-blue flame concentrated into a fist-sized ball circles the room, looking for its target like a heat-seeking missile. The beast applies more pressure. Two points sting as they pierce my throat. I hiss—a senseless reaction, as it pushes the fangs deeper.

Closing my eyes, I attempt to shut out the danger and run through the ways we could get out of this alive, but my fantasies are interrupted by the sound of approaching footsteps.

I drop Eve's hand; she whimpers in protest.

"Play dead," I whisper. Surprisingly, she becomes silent. I let myself go limp.

"Heel," a deep, masculine voice rumbles. The beast snarls around my throat. I continue to play opossum, but my heart beats double time. "You were warned," the same voice growls. A slight scrape against my neck and an animalistic whine make me rip my eyes open. The blue fire is attached to the rear of the beast, dragging it out of sight through the smoke.

I tremble as silence surrounds me like a precursor to my death. Then I jump as a seemingly disembodied hand grazes my ankle. Swinging up, keeping my core tight, I manage to head-butt him in his crotch, providing me with a small window of time to steal the holster on his waist.

Gasping, I drop the gun as my foot swings down, striking his head. He stumbles away. He must have inadvertently released one of my feet, and I'm now in a vertical split pose. If I wasn't a dancer who'd recently been in rehearsal, I would be in some serious pain.

"Fuck. You could be a little more grateful," his deep voice grumbles.

I blink at the newcomer and grab the sleeve of his long brown leather coat, pivoting on my foot. Warm chocolate brown eyes partially hidden by unruly, dark, wavy hair meet mine. Despite being upright, this guy is staring down at me—he's at least six-foot-three compared to my five-foot-six.

Stubble outlines his strong jaw. I'm not sure if it's intentional, but it suits him.

Eve stands up, and relief floods through me. She wobbles but manages a small smile.

I grip his firm biceps. "Please tell me you don't think I'm an alien."

He grins. "Why? Has the mothership not come to rescue you yet?"

I slap his arm, laughing. "No way! I was thinking *you* were the mothership! Wait. Is this really happening, or am I still dangling upside down with Beat-up Sneaks, Expensive Shoes, and Pink Stilettos having bizarre delusions of rescue?"

He chuckles, moving my hands to his chest, and stretches to release my other ankle. "No, you're very much being rescued. As for the strange delusions, I'm not sure. I'm assuming you're referring to the shoes as people?" He picks up one of the discarded sneakers, pauses, then gives me a closer look. I squirm; I feel like I'm in an X-Ray machine. "Huh. Aren't you a little too calm for being kidnapped?"

Eve grasps one of my hands, moving it from his chest to her shoulder; her fingers remain threaded with mine. Her smile wobbles, and tears form in her eyes. As they fall, they mix with the blood dripping from her forehead. "She's a bit odd. Doesn't really seem to process danger like the mere mortals we are."

The guy guides my foot to the floor as I huff, "I admit it *is* a weird personality trait. The more stressful the situation, the more sarcastic I get."

The stranger opens his mouth to reply, but Expensive Shoes, who suddenly comes into view as the fog dissipates, speaks first.

"Duncan. It's been…"

"Too long," my rescuer—who I assume is Duncan—mumbles, spinning around toward the familiar voice. I take a step backward and brace myself, then my mouth drops open in shock. Gone is the handsome man with striking green eyes. In his place stands a leering beast of a man. Inky tattoos slither across his chest and down his arms, which end in long-fingered hands with dangerous hooked claws.

"Lawrence," Duncan states, his tone bored and his posture relaxed. Lawrence grins, showing the same black fangs as his demon dogs.

"What the fuck?" I mutter, my mind reaching its quota for craziness this month. Eve clasps my hand and hides behind me, her entire body trembling.

Lawrence's curious gaze flicks to me. He tilts his head to the side. "I can see you now, my little Iris. What are you?"

I point at him as he steps closer; Eve's grip turns vise-like, so I can't go far, even if I tried to run. "I think we've established *you're* the 'what' here."

Lawrence studies my finger for a second before dismissing me and addressing Duncan. "Can you see it?"

Duncan nods.

My gaze scans the room. "See what?"

"Is she yours?" Lawrence drawls.

"Yes," Duncan replies stiffly, positioning himself closer to me.

My mouth drops open. "I'm most definitely *not* yours."

Duncan sighs and rubs a hand over his face.

Lawrence laughs. "Then you won't mind me taking her."

Lawrence shoots across the room in a blur; a sickening crunch of bones sounds in my ear, and strong arms wrap around me, forcing the air out of my lungs. Black, curved claws dig into my ribs as the world starts to spin, and darkness blots the edges of my sight. We stumble as blue stars erupt in my vision, and everything comes to a sudden halt. A blue net of electrical sparks surrounds me and Lawrence.

Duncan leans against the wall with his hands in his jeans pockets.

"Where are you going, Lawrence? I can't let you take the girl."

Lawrence wraps his hand around my throat for the second time. "He will be eager to find out what this pretty little Iris is. She doesn't even know."

I purse my lips. "Why do you keep calling me that? My name is—" He cuts off my words with a squeeze of his hand, and I thrash about, trying to stomp on his feet.

Lawrence sniffs my shoulder. "If nothing else, she will make a tasty meal."

I stiffen. They were going to eat me? I think I preferred being an alien.

"You and me both, sweetheart," Duncan mutters under his breath. He pulls a knife out of each pocket, the moonlight glinting off the sharp blades as he palms them. I frown. *Did I say that out loud?*

Duncan circles us like a lion deciding on its best direction for a kill.

Lawrence pivots, using me as a shield. Halfway around, I spot Eve lying still on the floor. Glazed hazel eyes stare at me, unblinking. Her temples have been crushed, resulting in a surreal-looking skull, like a deflated doll.

My hand flies to my mouth to stop the scream on the tip of my tongue. Focusing on Duncan, I push down my panic and force myself to breathe evenly. After two rotations, my suppressed terror has morphed into rage.

My heart pounds in my ears. Before I can lose my nerve, I lean back into Lawrence's body and wrap my hands around his neck. Tipping my head back, I try not to flinch when he smiles, his black, gleaming fangs elongating. He arches an eyebrow and tightens his hold on my waist, pulling me closer.

I lock my hands behind his head and give Duncan a surreptitious glance, hoping he can read my intent; otherwise, this net is about to get very claustrophobic.

Bending my back, I use my body to toss Lawrence over my shoulder.

The net vanishes, and he crashes against the wall. I blink. I'm not that strong… must be the adrenaline.

Lawrence springs to his feet, scooping up the gun I dropped earlier. A belligerent grin accompanies his obsidian eyes.

Three events happen at once; a thunderous *bang* reverberates around the room, perforating my eardrum, Duncan lifts his hands, and I instinctively jump in front of him.

Chapter Two

Natia

Tauruses have a winning mentality. They go into something with a do-or-die attitude, and giving up never crosses their minds.

Four years later.

Heavy rain obscures the abandoned warehouse as I squint through the windshield to analyze our surroundings. Dangerous possibilities lurk in the rain and shadows. The only working street light illuminates the front entrance to the warehouse with a neon orange glow.

"Where is he? Maybe we should issue department watches to our marks so they can turn up to their own demise on time," I grumble.

Duncan glances up from the unusual leather-bound book written in some kind of hieroglyphs, which he has perched on the steering wheel next to the clock on the dashboard. As our resident language expert, I'm not sure there's a language the guy can't read. "It's only been five minutes."

"If you were five minutes late for a bus, you'd miss it. If you were five minutes late crossing the road, you might get hit by said bus. Besides, I have a date."

Duncan scoffs then quickly stiffens as I shoot a glare his way. "Sorry... I was just..."

"Just what? Shocked that I could get a date?"

He scratches his chin. "Well, you are a bit... prickly."

"What the hell is that supposed to mean?" I give him a playful shove.

He chuckles. "Really, though—who is it?"

I give him a wink. "*The Real Housewives.*"

He snorts. "I see your priorities are in order."

We fall into companionable silence, each of us tracking any small movements. This particular demon is skilled in causing doubt and was being strategically placed in juries to ensure certain clients would be found innocent. We are luring him to the warehouse under the pretense of hiring him on behalf of a sports star who crashed his car into a house while high on drugs.

After New York, my world combusted with the knowledge that we aren't the only species at the apex of the food chain, and we were in fact being hunted, preyed upon, and used as fodder for a wide host of supernatural beings that enjoy toying with human lives. Decisions were made, life-altering ones, which led me and Duncan to a fast friendship and a joint interest in protecting humankind. We aren't without our own power; with the support of an international secret government agency, my enhanced senses, and Duncan's magic, we are a force to be feared and admired.

Something shifts in the distance. I squint as a dark figure emerges from around the corner before disappearing into the front entrance of the warehouse. "Is that our mark?"

Duncan follows my focused gaze. "I can't tell… Let's wait—"

I jump out of the car. "Let's not."

Duncan utters a curse and follows me, but waits outside. Entering the warehouse through the back door, I get my first glimpse of our target lounging against some old wooden pallets—a bald, stocky guy in his fifties with mean-looking tattoos decorating his skull and neck.

He resembles an ex-cage fighter with a name like "The Destroyer" or "Knuckle Duster." I move forward at a casual pace, my heavy footsteps echoing throughout the expansive room, announcing my presence.

Knuckle Duster (yes, that's the nickname I'm going with) pulls himself up to his full height, using the pallets as leverage, and saunters toward me, his hand prematurely outstretched. "You must be Dana. Where's your colleague? Fox, right?"

"Really, an *X-Files* reference?" Duncan chuckles into the earpiece.

I smile and keep focused on him. "He's running late," I answer.

His eyes flick to the tops of the swords sheathed at my back. He smirks and shakes his head as two other people stroll through the door and flank him.

"They think the joke is on us," I mutter under my breath so only Duncan will hear.

"Help?" Duncan enquires.

"Not yet. You need to be our surprise."

"So, Dana," Knuckle Duster drawls, "you're not here for business, are you?"

I halt my approach, leaving twenty meters between us. "Depends on your definition of business. For me, that's precisely what this is."

The man on the left skims his eyes over my body. "She's tiny, boss. Let's just kill her and go back to the bar."

"Agreed!" the woman on the right exclaims, examining her fingernails.

Knuckle Duster waves his hand toward me with a bored expression. "Go ahead."

The woman drops her hand and gives me a slow, sly grin. She prowls toward me, her lithe body making her movements almost cat-like.

I smirk, which wipes the grin off her face. Clearly, she expected me to be scared. My heightened senses feel the shift in air currents, alerting me to her attack, and the flex of her arm muscles gives away her first move. I duck as her fist whizzes over my head and hammer mine into her stomach, sending her sprawling.

She rights herself and flips her ice blonde hair over her shoulder. I meet her calculating gaze as she analyzes my body. Her movements are quicker this time, but I anticipate the strike, my forearms taking the brunt of a double kick. I catch her foot and twist to the side, flipping her over.

She hits the floor with a heavy thud and lets out a sharp breath as the air is knocked out of her lungs.

"Help?" Duncan enquires again.

Standing over her unmoving body, I reach for my sword.

Before I can raise my arm all the way, she snaps her legs around my neck, cutting off my air, and tries to pull me to the ground.

I lean back, taking her with me so she's straddling my shoulders like a kid at a concert.

She sends her weight backward, flipping me over her. I groan as my head bounces on the floor.

"I'm good," I grunt to Duncan, springing to my feet.

"Get in there," Knuckle Duster snarls to the woman's partner, shoving him forward.

I run toward the warehouse wall and push against it into a high backflip, landing in a crouch behind the man. He turns around, confused. I kick his head, knocking him to the floor.

Less affected than I thought he'd be, he gets to his feet with a grin right as I feel long fingernails digging into my neck from behind.

I grasp the hands gripping my throat, and using them as leverage, jump and wrap my ankles around the man's neck so I'm suspended between my two attackers.

I rotate my body to the left, and the man's eyes widen in surprise.

Two of the woman's manicured fingernails snap as she hits the floor, while I land with graceful precision on my feet.

I wince. "Sorry. Those looked expensive."

Removing my swords, I rotate them in my hands and simultaneously slice their throats.

Crimson seeps across the dirt floor, collecting in a central pool; the corpses' lifeless eyes stare at each other, as if they died in a lover's pact.

Knuckle Duster moves swiftly. Sensing a more powerful enemy, I abandon my swords and twist the whip disguised as a belt around my arm. He grins. What is it with men and whips?

"Help," I whisper to Duncan.

My first lash catches Knuckle Duster on the ear.

He yelps, as his blood drips like a macabre ruby earring.

Eyes narrowing, he stalks toward me. I try catching his other ear, but he grasps the whip and, wrapping it around his wrist, drags me to him.

His fist slams into my gut.

I grunt and lean forward to keep my balance as the force sends me skidding backward. The whip follows me like a snake, throwing dirt into the air.

Plucking a dagger from my boot, I stab it in the floor to slow my momentum.

Knuckle Duster is in front of me before I can fully stand.

"Duck!" Duncan shouts. Doing as I'm told—a rare occurrence, so take note—I duck and roll across the unyielding dirt, missing a shot of blue magic by a hair's breadth.

"Be glad my reactions are as fast as Lightning McQueen's," I breathe, hissing at the pain in my back from the road rash.

Landing next to the woman's body, I yank my sword out of her throat.

Minuscule air movements tickle across my palms, giving away Knuckle Duster's next attack. Leaning back in a move worthy of *The Matrix*, I dodge a jab of his elbow to my throat, swing my leg out across the floor, and trip him backward while wrapping the whip around his neck.

His substantial six-foot-plus form hits the ground, and I hear the tell-tale sound of bones cracking.

Duncan scoffs. "Okay, I do love your references… but you got me on this one. Who's Lightning McQueen? Sounds like some UFC fighter. Am I right?"

I hold back a giggle and try to adopt an air of confidence. "He's a racecar driver. Drives for Disney, actually." Duncan tilts his head to the side, and I roll my eyes. "It's Pixar! *Cars?*" he gives me a blank stare, and I sigh. "Whatever."

Lying on the floor, the creep tries to negotiate. "Can't we make a deal? My name is Eric. I can persuade anyone to do anything you want. My employer is powerful—trust me, he could get you *anything* you want."

"Eric? I think I preferred Knuckle Duster," I mutter, causing him to frown. Channeling my inner feminist tendencies—if you ask

Duncan, they're more accurately called my "psychotic" tendencies—I kick him where every man dreads.

He rolls to his side, groaning. A putrid, clear liquid oozes over his entire body. Shedding his human form, his skin turns a vibrant shade of purple.

Duncan and I tilt our heads to the right.

"Death or defense?" I wonder.

"You bitch!" Eric snarls, springing to his feet.

Ah. That would be defense, then.

He blocks my first strike by sacrificing part of his arm.

Sniffing the air, I wrinkle my nose. "I smell burning."

Duncan punches Eric in the face. I grimace as I hear cartilage breaking, and something splatters across my face.

Eric staggers back, nearly tripping on an errant piece of rubbish. "My master will make you suffer for an eternity. He'll strip the flesh from your bones and feed it to the hounds of hell!" he screams.

Interrupting Eric's threat to damn us to eternity, Duncan pulls on the end of my braid and brings it around so I can examine it.

I whirl on him. "You singed my hair!"

Duncan's lips turn up as he uses his nickname for me. "No, Locks, you just weren't fast enough."

Eric advances again, his face twisted with rage.

He lashes out and catches my arm with his claws. Several stinging scratches dribble blood.

Using my irritation to put extra force behind my thrust, I swing my blade high and slice perpendicular to Eric's neck.

His head, now a vivid purple with lilac freckles, hits the ground and, like a bowling ball, bounces twice, spins to the right, and hits the warehouse wall.

I sniff haughtily. "I disagree—your aim is off. Seriously, when's the last time you practiced with those fireballs you throw around willy-nilly?" I examine my hair again and groan. "You're lucky it was just the ends."

Surveying the room, I point my finger at Duncan. "Your turn."

He shakes his head. "No way, I mopped up the nest of vampires last week. Anyway, you're already covered in…" He points up and down at my black combat gear coated in demon blood and guts. I stare at the ceiling, trying to get my annoyance in check.

"Why can't they go *poof?*" I emphasize by clapping my hands in front of me. "Like in the movies?"

Duncan scratches his beard. "Which movies?"

I try to think on my feet. "Buffy?"

"You're joking, right?"

I put my hands on my hips. "They get 'dusted' by the slayer. It's clean, it's neat, and Buffy goes home without getting sweaty. In fact, half the time she goes on a date or out with her friends afterwards and nobody is the wiser about her efforts to keep Sunnydale safe."

He stifles a laugh as he grabs my injured arm. Healing warmth suffuses my skin as he passes his palm over the scratches. "You know the name of the town Buffy protects?"

"And you do, too, by the sound of it," I retort with a grin. He looks away, but not before I catch the blush creeping up his cheeks. Ha, I knew it. He's a closet Buffy fan. The stinging in my arm diffuses, and Duncan lifts his hand away to reveal pink, fresh tissue.

I move my arm back and forth, testing the tightness of the skin. "Your healing power never ceases to amaze me," I mutter.

After our unique meeting four years ago, where I narrowly escaped being eaten by demons, Duncan trained me to hide my unusual aura—the thing the demons were attracted to in the first place. Some humans have extra abilities; I'm blessed with the psychic ability to see auras. I can perceive things beyond the physical senses (taste, smell, physical sight, touch), and it gives me access to the visual perception of the astral body, also known as "psychosoma." My power just needed a little honing. Since then, I've come to understand most people are a single color or hues of that color, unlike me. Demons, on the other hand, give off a variety of auras; unnatural power generally results in an unnatural aura. My regular mental shields are strong, but they need to be stronger in order to keep my aura hidden. The most effective method is to mentally sing songs, much to the amusement of Duncan and anyone else who can read minds.

So, I have constant background music playing in my head, which has become as natural as breathing. However, when my emotions flare, I add another layer of protection by purposefully singing any given song. The great thing about music? There's something that fits every situation, every mood. Take the time I found my Uncle Charlie in a compromising position in the pool house with a former teacher of mine—"Love Shack" by the B-52's seemed appropriate, until I accidentally sang it out loud to a very embarrassed Miss Jacobs. Still, they were once childhood sweethearts—who am I to judge?

Bagging the two bodies, a severed head, arm, and torso in clear plastic like some grisly dry cleaning, I drag them to the spacious trunk. As I drop the head into the trunk, the demon's milky eyes spring open; I jump back and let out a tiny squeak—not a good look for my carefully cultivated badass image.

Grinning, Duncan peers into the trunk. "He's still dead, Locks. It's just an involuntary reaction after death."

22

I straighten my spine. "I knew that, it just caught me off guard." I slam the trunk shut and stalk to the front passenger door.

Grabbing a clean cloth from the glove compartment, I sit in the front passenger seat with my legs dangling outside the car and begin cleaning my swords.

Sliding into the driver's seat, Duncan rolls his eyes. "Can't you do that at home?"

I give him my death stare, hoping to convey his imminent demise should he continue this conversation.

He ignores me. Guess I need to work on my death stare.

Chapter Three

Natia

As a Taurus, when life gets chaotic, music is your stress reliever.

T he razor-sharp blade glistens as the cloth runs along it, and my feet bounce to the beat of Guns N' Roses's "Patience." Duncan shakes his head but gives me a few minutes to finish before starting the black SUV. I know, so predictable for a secret organization that kills supernaturals.

Laying my shiny swords on the back seat, I swing my legs into the car and sit awkwardly, trying to avoid getting the leather seats dirty, as no doubt I'll need to clean them, too.

Duncan glances at me. His lips twitch. "It's pointless, Locks; you'll need to clean the seats anyway."

Grumbling, I realize he's correct and relax. "In the upcoming bid for funding, we should suggest employing a cleaner for these tasks."

Duncan chuckles. "I can see them going for that instead of, say, the latest weapons technology or improved surveillance equipment." I concede the point but sulk the rest of the journey.

Twenty minutes later, I'm hauling the last of the bodies across the concrete floor in the underground garage of the Seattle SIP headquarters to the morgue for inspection and destruction. The SIP, or the Supernatural Intelligence Protection (evidently, they didn't employ a marketing company when naming the department), is a secret government agency that investigates and destroys supernatural beings who are a threat to humans. There are over one hundred SIP departments across the US, and several hundred on the planet. They prioritize cases with the largest body count or the ones associated with the most influential people and companies. Politics.

Heading up the Seattle office is Charlie, also my uncle. Think it's a coincidence that a family member is heavily involved in a supernatural organization? It's not. My initial kidnapping was meant to lure Charlie into a trap—they got sidetracked by my weird aura. To top the secretive nature of my family, my grandfather's multi-billion-dollar company is also responsible for many of the weapons used to combat the creatures we face on a daily basis. So, while the Waterfords are human, we are deeply embroiled in the supernatural world.

Uncle Charlie, Duncan, and three other men stand by and watch as I struggle with the weight. I glare at them. What happened to teamwork? Having your back? Gallantry? Grumbling, I start singing "Patience" out loud for the benefit of all present.

Duncan snorts. "She's been singing that since we decided she was on clean-up duty."

"'Decided,' my ass," I grumble under my breath.

Uncle Charlie's lips quirk as he shakes his head. "Debriefing—command room, now."

I stare down pointedly at the state of my clothes and point to the various unidentifiable substances in my hair. "Can I have ten minutes to get washed up?"

"You can have five," he replies crisply over his shoulder as he marches away.

Groaning, I hotfoot it to the showers.

Ten minutes later, I stroll into the command room, having scrubbed my skin pink and detoured to the kitchen for some chocolate Whoppers and water.

Uncle Charlie's eyebrow tics. "You're late."

"Sorry, couldn't find a towel. I could've come naked?"

Uncle Charlie's round face turns an interesting shade of red. No, wait… it's more purple, an unpleasant contrast with his silver hair and moustache. The rest of the team snigger but don't comment; infuriating your commanding officer further isn't wise.

Plonking my ass in the chair next to him around the lengthy oval table, I braid my long, damp, caramel-blonde hair. Uncle Charlie insists I cut it shorter—he believes it could be dangerous if someone were to get a hold of it in a fight. I countered I could whip it around to blind someone. Let's just say we agreed to disagree.

As well as myself, Duncan, and Aaden—the best intelligence and surveillance expert in the world (sometimes I wonder if his brain is coding in green zeros and ones like *The Matrix*)—Zee, Joan, and Jack, our newest recruit, are packed into the command room. I notice immediately that something is off about Jack—his red aura has become clouded. But what else is new, really? The guy has been nothing but rude to me ever since he arrived. He catches my stare and scowls. In my usual fashion, I give him a sickly-sweet smile then proceed to ignore him. True, I can be polarizing at times… but it's a

26

bit annoying to be immediately disliked by someone I barely know. All the same, I take another quick glance at his aura. Auras are generally positive, but they can become faint or clouded depending on someone's mood or recent experiences. I had covertly checked out Jack's personality test, but it didn't reveal anything negative from his past. Huh. Maybe he's just naturally sour?

Uncle Charlie's voice cuts through my musings. "How did you do it?"

Shit, I'd zoned out and missed what we're talking about. Sorting through the most probable questions, I decide on the obvious— "How did we kill the demons?"

I steeple my fingers together. "I took care of the man and woman first. After a fight with my whip, Duncan used his blue balls of power, I rolled and put him on his back, then he oozed this strange, clear liquid. Finally, I took his head."

Everyone stares at me with wide eyes, like I'm Medusa incarnate. "What?"

A blush creeps across Aaden's cheeks in contrast to his porcelain skin. Zee doubles over laughing, holding his stomach. He takes every opportunity to make fun at my expense—of course, I reciprocate. We have a love-hate relationship. Granted, it's at least seventy percent hate on any given day, but it fluctuates depending on how much he's annoyed me.

"What?" I repeat. Clearly, I didn't answer the actual question.

"I asked how… never mind." Uncle Charlie shakes his head.

His sunset aura brightens with emotion, and my own strengthens in response to my growing embarrassment. I start mentally singing "Gettin' Jiggy Wit It." Childish, I know.

Duncan snaps his fingers in front of my face. "Locks, pay attention."

I glower at him. Catching my expression, Aaden lets out a low whistle, his floppy charcoal hair obscuring his eyes.

I sing, *"Big Willie style's all in it, gettin' jiggy wit it!"* at the top of my mental voice.

Duncan, who is gulping his water, chokes and sprays it over the table, landing some on Zee. Perfect.

I pat Duncan on the back, mouthing, "One, one," to Zee, indicating today's score. He scowls, and his gaze promises retribution. I wiggle my fingers and smirk. "Bring it on."

Uncle Charlie clears his throat, gaining our full attention.

"Whilst Aaden was collecting intel for this operation, he discovered links to a much larger issue." He slides each of us a file. "Archan Reinheart is the CEO of Reinheart and Hunter. He and his partner, Michael Hunter, own the largest legal company in the US. They provide every kind of legal service available, from criminal to contract law. They're expensive, and with good reason—their success rate is higher than any other competing company. This was your mark's employer."

I open the file, revealing a typical executive photo. However, Archan Reinheart is anything but typical. He exudes strength, confidence, and a dark, dangerous sensuality. His dark blond hair is tied back to show penetrating hazel eyes, verging on gold. He has sun-kissed skin and full lips. I imagine undoing his hair, letting it fall around his face, then running my hands through the strands while placing soft kisses along his jaw…

Agh! Concentrate, Natia. Grabbing another Whopper, I nibble the outside. What can I say? Eating helps me focus.

Returning my gaze to the photo, I skim over his oval face with its square jawline then notice the suit, which does nothing to hide his sculpted body. Unwittingly mesmerized, I jump when Joan kicks me under the table, her ice blue eyes sparkling. Duncan glances at me. Checking my mental shields, I find the tiniest crack. He's a tough trainer.

Perhaps Def Leppard's "Pour Some Sugar on Me" isn't the most appropriate song to be singing right now. He raises an eyebrow, and I stare him down. Well, I try, but blink first. I tilt my head, deliberating if he's a snake or a fish, given they don't blink at all.

Uncle Charlie continues, "Reinheart has been a silent CEO for the last ten years. About eight months ago, he became active in the company. His return ties in with the disappearances in the area." He pauses, indicating the report of the recent spike of disappearances in Seattle.

Six men and women of varying ages, ethnic backgrounds, and social status have disappeared in the last seven months, the only link being they'd all been in contact with Reinheart and Hunter at some point. I think back to the fight. "Eric mentioned his powerful master. Could that be Reinheart?"

Uncle Charlie frowns. "Who's Eric?"

"The demon, his name was Eric."

Zee shakes his head. "You made friends with a demon? Only you, Natia."

"It would be one more friend than you have," I deadpan.

Uncle Charlie ignores us. "We need to infiltrate his inner circle and get close enough to find out if he's involved with the disappearances. But our primary objective is to find out *what* he is." We all stare at Uncle Charlie. "Our plant determined he's not human, but she can't identify what he is. She no longer has access to his inner circle, so we've pulled her out."

Surprised, I blink. "Who's our plant?"

"Lauren," Aaden responds.

I gaze down the table at him. "I thought she was on sabbatical leave?" Astonished I didn't know this, I turn back to Uncle Charlie. "How long?"

He schools his features. "Two months."

"She gained some access, but it was confined to... social occasions," Aaden explains.

I tense. "Define 'social occasions.'"

When Aaden doesn't answer, I whip my head to Uncle Charlie. He looks away. "She was his escort," he eventually says.

My jaw drops open. "You're joking."

Aaden raises his palms. "Not like that. She just escorted him to functions."

I turn back to Uncle Charlie. "And you believe that's where it ended?"

He nods once.

Chewing my lip and continuing my rendition of Def Leppard to lock down my emotions, I roll my head to ease the knots in my neck and shoulders then gulp half my bottle of water, wiping my lips on the back of my hand. "So what's the plan?"

Aaden and Uncle Charlie share a look and switch their focus to me. I immediately get an uneasy feeling. Aaden explains, "Your grandfather is merging with a company on the East Coast. He's employed Reinheart and Hunter to oversee the negotiations. You'll be one of Waterford Industries' representatives here in Seattle. Your grandfather will oversee the East Coast. You're expected to attend major meetings, negotiations, and any social events pertaining to the merger."

Like I said, a small but well-funded department of my grandfather's company provides the SIP with many of its weapons and invests heavily in weapons research on our behalf. So he knows about the SIP and what we do.

I stare at my uncle. "You can't be serious. I know nothing about mergers or legal stuff. I was an arts student, about as far away from business as you can get." He adopts a patient expression, preparing to indulge me in my rant. "Send Aaden or Joan—they're excellent strategists and will be able to keep up with the legal lingo!"

Aaden gives me a reassuring smile and pushes his dark hair back behind his ears. "Don't worry, I'm coming as your advisor. I won't let you make a fool of yourself. Well, not too much, anyway."

"You're the only one who can read his aura, Natia. We need to know definitively what he is, and you can sense his power signature— further clues to his origins. Duncan will be on hand if needed, and Zee's coming as your personal bodyguard," Uncle Charlie adds. Zee meets my eyes with identical horror. Appears he wasn't in on the plan either. Zee opens his mouth to argue, but Uncle Charlie puts his hand up, his classic signal for it's a done deal, don't bother arguing. Zee huffs in defeat.

Uncle Charlie squeezes my shoulder. "If we change the plan, we'll need a different cover story, given that Aaden and Joan aren't the grandchildren of Matthew Waterford. This would take time we haven't got, and given this cover contains elements of truth, it's more believable."

I shrug his hand off my shoulder and stare at his stern blue eyes, just a shade lighter than my own but crinkled in the corners with laughter long forgotten.

My voice is quiet, meant only for him. "I thought you valued my opinion and input... but clearly, I'm mistaken. You *know* what going back to the life of high and mighty society will cost me, who I might bump into. People betrayed me—that life is dead to me. I'll do it because my commanding officer is telling me to. But as your niece, I'm disappointed and hurt you didn't talk to me about this."

He grinds his teeth, offering no apology. Stubbornness is a Waterford family trait.

"It's unlikely you'll see him, Natia."

"Who?" Aaden asks.

I sigh. My past is exactly that—*my* past, and it should stay buried. But in the interest of full disclosure, my team should know.

"We will be entering the world of Seattle's elite, privileged assholes. Which includes my ex-fiancé, Dalton Miller."

Zee leans forward, his gaze boring into mine. "What happened?"

"We had fundamental differences in relationship philosophy."

Zee tilts his head, studying my no doubt tight features. "That shit. I'll knock him into next week and out of our path if we meet him."

Rubbing my forehead, a deep breath expands my lungs. Working with secret government agents means working with exceptionally perceptive people. Duncan gives my back a soothing rub as Uncle Charlie and Aaden describe the rest of the plan. We will be moving to my grandfather's penthouse apartment in Seattle tonight. My grandfather insisted Reinheart oversee the merger himself. He agreed. Our first meeting is at 10 a.m. tomorrow.

"When was the last time you visited your house?" Aaden asks me.

"Two days ago. I'm on top of my visits."

We each have homes we frequent at least twice a week. Mine is a guest house I've commandeered on my grandfather's estate. The rest of the time, we stay at HQ.

The SIP is located below a legitimate security firm, Crown Security Inc., which doubles as our cover identity. From the outside, the building resembles a typical business unit. The ground floor has a reception desk and various offices, while the lower level houses the SIP. It holds the command, medical, gym, and training rooms. The lowest floor is the living quarters.

"Natia?" I hear the hesitancy in Uncle Charlie's voice and meet his eyes in challenge.

"Charlie?" I reply, ice coating my tone. He winces. When he doesn't say anything further, I stand and head to my bedroom. I'm halfway through the living and kitchen area when Aaden catches up with me and grabs my hand, forcing me to stop.

"Natia... it needed to be on a need-to-know basis while we formulated a plan," he pleads.

I glance at Joan and Jack, who are leaning against the pool table with cues in their hands, not bothering to be discreet as they eavesdrop.

I stare at the floor. "Did it really, Aaden?"

Aaden's tall frame looms over me. I'm the smallest and, at twenty-five, the metaphorical baby of the team. All of the men are over six foot, and even Uncle Charlie is six-foot-one. I wonder if that's a prerequisite for joining?

Aaden squeezes my hand, and I meet his gaze. Even though I'm mad, my heart softens. His intelligent, steel gray eyes are filled with worry. "Natia, please... You know it has to be like this sometimes."

I'm too heated to continue a conversation about this. I pull my hand out of his grip and march to my bedroom to pack.

Tossing my dirty clothes in the laundry basket and clearing my king-sized bed of my laptop, Kindle, and journal, I throw my suitcase on the bed and consider my wardrobe. Given the majority of my time is spent running after demons and fighting, I own jeans, combats, leather pants, T-shirts, tank tops, a leather jacket, and a few dresses I wear on the rare occasions I go out—but nothing suitable for a boardroom. Duncan appears in my doorway, startling me. I can't decide if he teleports or just moves fast. I asked him once. His response? "I have a knack of being in the right place at the right time." Typical Duncan—dodging the question.

One of the most feminine statements I've ever spoken falls from my lips. "I have nothing to wear."

Duncan leans against the doorframe and arches an eyebrow. "I came to tell you that your new wardrobe has already been delivered to the apartment." My shoulders sag in relief. Wait, someone chose my clothes? Weird, but I can't muster the energy to care.

Duncan studies my face. "Are you worried?"

"Of course not," I grouch, throwing my arms in the air, "I can act like a professional business woman. Pretend I know what a merger is and understand the need for a legal team. I can sit in boardroom meetings for hours on end without falling asleep…" I groan. "This is ridiculous. I need to speak to Charlie. He's finally lost his marbles." I stomp forward. "Move," I uncharacteristically snarl at Duncan.

He ignores me. "Aaden will guide you—you'll be fine. Don't be angry with Charlie; he wouldn't have trusted you if he thought you couldn't handle it." He wraps his arms around me. I tense before relaxing into his warmth, taking a deep, steadying breath, and inhaling his unique scent of cinnamon, oranges, and fresh linens. His calmness strips away my anxiety and tension.

"Do you want me to come with you tonight?" he offers, resting his chin on my head.

I consider it. But if I'm going to pull this off, I need to be as independent, cool, and collected as possible. I bite my lip. "No, I'll call if I need you."

He pulls back and pins me with his stern eyes. "You better."

Yeah, he didn't need to work on his stares. He cups my face. "Don't let your guard down. We don't know who these people are, apart from dangerous. It's possible they can read minds, and if they can read auras, they'll find it odd you're shielding, but it's safer than them seeing it."

Four years on, and we still have no real clue as to the meaning of my unicorn aura (I nickname everything). What we do know is supernaturals are drawn to it—maybe out of curiosity, maybe because they know something we don't. Despite popular sci-fi fiction portrayals of mind reading as a common gift, in reality for humans, it's rare. Given the business we're in, we have a small concentration of people with this gift: Duncan, Uncle Charlie, and Aaden.

Duncan places a chaste kiss on my forehead and walks out. Three seconds later, I stick my head around the door to say goodbye, but he's already disappeared down the long, stone-walled corridor. My money is on teleportation.

I chuck the essentials in my suitcase, including my journal. I use it to write down my strong feelings and thoughts to help my mind deal with them, making it easier to shield my aura. I lean on my suitcase, stuff in the protesting contents, and wrestle with the zipper until it's closed. Sighing, I take one last look at my personal sanctuary, already mourning its temporary loss.

In the garage, I meet Aaden, Uncle Charlie, Jack, and Zee, who I shoot a 'you better behave' look. He gives me an innocent 'what, me?' face, and I let out a derisive snort. Yeah, right. As if he didn't have trouble with a capital T written all over him. Despite our constant butting heads, I begrudgingly admit I trust him implicitly with my life.

Jack stands beside Uncle Charlie with a scowl that matches his clouded aura. Charlie barks some final instructions while standing with his arms crossed in a defensive posture, clearly anticipating a fight. I don't have the energy for the battle he's expecting, so I stroll toward the car, my suitcase wheels whirling against the concrete floor. I sense his guilt and almost turn back. But he needs to feel the pain, too. Pausing at the open trunk of the car, I begin to lift my suitcase. I groan as my muscles protest, still sore from my earlier body-lifting excursion. Zee sidles up to me and, with little effort, drops it in the trunk. I turn to thank him, but he's already getting in the driver's seat; sometimes that man surprises me. I sit in the passenger seat, and Aaden does some final preparation on his laptop in the rear.

Resting my chin in my hand, I gaze out the window as the familiar buildings of the business park recede, then the lush green outskirts of Seattle fly past, giving way to excessive traffic and steel structures that dominate the skyline, darkening the streets and judging those below like looming gods. Aaden and Zee remain quiet. Drawing in the heavy, clogged air, my lungs weigh down with every breath, and a nervous fluttering in my stomach forewarns me of the danger we are willingly walking into.

Chapter Four

Natia

Tauruses are stable, possessive, and stubborn. They don't like change, and they need to feel secure.

Stepping out of yet another black SUV, a valet takes the car keys from Zee, and a cute bellboy named Mark with dimples and curly, chestnut hair takes care of our luggage. "Good evening, Miss Waterford. The apartment is ready for you."

Zee raises his eyebrows. "Looks like we're expected."

"Yeah, my grandfather will have called ahead to prepare the apartment."

Aaden helps Mark load the suitcases on the trolley. "They know who you are?"

I nod. "My grandfather is the owner."

Zee hands me the purse I'd left on the back seat. "Ah, owner of the apartment."

"No," I say, jogging up the curved steps toward the lobby, "owner of the building."

My boots click along the opulent marble floor with elegant, gold, decorative edging. The scents of lilies and roses tickle my nose from the tall, fresh floral displays outlining the spacious oval lobby, creating a splash of color on the otherwise soft, neutral backdrop.

Warm light dances around the room from the central demanding, grandiose, antique crystal chandelier restored by my grandfather when he bought the building. I step around the sofas positioned underneath it to reach the curved oak desk at the rear of the lobby.

An elegant lady in her forties wearing a stylish ivory blouse and navy pantsuit greets us. "Welcome, Miss Waterford. It's lovely to see you again."

"Hi, Jannette." I offer a polite, thin smile. I'm too tired for pleasantries.

I gesture toward the guys. "Jannette, this is Zee and Aaden. They'll be staying at the apartment and will need full security access."

Zee steps forward, startling Jannette. She quickly recovers and appraises him. I cock my head, trying to view him from her perspective. Zee's broad shoulders complement his generous six-foot-plus height, and a well-defined chest stretches his black T-shirt, his muscles honed from years of fighting and training. His short, dark hair matches the five o'clock shadow that seems to sit permanently on his rugged face, giving him a slightly dangerous look, matching his personality. His spring green eyes have flecks of brown in the center. He's appealing, but Jannette is missing one important detail—he's a cocky jerk. There's time for her to learn, I suppose.

Zee smirks and preens under our attention, and Jannette blushes while I roll my eyes; like he needs an ego boost. Ten minutes later, Zee and Aaden's handprints have been scanned, giving them access to the private elevator and a set of doors to the apartment.

Upon entering the apartment, Zee strides down the hallway, I assume for security reasons rather than being nosy—but it's probably both. Aaden stands still, taking in the large open-plan living area with enormous, curved oatmeal-colored sofas in front of a wall-length fireplace. The entire apartment is a blend of rich gold and cream tones.

38

Taking Aaden's hand, I pull him to the balcony doors.

"Let me show you my favorite view in Seattle and give you a tour of the apartment." Stepping out onto the balcony, we're greeted with a magnificent view of Elliott Bay. I lean over the rail, watching the ferry boats and twinkling lights.

"It's stunning… Did you stay here often?" Aaden asks.

Turning away, I warm my hands over the yellow flames licking the air from the stone fire pit in the middle of the chairs and loungers.

"Often enough to call it a home. We used it when we traveled since it's closer to the airport."

Aaden's eyes gleam. "Did you travel often?"

"Yes. I'm lucky. Hong Kong, Australia, UK, France, Singapore, and more."

"That's incredible."

Zee pokes his head through the door and glances around the balcony. His eyes narrow on the steam escaping from a hot tub large enough for twelve people. A slow grin spreads across his mouth.

"Fancy a dip later?" He wiggles his eyebrows.

I roll my eyes. "Keep dreaming."

He chuckles. "Oh, I will."

My aching muscles beg me to get in and allow the jets to massage the sore spots. Before following Zee inside, I promise the tub we have a date soon.

We grab some water from the fully stocked kitchen, and Aaden picks some restaurant menus off the refrigerator and raises his eyebrows. "Wow, how the other half live…"

I don't explain all the ways he wouldn't enjoy "the other half" of life. I know my childhood was privileged. My grandparents gave me an excellent education and loved me unconditionally. But my life was full of constraints, expectations, judgments, and the lack of freedom to make my own decisions. Leaving Seattle for New York to follow my dreams and study dance at a prestigious arts school, I put an entire continent between me and that life.

I wave my hand between the two main floor guest bedrooms. "And here are your accommodations, gentlemen." I show them where the clean towels are kept and leave them to choose their bedrooms. Naturally, Zee argues about it despite them being almost identical. I shake my head. He would argue the sky is green, just for the sake of it.

Upstairs in the master suite, I fling open my suitcase and prepare to unpack when Zee appears in the doorway with his luggage. I glance at his bag then his face, raising an eyebrow in question.

"I'm taking the bedroom next to yours. It's closer—I can protect you better."

My fists clench at my sides. "No way. The bodyguarding is for *outside* of this apartment. I'm not sleeping next door to you. The bedrooms have adjoining doors."

He grins. "I know. Scared?"

A little, but showing weakness to this man would be dangerous. My chin lifts. "Not at all."

"I'll be next door then," he says, wearing a self-satisfied expression as he stalks away. Narcissist.

Realizing he's manipulated me using my inability to back down from a challenge, I growl. I hear him laugh. My mental shields kick in, selecting "Boombastic" by Shaggy. Can't beat that for clearing your mind. Aaden jogs up the stairs, taking two at a time, and stalks into my bedroom. He must consider personal boundaries optional.

His face wrinkles at my song choice. "What did he do?"

"Manipulated me into letting him take the adjoining bedroom."

Aaden rakes his hands over his face, and he lets out a tired sigh. "You've got to be kidding me... I'll handle it." With that, he storms out.

I walk into the closet with my clothes slung over my arm, ready to be hung up. I stall as clothes for all occasions greet me, including smart and casual outfits, fabulous cocktail dresses, and the necessary business wear.

What has me frozen is the coordinating underwear hanging with each outfit. My jaw drops open—underwear? *Underwear?*

Aaden and Zee come running into the closet. Zee whistles, focusing his attention on the underwear.

Spinning around and turning Shaggy up in my head, I repeat the mantra, "I must not kill my bodyguard."

"What the hell are you doing in here?"

Aaden blushes. "Erm... you were shouting 'underwear' at the top of your voice..."

I rub my hand over my face. I couldn't even differentiate between voicing my thoughts and internalizing them. Herding them out of the bedroom, I mutter, "I'm tired."

"We need to go over the strategy for tomorrow's meeting," Aaden pipes up before I shut the door.

"Can we do it in the morning?"

He sighs. "Set your alarm for 5 a.m. We have a lot of prep to do."

I groan as Aaden closes the door. Collapsing sideways on the oversized bed fully clothed, I fall asleep within minutes.

Waking at 4 a.m. in the star position I'd fallen asleep in, I climb between the sheets and roll on my side, trying to reach for that last hour of sleep. At 4:20, I give up and drag myself to the bathroom, stripping my clothes off as I go. Eyes barely open, I turn on the large walk-in shower, big enough for... well, more than two. Who needs that? I get the two people... but more? Sounds complicated.

Switching on the soft glow of the ceiling lights designed to resemble the stars at night, I undo my braid. My hair touches my hips. Maybe Uncle Charlie has a point. I shrug. Priorities.

Rifling through the contents of my bag, I locate my toothbrush. Digging deeper for the toothpaste, I groan when I can't find it. Glancing around the bathroom, I spot my favorite shampoo, conditioner, and body wash perched on the vanity unit.

I smile—bless my grandfather for his thoughtfulness. We hadn't spent much time together after my grandmother died of a sudden heart attack. I coped by throwing myself into my studies, taking extra classes, attending more rehearsals, and exhausting myself so I couldn't think of anything but work—effectively abandoning by family. My grandfather's heart broke, and I wasn't there to help him pick up the pieces. I was selfish, hardening my own heart against the pain. Even now, five years later, his aura holds remnants of his overwhelming grief, as does mine. We avoid the subject, and I try to avoid the guilt, shoving it away when it comes knocking.

Smelling like coconut and citrus, I step out of the shower and wrap a huge, soft, white towel around my hair then pull on a fluffy robe. I pad down the stairs; it's 4:45 a.m. I'm hoping I have fifteen minutes before the guys wake and start bombarding me with information.

No such luck.

The wall-length fire is lit, bathing the room in a soft light. Both men sit on a sofa with coffee cups in hand, Aaden's laptop open, and various documents strewn across the table.

I ignore them. Coffee *then* strategy. No... coffee *is* my strategy. I snicker at my own joke. Zee and Aaden turn to me.

"What, I can't find something funny?" They shake their heads in unison, probably correctly concluding I'm a little crazy, made worse by the early hour and lack of caffeine.

Nursing my coffee, I sit on the opposite sofa.

Aaden pushes a plate piled with various Danish pastries toward me. "Sleep okay?"

I nod but ignore the food. "What's the plan?"

Aaden hands me a few documents to read. "It's a preliminary meeting—should be straightforward."

"As for Reinheart, it's time to dig deep for the Waterford charm and make nice," Zee adds.

I nod. "I'll find something to talk to him about and take a read of his aura."

"Lauren describes him as an arrogant ass. Be prepared, and try not to let the stronger parts of your personality out," Zee continues.

I raise my eyebrows. "Are you insinuating I can't play nice?"

"I'm saying your default position of stubborn sarcasm is not ideal for getting to know someone."

Bristling, I glare at him. "I can be nice."

Aaden and Zee laugh.

"What? I can."

They laugh even harder. Zee's phone tinkles and vibrates on the coffee table. "Boss man" appears on the screen, and Zee grabs it.

"Hi, boss." He listens for a few seconds as Uncle Charlie talks then presses the loud speaker button and places his phone in the middle of the coffee table.

"Can everyone hear me?" Uncle Charlie asks.

"Yes. Go ahead," Aaden says.

"Natia?" Uncle Charlie enquires.

"Here," I grunt, like I'm answering a teacher at school.

"We have another disappearance. Mary Conway. Last seen five days ago. She's a legal secretary for a subsidiary company offering pro bono work for Reinheart and Hunter. Her neighbor reported her missing last night."

I rub my hand over my face. "Where was she last seen?"

The line crackles with the ruffling of paper. "Last Tuesday night, she had drinks with a colleague at a local cocktail bar. She set off walking home about 7 p.m., but she never reached it. Jack's here—I'll send him and Joan to her apartment, as you have your meeting today."

I groan at the mention of sitting in a meeting all day. I should be at Mary Conway's apartment trying to piece together what's going on.

Uncle Charlie sighs. "Natia, I know you're frustrated, but your job is to infiltrate this from the top. Leave us to do the groundwork."

"Yeah, Natia. Leave the hard work to me and Joan," Jack grumbles through the phone, his disdain spilling from every word. What a jerk.

Charlie leaves me with his version of a pep talk. "I'll update you with what Jack and Joan find. Do your job, but be careful, Natia."

We finalize a few bits. Zee's my official bodyguard. We decide not to take weapons to our first meeting since it may give a bad impression. *"Hi, my name is Natia Waterford. Oh, don't worry about the Sai swords strapped to my back—they're this season's accessories."*

Zee is the SIP's combat trainer, and from his teachings, I've become an excellent hand-to-hand fighter. Through a mixture of martial arts, he's taught me how to use my unusual strength and senses. I can feel subtle changes in air currents, helping me predict someone's location and moves—almost like a foresight. Not minutes before, but enough to give me an advantage. But I prefer my swords—they give me the badass look.

Back in my bedroom, I dress and put on my disguise. Clothes, makeup, hair—it's all designed to hide my real self. Now, I'm Natia, Matthew Waterford's granddaughter, rather than Natia, badass agent for a secret government agency.

I keep my makeup natural and wear a light mocha-colored, knee-length, fitted dress. The material gathers on my hip, accentuating my curves. I team the dress with the matching ivory, silk underwear and nude heeled pumps and leave my lightly-bronzed legs bare. My grandmother's diamond stud earrings are my only jewelry. I used to watch her get ready for parties and made her promise from the age of five I could one day wear the pretty earrings that sparkle. Smiling at the memory, I twist my hair into a classic chignon. With one last look in the mirror, I take a deep breath—game time.

Zee and Aaden stand at the door dressed in designer suits, Zee in the classic bodyguard black and Aaden in smart charcoal.

I look them up and down with appreciation. "Wow, you both clean up well."

Zee puts one hand on the knot of his tie and does a twirl. "You're not the only one who has a new wardrobe." They look me up and down as if they've never seen me before. Zee's gaze hovers over my breasts.

"What?" I look down at my dress, panicking that I've managed to stain or damage it in the thirty seconds since leaving my bedroom.

Zee gives me a wicked grin. "I remember the underwear that goes with that dress."

Asshole.

Aaden swings the apartment door open. "Ready?"

Glancing at the ceiling of the elevator we've just entered, I let out a long breath. "As I'll ever be."

Chapter Five

Natia

Taurus: Masters of the poker face because, under the chill surface, there's an anxious person ready to snap.

Stepping out of the limo Reinheart and Hunter sent, I crane my neck to look at the skyscraper; glittering glass panels reflect the rare sunlight we've been blessed with during this winter season, but the building appears to repel the warmth and light. I pull up the collar of my white wool coat against an icy breeze as goosebumps spread across my neck and arms.

Chanel, the human version of Barbie, greets us. I shake her well-manicured hand, then she speaks down to me in a condescending tone, fulfilling her stereotype.

"Good morning, Miss Waterford. Mr. Reinheart is waiting for you on the rooftop for breakfast." I school my features as she continues. "Your associates can get settled in the boardroom." I take a deep breath. Shit, this is the kind of opportunity we needed.

Chanel ushers me to a small glass elevator on the left of the lobby, while the guys are shown to the main elevator. Zee changes course and steps toward me. I give a subtle shake of my head. He meets my eyes, looking torn. He knows I'm more likely to get information from Reinheart alone. Clenching his fists, he shakes his head and returns to Aaden, who points at his temple, reminding me to shield my aura.

A tall man in a black suit waits for me in the elevator. I stop myself from rolling my eyes. Are all bodyguards issued with a special introductory bag containing the essential items of a black suit, white shirt, black tie, and a little communication device behind the ear? I bet he has sunglasses also, maybe even a little tool that zaps your memories; wait, that's *Men in Black*.

The doors close as he pushes the button for the roof, and the one below it reads seventy-four, making me swallow hard. My stomach drops as the lobby shrinks, and we begin to rise above the surrounding buildings, opening up to a spectacular view of Seattle.

"Come here often?" I quip. I instantly scold myself—really, Natia, that's your opening words to someone who may be in Reinheart's inner circle? He raises an eyebrow but otherwise ignores me. Seems I'm not the only one who hates pleasantries. We ride in silence, and I channel my inner diva with Aretha Franklin's "Respect."

The elevator comes to a smooth stop. Stepping out onto the roof, I gasp. The sides are lined with a tall, curved glass barrier, sheltering the lush green plants, bright exotic flowers, and trees that line the path leading to an oak gazebo. Oversized ivory drapes wrap around the legs, revealing a small table and two chairs. I look over my shoulder to the elevator, expecting the bodyguard to be behind me, but both have disappeared. The hairs on my arms stand on end, and I begin to regret the decision to not bring weapons. Forcing myself to relax my shoulders, I explore the roof. Roaming the path to the left, I find a glittering infinity pool. Yep, this guy has the serious millionaire ego thing going on.

A deep, smooth voice drifts over the skin at my nape, causing a small shiver to expand from my spine across my body. "What do think of my small paradise, Miss Waterford?" I hadn't felt the small changes of the air currents alerting me that someone was at my back.

I keep my body relaxed and resist the urge to turn around, continuing to touch the various plants. "It's extraordinary... a colorful oasis in the middle of harsh, gray, manmade, steel structures. A small haven to chase away the suffocating, stale air and oppressive, draconian darkness of the city. You've given life to a normally devoid part of the universe." I caress a vivid purple bloom hanging from a tree and run my thumb over its velvety texture.

Slowly, I turn to face Archan Reinheart, who's standing less than a foot from me. Leaning back, I suck in a small breath, inadvertently inhaling his scent. It's an intoxicating mix of rich dark chocolate and sandalwood, with a hint of vanilla. He watches me with curiosity. His eyes are a mesmerizing, rich gold with small, lighter flecks sprinkled around the pupil. He drops his gaze to slowly scan my body. Perusal complete, he refocuses on my face.

In the interest of equality, I grace him with the same blatant inspection. His blond hair is clipped back like in his photo. My eyes trace his sensuous, full lips then fall to the corded muscles on his neck, giving an indication of his toned body. I imagine his smooth skin beneath the crisp, white shirt and finish by running my gaze down his narrow waist and long legs. Power surrounds him like a cloak, seductive and dangerous. Retracing my path, I'm hoping I've made him as uncomfortable as he's made me. His mouth curves into a wicked grin. Guess not.

I extend my hand and hold his eyes in challenge. "Nice to meet you, Mr. Reinheart." He takes my hand, but instead of shaking it, he holds it inside both of his. Calloused fingers encircle my wrist, and power thrums across his skin. Heat caresses my hand, trails up my

49

arm, surrounds my neck, then drips like honey down my back. I fight to keep my breathing steady and calm. What the hell is that?

Smiling, he lets go of my hand just as the heat reaches the base of my spine. "Please, call me Archan."

Switching songs to AC/DC's "Highway to Hell," I think I see his lips twitch. His aura flickers like a flame, reds, blues, and oranges licking up his skin. I've never seen anything like it. Conclusion: definitely not human.

He moves with a lazy, feral grace toward the gazebo. "I thought we could share breakfast before the meeting," he rumbles over his shoulder.

Walking behind him, I keep a small distance, studying the movement of his muscles beneath his expensive tailored suit. And yes, I ogled his ass just a little. "Why?"

Reaching the table, he pulls out a chair. I guess gallantry isn't dead after all. I sit down on the plush rattan chair as pleasant warmth surrounds me from the overhead heaters.

"Your grandfather requested I look after you during the merger. I have looked into your background, and you do not have the education needed to represent your grandfather's company. Despite my objections, he insisted you take part. Dancing does not give you the skills to understand how a merger works. Dance is a…" he pauses, appearing to choose his words with care, "*specific* skill that does not involve the traditional core skills for business. Having not worked in the real world long, I need to prepare and advise you on what to say."

He rounds the table and sits opposite me. I straighten my spine. What an asshole. He tried to remove me from the team, insinuated my studies were useless, and indicated my IQ is questionable. A growl creeps up my throat. I swallow it and focus on the addictive sound of AC/DC's vocalist in my head.

Crossing my legs, I start tapping my foot to the tune. "I see... so you would have me work from a script, saying what you want me to say when you want me to say it?"

His gaze flicks to my foot.

"Yes," he responds as he starts to pour tea into my cup. I put my hand on top of his to stop him, and warmth drifts over my palm. He raises an eyebrow.

"I drink coffee."

He continues to fill my cup. "Tea is better for you."

Presumptuous jerk. I sense people do as he commands without question. Unfortunately for him, I've dealt with arrogant, egotistic men all my life. I stand, intending to return to the elevator to find some coffee. He narrows his eyes.

"Sit," he demands, an undertone of annoyance in his authoritative voice.

I arch an eyebrow. "I'm here for breakfast, and I drink coffee, not tea."

His jaw tics as a "Man in Black" appears behind me from seemingly nowhere.

"Bring Miss Waterford coffee. She is not able to recognize the sophistication of tea." I blink and move him to number one on my shit list. I'll update my journal later.

I sit, a little stunned. Walking away now would seem childish, despite my overwhelming desire to stick out my tongue at him. Ha, I bet that would get a reaction, but it would augment his opinion of my low IQ.

Archan picks up a silver knife and slices some of his croissant. "What do you know about the process of a merger?" I send a silent thanks to Aaden for his preparation this morning and take a small bite of melon.

"We're at the planning stage. The letter of intent has been signed, allowing us to enter the negotiations. Today, the advisors will introduce themselves, an approximate timeline will be agreed upon, and if time allows, discussion about the strengths, weaknesses, opportunities, and threats of the merger will start. I believe the common term is SWOT." I pause, holding his gaze. "Your role is to oversee the legal matters of the merger, not to interfere, and you *aren't* an advisor."

His mouth twitches. "You have done your homework, Natia—"

I interrupt. "Miss Waterford."

His eyes narrow. "Miss Waterford." The conspicuous man in black appears with a pot of coffee, and not a moment too soon. I pour myself a cup and take a sip. I grimace—it's decaffeinated. I glare at him, and his gold eyes dance with amusement. Well played, Mr. Reinheart.

Archan focuses on my face, giving me his full attention. It's unnerving. "Why are you really here, Miss Waterford?"

A swell of power makes the hair on the back of my neck prickle.

I take another sip of the disgusting, brown, *pointless* liquid before pushing it away. "I don't understand the question," I answer calmly. Humans wouldn't normally be able to feel the weight of the power currently being thrown at me.

He tilts his head, as if trying to read my thoughts. "Do you have another agenda?"

"I'm a shareholder, here to oversee the merger of my grandfather's company and ensure the heart of the business remains intact," I drone, as if his intelligence can't cope with big words. I eat a few pieces of strawberry. "What about you, Archan? You were nowhere to be seen until a few months ago. What have you been doing in your spare time?"

His eyes narrow. "I've been on sabbatical, learning new hobbies and relaxing. But it was time to come back."

I snort. "Well practiced, Archan. Are you going to be honest, or should I accept your well-constructed response, which answers nothing?"

He puts down his cup and leans back in his chair, inspecting me with more interest. "I had other priorities. Several projects needed my full attention." His eyes follow my hand as I spoon more fruit into my mouth, making me self-conscious. "What about you, Miss Waterford?"

"Excuse me?"

"Why did you choose to dance?"

"It's something I enjoy and I'm good at. I wanted to dance for a famous company."

"Well practiced, Miss Waterford. Are you going to be honest, or should I accept your well-constructed response, which answers nothing?" he says, throwing my words back at me. Guess I deserved that.

I glance at his smart black leather shoes. "Dance is a way to lose myself, but find myself at the same time. I have a second heartbeat that thumps only to the beat of my dance. When I dance, I breathe, the world disappears, and I follow my heart without fear. My feelings are exposed, and passion makes my walls nonexistent… I don't feel pain, I only feel free."

I look up. Archan's stare is so intense, I have to fight the urge to squirm. I return his stare, both of us caught in the moment. A strong wind whips around us, causing my napkin to lift from the table. I snatch it before it flies away. Archan frowns, glancing around. I do the same, but the source of the sudden gust alludes me—maybe there's a gap in the glass barrier?

Needing decent coffee and a reprieve, I stand and smooth down my dress; his eyes follow my hands, and heat flares in his gaze. Striding toward the elevator, I switch the song to Liam Payne's "Strip That Down." I immediately give myself a mental slap. Archan enters the small elevator behind me, and his arm brushes mine. The small space becomes charged with his power, transforming into something magnetic and dangerous. His exotic scent permeates the air, infiltrating my senses, making it difficult to breathe. Heat touches the base of my neck, strokes over my shoulders, then drops down between my breasts. I close my eyes and bite my lower lip in an effort to contain a moan.

"After you, Miss Waterford," Archan's smooth voice drawls. I snap my eyes open to find a hallway in front of me. Archan's eyes glitter. Scowling, I force myself not to run, noting we're on the seventieth floor. I was only in the elevator for five floors? Archan puts his hand on the small of my back, guiding me along the corridor to the boardroom. I walk faster to break the contact, but he matches my speed.

Aaden sits near the head of a large table while Zee stands behind him, adopting the typical bodyguard pose—hands clasped in front of his body, feet slightly apart. His stare tracks me. He looks bored, and the meeting hasn't even started; I suppress a giggle.

Spotting that Aaden has a cup of coffee in front of him, I search for its source. Archan signals the start of the meeting by asking everyone to take a seat. I have two choices: continue to search for the elusive coffee and ignore him, or conform and sit. Screw it, when everyone sits, I spot the coffee at the back of the room and make my way to pour myself a cup. I put in extra cream and sugar, salivating at the rich smell.

I turn around to find several people looking at me with a mix of irritation and surprise. I give them my brightest smile. "Apologies, I've come from a breakfast meeting with Mr. Reinheart, and he couldn't provide regular coffee." I catch Archan's eyes. He gives me a barely perceptible nod, acknowledging my small win.

I take the only empty seat between Aaden and Archan. Well shit, sitting here is going to be about as fun as meeting your dad at a strip bar on a night out. As I drag my chair under the table, my bare leg brushes against Archan's. I hiss softly as electric tingles dance up my leg. My eyes snap to his. He stares down at the table, but one corner of his mouth twitches. I tuck my legs under the safety of my chair.

Aaden elbows me. "Are you okay?" he whispers, leaning forward so his hair slides in front of his eyes. I nod, but he frowns, not buying it. What have I started? I've antagonized a powerful and dangerous man. His power hums around him, like I'm sitting next to a transmission tower, but I sense he's keeping its full force muted. My traitorous body doesn't help, happy with the sensations from his touch. I convince myself it isn't him and any attractive man would have the same effect. I aptly pick "Stuck in the Middle with You" by Stealers Wheel. Aaden snorts softly; at least someone is entertained. I tap my fingers on the table to the rhythm, and Archan glances at them then at me. Oops.

The meeting follows the format we prepared for. Introducing myself as Matthew Waterford's granddaughter, I describe my role as an overseer to protect the company's family culture. Edward Pearson, a man from Grant Ltd., the company we're preparing to merge with, enquires about my history and involvement with the company. I tell him about my internship in the accounts department and how I was later involved in decisions about the direction of the company (provided weapons development counts).

I'm leaning over the table involved in the discussion when Archan reaches for his glass of water, brushing his hand against mine. I flush and lose concentration mid-sentence, but manage to continue to make eye contact with Edward. Edward's brows knit together, then his expression changes as he studies the rest of my body. Excellent, now he thinks I'm interested in him. I kick Archan under the table, and he grunts quietly, not expecting it. Great, he's reduced me to childish behavior.

The meeting wraps up at 4 p.m., and we agree to meet at ten tomorrow morning to begin SWOT analysis (*get me with the lingo*). Archan stands at the door, thanking each person for coming.

As Aaden packs his laptop away, Edward makes his way over. Smiling, he holds out his hand. "Miss Waterford, it was lovely to meet you. I hope you don't mind me questioning you. It wasn't to be rude—I'm genuinely interested."

Shaking his hand, I give him a friendly smile. "No problem, Edward. Please call me Natia." Archan's head snaps toward me. I resist the urge to smirk. I don't know what the score is in this competition, but I need to remember we're here to find the missing people and figure out what Archan is. I'm supposed to gain his attention subtly, in a formal way. He turned the original plan on its head the second he invited me to—more like *tricked* me into—breakfast this morning. The second I met him, my false persona of "polite society Natia" fell away. His arrogance grates on me, but I think I have more chance of getting closer to him this way. He's used to being bowed down to, and he seems intrigued to have someone push back. That is, until he's had enough and pushes me off the roof.

Wishing Edward farewell, I head out with Aaden in front of me and Zee behind, doing his bodyguard thing, I suppose. I shake Archan's hand.

"Thank you, Archan, it was… interesting to meet you."

He smirks. "And you, Miss Waterford. See you tomorrow."

"The meeting starts in the boardroom at 10 a.m.?"

His smirk turns into a wide grin. "Indeed, it does."

Chapter Six

Archan

Unknown origin.

Zac's intel showed the girl had studied at a prestigious dance school. Her tutors talked about her dedication, energy, innovation, and her excellent form. On graduating, she earned a place with a famous company in New York and had a promising future. One month later, she left and changed her career direction, joining her uncle's security company.

I watched her step out of the elevator into the oasis I had created. She was nervous, but her body language didn't betray her. She held herself with a quiet confidence, rare at her age. Her eyes continuously scanned the area, looking for threats.

She didn't realize she was about to meet the biggest threat she had ever faced.

Her sun-kissed, smooth skin shone in the light, and her long legs were accentuated by the heels she wore. Her dress showed her perfect curves—I couldn't take my eyes off her. She has natural caramel-blonde hair, which I itched to pull free of its conservative arrangement and let the long curls I'd seen from her photos cascade over her breasts.

Standing behind her, I made sure to put her off balance. The shock of my being close unnoticed was evident in the infinitesimal jolt her body gave. Her hand twitched, as if reaching for a weapon—interesting. She studied the garden, soaking in the smallest details and surprising me with her assessment; most people droll on about the pool and the "greenness" of the garden. She caressed a flower like it was a rare diamond. Then her raw and exposed answer of why she danced startled me into silence; I'm curious how she would look, lost to her body's movement, which shrinks the world to become a second heartbeat thundering only in her chest. Her passion for dance makes her decision to abandon it even more confusing.

Her sparkling turquoise eyes examined me with calculated curiosity. I wondered if they would change color with emotion. I'd smiled to myself—time to find out.

Taking her hand in mine, I'd let my power drift over her skin, a little stronger than intended. My power seemed to be pulled to her. She managed to hold herself still. However, her eyes deepened to a captivating azure. Coconuts and sunshine drifted on a slight breeze. But her natural scent is the untamed wildness of an approaching storm with the freshness of the earth after the rain.

She shocked me, having done her homework about the merger; she still needs guidance, which she may not accept. She was stubborn and seemed to delight in challenging me. Nobody has done that in a long time. In thirty minutes, she managed to awaken my body and mind, which has become numb in a world saturated with sensation. She didn't realize she had set a game in motion, one that will end with her being mine.

I felt her probing my aura. She wouldn't see anything—humans can't. Her mind was fascinating, though. She had strong shields, blocking her thoughts and aura. To add extra layers to her shields, she sang. It was most amusing. And singing about taking off her clothes was certainly distracting. To break her shields, I'll need to overwhelm her with emotions.

I watched her hips sway toward the elevator. She seems unaware of her own natural sensuality. Natia is definitely a puzzle—one I intend to unravel. If anything, she will break the monotony that plagues my long existence.

It has taken a long time for us to reach this point—we are closing in, and Michael has strong leads on our target. The fate of the world is in our hands, and it must go our way. There is no other option.

Zac enters my office, smiling. "Three left to go," he says, referring to the number of places left for us to search.

I stare out of the window at the storm clouds rolling in from the sea. "What about Mary?" I ask him.

"Her disappearance has been reported to the local police. They haven't linked anything to us. They're still treating the missing people as separate cases."

"Good. We don't need any more complications."

"Speaking of complications, what did you find out about Miss Waterford?"

"You need to assess her. I can't get a read on her thoughts or her aura."

Zac frowns as he folds himself into the chair opposite me. "Her aura?"

People don't and, for the most part, can't hide their aura, but Zac is excellent at seeing through shields.

"She is hiding it."

"And she's human?" Zac questions.

"I believe so. But she's unusual. She reacts to the slightest movements and holds herself like a fighter."

"She does work for a security firm," Zac points out.

"Her advisor and bodyguard also shield their minds, but not their auras. One employee could be a coincidence, but three?" I don't elaborate any further, wanting Zac's opinion without bias. "Assess her, and get Barney to do a more extensive background search."

"Anything in particular you want him to look into?" Zac asks.

"Her parents… they are absent from her life. I want to know why. Also dig deeper into why she left New York."

Zac raises his eyebrows. "You like her?"

I tilt my head in contemplation. "I like the idea of breaking her walls to find out what she is hiding."

"You think she's involved in the game?"

"No. But she isn't telling the whole truth. I need to understand her."

Zac rolls his eyes. "Ever the puzzle solver."

I change the subject. "What about Khalkaroth? Any further sightings?"

Zac clasps his hands behind his head and leans back. "No. We found his location, but he'd already taken off when we raided the apartment. He'd set some interesting traps, though."

"Anyone hurt?"

Zac shakes his head. "The lunar pythonares made for an interesting hour, but everyone's fine." I suppress a shiver—I hate hell snakes.

"Do you think he has her?"

"I don't think he ever did. Someone's feeding us false intel. That said, if he finds her first, he will protect her, making our lives harder."

Rain begins to pelt the windows, as if the world is mourning the innocence it may yet lose. "It won't matter. Once we have it, she will come, willingly, to her own destruction."

Chapter Seven

Natia

Give a Taurus a comfortable couch and plenty of food. It doesn't take much to satisfy them.

Standing under the hot shower, I lean my back against the cool tiles. The contrast helps erase the lingering sensations Archan has provoked in me. Humming softly while lathering my hair with shampoo, I hear a soft groan. Shrieking, I bump my head on the tiles. Shampoo stings my eyes, preventing me from opening them. Zee's distinct laugh echoes around the room. Grabbing the shampoo, I throw it out of the shower, aiming in his general direction. I hear him catch it.

"Is that an offer to help wash your hair?" he rumbles.

"Get out!" I bark, frantically rubbing my face. When I open my eyes, he's gone. I swear, I'm going take his balls and shove them up his ass. My foot touches something. I look down to find the shampoo bottle standing upright at my feet. I scream. Scrap that, I'm going to take his balls and mince them into food for stray dogs. The door flies open, and Aaden runs in. Fantastic, it's See Natia Naked Day.

He scans the bathroom for the unseen threat. "What's wrong?" In all fairness, his eyes don't linger on me. He can keep his balls. He reaches to turn on the main light.

"No!" I squeak. "It's Zee. I'll deal with him later."

Aaden huffs and stalks through the bathroom, going through the door to the adjoining bedroom. I roll my eyes at my own stupidity; I forgot the bathroom is shared.

Finished up, I braid my hair and pull on a pair of sleep shorts with little unicorns and match it with a tank top that reads, "Me, crazy? I should get down off this unicorn and slap you." I like dressing to express how I feel.

The second my foot hits the stairs, Zee is standing at the bottom, wearing a cheeky grin.

"Sorry, Natia, I didn't realize it's a shared bathroom." At least he apologized—the fact he sounds unrepentant isn't something I can change.

I stand on the top step with my hands on my hips. It's not often one of the guys has to look up at me. "Apology accepted, but you need to move downstairs."

Zee's eyes harden. "No."

He stalks off to sit at the dining table. I look up and ask heaven for what purpose they have sent Zee—I get no response. As I head into the kitchen, Aaden calls out, "We ordered Italian, come sit with us."

"*È meglio che tu abbia ordinato lasagna.*"

Aaden raises his hands. "Of course I ordered you lasagna. I like my balls where they are." He knows me well. I grab a beer and sit next to Aaden so I can gaze over the bay.

Zee taps a notepad in front of me. "Charlie called. Jack and Joan didn't find anything at Mary Conway's apartment. But it has been expertly cleaned; someone eradicated every speck of dust, fingerprint, and DNA."

"Any CCTV?" I ask.

Aaden shakes his head. "It's broken. The building supervisor was surprised, claimed it was working the day before."

"What happened?" Zee asks me.

I tilt my head. "When?" Zee and Aaden give me a hard look. "Oh, you mean breakfast." I take a long drink of my beer. "I don't think he suspects why we're here. At least, I don't think he suspects the *real* reason we're here, but he may be suspicious we're here at all. Does that make sense?"

Aaden nods. "Did you find anything out about him?"

"Nothing verbally," I answer.

Zee sniggers.

I roll my eyes. "Child."

"You would disagree if you had opened your eyes in the shower when I replaced your—" I smack him over his head. "Ow."

"Behave like a child, and I'll treat you like one," I admonish him.

I turn back to Aaden. "I got an odd read on his aura. It's inky with blue, orange, and red flames licking the outside... Really, I've never seen anything like it."

My eyes trace the droplet of water trickling down the side of my beer bottle. "Power hums over his skin, but he's masking his real power. I think he can read minds—I felt a small pressure. But it could have just been the pulse of power he pushed over me."

Aaden and Zee stare at me with wide eyes. I glance between them, praying they aren't going to delve any further. Aaden opens his mouth, but Zee beats him to it. "Where?"

Aaden shakes his head. "Blunt much?"

I take a few more gulps of beer to combat the sudden dryness in my throat. "Mainly my hands and arms."

"What did it feel like?" Aaden asks.

"Why the hell does that matter?" I snap. I tip my bottle back again, but it's empty, so I swipe Zee's half-full bottle from his hand. A lazy grin appears on his face as he watches me drink it. I narrow my eyes. "Any comments, and you won't wake up in the morning." He holds his hands up, feigning innocence.

Aaden lets out a sigh. He's still waiting for an answer.

"Heat, and small electrical sparks on my skin," I mumble.

"Not human then," Aaden aptly concludes. "What else happened?"

"He wouldn't give me proper coffee at breakfast."

Aaden chuckles. "Yeah, we guessed when you announced it to the entire room." I'd forgotten about that.

"He indicated I'm a brainless brat who could only dance for a living, I have a low IQ, and I'm only here because my grandfather is entertaining my idea of being one of the 'big guys.' As such, I should only speak when Reinheart tells me to and say what he tells me to. It threw me a little," I admit.

"I bet," Aaden says, "how did you respond?"

"I spouted what you told me. Thank you, at least I could defend myself."

Aaden pats my leg. "You're welcome."

Zee's forehead creases. "You've entered a power game."

I nod. "It's a good thing. I can't keep my personality in check with the arrogant jerk. I suspect everyone says yes to him—I'm a novelty."

Aaden rolls a wooden coaster around in his hand. "This is good; you have a way in."

Zee shakes his head. "I disagree. If your senses are correct—"

I narrow my eyes. "My senses are always correct. Well, like the pill—99.9% of the time."

66

Zee raises his arms in the air. "Exactly. You're sensing he's powerful like nothing we've seen before. This isn't the right way to get his attention."

"It's done now. I can't reverse time." Changing the topic, I ask, "What did you both find out?"

Aaden answers, "While you were dining like a queen?"

I snort. "Without coffee."

"You're not letting that go, are you?" Zee teases.

"Not likely."

Aaden starts again. "All of Reinheart's men are shielding their minds. I didn't catch a single errant thought. Zee asked to examine the general layout and the location of the exits for security reasons. They refused, until Zee threatened to take you home and contact your grandfather, stating safety concerns."

I glance at Zee, impressed. He smirks. "I rock at being your bodyguard, admit it."

I shake my head, smiling, and Aaden continues, "Zee noted where the security cameras and exits are located. He also discovered Archan's office and personal apartments are on the top two floors."

I frown. "He lives there?"

"Only when he's in the city," replies Aaden.

"What about the rest of the time?"

Aaden shuffles through his papers. "He owns an estate on the outskirts of Seattle. We tried to do some reconnaissance, but the estate is gated and well-guarded."

"Did Lauren ever go there?" I ask.

"No. She never went to his apartment either."

"What's our plan for tomorrow?"

"You need to gain access to his personal apartments and," he hands me a small memory drive, "plug this into his computer. It'll automatically upload his personal files, including any buried ones."

I turn the small memory stick over in my palm. "How sure are we that's were his computer is?"

"You doubt me?" Aaden puts a hand on his heart, looking hurt I've questioned his technological sleuthing skills.

I place my hand on his heart also. "Of course not. How long will it take to upload the files?"

"Yeah, yeah," Aaden chuckles, looking a bit flustered. "It depends on the size of the files. But no more than two minutes."

Furrowing my brows, I try to think of a plan to get me near his computer.

"Uh oh, I can see the cogs in her brain turning," laughs Zee. I smack him over the head again, and he laughs harder. Ugh, he's impossible.

Two loud raps on the door echo in the room; Zee tenses and jumps up, and I put a hand on his arm. "It's the food."

He stalks over to the door, peeks through the privacy hole, and asks for the password—only a select number of staff know it. I changed it on our arrival.

"Bunnyhops," the voice through the door mumbles. Zee quirks an eyebrow at me, and I nod, trying not to laugh at his expression.

My mouth waters at the delicious, rich smell of lasagna. Sitting with my legs crossed at the ankles in the middle of one of the curved sofas, I balance my plate in between my knees and scrape the top layer of crispy cheese to the side to eat first. My stomach rumbles in pleasure as I scoop up the spicy tomato sauce that Alessandro's is famous for. I moan as the complex taste explodes on my tongue.

Finally, I tuck into the soft pasta. The great thing about lasagna? I can repeat this two more times. It's like having three meals.

I mull over how to get to Archan's computer. By the time I'm on my last layer, I have an idea, and I look up—only to find an amused Aaden and Zee staring at me.

"What?" I glance at my boobs, checking they aren't cradling any lasagna bits. Nope, all clean. I return my gaze to the guys, puzzled.

Zee studies my plate. "Why do you eat like that?"

"Like what?"

He nods toward the remnants of my food again. "You know, in layers?"

I push the final bed of pasta to one side. "Eating in layers is like eating the individual parts of the food. I can taste each one carefully, plus it makes my food last longer."

"Isn't the point to eat the ingredients together?" Aaden asks. "They pay top chefs to find flavors that complement each other."

"They do all go together, in the end!" I quip. "Enough about my superior eating habits; I have an idea for how to access Archan's computer."

I outline my ingenious plan. They agree it's good, but Zee's uncomfortable about leaving me alone with Archan again. I think he feels he's failing as a bodyguard. I remind him of my kill count this year, and he huffs—I take pride in knowing mine is higher than his.

Chapter Eight

Natia

A Taurus will always find things out; they might not say anything right away, but they can put two and two together.

We enter Reinheart and Hunter at nine the following morning, and Barbie immediately rushes forward. Honestly, I can't remember her real name; if she hadn't lived up to her stereotype, maybe I would have made an effort.

"Good morning, Miss Waterford. You're early for the meeting. I'll check if the room is ready." She points to a white, tufted, leather sofa situated under an enormous abstract canvas in tones of gray. "Please take a seat. Would you like some coffee?"

I smile—now I'm offered coffee? "That's okay, I have a breakfast meeting with Mr. Reinheart at nine." I glance at my watch. "Oh, I'm a little late."

Barbie stares at her handheld tablet, and her fingers tap on it quickly. A line appears between her brows. "I can't see anything scheduled. Let me check with Mr. Reinheart."

"Of course, go ahead." I cross my fingers. My plan hinges on Reinheart's willingness to play this game. Sitting between Zee and Aaden on the sofa, I take a deep breath. Aaden offers me a reassuring smile, and Zee remains stoic, as any good bodyguard should do.

I look at Barbie, who's leaning over the ultra-modern glass reception desk for the phone. "Fake or real?"

Aaden looks between me and Zee. "What's real?"

"Fake," answers Zee, understanding my question.

"Agreed... How can you tell?" I ask Zee, while Aaden just stares at us, bewildered.

"The shape—real ones aren't shaped like cantaloupes; they're more like pears." He tips his head to the side. "Also, there's too much volume on the top. How would you know?"

"Weight ratio. Skinny women rarely have naturally large breasts. Also, while she's only in her twenties, gravity should have begun taking course by now."

"Oh, b-boobs," Aaden stammers, blushing.

Barbie struts toward us, wearing a small scowl. "Sorry to keep you waiting, Miss Waterford. Mr. Reinheart forgot to put it on the calendar. He's waiting for you." She indicates to—yes, you guessed it—another "Man in Black."

A six-foot-two hulk of a man with dark wavy hair beams at me and sweeps out his hand. "Your carriage awaits, Miss Waterford."

I blink—they speak! He leads me to the small elevator I rode in yesterday; I add crossed toes to my fingers that we're not going to the rooftop. He leans across me and presses the button for the seventy-third floor. My stomach drops with the acceleration. Checking my mental shields, I'm happy the background melody is doing its job. No need to bring out the big guns yet.

I'm about to turn to the man, when he holds out his hand. "Nice to meet you, Miss Waterford. I'm Zac." I stare into his stormy blue eyes and grasp his hand. It's warm like Archan's but has a different buzz of power—it's not as strong, but still packs a punch. Feeling a firm tug on my shields, I manage to keep my smile in place and study his aura. It's gold mixed with ink and constantly moving. Who are these people?

"It's lovely to meet you also," I say, as the elevator doors open, revealing Archan with his hands in his pants pockets, his expression neutral. Letting go of Zac's hand, I step out of the elevator and turn around. My mouth turns up. "Thank you, Zac. Please call me Natia." I couldn't help myself. Archan stiffens just a little.

The elevator doors close behind me. I can't go down the hallway any further, as Archan is standing less than a foot away from me, and I refuse to back into the wall. His unnatural warmth and scent envelop me. He's dressed in black slacks and a crisp, white shirt with his sleeves rolled up to show muscular arms and a dusting of hair; the first few buttons at the top of his shirt are undone, revealing smooth, tanned skin and the hint of a tattoo. His damp hair curls at the base of his neck. My fingers twitch as I imagine running my hands through it…

Grr, concentrate, Natia!

Looking down to compose myself, I grin. He's barefoot which, for some reason, is really entertaining. I raise my eyebrows, letting my eyes flick to his feet then back to his face. "You're not ready for our breakfast meeting, Archan?"

He moves to the side, indicating I should go ahead. "I am not aware we have one, Miss Waterford."

He sounds amused. Good. I need to not piss him off—too much. His footsteps sound close behind me, making me feel like I'm being stalked. The hallway opens up to reveal a large open-plan area with a huge kitchen, dining, and living area. I stop to take in the room.

He sidesteps me. "I am afraid you will have to put up with my cooking; I was about to make an omelet." He pulls out ingredients from the well-stocked refrigerator and pours two glasses of orange juice, placing them on the solid wood breakfast bar, which curves around the kitchen.

"Do you have coffee?"

"Of course," he answers, as if it's a stupid question.

"Is it caffeinated?"

He smiles a genuine smile; it reaches his eyes, which sparkle with amusement. I almost stumble. That look should not be allowed on a human being—wait, he's not human. It still shouldn't be allowed. "Yes, Miss Waterford, it is."

I distract myself by studying the room more closely. Warm oak floors match the kitchen, and soft lighting is recessed into the floor. Six mismatched maroon chairs surround a circular table, with three orb light fixtures hanging from the ceiling at different levels over its center. A pale taupe rug sits in the middle of a sunken sitting room, accompanied by three large wine-colored sofas surrounding an oak coffee table. Paintings line the walls, none of which I associate with "skyscraper living." Natural light floods the room from the floor-to-ceiling windows framing the far wall. The overall effect is one of warmth and comfort. Spying a set of double doors to the right of the room, I wonder if it's his office.

I stroll toward one of the breakfast bar stools.

He rounds the bar, moving behind me. "I'll take your coat."

I resist the urge to roll my eyes. Here we go with the demands, not requests. He brushes my neck with his hand as he lifts my coat. I've readied myself for his games, which seem to include driving me crazy with small touches. However, my shields need a boost… let's see—"U Can't Touch This" by MC Hammer. Classic and appropriate.

He returns from wherever he disappeared to put my coat. "You look radiant today." Spinning around to face him, I catch his gaze at my ass before he raises it to my face, looking unrepentant. Today, I've chosen a knee-length navy pencil skirt and a wrap-around white blouse. Zee's memorized the underwear that coordinates with each outfit, telling me, "the lace underwear contrasts beautifully with my tan skin." I've kept my grandma's diamond studs but added a pearl drop necklace, and my hair sits in a simple French twist.

I blush and sit on the stool as he goes back to cooking. "Thank you."

Chef gadgets galore line the kitchen surfaces. I'd say it's for show, except he seems at home in the kitchen. The brewing pot of coffee fills the air with its divine smell as Archan chops the various ingredients, his back to me. Mesmerized by the flex of his arms and shoulders, I almost miss his question. "Why do I have the pleasure of your company this morning?"

Clasping my hands in front of me on the breakfast bar, I lean forward. "You wanted to discuss the meetings beforehand. I assumed I needed to come early to talk to you."

The frying pan sizzles, and the smell of peppers and onions fills the room. "I thought you have this handled?"

Time to stroke his ego—not my natural ability. In my opinion, either you deserve the praise or you don't.

"If you can spare me some time, maybe I can contribute more to the merger?" There, not a blank check to tell me what to do, but an "I'll listen to your opinion, buddy." He goes quiet while beating the egg mixture in the pan. Finished, he turns and leans over the breakfast bar toward me, leaving barely a foot between us.

He studies me with an unwavering focus. "Is that so?"

My mouth goes dry. I need a yard stick to keep this man at a safe distance. I sip my orange juice to hide my reaction.

Looking pleased he's unbalanced me, he pours my coffee and hands it to me. "Which part would you like to discuss?"

"I'm assuming the team will focus on strengths and weaknesses today, as that often leads to the opportunities and threats—"

He interrupts, "Is that because it is in the order of the acronym SWOT?" Taking a deep, steadying breath, I attempt to push down the growl working its way up my throat. It fails. He turns, eyebrows raised. I smile—that's right, I bite, too. I sit on my hands to prevent myself from strangling him.

"As I was saying, I have a list of what I consider to be some of the strengths and weaknesses." I narrow my eyes, daring him to question my IQ further. When he doesn't, I reach for my handbag on the floor. Flustered, I bend too quickly to pick up the bag and lose my balance, starting to topple off the stool.

Out of nowhere, Archan grabs me around the waist, pulling my back against his front. How did he get there so quickly?

Warmth radiates down my back, and I become hyperaware of his hands resting just below my breasts. He brushes a stray hair from my neck, and I look up at him. Bad idea—his mouth is inches from mine. He studies my lips and gives me a crooked grin; my breath hitches, pushing my abdomen tighter against his hands.

"The list?" he questions, his voice husky.

"Oh, of course." *Get it together, Natia.* Releasing me, he scoops up my bag and places it on my lap. I pull out the handwritten list Aaden and I made last night and hand it to him.

He puts it on the breakfast bar. "We can talk about it while we eat."

Handing me a plate with cutlery, he sits next to me with his own food. I scrape off the cheesy top layer while he reads my notes.

"You have some good key points…" He sounds surprised.

"Thank you, I try."

Cheesy layer finished, I begin to deconstruct the omelet, separating out the ham, onions, and peppers.

"Do you have an example of this?" he asks.

I lean over his shoulder, and he points to where I've written about the companies having conflicting departments in some areas of the business. Well shit, there's only one I can think of.

I tilt my head as if in contemplation. "The weapons department at Waterford Industries and the humanitarian department at Grant Ltd."

After studying the small pile of green peppers I've successfully separated—he makes an *excellent* omelet—I look back to him, waiting for the next question.

He stares at my plate. "Do you like green peppers?"

"Yes." Popping a forkful of them in my mouth, I hum in appreciation. The seasoning is fantastic, and the peppers have just the right amount of crunch. He's made my coffee with the perfect amount of cream and sugar, too.

My mouth fails to consult my brain before I say, "This is wonderful. You can cook me breakfast anytime." I then give myself a well-deserved mental slap.

A wicked grin spreads across his face. "No problem. I should get to call you Natia, though, if we are getting that personal."

I start Queen's "Under Pressure." He flicks his gaze to my plate, as if trying to figure something out.

"How could you turn this weakness into an opportunity?"

"Waterford needs to be transparent with who they supply weapons to, making sure they liaise with Grant Ltd.'s humanitarian team to ensure their philosophies match. We could use the press to show we're arming the correct people." Peppers and onions now eaten, I start on the egg.

"Is it possible to be transparent about everything the weapons department is doing?" he asks.

A forkful of egg pauses halfway between the plate and my mouth. Alarm bells ring in my head. What's the probability he's focused on the one department Waterford Industries can't be transparent on?

I feign confusion. "Why do you ask?"

"No reason. You'll be fine today."

He stands and puts his dishes in the sink. "I am sorry to leave you before you have finished eating, but I need to get ready if we are going to be on time for the meeting. There is more coffee in the pot—help yourself." He strides up the stairs to what I presume is the bedroom.

Rummaging through my bag for the memory stick, I eye the double doors. *Please let it be his office.* Approaching the walls and feigning interest in the art, I edge along until I'm in front of the doors. I glance at the cameras, making sure they're in the correct position, before putting my hand on the door handle.

Please don't squeak, please don't squeak.

Pushing open one of the doors a crack, I peer in and breathe a sigh of relief when I see his computer on his desk. I glance at the stairs and strain my hearing. Faint footsteps sound above my head; he's on the opposite side of the apartment, away from the stairs. I dart into his office and plug the memory stick into his computer, and the white light starts flashing. A bead of sweat tickles the back of my neck. I'm hyperaware of every noise as I take in the numerous artifacts in the display cabinets. *Is that a diamond crown?*

Footsteps sound across the floor toward the stairs, but the light is still flashing—the upload isn't complete. Leaving the memory stick, I dash into the living area and close the door. I stare at the art, as if it's what I've been doing the entire time.

He strolls over and stands beside me. "Do you like art?"

I tip my head at a familiar painting, which may be an original. "I don't know any modern artists, and I don't take part in the collector's scene. I like what I like, and I don't feign interest in things I don't find beautiful." His eyes widen. I refrain from rolling my eyes. "Just because I come from a family of wealth doesn't mean I must pretend to like things I don't appreciate and ignore those I do find pleasure in."

"That is not what I am thinking. It is rare to find someone so honest, particularly with your status. Most succumb to the pressures of their peers. I agree, you should never hide how you feel because of other people's expectations."

I point to the painting. "Is that 'The Birth of Venus?'"

"Yes, you know your Greek gods?"

"Some. Did you have a copy made? It's an amazing replica."

His lips twitch. "Something like that."

Studying the painting some more, I ask, "Could you get my coat for me, please?" I hold my breath waiting for his answer, hoping this gives me time to retrieve the memory stick.

"Of course." He strides down the corridor we originally entered. I scurry to retrieve the memory stick and rush back to the living area a split second before he rounds the corner. I'm not able to shut the door without the click being noticeable, so I leave a small gap, hoping he won't notice. Walking toward him, I head him off to collect my coat. He hands it to me and strides straight toward the office. I freeze. He enters without pausing, and my heart beats erratically until he returns with his suit jacket.

"Ready?" he asks, mimicking Aaden's words to me only hours before. If I only realized how not ready I was for this day. But I guess you never know when your world's gonna get turned upside down.

Chapter Nine

Archan

Unknown origin.

ntertaining myself with the occasional brush against Natia, I listen to her small gasps and watch her body react. It is the only way to survive the dullest meeting of my life. The wild scent of a storm drifts over to me. I breathe her in—she's so responsive but on her guard, reinforcing her shields and patching the smallest of cracks.

Her hesitancy when discussing the weapons department confirmed my suspicion—she knows more than she is letting on. Zac strides in as we are wrapping up today's meeting.

"Hi, Zac." Natia beams at him. A genuine smile lights up her face, one she hasn't graced me with yet.

"Hi, Natia," he says coolly, purposefully not meeting her eyes. She blinks and looks a bit confused before turning away and talking with her companions. Zac pulls me aside to show me a security video from this morning, and I immediately use my abilities to reach out to his mind, establishing a mental link so we can converse privately—my favorite way to communicate.

"This is the security feed from your personal apartments this morning," he says.

I watch as Natia arrives and we go to the kitchen. The security cameras turn to focus on our exchange. Zac fast-forwards the feed to when I go upstairs. Natia searches her bag then stands, but the cameras don't follow her movement like they should. She disappears from view, just outside the office. Zac switches to the office feed, which is focused on the back left corner—it should be on the doors.

"You think she was in my office searching for something?" I ask Zac.

"I think it's suspicious that the second you both entered the boardroom, the cameras were no longer faulty."

"Did you get anything when you touched her?"

"No. Her mental shields are blocking her memories, her thoughts, her aura... I can't even view the previous five minutes. That's unusual. Some people can bury strong memories and ones they view as important, but to block everything is something else."

Zac is perplexed. We are on the last leg of our mission, when Natia suddenly appears under the pretense of representing her grandfather's company. I glance at her.

"Has she been honest with you when answering your questions?" Zac asks.

I think back on our exchanges. *"She hasn't lied. But she's a master at manipulating her words, answering part of a question, or deflecting it and not answering at all. But woven in is brutal honesty... It's confusing."*

"What do you want to do?"

"I will distract her tonight. Get Leo to pay her apartment a visit, bug it. Let's see what she's hiding."

"She seems to be resisting your usual charm." Zac sounds amused.

"It's called playing hard to get, Zac. She wants me. It is novel to be challenged. But she is just like the rest of them. I'll easily break her."

Zac snorts as he exits the room. I rise to shake hands with the various advisors, when I notice Edward approaching Natia.

"Hi, Natia, how are you? Coping with the tedium of the meetings?" he enquires.

It's probable the only thing keeping her awake was me. She recited an interesting mix of eighties songs. It became clear Aaden can read minds when I caught a glimpse of a note he wrote to Zee, informing him of her amusing choices.

"I'm coping fine, thanks, Edward." She sounds tired. I study her face, noting the slight darkening under her eyes.

"I would love to sit down with you and discuss some of your ideas."

I stiffen. Her response better be negative; otherwise, I'm going to have to deal with the vermin.

A small frown furrows her brows. "I don't think that's wise outside of this boardroom."

Edward sighs. "You've outed me. I was… hoping for a date?" At least he is honest.

"I appreciate your offer, but I'm already spoken for."

He looks deflated as he picks up his suitcase. I smirk at the lie. "I see. Well, he's a lucky man. Goodbye, Natia."

Aaden shakes my hand without comment. Zac folds his arms and stares at Natia, not disguising his distrust. Taking her hand, I push power along her skin. She flinches. I suspect she has a strong psychic ability, making her extra sensitive to my power.

"I can't meet for breakfast tomorrow, so we will have dinner tonight instead," I tell her.

She stares at me in defiance. "I have plans tonight. I can manage without you."

"Fine, we will have dinner now."

She offers me a deranged smile. "Thank you for the offer, but I have matters that require my immediate attention before my evening plans. I will see you tomorrow."

82

I release her hand and return her stare. Zee steps so close his chest brushes her back. I glance over her head, and my lips twitch; as if he could keep her safe from me. I allow a wave of power to roll across her, and her skin glows from the effect. She digs her nails into her palms, battling the senses that are no doubt telling her to run.

"Then I hope you have a pleasant evening," I concede.

She pushes Aaden to move faster toward the elevator.

Barney and Zac pile into the boardroom and shut the door, and Zac immediately hands me a report. "We have Krian in the basement. Khalkaroth loaned the apartment from him."

I sit on the edge of the table and glance at the report. "She's taken a copy of my files?"

Barney nods. "I don't know how deep the program went to access your personal files. But assuming it's everything, they have the video and research files. The safe house location isn't named on any of them." I don't know if I'm impressed with the ingenuity or angry at her defiance.

Zac pours himself a coffee. "What do you want to do next?"

Tie her to my bed and make her body beg for release is my initial thought. "Put a tail on her. I want to know where she is at all times. Did you bug her apartment?"

Zac and Barney look surprised. "Yes, but they have a device blocking it. We aren't going to bring her in and interrogate her?" Zac snaps.

"It would attract too much attention. She is the granddaughter of a wealthy and powerful man, who also happens to be our client. This will take more finesse; I'll break her *my* way. Speaking of interrogation, let's go and see our old friend Krian."

Bypassing the slow and torturous elevator, we teleport to the basement. We don't bother to be discreet—it's not like anyone will see us down here.

"Why do you think she is here?" I ask as we walk down the clinical white corridor toward the holding cell.

"It's not the merger. She could be investigating the disappearances in a criminal manner. But she's not law enforcement, so it's more likely she's involved in the game."

The game has become our obsession—so called because each chess piece, moved with care and precision, progresses us closer and closer to our goal. Each side is constantly searching for the fated end pieces, which will end the game one way or another. It's a twist on the classic good versus evil, with the fate of mankind hanging in the balance. And now, the wait is over, and the finale is close. Natia's appearance at this stage may mean she is working against us—which makes her the enemy.

I loosen my tie and remove my watch. "With what goal?"

"Maybe she's a hunter?" Barney guesses. I let out a quiet, frustrated sigh. Enemy hunters, seeking our goal of the final pieces of the game, must be dealt with. The anger seeps through me as I think of the possibility that our files—*my* files—could have fallen into enemy hands. If Natia is on the enemy's side, and a hunter at that… she will most definitely regret it.

"You don't think she's working independently?" Zac questions, halting outside of the glass wall.

Barney shrugs.

"Did you find anything more when you did another background check?" I ask him.

"Nothing about her parents. But there's an unofficial police report in the file I gave you. Officially, her friend was kidnapped and murdered a few weeks before Natia moved back to Seattle. Unofficially, Natia was also kidnapped. I suspect supernatural involvement."

It only adds to the enigma that is Natia Waterford.

"What do you want to do?" Zac asks.

Unofficial reports mean Natia's into this deeper than I thought. Covering up supernatural activity involves special forces. Is she part of those forces? That would improve her situation considerably. Still, stealing my files leaves her motives unclear, and I don't like unclear. "She's an unknown… Until that changes, we keep her close. She mentioned she has plans tonight. Find out where she is, Barney." Barney teleports out.

"Hmm…" Zac starts.

"What?"

He shakes his head and looks back at Krian in his unassuming, pathetic, wrinkly human form. "She's dangerous—eliminating her would be best."

I stiffen at the thought of him "eliminating" her. "You know as well as I that simply removing the problem doesn't address the root cause."

"She has the files."

"And if we kill her, we won't know why she stole them, who she is working for, and who she's shared them with."

Zac sighs, his need for violence refocused on the demon in front of us. He retrieves the lunar pythonares and studies her face. "She's a beaut'." The man has a weird fascination with anything snake related.

"You hold her, I'll hold him." I nod to Krian and enter the room. The chains around Krian's ankles go tight against the floor, and the cuffs around his wrists magnetize to the metal table in front of him.

I sit in the chair opposite him and fix him with a cold stare. "Where is Khalkaroth?"

Krian's eyes go wide as he glances between me and the snake coiling around Zac's waist. "I don't know. He left a few days ago, didn't tell me where he was going!"

I glance at Zac, who nods as he strokes the hellish snake creature on its head.

"Did anyone else visit the apartment?"

He shakes his head. I flick my eyes to Zac, who's frowning.

I sigh. Violence is a necessary evil—but I grow tired of it. "Krian, uncharacteristically, I am asking for this information rather than taking it. Do not mistake this for patience. Lie again, and we do this the hard way." Without moving, I clamp invisible ice fingers around his throat, cutting off his air.

He squirms in his hard metal chair. Fear grips him, stripping away his human form. Twin black, curved horns extend about six inches from his forehead, and his pale skin morphs into a deep claret, his glassy blue eyes fading to reveal his true black ones. Every species of demon has a different true form. Krian is one of the most common and now resembles a classic human demon. I release his throat. He shakes his head again.

Zac steps forward and lays the lunar pythonares on the table in front of Krian; she hisses as her hot yellow skin touches the cool metal. Krian leans away, trying to avoid the stare of the hell snake. Zac snaps his fingers in front of the snake. "Stay." Obediently, she coils her long, thick body on the table but never moves her unnatural gaze from Krian, who is too busy paying attention to the snake to notice the much bigger threat.

Zac's eyes grow blank as he touches his fingers to Krian's temples.

Krian jerks before he begins to scream in agony.

Blood trickles from his nose. The hell snake edges closer and flicks her black tongue with interest.

Zac releases Krian and nods to the snake. Immediately, her jaws snap open, revealing dangerous, gleaming fangs. Krian shudders and tries to back away, but his shackles keep him glued to the table, as the lunar pythonares slithers nearer. From its open jaws, another mouth protrudes and slowly drops open, stretching its maw impossibly wide, with hundreds of needle-sharp teeth.

She strikes Krian's ear, taking it clean off and swallowing it whole. Zac removes a wet wipe (one of the best human inventions of the twenty-first century) from the side table and cleans a small blood splatter from his wrist.

Krian cries out again when the snake takes his nose. Letting out an annoyed huff, Zac brushes his fingers against Krian's temple, cutting off the noise.

We leave the snake to her meal and step outside.

Zac bins the wet wipe and sits back to watch the snake. "He doesn't know where Khalkaroth is. But Khalkaroth did have a visitor. However, his memory has been tampered with to protect their identity."

"Must be someone higher level," I muse.

Zac nods, looking fascinated with the snake's ability to swallow whole limbs. "I'll put some feelers out, starting at the top."

I put my watch back on. "Keep me updated."

Chapter Ten

Natia

Taurus: Stubborn ass.

Entering the apartment, Zee changes the password and checks each room. Aaden and Zee picked up on the undertones in the final parts of the meeting and reached the same conclusion—they knew. Aaden attaches the memory stick to the laptop on the dining table.

Zee jogs down the stairs. "All clear. You said your grandfather has anti-surveillance technology in the apartment?"

"Yes, it's in the master bedroom at the rear of the wardrobe, in a safe. The combination is—" Zee slaps a hand over my mouth and pushes me a piece of paper and a pen across the table.

"Write it down," he mutters, taking away his hand. I jot down the code, and Zee immediately runs upstairs.

Aaden sighs. "They're encrypted."

"Can you unencrypt them?"

He throws me a sardonic expression. "Do you know who I am? It'll take a few hours, though." I huff. I'm desperate to see the files.

Zee returns and sits next to me at the dining table. "He pushed for you to be alone with him tonight. Maybe we should pull the mission and find an alternative approach."

I shake my head. "We just need to be careful. I'll avoid being alone with him; we have the files, let's see what they reveal," I press, as my phone starts ringing. It's Uncle Charlie. My heart sinks—I already miss him, but I'm not ready to forgive him. I answer with every intention of keeping it professional.

"Natia Waterford," I answer in a crisp voice.

"Don't be coy, Natia. You know full well it's me."

I grind my teeth. "How can I help, Charlie?"

"You're to return to HQ tonight," he commands. What is it with men trying to push me around?

"Why?" I challenge.

"Your position has been compromised. Reinheart knows you aren't there for your grandfather's company. Pack, Natia." He can only know this if Aaden or Zee has informed him. Aaden looks away, suddenly engrossed in watching his laptop screen count the percentage to complete bar.

I try reassuring Uncle Charlie. "I've managed to gain his attention, allowing me access to his apartment. This is the closest we've come to him—how many more people need to go missing before it's worth the risk? Mary has just been taken; if we act fast enough, we may be able to save her. I'll be careful. Zee won't let me out of his sight."

He exhales heavily, and I imagine his eyebrow tic is in full force. "It's too dangerous."

"You're making this decision because I'm your niece, not as a colleague," I challenge.

"You're my subordinate, and you *will* return now."

Furious, I disconnect the call. The phone starts ringing again, but I switch it off, slamming the phone down on the table.

I swing my gaze to Aaden. "I'm not going back, but I understand if you want to."

Zee sighs, tips his head to stare at the ceiling, and runs one hand over his buzz cut while grasping my hand in his other. "If you're staying, I'm staying." At least I have my bodyguard.

Aaden taps his fingers on the table. "I'll stay. But I still think you're in danger."

I snort. "When am I not?"

Aaden's software will take twelve hours, and it's seven in the evening. Rolling my shoulders to release some tension, I head to my bedroom and grab my journal. I need to deal with my excess emotions, or else I'm going to burst. Lying on my stomach sideways across the bed, I start with Uncle Charlie. I begin to write, focusing on letting out every thought and feeling, just like Duncan taught me.

I'm upset and hurt he didn't discuss this assignment with me beforehand. I'm angry he's thrown me back into a life I hate. I'm disappointed in the person that's more of a father to me than an uncle, and I miss him.

Archan's turn. I roll over and stare at the ceiling for ten minutes. Lost for words, I decide I need some air and trudge downstairs to an empty room. I assume Zee and Aaden are in their bedrooms. Opening the doors to the balcony, I lie down on one of the loungers and look at the stars. The night is clear, and the air is crisp, cool, and cleansing. My skin tingles with goose bumps as the breeze drifts over my skin.

Archan's an arrogant pig who enjoys making me feel uncomfortable. He plays exhausting power games and belittles my intellect. He sees my passion for dance as worthless. I'm angry, pissed, and confused at my body's response to him. He makes me feel alive and on fire—something that hasn't happened in a long time... since Dalton. The attraction I feel is unrivaled, but it's not real—it's fabricated by him. It's a ploy to get me to submit and let down my shields. I could fall fast and hard and land on my ass, not my feet. He's the only person to have ever made cracks appear in my control.

Sighing, I flip through the pages of the journal and stumble upon the bucket list I've hastily scribbled in one of the margins.

1. Dance in the rain.

2. Be kissed in the dark by a stranger.

3. Have a champagne breakfast on the Eiffel Tower.

4. Take a carriage ride through Central Park.

5. Take part in a flash mob.

6. Snuggle in front of a fire while in a log cabin in the snow.

7. Skinny dip in the ocean.

8. Have dinner on a yacht by moonlight.

9. Be kissed slowly from ankle to neck (the opposite way to the norm—just to be awkward).

10. Have sex in an elevator.

There's more, but I try to keep my list below ten—makes it more achievable. Not that I've done any of the things on the list since I started the journal three years ago; most of them involve a partner. I let my mind wander.

I suddenly hear Aaden's voice. "Are you okay?" I snap my eyes open. I must've drifted off to sleep.

"I'm fine."

"You know, it's in the 'Man's Handbook' that when a woman says she's fine, she actually means the opposite." He chuckles. "Then the man has two options: ignore the fact that she isn't fine, or try to make it better. Which one should I choose?"

Tapping my fingers on the side of the chair, I look up at him. "I need to go out."

His eyebrows squash together. "Out? How does that help?"

Jumping up, I pat his shoulder and push past him. "If you're coming, put on your dancing shoes."

After a quick shower (where I made sure the adjoining door was locked), I pass through the wardrobe, ignoring the fancy clothes, and grab my suitcase tucked in the back. Scrambling through my untidy packing, I locate my ruby dress. It has a plunging neckline held together by spaghetti straps that crisscross several times over my back, finishing at the base of my spine. The bottom ends with a flowing, knee-length skirt. I slip on a pair of silver-heeled sandals, replace the diamond studs with small silver hoops, and let my natural curls cascade down my back. The matching red panties, which are small shorts really, allow me to keep my dignity while dancing. I'm texting Nick—my old dance partner—to ask him if he will meet me at my favorite salsa bar as I open the bedroom door, where Zee is leaning against the wall, his arms crossed.

I frown. "What's up?"

"This isn't a good idea. You've pissed off a powerful man who has a penchant for making people disappear." He doesn't even check me out; wow, he must be worried.

"Are you coming?" I ask.

"I have no idea where you're going, but if you're going out, yes."

I wink. "Then I have an excellent bodyguard with me."

He raises his arms in a 'what can I do?' gesture. He's wearing dark blue faded jeans and a deep red shirt.

I grin. "We match."

He looks confused, so I wave a hand between my dress and his shirt. His shoulders relax a little. Downstairs, Aaden sits at the dining table, staring at his laptop.

"Looking at it won't hurry it along; you can't threaten it," I tell him.

Aaden turns and smiles. "You look beautiful, Natia."

Zee swivels on his heel and studies me. "What underwear are you wearing?"

"What the hell has that got to do with you?" I shoot back.

"I don't remember that dress, so I don't know what underwear you're wearing."

I wiggle my eyebrows. "Wouldn't you like to know?"

"It's an essential part of protecting you."

"How?" This should be good.

"If you get kidnapped, I'll be able to describe what you're wearing. Or, if you need resuscitating, I'll know if your bra opens from the front or the back, saving precious seconds."

Shaking my head, I open the front door. "I'm not wearing a bra."

He trips, and I can't help but giggle.

Chapter Eleven

Natia

Tauruses enjoy beautiful music, heady conversation, and sensual hands on their bodies.

Music vibrates through my body, and my hips begin to sway. Zee and Aaden look decidedly uncomfortable—dancing isn't their thing. I remind them that it's a bar and that they do indeed sell alcohol.

Standing near the entrance on the higher level, which houses the bar, I scan the dance floor and find Nick with a petite brunette. I love to watch him dance, his movements fluid and expertly executed. The song finishes, and he places a chaste kiss on her forehead. I'm curious—does he have a girlfriend? I hope so. After a horrible breakup a few years ago, he lost his confidence. He spots me, and I rush down the stairs to meet him. We share a hug, then he holds me at arm's length.

"You get more beautiful every time I see you," he gushes.

I laugh. "Hi, Nick, how've you been?" I slide a glance at the petite girl, who's now dancing with a group. She's gorgeous, with shoulder-length chestnut hair, a curvy body, and olive skin. She has a heart-shaped face and deep brown eyes.

He grins, following my gaze. "I'm working on it." He suddenly looks over my shoulder, and I turn around. Zee is standing right behind me, leveling Nick with a menacing stare.

I wave a hand between them. "Zee, this is Nick, my old dance partner."

Nick offers Zee a hand. "Nice to meet you, Zee."

Zee nods, glares at him for a few seconds, then stomps to the bar, finding a seat overlooking the dance floor with Aaden. Guess he's still upset about me leaving the apartment.

"Don't worry… he's overprotective, that's all," I murmur, explaining Zee's behavior.

Nick nods and changes the subject, putting a hand on my arm. "So… have you seen Dalton since you've been back?"

Ice fills my veins as the betrayal of my childhood sweetheart—and ex-fiancé—comes rushing back. He cheated on me with my best friend one month before I went to New York. His excuse was he "couldn't do long distance relationships." I understood, but cheating on me—with my *friend*, no less—wasn't the way to end our relationship. I deserved more respect. He was my best friend—we'd shared everything, and at the time, I was heartbroken. My life has moved on so much since then, my world expanding to encompass the supernatural one; stuffy Dalton with his prim ways would never have fit in it, which is maybe why I rarely think about him anymore.

"No, why?" I ask, trying not to sound too sharp.

"He split from Jessica about six months ago. He talks about you a lot." It would be petty of me to feel happy they hadn't worked out. Instead of thinking about it, I change the subject.

"Dance?" I ask Nick, but he's already dragging me to the dance floor.

"I hope you can keep up," he quips.

He embraces me as a classic salsa tune starts playing. We laugh as he leads me into multiple turns, lifts, and various moves that make me feel feminine and sexy; it's like I never stopped dancing. The crowd parts to give us room to move, and I feel so alive and free. After three more songs, I tap out. I mime tipping my hand back over my mouth, silently telling him I need a drink. Nick nods and saunters off to find his little brunette.

Making my way over to the guys, Harry the barman hands me a peach schnapps and lemonade.

Aaden chuckles. "I always thought you'd be a bourbon kinda girl."

I swirl the ice in the glass. "You should know by now, Aaden, I don't conform to people's expectations."

Zee stares at me with an expression I can't place. "I didn't know you could dance like that."

I scowl. "What did you think studying dance for three years would lead to?"

"I thought it was ballet and pompous shit."

I laugh. "Common misconception. There are many types of dance, Zee; otherwise, we'd all be pointing our toes and performing pirouettes in a nightclub. Although I think you'd look sexy in a tutu." Aaden chuckles, and I turn to him. "You, too, twinkle toes. A nice pale blue tutu would complement your eyes."

I down some water then start sipping my peach schnapps. We chat about inconsequential things. Aaden tells us about growing up on a pig farm and reveals his parents' disappointment that he became one of the best technological intelligence analysts in the world rather than taking on the family pork business; his younger brother reluctantly took that role. Zee shares that he used to work as a volunteer rescuing animals from abusive owners, which is quite the revelation. They grill me on my childhood, where I reveal my teenage obsession with Justin Timberlake and all things Disney. It's easy for them to gather that my grandparents raised me. However, my parents' abandonment still remains a mystery to me. The weak-assed excuse they weren't ready for parenthood has always sat uncomfortably with me.

An hour and three drinks later, I encourage the guys to join me on the dance floor. They stay rooted to the spot, under the guise of having to watch from the bar for my safety. I roll my eyes and begin to make my way around the crowded dance floor, looking for Nick. He's nowhere to be seen, and neither is the brunette—excellent.

I start swaying my hips with my hands in the air, losing myself to Ed Sheeran singing about how he likes the shape of his woman. My eyes are closed, lost in the lyrics, when warm hands grip my hips from behind. Assuming it's Nick, I step back, tucking my body against his, and blindly wrap my hands around his neck.

"You get lucky?" I ask, chuckling.

A deep, smooth voice whispers in my ear. "Not yet, but I've got my eyes on the sexiest woman here." His mouth is so close, he's almost nibbling on my ear. I gasp and spin around.

Archan chuckles. "Lost for words, Miss Waterford?"

He pulls me against his hard body and guides us deeper into the crowd. I scan the room for Zee and Aaden.

"Don't worry, your protectors are fine." My heart starts thumping so loud and fast, he must feel the vibrations from my chest. We begin swaying as he looks down at me.

"You are exquisite when you dance… your every move beautiful, graceful." He leans down and pulls on the ends of my hair, tipping my head back. "And I love your hair down." He releases my hair and places his hand on the bare skin at the base of my spine. Velvet heat spreads from his hands, over the curve of my ass, then down the back of my thighs. It caresses the sensitive flesh at the back of my knees before continuing down my calves. Liquid fire pools in my belly.

He watches my reaction, and his ethereal gold eyes swirl with desire. A look of pure masculine satisfaction spreads across his face. My mind goes blank. Hooking a hand under my thigh, he brings it up to his hip. Keeping the other on the base of my spine, he dips my body, arching my back until my hair touches the floor. His breath plays over the exposed skin between my breasts, and my nipples pebble.

"Stunning," he rasps, as he brings me back up. I tip my head back to stare at him. Our breath mingles as his gaze traces my lips. The music changes to an upbeat song, snapping me out of my trance.

I stiffen in his arms. "What are you doing here?" My voice is embarrassingly husky.

"I am joining you."

"You weren't invited."

"I don't need an invitation to come to a public bar. I am glad I came. Seeing you dance is something I won't soon forget. Now, are we going to continue to dance, or would you like a drink?"

He's offering options? I want to refuse both, but I need to check if Aaden and Zee are okay.

"Drink."

He steers me off the dance floor, his grip on my hand firm but painless. As we approach the bar, I notice Aaden and Zee are missing. My anxiety steadily increases.

Once at the bar, Archan asks, "What's your pleasure?"

I roll my eyes so hard I glimpse my own ass. "Dear god, is that the best you've got?"

He gazes down my body. "Not even close."

Harry appears before us and wordlessly starts mixing my peach schnapps. "A bottle of water, too, please, Harry."

Harry hands me my drink. "No problem, Natia." I catch the tic in Archan's jaw and grin. Mixing my drink with a straw, I turn, only to be greeted by a wall of muscled chests. I freeze and swallow reflexively. Where the hell did they all come from? A girl likes to feel special, but not cornered. I put my drink down, my senses on high alert and my body bracing itself for a fight.

Archan puts a hand on my shoulder. "Relax, I just want to chat, and I have brought a few friends for you to meet." He introduces a man of about six-foot-four. What are they feeding these men? He has short, cropped, dark hair and deep brown eyes. He gives me a lopsided grin.

"This is Barney, my head of intelligence." Barney raises his beer bottle in a silent greeting. He moves on to the next man. "You have already met Zac; he is head of security."

I raise a hand in a small wave. "Nice to see you again, Zac."

He smiles, but it looks more like a grimace, with hostility still lining it. "And you, Natia."

I turn to the last man. At six feet, he's relatively short in comparison to the rest of them. He has light gray eyes, short ice-blond hair, and an athlete's body.

He raises his hand to shake mine. "I'm Nathan. It's nice to meet you." The slightest tingle of pain jumps across my hand as I shake his. I try not to react.

"And what are you head of?"

A corner of his mouth lifts. "Acquisitions." Well, that's a little less intimidating than the other two.

Leaning my back against the bar, I twist to look at Archan. "What would you like to talk about?"

"I would like to get to know you more." He leans against the bar next to me and fixes me with that dangerous stare.

"Ah, well if that's all, then I like long walks on the beach, Italian food, and picnics in the park."

The men chuckle.

Archan ignores them. "How about why you stopped dancing and joined your uncle's security firm?" I stop breathing for a few seconds. That's a very specific question. I make sure to follow the song playing in the bar to reinforce my shields. Shit, did I forget to do that on the dance floor?

"Dancing didn't give me the necessary intelligence to become a useful member of society," I spout, throwing his words back at him.

He pierces me with a look. "I disagree. Watching you dance tonight has been an education. Not much surprises me, and even less makes me change my mind. But your passion should be shown to the world. Why did you quit?"

He's not going to let it drop, so I answer with honesty. The best lies hold elements of truth. I look at the floor to disguise my emotions. "I adore my grandparents, but when my grandmother died, I became distant from my grandfather, and I already don't speak to my mom and dad. I felt alone in New York—it's a world away from home, so I decided to come back. Uncle Charlie offered me a job. I've been able to reconnect with my grandfather and build a life that involves my family."

When I look at Archan, numerous emotions pass over his face: distrust, anger, confusion, and the last thing I would expect—empathy.

Zac interrupts our staring. "What do you *do* exactly?"

"Uncle Charlie invested in training me to become a security officer. He knew I would get restless in an office job. I love my job." I'm proud of myself for reciting my prepared answer. It deflects the question, and most people don't realize I haven't answered it, yet it's still the truth.

But Zac isn't fooled, and he all but rolls his stormy eyes at me. "He trained you to do what, exactly?" Archan slides a hand around my waist and draws me to his side, resting it just below my hip. Heat spreads around my stomach then brushes the underside of my breasts. I hitch in a breath, and the liquid heat that pooled in my lower belly earlier is back.

I know what he's doing, and I hate him for it. I'd prefer the traditional methods of torture. Kidnapping, beating, fingernail pulling, teeth being taken out, someone even threatened to cut off my hair once. I admit, I reacted to that one… Does that make me vain?

This is a seduction to get me to spill my secrets and destroy my shields. Zac repeats the question, raising an eyebrow. They think they've broken me with this crazy sensation torture. They've underestimated me.

"I protect people from bad things," I declare.

Nathan, who watches the exchange with calculating eyes, asks, "What kind of bad things?" I've slipped up. People aren't protected from things—they're protected from other people.

"Murderers, rapists, kidnappers—"

Barney interrupts me, "Those are people, not things."

I screw my face up, feigning confusion.

"Speaking of kidnapping, what about yours in New York?" Archan demands. My entire body stiffens as flashes of Eve's crushed skull skip across my mind. Very few people know I was kidnapped; the SIP erased any trace of my involvement in Eve's murder.

"What do you mean?" I snap. Zac tilts his head.

Archan's eyes harden. "I mean when you were kidnapped by 'bad things' and your friend's skull was crushed."

Turning to face Archan, he mirrors me while running his hand along my waist. I glance down. A cold sweat breaks out across my skin as I imagine black claws extending from pale, translucent hands, crimson blossoming across my abdomen. I know I'm imagining it, but burning bile still rises up my throat.

I flick my gaze up. My mind flashes between Archan's bronzed face and the sickly pale skin with black eyes that haunts my dreams. "It's true, my friend was murdered. What about it?"

Archan's grip on my waist tightens. "Lawrence?"

My jaw drops, and I slam every bit of energy I have into my mental shields. He winces. "Get out of my head," I hiss.

"Then be honest. How did you escape Lawrence?"

"With injuries," I grind out.

Archan frowns and glances at Barney. "Wait. This was four years ago?"

"Yes, August." I guess Barney must have been investigating my life. Archan holds my chin in his hand and stares into my eyes.

"You're her," he mutters.

I tuck some hair behind my ear. "Excuse me?"

Zac barks out a laugh. "Of course she is."

I scowl at him, and Nathan explains before I explode. "Lawrence is looking for a girl that injured him about four years ago. Long blonde hair, toned, curvy body, and blue eyes."

I shake my head. "Impossible—he's dead."

Archan's grip tightens. "No, Natia, he is not. He was injured and pissed, but not dead. He's been searching for you for four years. Recently, he put a bounty out for you. My question is why is he so obsessed with finding one girl?"

Gold eyes pin me in place, demanding an answer. "Maybe I left a lasting impression and he wanted another date?"

"What are you hiding?" Archan demands.

"Nothing you need to know."

Barney starts laughing. "You're right, she is excellent at interrogation. Not one lie or straight answer."

My head is reeling from the news that Lawrence is alive. I huff. "Is he some drinking buddy of yours?"

All four men laugh silently. "I have been known to have a drink with hell's royalty, but no, I'm not his 'buddy,'" Archan chuckles.

"Royalty?" I squeak.

"Lawrence is the prince of the seventh level of hell."

"Violence," I mutter. Archan nods. Lawrence is alive, he's the *literal* Prince of Violence, and he's hunting me. It's too much to take in, so I box it off to deal with later.

"Tell me why you took the files," Archan demands.

I glance at all four men—correction, four powerful beings. They know and have even admitted to socializing with hell's royalty. Evidence of their malicious intent is mounting, but I can't come right out and declare, "because I suspect you of kidnapping seven people." So I opt for the less inflammatory reason.

"I want to know what you are."

"And you think I would leave that information lying around on my computer?" he scoffs.

I cock my head to one side. "Well no, not when you put it like that."

"Be honest. Is that all you were looking for?" Zac presses.

"Quid pro quo—if you want me to be honest, then you need to be."

Zac steps closer, making me back into Archan even further. "You don't have control here, Natia. Answer the question."

"I'm sorry, I don't have time for this bullshit, and I didn't bring any crayons to explain it to you, Zac," I whisper fiercely.

"Tell us what you're hiding," Archan murmurs in my ear; a shiver travels down my spine from his warm breath.

I've had enough of this shit. Maybe it's the alcohol, but I make a conscious decision to stop being scared. He wants to play games? Fine, I'll play. I step into Archan's body, ignoring the intense sensations, wrap my hands around his neck, and tilt my head back to stare at his molten gold eyes, which widen in surprise.

Running my fingers through his hair, I pull his head down to me, leaving inches between our mouths. His lips part. "And if I say no?"

"There are ways of breaking you," he whispers softly.

I laugh a little hysterically. "You're welcome to try. There's little you can do that hasn't already been done to me."

He smirks, not a pleasant look—one promising pain. "I have an active imagination, Natia, one that is well-versed in breaking people. We can do this the nice way, or not."

I step back and lift my wrists out to him in mock surrender. "Let's go."

He stares at me, and I raise an eyebrow. "No? Then leave me the fuck alone."

I push his hands off my waist. Using my considerable strength, I try to push through Barney and Zac, but they're like marble statues.

I huff. "Excuse me, I need the restroom."

Barney sips his beer and looks down at me. "I'm sure it can wait."

"Nope, it really can't," I say sweetly. Then I use the age-old excuse sure to make every male, regardless of their origins, cringe. "I'm on my period. I need to go to the restroom. Now."

Zac chuckles—the evil pig. "You're a grown woman, Natia, not a teenager battling her way out of a difficult math class she can't be bothered with. And we aren't fresh-faced twenty-year-old men who blush at the sound of a woman's private business."

Correction on my part—it works on all males apart from these insensitive asses.

"You okay, Natia?" Harry says from behind me.

I glance over my shoulder at my knight behind the bar, equipped with a white cloth rather than a sword. "Yeah, Harry—thanks. I was just leaving. Who's on security tonight?"

"Rob. You need him?" Harry replies as he scrutinizes the dangerous males surrounding me. I pass my eyes over Archan, Zac, Barney, and Nathan.

"Let her go. We don't want to cause a scene," Archan mutters.

"That's okay, just tell him I said hi!" I shout over my shoulder as Zac and Barney separate.

As I'm walking away, Archan proclaims, "You can run, but I will find you. This conversation is not finished." A crash of power steals my breath, and the hair on my arms and the back of my neck stand on end: a warning.

I scan the bar for my guys, but they're nowhere to be seen. I walk through the stock room and, needing a crowd as a diversion, pull the fire alarm before exiting out the rear of the building.

Chapter Twelve

Natia

Tauruses bury their anger until they have a big explosion of rage.

Covering my ears against the insistent whine of the alarm, I phone Zee. He answers in a panicked voice. "Where the hell are you?"

"In the alleyway, next to the bar," I explain. He hangs up.

The air shifts—I'm not alone.

Stepping toward the end of the alley, I squint at the outline of a gray aura. It's not Archan or any of his men. The power feels off, malevolent. Moving toward me, he wraps his body around each facet of darkness, avoiding the green glow from the exit sign. Thin, black-tipped fingers slink out of the shadows.

"Who are you?" a raspy voice asks.

"Seems like that's the question of the day," I mutter.

He steps forward. The shadows follow him, forming an inky cloak around his body. Lank, chin-length black hair obscures his flat green eyes, as they roam over my bare skin. "So, you're his new toy. You're different than the others. Less polished, but... I see the appeal."

"I'm nobody's toy," I grind out between my teeth. His pale, thin lips curve up, and he throws his head back, exposing his gangly neck. He bellows, puffing out his putrid breath, which smells of sour milk and stings my nostrils. An icy finger caresses my bare arm, creating a deep-seated chill, like I've been swimming in a pond in December. Lifting his finger to his mouth, he licks it.

A small smile spreads across his face. "You taste… different. There's darkness in you."

Anger flares inside me.

My fist connects with his sharp chin, and his eyes widen as his head snaps back.

I kick him in the chest, causing him to huff out a breath. Before I can pull my foot back, he captures it and twists my leg to the left.

Forcing my body to follow the push and avoid my leg snapping in half, I lose my balance and land on my ass, hard. A white-hot flash of pain explodes in my skull as it cracks against the concrete.

I bounce to my feet before he can land another blow, but he's too close and too fast for me to anticipate his movements.

Stepping on the bins, I jump and flip, landing behind him. He spins around with a waist-high roundhouse kick, his knee-length coat flapping around him. Returning the favor, I catch his ankle, and my hand slips to his large, leather, lace-up black shoe; it slides off to reveal an elongated, bony foot with black-tipped toes the same length as his fingers. I drop it and wrinkle my nose—I'm not a foot person when they're normal-looking, never mind a foot resembling something from a zombie movie.

"You should see a podiatrist about that," I state, pointing at his bare foot in the shallow puddle.

His black eyebrows curve in confusion. Guess it's his normal. He throws a punch at my face. I duck, and he groans as his fist crumbles some of the brick wall. That would have broken my nose.

Going to the balls of my feet, I jab my elbow into the base of his skull. He laughs, distracting me. Spinning around, he pulls me into a punishing embrace, immobilizing my arms.

He slowly sniffs my hair, and his eyes widen to form perfect discs, the green fading to glistening crimson. "I like you. Not a toy after all."

Instead of replying, I head-butt him, causing the dizziness already circling me to nearly take my consciousness. He grunts then gives me a wicked smile.

I groan. "Awesome... turned on by pain, aren't you?"

"No, turned on by a woman who can fight. I don't do passive fucking."

I shudder. "No way in hell. Let me go—now."

He starts laughing manically. "Oh, sweet girl, in hell is exactly where it will happen." I growl at him as faint footsteps grow closer.

He glances down the alley. "We'll finish this dance another time. In the meantime, give him a message for me." He whispers in my ear then releases me. Stepping back into the shadows, he grins, displaying his sharp yellow teeth, and disappears just as Zee and Aaden reach me.

Aaden touches the back of my head and brings his hand forward—dark blood shines in the dim light filtering into the alley from the distant street lamps. He narrows his eyes.

"He hurt you?"

I shake my head, which is stupid, as it makes me stumble. They each hook a hand under my arms.

"You don't need to drag me. I can walk," I grumble, trying to wrench myself from their grip. "What happened to you two?"

Aaden answers, "We saw Archan dancing with you, but instead of coming to help, we felt compelled to go outside. Then we couldn't get back in. There was an invisible wall around the bar we couldn't penetrate."

Hurrying two blocks in the opposite direction of the apartment, we turn left to walk two more blocks, then left again for three blocks, leading us behind our building. We make it back without incident, and Zee performs his usual safety checks. I glance at Aaden's computer—seven hours to go.

Zee points at the sofa. "Sit."

I bristle. "No, you sit."

"So help me God, Natia, sit before I make you."

I cross my arms. "You wouldn't dare."

He stalks toward me; apparently, he would. He opens his arms wide, ready to wrap them around me. I duck and grab his legs, throwing him over my shoulder. It sends me back on my ass, jarring my tailbone. I quickly push to my feet to put distance between me and a growling Zee.

"What the hell, Zee?! What's with the manhandling?"

"You need to start taking this seriously. You're in danger! Archan knows something isn't right. There's no hiding from this now, and all because you wanted to *dance*."

My vision goes a little blurry as my eyes sting with the first prick of tears. I point at him. "You aren't the one who has to play constant mind games while risking your life creeping around with what I believe is the most powerful being we've ever come across. You aren't being interrogated while having your body played against you. It's not something we prepared for. My body can be tortured until the point of death. This is mind fucking—it's intimate, a violation, and it's screwing with my brain."

Zee lets out an empty laugh. "Like you don't want it. I see the look on your face when he touches you. That's all you, Natia."

My jaw falls open. Speechless, I turn and stalk up the stairs toward my room, not trusting myself to open my mouth; I know I'll say something I'll later regret.

"I expect you down here in an hour to fill us in on your little chat with the Prince of Darkness. That should give you enough time to take care of your pent-up frustration," he spits out.

No. No way he just said that. I turn around and take my time to walk back down the stairs. My anger, hurt, and embarrassment rage inside me.

"Natia," Aaden warns.

"Repeat what you said," I seethe, stalking toward Zee. He stands with his arms crossed, looking every bit the arrogant asshole he is.

"I said—" he starts, but a wave of power whips my hair around my face and rustles my dress. Behind me, a glass vase smashes on the floor, and the crash echoes around the room. Zee is thrown against the refrigerator by an invisible force. I stare down at him, frozen.

His mouth falls open. "What the fuck just happened?"

Chapter Thirteen

Natia

Taurus. If something is wrong, they will always blame their own carelessness instead of other people.

I'm lying in the fetal position on the bed when the mattress dips, and I feel a warm, comforting hand squeeze my shoulder, accompanied by the scent of cinnamon, oranges, and fresh linens—Duncan.

"They called you?" I mutter into the pillow clutched to my chest.

"Charlie did when you refused to go in. You should have called earlier."

"I thought I was handling it."

He begins rubbing my back in soothing circles. "What happened?"

"I was angry, embarrassed, and confused. I wanted to hurt Zee... I was overtaken by a rush of power, and when it cleared, Zee was on the floor," I pause, "it's unforgiveable."

Duncan puts a hand under my chin and tips my head to face him. "Did you actually want to physically harm him? Or did you just want him to experience the hurt that you're feeling?"

I crease my brow. "I'm not sure." I pull my chin out of his grip and look away. "What's happening to me?"

"It's likely you're an elemental witch with an affinity for air."

I blink—a witch? Witches run in families like Duncan's, where generation after generation pass down their magical gifts and knowledge. My family has a few supernatural quirks—a mind-reading uncle and my shielding—but no obvious manipulation of magic.

Duncan continues, "I'm not sure why it's only happening now. Maybe stress triggered it? I'll need to work with you to master it. But right now, it's time to get up. We need to look at Archan's files."

I stretch my body, extending my toes and arms, and contemplate telling Duncan about Lawrence. But I know Duncan will hunt him, and we've got enough going on without opening this box. It can wait.

My heart beats faster with every step my bare feet take down the stairs. I'd hurt Zee—how could he ever trust me? Standing in the living room, I hug my chest. Aaden and Zee are hunched over the laptop at the dining table with their backs to me.

"Hi," I murmur. Duncan places his hands on my shoulders and pushes me forward.

Aaden looks at me over his shoulder with a small smile. "Hey, how are you feeling?"

"Erm, tired, I guess."

He nods at the laptop. "We've just started looking at Reinheart's files."

I sit opposite Zee and try to catch his eye. He ignores me. If he never spoke to me again, I would deserve it.

Duncan looks over Aaden's shoulder as the video starts to play. A woman stands in an indistinct alleyway, one end blocked by a brick wall. She appears nervous, scanning the walls, her hands in her coat pockets. Two minutes later, a man walks toward her and stops in front of her, his back to the camera. She passes a small package to him, which he puts in his coat pocket. He keeps his head down as he

113

leaves, hiding his features in the shadows. The woman waits three minutes then walks out to the street. Something pulls at my memory; I tug on the thread, trying to trap the thought.

"Kelly Peterson," I breathe, snatching the folder containing the disappearances. Finding a photo of Kelly, I lift it to the screen.

Duncan's eyes flick between the screen and photo. "You're right."

"The video is dated May 15th. She was reported missing by her neighbor on May 17th... maybe because she lives alone?" I muse.

I take out the next file—Ben Hamilton. "Play the next video." This time, it shows a blue sedan in a parking lot, with a lone driver. Six minutes go by before a red hatchback appears with a man behind the wheel. The blue sedan driver gets out of the car—it's Ben Hamilton. He holds a package slightly larger than his palm as he walks to the red hatchback and gets in the passenger seat, handing the parcel to the driver. As we watch, Ben frantically waves his hands, as if having an argument. Shortly after, he gets out and runs back to his own car. The red hatchback wastes no time squealing out of the parking lot, and Ben follows seconds later.

"It looks like they're all meeting the same person," Aaden says.

I nod slowly. "It's difficult to tell from those videos... Let's check the rest and see if they follow the same pattern."

An hour later, we've watched and analyzed all six videos, each one featuring one of the victims and the same man. We've determined he's six-foot-three, well-built, and weighs about two hundred and twenty pounds. He meets our victims in alleyways, parking lots, and bars, and he always manages to keep his face away from the camera or uses the shadows to hide his features.

"We have seven disappearances." I flick through the file. "Mary Conway is our last victim, but there's no video of her."

"Maybe Reinheart hasn't uploaded her file yet?" Duncan suggests.

I tuck my feet under me on the chair. "The victims met with our mystery man, gave him a small parcel, and disappeared within two days. Is Archan having them killed?"

Aaden scratches his left ear, a habit when he's thinking hard. "If he has videos of them, he knows they're handing off a package to the same man. Why not pick up the man for questioning?"

"Maybe he works for Archan and he's drawing out traitors... people stealing from him?"

Duncan turns to me. "If he's making these people disappear and knows you have these files, you're in more danger than we thought. I think Charlie's right; we should find another way."

I shake my head. "That's what we do, Duncan. Put our lives before others that don't understand what they're up against. We are meant to protect innocents who have no clue about this whole other world that slithers around them. That means we don't get to run at the first sign of danger."

Zee, who's been silent so far, smashes his fist on the table, making the laptop jump. "You can't be serious. You're not suggesting you continue with this mission? He'll kill you and make you disappear. He's already smashed your head and bruised your face."

I frown. "What are you talking about?"

He runs his index finger over my right eyebrow, making me flinch. He grimaces, and a look of frustration and anger settles onto his face. "Is your memory that short? Go look in the mirror. The remnants of last night are still on your face."

Realizing his assumption, I point to my injuries. "This wasn't Archan—this was a demon. He was waiting outside the bar. He thought I was Archan's new plaything. This was our subtle way of discussing the differences between enemy and plaything."

Duncan frowns at my face. "That's not exactly subtle."

I raise an eyebrow. "You should see the other guy."

"We didn't see anybody," Aaden says.

Running a hand over my head, I touch the egg-shaped lump and wince. Duncan combs his fingers through my hair, finding the source of my pain. Warmth suffuses my head, and the pain eases. "I've already done what I can with your face. You just have some bruising, but it should be gone in a few days. Does anywhere else hurt?"

I shake my head.

"Can you describe him?" Aaden asks.

My mind runs through his distinctive features. "I don't know what type of demon he is, but he had long, bony, black-tipped fingers, sharp facial features, crimson eyes… oh, and a pointy, long foot with black toes."

Duncan frowns. "Foot? He was one-legged?"

Snorting at the image of a hopping demon, I shake my head. "No, his shoe slipped off in my hand."

Duncan grins. "You touched his mangy foot?"

I mock shiver. "Don't, Duncan. I'll have nightmares for weeks. The guy needs to put socks on his Christmas list."

"Not sure demons get visits from Santa," Duncan mumbles.

"How about his build?" Aaden asks.

"He's tall, about six-foot-two or three, and well-built. He also seemed to move with the shadows, or rather the shadows move with him. In fact…" I glance at Aaden's laptop screen, paused on the last video, showing the mysterious man. They follow my gaze.

Zee exhales. "So, you've met our potential kidnapper."

"I can protect myself, Zee. We need to stop whatever is going on. You know we won't have another opportunity to get this close."

"There lies the problem, Natia—you're too close. How can you be effective when you can't think straight when he's around you? He's trying to bring down your shields, and when he discovers your true aura, what then? If I remember correctly, the last guy tried to drag you to hell. What if he figures out what you are?"

"Then he can let me know," I quip.

"So you think he'll shrug his shoulders and let you go? You're walking into the lion's den with a stick to protect yourself. You're out of your league." Inhaling deeply, he meets my eyes. "I can't be part of this." Snatching his coat from the back of the chair, he storms out of the apartment, slamming the door behind him.

I lurch to my feet, and Duncan grabs my arm. "Let him be, Locks. He's scared for you. Let him work through his frustration. He'll be back."

I sit next to Aaden, pulling my knees up to my chest and circling them with my arms. "Is there anything else?"

He nods. "Some text files."

He opens the first one; it's about the possible whereabouts of an artifact they must be hunting for. Notes show locations they've already checked. There are three left to search.

I frown. "Do you think the victims were handing our mystery demon what they thought may be this artifact?"

Aaden swings back on his chair. "Good theory. The real question is when Reinheart finds this artifact, what's he going to use it for?"

"Good point…" I put my hand on the back of his chair and push forward. "Stop swinging on your chair, you'll fall and hurt your head."

His lips quirk up. "You sound like my seventh-grade teacher."

Ignoring him, I point to a file named "Pan." "What's that?"

Aaden opens it and finds that it's actually an extensive document about a person.

"Unusual name," I muse as we scan the text. I point to a map with dates. "This Pan has led them on a worldwide hunt. If I didn't know better, I would say they don't have a clue where he is."

Aaden nods. "So, they're searching for an artifact and a man called Pan."

I drum my fingers on the table. "We don't know if they're responsible for the disappearances. But everything is linked. So we research the shit out of it and join the search for this artifact and Pan."

Duncan taps his fingers on the screen, and Aaden scowls, quickly wiping the fingerprints off with the sleeve of his sweatshirt. Duncan lifts his hands in apology. "Sorry. There's a picture file—can we look at that?"

Aaden double clicks the final file. A document with strange symbols fills the screen, and Duncan leans away, exhaling sharply. I narrow my eyes. "What?"

"It's the Septuagint."

I stare at Duncan, waiting for him to elaborate, but he looks lost in thought, so I prompt him. "The what?"

He blinks. "It's a page from a manuscript written around 300 BC. Essentially, it's the Old Testament written in Greek. Scroll down, please, Aaden."

Aaden moves the page to a photo of another ancient-looking paper. Duncan scrubs his hand down his face. "Shit."

"What?" If Duncan's nervous, I'm terrified.

"This is a page from the Dead Sea Scrolls, ancient Jewish religious manuscripts... some dating four hundred years before Christ. Can you send me a copy of these?"

Aaden attaches the files to an email.

I fold my arms across my chest. "What the hell is going on?"

"Whatever it is, it's bigger than some disappearances, Locks."

"How much bigger?"

"Think biblical style."

My mouth forms a soundless *oh*.

Aaden sighs. "We have missing people, a mysterious artifact, a man named Pan, and ancient religious documents. I'm all ears for how this story plays out."

"Don't forget the bunch of unidentified powerful beings in the middle of all this," I mutter.

"And a shadow demon," Duncan adds.

I groan. "So not complicated and confusing as hell?"

"Don't mention hell—that's the last thing this situation needs," Duncan mutters. We sit for a few minutes, assimilating the information.

Aaden breaks the silence. "We need to talk about last night... about what happened with Archan." I stiffen; Duncan puts a hand on my shoulder, centering me.

I twist my hands on my lap. "He questioned me about leaving New York to work for Uncle Charlie. I think he bought my reasons, but his men drilled down into what my job is."

Duncan frowns. "What men?"

"He brought three of his men along. Barney, his head of intelligence. Zac, who I've already met; he's head of security and an ass. And Nathan, who's head of acquisitions. That seemed strange at the time, but now we know they're searching for an artifact, it makes sense."

Aaden scratches his left ear. "What did you tell them?"

"That I protect people from bad things."

Duncan winces. "You slipped up. Did they notice?"

"Yes. Nathan zoned in on the word '*things*.'"

Duncan runs his hand through his wavy hair. "Shit. He'll keep going until you break."

"I know." I put my head in my hands, exhausted, but not admitting Archan glimpsed my memories of Lawrence. "It's done now. I just need to be extra careful with my shields. He asked why we stole the files. I told him it's because I wanted to know what he is. Which he thought was amusing."

"So we keep going?" asks Aaden.

"We have no choice. He'd come looking for me anyway. At least this way, we have some control."

"Agreed," says Duncan, "I'm staying. When you're not attending meetings, we'll work on your new powers and strengthening your shields."

"Why do you think she suddenly has powers?" Aaden asks Duncan in his typical no-nonsense fashion.

Duncan grins. "Not sure, but they can only be a blessing for Natia in this situation."

Aaden focuses his steely gaze on me. "Have you tried accessing them again?"

I shake my head. "No, I'm really not sure how I did it to begin with."

"You were pissed," Aaden says. I tilt my head in acknowledgement. "Don't you find the timing suspicious?" he pushes.

I frown, while Duncan nods and says, "A little."

"Wait, why is it suspicious?"

"You've shown no magical capabilities beyond aura reading, strength, and sensitivity to air currents before now. Most people come into their powers around puberty," Duncan explains.

Rubbing my hands down my face, I consider the implications. "So either I'm a late bloomer or something else is happening to me."

Duncan squeezes my shoulder. "Whatever it is, we'll face it together, Natia. You're never alone."

Images of the SIP testing people's strength and powers float through my mind. Anything unusual, and they're all over it—and not necessarily in a good way. I may be human, and they may value abilities, but they don't tolerate unstable agents. They'll want to know why I have power, where it came from, and what I plan to do with it. If I can't demonstrate I have control, they may incarcerate me. "I don't want to tell the SIP yet, not until we know what it means for me." I know Duncan will protect me, so I aim this at Aaden.

He nods. "It's okay, Natia. I won't say anything. I'll contact Charlie and update him with the progress we've made with the files. He'll find it difficult to justify pulling the mission when we've gotten this close."

"What about Zee?"

Aaden pushes his chair back. "I'll handle Zee. Go get some sleep; meeting's at noon today. You have," he peers at his watch, "three hours."

Duncan follows me upstairs, and I sit cross-legged on the center of the bed. The mattress dips as he sits on the edge. "Tell me about Reinheart and how you feel when he's trying to break your shields." I flush and look away.

Duncan wraps an arm around my waist, and my head collapses onto his shoulder. "He's playing with you. It doesn't mean you're weak—it means he's strong."

I gulp. "He... touches me with his power. It's hot, sensual—intoxicating. My mind blanks, and all I can feel is his essence thrumming under my skin. His brief touches unsteady me. It's a dangerous combination." I tip my head back to look into Duncan's eyes. "This is what scares me... I don't know how much is me and how much is his mind fucking." I bury my face in his neck.

A knock on the open bedroom door makes me lift my head. Zee is leaning against the doorframe, his hands in his jeans pockets.

"How much did you hear?" I ask, panicking we're going to repeat our earlier argument.

"Enough to know you need support, not judgment. I'm sorry... I crossed a line. If you hate me, I understand. But I'm here for you. If you want to finish this assignment, I'll support you."

I stand, closing the space between us, and put my arms around his waist. He tenses.

"Forgive me?" I ask.

"What for?"

"I kinda threw you across the room."

He laughs, and his muscles relax beneath my fingers. "I deserved it, and if that's what you can do with your new power, it will help protect you. Work with Duncan to harness it, and we can spar to keep your fighting skills honed."

I give him one last squeeze. "Okay, sleep first, then the lion's den. But remember, our sticks are bigger than theirs, and we swing them faster and stronger than the largest cat."

Sleep claims me fast. I dream of golden eyes and my skin being covered in blue, red, and orange flames burning me from the inside out, balancing a fine line between pleasure and pain. When I wake, I'm covered in sweat.

I can't escape this man.

Chapter Fourteen

Archan

Unknown origin.

Leaning back on the sofa in my apartment, I glare at Zac, Barney, and Nathan.

"She must be involved. Her excuse of wanting to know what I am is only half the truth," I start. Tension creases Zac's eyes, and I put a hand on his shoulder. "Stop beating yourself up, Zac. We all missed it."

He looks to Barney and snaps. "How close are we? They have the files, the last locations, and they most likely know we're searching for Pan and the artifact—the Jar."

Barney takes his phone out of his back pocket, and we wait while he scrolls through his emails. "We're close to finishing the search of the Iron Mountain; Dina only has access four hours a day, so it's taking time."

"And the others?" Zac demands.

"We're working on the natives of North Sentinel Island. They're hostile.

Michael's in Poland and has made some progress."

I stare at the floor. "What do you think Natia is after?"

Nathan exhales and runs a hand over his head, causing the groomed, short curls to dissolve into a mess. "The Jar, possibly Pan's protection…"

"We track her," I say. "If she finds it, she will lead us to Pan, and we'll destroy them both."

Zac grabs his beer and takes a long drink. "What about Lawrence? He doubled the bounty for her last night."

Barney laughs. "From those glimpses of her memory, I don't think they're friends. He's either pissed off and wants to kill her himself, or he's infatuated with her. I would vote the second one, given how alluring she is."

Zac rolls his beer between his hands. "What about her shields? If I break them, I can scan her memories and maybe find Pan's location. Screw who her grandfather is."

I work to relax my fists when I see the whites of my knuckles. I don't want anyone else's hands on her, plus Zac can easily destroy an unwilling mind. "No. I will do it my way."

Barney huffs. "It's taking too long."

I give him a hard stare. "Are you challenging me?"

A look of panic crosses his face. "Of course not."

"I'll have cracked her shields by the end of the week. Then you can take a read, Zac, and we will know for sure who she is. Get someone to watch her apartment; put a tail on anyone who isn't delivering food or cleaning. Don't interfere with her actions, but get Leo and Jed to follow her. I want an hourly report."

I stand and walk to the window to look out over the twinkling city lights. Humans have come so far in the last hundred years, but I'm not fond of the skyscrapers. The concrete jungle is littered with imitation nature; plastic plants falsely shine in the artificial light, struggling to give the illusion of life. Most people don't even notice. Natia's reaction to my rooftop surprised me; she took in every branch, every bloom. Her hands touched the garden as if she could draw strength from the life before her. Zac pulls me out of my musings. "What about the messengers? They're restless."

"They will have to be patient, unless they want to end up like Kelly. We will continue to protect them, but they will need to stay in the house under guard."

Barney sighs and shakes his head. "I can't believe we lost her."

"It's not your fault. We've protected the rest."

The men and women we sent to Khalkaroth were supposed to get us closer to Pan's location. We suspect he's protecting Pan and trying to locate the only object we can use to track this person—the Jar. But the more false artifacts we lure Khalkaroth out with, the more suspicious and careful he becomes with his movements. Our last messenger, Mary Conway, disappeared following her exchange. We suspect he's realized our intentions, so Mary was our last messenger. Which means Khalkaroth could have sent Natia in his place to steal the Jar he believes we have or sabotage our efforts to find Pan. It's an unusual tactic for the normally brutal demon—but maybe he's learning the art of subtlety? She certainly fooled me into trusting her not capable enough to steal from my own apartments.

I glance at the office doors, remembering that they were open slightly the morning of our breakfast. I dismissed it at the time, believing Margret, my cleaner, had mistakenly left it open. I should have known after eight years of no errors she wouldn't have done that. But sweet, innocent, beautiful Natia never entered my mind—if her naivety is an act, she plays it well, her cheeks wearing the glow of her embarrassment more times than not, and she showed no signs of panic, which would have given away her intentions. It doesn't fit that he sent her, but I need to be sure—if she is working with Khalkaroth, she will regret the day she walked into my life.

"See if you can tie any of Natia's group or security company to Khalkaroth," I say.

Nathan turns to me. "You think she's working with him?"

"No, but we can't take any chances," I state. "Let her snoop around. We don't have the Jar, so there is nothing to lose. But it will keep her busy while I work on breaking her shields."

Barney and Nathan leave, and Zac joins me to look out over the city.

"She's captivating."

I glance at him. "Natia?"

"Yes. I can see why you like her. She isn't put off by your dominating nature. She challenges and intrigues you, but you need to keep focused. Even if she isn't involved, she's a distraction, a dangerous one. As much as you think you're breaking her, she may break you in return."

"It's been so long since someone aroused me like she does. I find myself wanting her to choose to let me into her fascinating mind."

Zac stares at the city. "We don't have time for a fairy tale romance."

I laugh coldly, a sound that seems so at odds with the warmth Natia provides me with her presence. "I'm not looking for love, Zac. I'm not capable of it. I'm looking for an equal, a participant in sex, not someone who panders to me."

Chapter Fifteen

Natia

When a Taurus is angry, anything that gets in their way will be destroyed.

The next morning, we enter Reinheart and Hunter with no issues. Duncan stays in our SUV a few blocks away. Following the plan to keep me as far away from Archan as possible, I arrive ten minutes late. Aaden sits at the opposite end of the table from Archan. As expected, there's an empty seat next to Archan. Zee stands behind it, as if waiting for me. When I enter, Aaden jumps up and moves to the empty seat, I sit in Aaden's seat, and Zee moves behind me. Archan's eyes track this game of musical chairs with mild interest.

Laugh it up, buddy, but your hands, legs, and anything else you want to touch me with are staying at least three feet away from me at all times. I slap myself mentally, but at least I didn't say it out loud.

"Nice of you to join us, Miss Waterford," Archan drawls.

His eyes rove over my face then seem to stop, his gaze lingering on the fading bruise above my right eye. A muscle in his tense jaw jumps, and a hint of fury flashes through his eyes. I try not to mistake his expression for one of concern—I'm sure he's still just furious about last night, nothing more.

"Apologies, gentlemen. I needed the ladies' room." And just like that, my lateness is old news. Zac stands behind Archan with his arms crossed and glares at me throughout the meeting. I've already decided to stop being intimidated by Archan and his men, so I glare back and give him my best deranged smile. Starting with "Hit Me With Your Best Shot," I alternate a variety of eighties songs and drift in and out of the meeting, contemplating the case, Archan, and my mental health, until Edward nudges my elbow. I narrow my eyes at him.

He leans away from me. "Erm… we were asking your opinion on a name for the new company."

I furrow my brow. "It's been agreed the company will remain Waterford Industries."

"We think it would be more appropriate to have a name that represents both companies," the balding, stout man across from me explains.

This is where I draw the line. My presence may be fabricated, but I'm passionate about making sure my grandfather's business is protected.

"So you're saying Waterford Industries, with a net worth of two hundred billion dollars, should change its prestigious name—which is known worldwide for its excellence—for a different name because of a merger with a company one hundredth of its size?"

The man's face turns red. "I see your point, but—"

Leaning over the table, I twist my head and read the name on the folder in front of him. "James, is it? Waterford Industries will not be changing its name. If this is a deal breaker, take your fancy briefcase and go back to your failing company. Good luck with job hunting."

James's face reddens further. Even his semi-bald head is turning pink. "You are overstepping, Miss Waterford. You have no authority here."

"Actually, Mr. Ledmen, Miss Waterford has the power to stop this merger if she feels her grandfather's company's identity is being compromised. I would say this is a clear case. Do you wish to proceed with the original plan of the company remaining as Waterford Industries, or shall we conclude business?" a deep, smooth voice drawls from the head of the table.

My eyes snap to Archan for the first time, breaking my own rule. His gold eyes are focused on me. I struggle to catch my breath then jump when a warm hand touches my shoulder.

Zee bends next to my ear. "It's only me." I lean my head back to look into Zee's eyes, acknowledging the spell is broken. James glowers at me. Guess he doesn't like being argued with. Archan's interference hasn't helped—as if the little woman needed a rescuer. I risk a glance at Archan, checking his aura. The red is the most prominent at the moment; healthy ego is my assessment. Could the man get any more dominating?

Heat wraps around my calf. It slides up my leg in slow circles, and sensual phantom fingers caress my upper thigh. I bite my lip to stop a moan escaping and level a glare at him. His lips twitch. Asshole.

Zee kneels to whisper in my ear. "Duncan called. They've found Mary Conway's body. He's been called to the scene. What do you want to do?" Without hesitation, I slide my notes into my bag.

"Excuse me, gentlemen. Something needs my urgent attention." I catch Aaden's eyes; he's wondering if he should stay or come. I can't torture him with a meeting I'm not in, so I give a subtle nod of my head.

"Is there anything I can help you with, Miss Waterford?" Archan enquires, his casual tone at odds with his expression.

"Thanks, but I'm afraid this is outside of your area of expertise."

He gives me a predatory grin. "I hope you resolve the issue and return to us as soon as possible." He's challenging how fast I can solve problems in front of a boardroom full of people. Screw him— this is more important than power games.

"Don't expect my return today. I'll see you after the Christmas period, gentlemen. Happy holidays."

Barney meets us outside of the door, his warm brown eyes crinkling with false concern. "The limo is at the front; it'll take you anywhere you need to go." Yeah, right. As if we're going to make it easy for them to know our business.

I give him my best fake smile. "Thanks, Barney, we have our own car." Zee, Aaden, and I enter the elevator and stay silent until we're in the SUV with Duncan.

"Did you bring my change of clothes?" I ask Duncan. If we're going to a murder scene, we might encounter problems, and I can't fight in a fitted dress and high heels. Well, I could, but it could be embarrassing if the dress rips to show my underwear. It would cheer up Zee, though. He hasn't been his cheeky self since I threw him across the kitchen.

"In the rucksack under the passenger seat. I brought your favorites," he replies. I'm in the back seat with Aaden, while Zee is up front with Duncan. I pull out my deep red leather pants, matching jacket, and black tank top. The leather of the jacket is buttery soft; Duncan bought it for me when I was given my first official assignment. The pants I already owned. They offer good protection during a fight, but together, they are a little much for a crime scene.

I catch Duncan's eyes in the rearview mirror and raise an eyebrow. "You mean *your* favorite outfit?"

He chuckles. "There's a sweater if you don't want to wear your jacket. Your boots are under the driver's seat." Aaden reaches underneath and pulls out my mid-heeled black boots. Now these are my favorites.

I smack Zee over the head, and he yelps. "What the hell was that for?"

I kiss him on the cheek. "For when you look in the mirror and try to watch me get changed."

A wicked grin curves his lips. "If I've already been caught, that means I *can* look." I give him my best psychopathic stare. He holds his hands up and turns to face the front. *Huh, maybe that's my best look for scaring people?*

I only have to slap Zee three more times for looking and commenting on my underwear. The man's a pervert obsessed.

Duncan parks beside a familiar red sedan. "John is here. He called Charlie. He knows we're investigating the disappearances," Duncan explains. Detective John Patton is our contact at the Seattle Police Department. He's aware of the existence of supernaturals but tries not to get involved. He says he has enough nightmares with the things humans do. I don't blame him. Some cases haunt you months later. Some you never let go.

Mary Conway's body lies face-up on the sidewalk of an uptown street lined with 1920s brownstones. The gods have blessed Seattle with sunshine today. Fluffy white clouds pass through the blue sky, and a chilly breeze picks up strands of hair on my neck, making me shiver. Remnants of a heavy power clog the air, making my skin crawl. I look up and down the street. It's two o'clock in the afternoon, and there's no one on the sidewalk. Even beyond the crime scene tape, there are no reporters, no nosy citizens.

"Afternoon, Natia, Zee, Aaden, Duncan. I didn't expect so many of you," John greets us, looking puzzled.

"We were in town," I explain, avoiding specifics. I step next to the body. The crime seems more brutal in the sunshine. Bending to look at Mary, my torso casts a shadow across her face. Each dead body still hits me hard. I've never become "used to it," as some people do. Most people see it as a weakness. Duncan says it's because I'll never accept or excuse the evil that walks the Earth.

"Details?" I ask, taking in Mary's face. Her dull hazel eyes are fixed on the sky. Mascara stains her cheeks in distressed black streaks, and her lips have a faint tint of bright pink lipstick, keeping them artificially colored despite death.

"About 1:00 p.m. an anonymous caller reported a body on this street. Dispatch arrived four minutes later. They recognized her as Mary Conway and called me, then I called you on my way here. The scene is well preserved—the beat cops are good."

"Why is there no one on the street?" Zee wonders.

"The gas company got a call about a possible leak and evacuated the street about 12:30 p.m."

I cross my arms. "Assuming the caller of the gas scare is our killer, it seems he wanted her in plain sight in the middle of the day... but he also didn't want her to be found by just anybody, if he cleared the streets."

Zee undoes his tie and gives me a meaningful look. "If he thinks you're working with *AR*, maybe it's meant for you."

John sighs. "AR? Never mind. I got the gas company to keep the area quarantined for the next two hours." Aaden appears with the camera we use for crime scenes and hands me a pair of gloves.

Snapping them on, I nod at John. "Good, we have time to process the scene."

Crouching, I study Mary from head to toe. "Are these the same clothes she went missing in?"

He flicks through his notepad. "Yes."

I lift her right arm with no resistance. "Rigor mortis has passed… She's been dead at least twenty-four hours." Turning her left arm over, I notice symbols on the inside of her wrist, which look as if they were recently tattooed; the skin is still raw and damaged.

I glance at Duncan. "Do you know what these mean?" He crouches opposite me, and Aaden hands him a pair of gloves. Duncan draws his eyebrows together, taking hold of her wrist, and examines the symbols.

"No… I don't remember ever seeing anything like these."

I blink. Duncan always knows the languages, even the demonic ones we sometimes come across. Aaden snaps photos of the symbols. Examining the body further doesn't reveal any obvious cause of death. I repeatedly circle the crime scene, scrutinizing every inch of ground for evidence, and find nothing. John leaves to respond to another call, and we agree to meet for the autopsy findings tomorrow.

With thirty minutes to spare, we decide to take a wider look at the street. Aaden and Zee go left, while Duncan and I turn right. Two hundred meters from the crime scene, I spot a little girl about four years old dressed in flannel pajamas walking on the opposite sidewalk, crying out for her mommy. I jog toward her, but she runs away, her dark curls bouncing and slippers squeaking.

"Hey, sweetie, it's okay. Let's see if we can find your mom," I call out.

She ignores me, scampering down an alleyway.

Following her to the mouth of the alley, the hairs on my arms prickle with the presence of power. "Why do things always lead down a dark alley? Why not a meadow full of flowers?" I ask Duncan, as he joins me in the narrow, claustrophobic space.

We emerge into a large, well-kept communal garden surrounded by tall trees. Duncan laughs. "Not quite a meadow, but close."

My eyes scan the garden for the missing little girl. Sunlight dances across the grass and through the leaves of the evergreen trees. Several white wooden benches surround the open area. It's a small paradise in the city. The air currents shift, twisting and racing over my palms. I whip around as three enormous Renevate demons appear from behind the trees, muscly chests bare, legs cloaked in billowing, dark trousers. Their short, spiky, white hair crowns a blocky head and is a stark contrast to their naturally black skin. Milky eyes study us as they spread out, circling us.

Awesome—because my day didn't have enough excitement already. "If I'd known I had a wish today, I wouldn't have wasted it on agriculture."

Duncan chuckles. "Aw, Locks, not scared of a few Renevate demons, are you?"

"Nope, just marveling at the universe's sense of humor, and my ribs still ache from the cuddle the last one gave me."

Renevate demons are fast, strong, and committed to killing their target, even if it means their own deaths. They're always controlled by a more powerful being. But the big problem is the two sets of hands; they hold you with one set while strangling you with the other. I curse under my breath—I've left my swords back in the car, meaning hand-to-hand combat is inevitable.

"Great… Dip, Dippy, and Dippier," I quip as I spin in a circle.

Duncan gives me a half smile. "Which one do you want?" I give them a once-over. The largest is the one on the right—Dippier. The other two are a little smaller.

I point out the largest one. "I'll take Dippier." He flashes me his white, razor-sharp teeth in what I think is his attempt at a smile, but the grimace more closely resembles a rabid dog.

Duncan pulls a small dagger out of his boot and hands it to me. "Good choice, Locks. He seems the most pissed off."

Spoiling the plan, Dippy launches himself toward me.

Dip runs at Duncan. Seems like my original target is either the leader or a wimp.

Sprinting toward Dippy, I drop to my knees and slide across the grass at the last second.

Leaning back and pushing the dagger up, I tear through Dippy's abdomen and miss being covered in demon guts by millimeters.

Rolling to my feet, I stand in one fluid motion and shout to Duncan, "Remember, it's your turn!"

He chuckles. A power bolt breezes past me in a blare of crackling blue light and buries itself in Dip's face.

A wave of blood splatters the white wall with crimson in a gruesome, vivid contrast.

My face is still sizzling from the heat of the blast, like I've spent too long in the sun.

"You dare singe my eyebrows, and I'll chop off your—"

Dippier throws his fist toward my face.

I duck and bring my leg up at an almost one-hundred-and-eighty-degree angle, kicking his head. My foot bounces off his skull, unbalancing me.

"Are these guys made of concrete?" I shout at Duncan.

Dippier takes advantage of my wobbling and wraps an arm around my throat.

Twisting my body, I hammer my elbow into his solar plexus. He grunts but doesn't let go.

Wrapping his other arms around me, he pins me to him. It's my turn to grunt. I expand my chest, giving me more time before he cuts off my air. Duncan stalks toward me, calmly assessing the situation. He can't throw one of his magic balls (*yes, I just said that*), as the demon is behind me. My lungs burn as my body begs for oxygen, and my cracking ribs complain.

If you have a plan, Duncan, now is the time to execute it.

I'd pictured my death as an epic battle, one that included my swords—like the ones you face at the end of a level on a video game. Not being flattened like a panini by an overgrown demon with too many arms.

Footsteps pound down the alleyway. *Please be Zee and Aaden. Who am I kidding? Lady Luck is on sabbatical.*

Four more Renevates spill into the clearing, with one blocking the exit.

Duncan points to my left hand, held fast to my side.

My eyebrows squash together. I'm not good at hand signals. He makes a crude stabbing motion. Ah, that one I think I know.

I close my hand, feeling the hilt of the dagger, and mouth a silent *oh* in realization. I can stab the demon, but I'm going to have to slice through the side of my thigh—it's that or die.

Flicking the dagger around in my hand so the blade faces backward, I thrust it into the demon and hiss at the sharp stinging along my thigh. Mercifully, the monster releases me.

Whirling around, I ram the blade into its neck.

He holds the gash as his blood spills out of his throat like a waterfall before crumpling to the ground.

Going back-to-back with Duncan in the middle of the clearing, I breathe through the pain, and the adrenaline begins to numb it. Balancing my core, I assume my fighting stance, ready for the next kill.

Chapter Sixteen

Archan

Unknown origin.

"I'd rather watch paint dry," is the human saying being clearly demonstrated as I listen to the inane argument these pompous men are currently spouting. My phone rings, interrupting the meeting. I look down—it's Jed. He wouldn't call unless it was urgent.

"Yes?" I snap.

"She's being attacked by Renevate demons. What—what do you want to do?" He sounds more than a little panicked.

"Help her, and stay on the phone." I stride out of the boardroom, offering no apologies, leaving them to argue over inconsequential things. I'd envied Natia when she had left. It's obvious she belongs in a boardroom about as much as me.

"Get the car," I snap at Barney.

"It's ready," he states. Riding in the elevator, I curse the slowness of the blasted thing. A distinct, feminine voice cries out through the phone, followed by the faint sound of bones breaking. Fuck, I should have followed her when she left.

Trying to keep calm, I ask Jed, "Update?"

"Two down, two to go."

"Casualties?" I ask, my voice steady in contrast to my twisting insides. If anyone is going to kill her, it will be me. But not before I have quenched this need of her.

Nathan waits in the passenger seat with the engine running. I jump in and start driving just as two doors slam behind me—Zac and Barney.

"The girl is okay. She's killed three of them, and the man is some kind of warlock," Jed reports.

Pulling the car into the street, I glance at the location on the GPS Nathan must have entered. I ignore the directions; it would take us through city traffic. Instead, I weave through the back streets and power past the gas company waving us down. Pulling up behind Jed's car, I jump out and sprint down the alleyway.

Jed and Leo stand in a clearing, surrounded by seven Renevate demons in various states of destruction. Blood coats the ground, entrails lay entangled on the white benches, and the walls are splattered with scarlet, as if a child has been let loose with a tin of paint.

I blink at the sight of Natia straddling the heaving chest of the only living demon, which is twice her size. His four hands have been severed and litter the ground like spare parts. She glances at me and rolls her eyes. Apparently she's stronger than she looks and is not only familiar with my world, but comfortable in it, too.

"Who sent you?" she interrogates the demon. He simply cackles. She twists a knife lodged in his outer thigh, making me inwardly wince as he shrieks.

"Let's try this again. Who sent you?" she barks.

"Khalkaroth," the demon grinds out. She twists the knife again, tearing through muscle, a brutal and precise move meant to maximize pain without killing someone.

"Why?" she presses.

"To kill you," he gurgles, as blood dribbles from his lips.

"How unoriginal and anticlimactic. Why does he want me dead?"

When he doesn't reply, she pulls the knife out of his thigh and plunges it into the other, twisting it deep. The demon screams. I smile—this woman is merciless.

"Why does he want me dead?" she demands again.

The demon flicks his gaze in my direction. "I don't know."

Natia glances at me, missing nothing. "You lie. Try again."

"He wants to win. He wants it unleashed." I study Natia's response. The answer makes complete sense to me, but if she's as clueless as she says, it should be a mystery to her. Her face scrunches up in genuine confusion. Tension I didn't realize I was carrying leaves my shoulders.

"What is *it*?" she demands.

He spits some blood toward her, and she leans away. "The final evil." His body starts to convulse. Natia removes the knife and slices cleanly through his throat.

She wipes it on the grass and pushes to her feet.

I assess her for injuries; her neck is red, and she's clutching her abdomen. I assume one of them got their hands around her throat and ribs. I could strangle her myself for the danger she's walked into.

"What the hell are you doing here?" she rasps. The damage to her throat must be worse than I thought.

"It appears you needed some assistance." I point toward Leo and Jed.

She narrows her eyes on Leo. "You work for him?"

Leo scratches the back of his neck. "I didn't think to mention it at the time." Zee, Aaden, and an unfamiliar man, who I assume is the warlock, run toward us. They stand next to Natia in a line of protection. It's an instinct she provokes in people, including me.

Jed, Leo, Nathan, Barney, Zac, and I stand opposite them—she should be intimidated. Instead, she is furious and sexy as hell. As I struggle to decide if she's brave or stupid, she steps toward me, and the warlock grasps her arm. My power flares.

Grinding her teeth, she shakes him off. "No, Duncan, we need to know what these assholes are up to." I'm distracted by her outfit, showing every perfect curve of her body. Her hair has come loose and cascades down her back.

This is the real Natia.

She strides toward me, her boots coming toe-to-toe with my shoes. Tipping her head back, she stares defiantly into my eyes. She's close enough that I can feel her breath on my skin.

"I'll ask again. What the hell are you doing here?"

Zac initiates our mental connection.

"She's pissed."

"Agreed."

"Do you want me to do something?" he asks, sounding amused.

"No, I like her feistiness," I admit. *"I can't decide if she's brave or crazy."*

Zac tips his head to the side. *"She has a lot of courage, she's a fighter, and she has never backed down from you. She might be a little insane, though."*

I chuckle. The rest of my men initiate our mental link. I allow it.

Leo examines her like she's something to eat. *"Her ass is fucking perfect in leather."*

Jed laughs. *"Hell, yes! Sign me up for some of her."*

Barney interrupts before I strangle Jed. *"She's bleeding."*

Examining her, I spot the blood seeping from a wound on her thigh, camouflaged in the deep red of her leather pants. I reach out to touch her leg, but she knocks my arm out of the way.

"It's a flesh wound," she snaps, not a hint of pain in her voice. She must still be riding the adrenaline from the fight. "Have you lost your ability to speak, or is it beyond your intellect to answer a simple question?"

My mouth twitches. "Dinner?"

She frowns. "The main meal of the day, often taken between late afternoon and early evening. Your point?"

Gods, this woman never says what I expect. "We will discuss this over dinner."

She rolls her eyes. "Cam's Heaven Diner, two blocks east. If you're not there in ten minutes, I leave, and my team is coming. I don't care if your goons come or not."

Jed crosses his arms. "Babe, who are you calling a goon? We saved you."

She blinks at him, as if he hasn't been important enough to notice until now. "You helped." She waves her hand, gesturing to the gruesome scene. "And you guys can clean up."

Duncan chuckles, and she points at him. "It's still your turn next time."

Spinning on her heel, she marches down the alley and lifts her sweater over her head, revealing a loose tank top. I watch her perfect hips sway down the alley. Turning back, I find all my men looking, too. I can't blame them.

We wait until Natia and her team have left before speaking.

"So, there's definitely more than meets the eye with Natia," Nathan points out. "She didn't bat an eye dealing with demons. She's part of the supernatural world."

I nod and ask Jed and Leo, "Do you know why the Renevates attacked them?"

Leo turns to me. "No, but the demon was telling the truth—she was their main target. They kept zoning in on her. Given she came to investigate Mary's murder and was talking with the local detective, it would seem logical Khalkaroth sent them, which means she isn't working for him. She held her own; she's a damn good fighter, elegant and graceful, but strong. She knows how to immobilize and interrogate. She doesn't work for a security firm, unless she's protecting the president." His voice holds respect, difficult to gain from Leo; she must have truly impressed him.

Jed grins. "She's flexible… I couldn't keep up with the angles her legs were achieving, but I have a few ideas—"

I snap my hand around his throat. "You won't touch her. Do you understand?" He winks at me.

Before this turns into a fight, Zac brings us back to our mission. "What now?"

I release Jed, who's still grinning at me. "We meet on her terms, let her think she has the upper hand. I am going to persuade her we should work together. It will be easier to find out what she's up to. Jed, you have the best skills to infiltrate her group, so you'll be working with her directly. I warn you—touch her, and you will lose your hand."

My men gape at me, shocked. I've never been possessive over a woman before. I don't explain, mainly because I can't. I don't understand this need to dominate and possess her.

Barney glances at the demon Natia tortured. "She seemed genuinely confused when the demon mentioned releasing the last evil. Either she's an excellent actress, or she's clueless. What are you going to tell her about our mission? The Jar? Pan?"

"As little as possible. We will see what she has figured out so far and feed her enough information to keep up the pretense of a working relationship. She can give us information we wouldn't have otherwise known."

Barney scratches his head, grazing his cropped hair. He almost looks comical when he does it. "What information?"

"She has a relationship with the detective that we do not. She will be privy to the conversations not in the reports."

Nathan looks around the garden, surveying the destruction. "Have you noticed she doesn't lie?"

"She does. She's just good at it," Zac answers.

Nathan puts his hands in his pockets and frowns. "No, she doesn't, Zac. I admit she's clever at deflecting questions, but she doesn't lie. I can't decide if it's part of her personality… or something more."

Leo frowns. "Like what?"

"There are some beings that can't lie," Nathan answers slowly.

I chuckle. "You're suggesting she's not human?"

Nathan thins his lips as his gray eyes flash. "I'm suggesting she's unusual."

Zac nods, rubbing his chin. "Do you think you can still crack her shields?"

Briefly, I flood the garden with my power, wiping it clean of the destruction and chaos left behind from the battle, then shove my hands in my pants pockets and walk toward the street. "Yes. She won't be on her guard if she thinks we are on the same side. Let's go—we don't want our little badass warrior getting stroppy and leaving the diner."

Chapter Seventeen

Natia

Tauruses—their little secret? When they need help, it's hard for them to admit it because they hate looking weak.

I sit alone facing the door in the deserted diner. Duncan sits two tables down, while Zee and Aaden sit three tables up. Cam's Heaven is a typical American diner, with booths, plastic red-and-white-checkered tablecloths, neon signs, and waitresses who use the word "honey" in every other sentence. The food here is amazing—Archan will hate it. I'd be surprised if he's tasted a french fry or corn dog in his life.

The waitress arrives; I open my mouth to send her away, but I change my mind and order for us both. He's about to get an education in true American cuisine.

Zee rolls his eyes. "What? I eat when I'm stressed. It's a thing, go look it up," I grumble.

Precisely ten minutes go by when the bell jingles, announcing the entrance of Archan and his goons. The swell of power from them as a collective sucks the air out of the room and appears to shrink the diner to an eighth of its size. A look of surprise crosses his face when he sees I'm sitting alone. *That's right, buddy. I'm not scared of you… much.*

He takes his coat off and peers at the torn, red, plastic bench opposite me. I struggle to keep from laughing at his expression. Deciding the plastic doesn't deserve his rear end, he lays his coat across the seat and sits on it. The waitress appears with two cups of coffee. He smiles and takes note of her name tag. Or he might just be staring at her boobs. "Thank you, Ali."

She gives him a toothy smile. "No problem, honey. I'll be right back with your order."

"That's more manners than you've shown me in hours of numerous meetings *and* an interrogation," I mutter.

His lips tip up. "Will 'please and thank you' get me what I want?"

I arch an eyebrow. "Depends what you want."

"From you? Many things."

"Name one, with a please and a thank you, and I'll think about it."

He leans forward, an amused gleam in his eyes. "A kiss, please, and I promise to thank you afterwards." He glances at the low neckline of my top as butterflies bounce around my abdomen, making me flush. I resist the urge to wrap my arms across my chest.

"No."

"It's only a kiss. Scared?"

Warning bells go off. *Don't fall for it, Natia.* My stupid brain doesn't beat my mouth. "No."

"Then you won't mind giving me a kiss."

I glance at Zee, knowing he'd used this exact tactic a couple of nights ago when he took that stupid adjoining bedroom. He shakes his head. "You need to learn," he grumbles.

"I know," I mutter. "Fine, let's get this over with."

The screech of metal against cheap laminate suddenly echoes in the diner; I turn to see Duncan standing behind me, glaring at Archan. "Natia, you don't have to indulge this asshole. I believe you'd agree that we're here for more than power games, wouldn't you, Mr.

Reinhart?" Duncan snaps. I look back at Archan, who blinks and slides his gaze between me and Duncan as if dissecting the pair of us.

I reach out and touch Duncan's arm. "Duncan, it's fine. He's right—it's only a kiss, and he doesn't scare me." I meet Archan's eyes and smirk, hoping he can't hear my hammering heart. "If this is what it takes to get him to move on, then fine. It's not a big deal."

Duncan nods slightly and sits back down, keeping his eyes locked on Archan.

I lean across the table, squeeze my eyes closed, and pucker my lips in the least romantic way I can think of. Calloused fingers grip my jaw gently, and his breath tickles my mouth. My lips part, and my trapped heart feels like it's trying to climb out of my chest. He chuckles. I open one eye to find his dancing with amusement. Releasing my jaw, he tucks a strand of hair behind my ear.

"Not here, and not like this. It will be at a time of my choosing."

I bump back against my seat. "That's not what we agreed."

"You should learn to negotiate terms before surrendering."

"You had your chance. You missed it. *Your* loss."

"I am certain it would be my loss if I had, indeed, missed my chance. It will be at a time of my choosing."

"How is it you're still dominating when you're saying 'please?' Do you practice at night in front of your mirror, quirking your eyebrow and giving it your best sardonic expression? Or do you have one of the men role-play?"

Several of his crew laugh. "She has you there, boss," an unfamiliar voice chuckles.

Archan changes the subject. "How is your leg?" he asks, faking concern.

"Fine. Duncan patched it up." He'd used magic to bind my skin together and reduce the pain in my ribs and throat. "Why were you following me?"

He sips his coffee. "I wasn't." I count to three in my head—that's meant to help, right? It's not working. I continue, reaching twelve before Archan breaks into my Zen counting. "My men were following you."

Ah, we're playing word games. I'm a master at this. "For what purpose?"

The corner of his mouth twitches, like he knows he's about to give me an answer that'll piss me off; of course, he doesn't disappoint.

"Many purposes."

I tip my head back to look at the ceiling. He follows my gaze. "What are you doing?"

I continue to stare upward. "I'm pleading with God for the patience to deal with you. It's taking him some time to get back to me, given the enormity of the task." He laughs, a full belly laugh, and I smile at him. I can't help it—the sound is infectious, and my temper cools.

Sighing deeply, I tap my finger on the table. "This is getting us nowhere. Either you're honest with me, or we end this meeting none the wiser about each other's goals." He tilts his head, a minuscule movement.

When he speaks, he surprises me. "We each get five questions the other has to answer honestly—no avoidance or twisting of the questions, either." He arches an eyebrow.

"Fine, I'll go first." I consider the wording of my question. "Did you, your men, or your company have Mary Conway killed?"

"No." His answer is instant, no hesitation. Truth—good start.

"What about the other six missing people?"

Again, his answer is honest. "No." But he doesn't query that there are more missing people.

"Did you have anything to do with the disappearances of the six people?" He hesitates; my hand freezes as I'm about to sip my coffee, my lips perched on the edge of the cup.

"Yes."

Setting my coffee on the table, I stare at him. When he doesn't elaborate, I grab my leather jacket from the back of the booth and stand.

Aaden, Zee, and Duncan rise out of their seats. Archan grabs my hand. Warmth surrounds it, but it doesn't spread.

I look down at him. "I can't play any more games. Someone was murdered."

"Sit. I'll tell you about the disappearances." I give a small nod of my head to my guys and return to my seat.

"The others are safe—they are under my protection. They can leave when they want, but they stay because they know the danger they are in."

"Do you have proof?"

Archan looks to Nathan, who pulls out a tablet. Letting go of my hand, Archan taps his fingers on it a few times and turns it toward me. It's a live video feed of a combined living/kitchen area. People are eating at the breakfast bar, two are cooking, and some are watching TV. The girl on the end of the sofa reading a book has her legs over the guy next to her, and he's stroking her foot.

"They are in a hidden location. I won't tell you where, so don't ask." I glance at him, sensing no deception.

"This could be fake or an old feed." He subtly rolls his eyes. It's a very human gesture I've not seen him make before. Maybe I'm rubbing off on him?

"Give me the name of one person who disappeared."

I think back to the reports. "Arnold Manners."

He takes out his phone and pushes one button; whomever he calls is on speed dial. "Get Arnold to come to the living area," Archan commands. A man I recognize as Arnold Manners from his photo comes to the screen and waves. Archan raises an eyebrow.

I take the phone from his hand. "Ask Arnold to rub his right eye." Five seconds later, Arnold rubs his right eye, and I return the phone to Archan.

"Satisfied?" he asks. I nod, and Nathan returns to his seat with the tablet.

As I consider what I've seen, Archan shuffles the sugar, salt, and pepper shakers so they're in a precise line. I should have known he would have a touch of OCD.

"My turn," he says.

I shake my head. "I've only had three questions."

He ignores me. "Why are you here?"

"To find the missing people."

He looks up from the shakers. "So, now you know where they are, is your job done?" He appears hopeful—idiot.

"No, I've spent the last two hours looking at Mary's body. Someone wants these people dead. I'm assuming Mary didn't come to you for protection, or you reached her too late." He thins his lips but doesn't answer. Instead, he asks his next question.

"Why do the Renevate demons want you dead?"

152

I swirl the last of my coffee in my cup. "I have no idea. My assumption would be because we're investigating the missing people." He nods, seeming satisfied with my answer.

"What does the secret weapon department of Waterford Industries do?"

I try, and fail, to stop my heartbeat from increasing. "There's only so much I can tell you."

He clenches his jaw. "Tell me what you can."

I take a deep breath, picking my words so as not to lead him to questions about the SIP. "My grandfather supports a group that investigates supernaturals. He has a small department that develops weapons to help kill them."

"And you are part of this group?"

"Yes."

"Is it your mission to kill all supernaturals?"

I shake my head. "Of course not—I'm not a bigot. Like the authorities that deal with criminal humans, we focus on those supernaturals that mean us harm."

I put my hands under the table and cross my fingers, praying he doesn't probe further. Thankfully, he leaves it alone, but throws me a second curveball.

"How do you know Khalkaroth?"

I screw my face up in confusion. "I don't. The first time I heard his name was today. Who is he?" Archan stares at me. It's another staring match I lose. *Maybe there are classes I can attend?*

"The demon who killed Mary Conway and Kelly Peterson."

My body chills. "Kelly Peterson is dead?"

A muscle jumps in his jaw as he flicks his eyes to Barney. "Yes."

I frown. "Is Khalkaroth the shadow man from the videos?"

He nods.

My frown deepens. "If you were able to video him, why haven't you caught him? Unless that wasn't the purpose?"

"We were following him. He is hiding something important."

"Some*thing* or some*one*?"

His eyes narrow. "Someone."

"Pan?"

He falls silent as his shoulders tense.

"My turn," I say, even though I have no idea if it is. "How old are you?"

His lips tip up. "Thirty-four."

Yeah, right. And my ass isn't bruised from being slammed on it several times in the last few days. I don't go cliché and spout the famous vampire question, *"How long have you been thirty-four?"*

Instead, I try, "How old is your soul?" He adopts a neutral expression; I've asked the right question, as he evades it.

"Old enough to have lost too many people I care for, and hardened enough to no longer care." Not sure what to make of that, I go back to the case.

"Who's Pan?"

His face darkens. "You've read my files?" I nod, before he continues. "Someone dangerous. Don't go looking for them, Natia—you will get hurt."

He should know by now that I don't do as I'm told. "What's the name of the object you're looking for?" I ask.

He pauses before answering, considering me. "The Jar."

"The Jar? That's it?" He doesn't quantify this any further. "So you're looking for the Jar, and Khalkaroth is looking for the Jar while also hiding Pan. What's so important about this Jar?"

"It will help us locate Pan."

I drag my bottom lip between my teeth; he follows the motion. "That's all? It will help you locate someone?"

His eyes bore into mine. "No, that's not all. It's part of a much bigger problem. If it falls into the wrong hands, there could be serious consequences."

"For you?"

He shakes his head. "For the world."

You can hear a pin drop in the silence that follows. Even the grill from the kitchen seems to have paused. If it's as important as he says, we need to find it before Khalkaroth. Last question—I sense I've gotten what I can out of him regarding the Jar and Pan, so I opt for something different. "What are you?"

He glances out the window. "An ancient. Damnation to some, salvation to others." I'm about to ask what the hell an ancient is, when he cuts me off. "My turn, last round. What are you?"

"Taurus."

He levels me with his stare. I huff, answering the question with honesty. "I'm a protector of sorts. I dedicate my life to killing those who harm innocent people, specifically those of supernatural origin."

"You're evading the question."

I frown. "I've just told you what I do."

He narrows his eyes. "Exactly. You've told me what you do. Not what you are."

I roll my eyes. "Human."

"Why do you hide your aura?" He leans back in his seat.

I nibble the inside of my cheek. "People can use it to help them interrogate you, gleaning information from its changes. I hide mine for my protection."

He swaps the salt and pepper shakers around on the table then lines them up perfectly again. "You need to stop investigating this."

I shake my head. "I've already told you I can't. I have a responsibility to find Mary Conway's murderer."

He surveys the world outside, and his features tense. "Then you'll work with Jed. He can help protect you."

I bristle. "I don't need one of your goons. I can handle myself."

He narrows his eyes. "What about today? Would you have survived the Renevate attack?"

I go quiet. "Fine, but we need ground rules if we're going to work together." The waitress arrives with our food. Archan doesn't look the least bit surprised I ordered for him. Damn, he's beginning to see order in my chaos. I've ordered us the same, except my chiliburger is extra spicy. The waitress looks between us.

"Hey, honey, who's extra hot?"

Archan gives me a wicked grin. I roll my eyes as my stomach rumbles. "That would be me," I say, blushing as I take the plate from her. She slides the other plate in front of Archan and tops off our coffee. My mouth waters at the smell, and I close my eyes. When I open them, Archan is studying me.

"What?" I ask.

"You don't hide the pleasure you find in the small things."

I pop a crispy, salty french fry in my mouth. "Food is no small thing."

Ignoring him for a few minutes, I take the bun off the top of my burger and place it on a paper napkin. I eat the pickles first, enjoying the crunch and relaxing with each bite.

On my last forkful of bacon, I glance at Archan. "So, ground rules."

156

I look at his plate; he's eaten all of his food and is watching me with amusement. One, he likes the food? Two, how did he eat that fast?

As if answering my thoughts, he says, "I don't eat fast, you eat slowly." I'm about to chew him out (pun intended), when he points toward my deconstructed burger.

"It wasn't a criticism—you savor your food. You like tasting each individual flavor." I study his face. Nobody has ever gotten that without explanation. I pop a few more french fries in my mouth. If I'm eating, I can't announce anything stupid like, "You're the only one who gets me." Although, it might stop him from flirting with me when it appears I'm proposing marriage. Who am I kidding? He'd pop out a diamond ring and challenge me to do it, and me being me, we'd be married in Vegas before the night's over by Elvis with a gut.

"The rules?" he prompts. His knee brushes mine under the table, and I immediately glare at him. I brush the excess salt off my fingers over my plate.

"These crazy touches—they need to stop." I point my finger to the floor through the table.

He gives me a sardonic look. "Are you sure?"

"Yes, unless I ask for them." I drop my head in my hands, as the rumble of masculine laughter surrounds me. "Real mature, guys," I mutter.

Archan pulls one of my hands off my face, giving me a soft smile. "Not even I can force chemistry to exist where it doesn't. If you're affected, it's because you want to be," he purrs. Heat burns my cheeks.

"So what *can* you do?" His eyes glitter with unspoken desire. "I don't mean… ugh… I mean do you have any power other than driving me freakin' crazy?"

"With your temperament, I'm not sure that skill is owned solely by me."

I point at him. "You're avoiding the question."

He sighs and glances around at his men before settling his gaze back on me. "I can heal."

"Like Duncan?"

Archan's head snaps to my best friend, who glares at me. I shrug, it's not like they don't know he's a warlock. They saw him fighting demons with magic, for God's sake.

"What about the weird warmth thing?" I ask, trying to break the intense three-way stare off.

Archan grins. "It's an extension of my power, but you do seem extra sensitive. Are you always that sensitive?"

"Quit the flirting."

"That wasn't part of your rules, and you're avoiding the question *again*."

I massage my left temple, fighting against the dull throb. "I'm sensitive to magic, yes. I can read auras and have an acute awareness of people's movements."

"And your fighting skills?"

"Come from training with the best of the best."

Zee snorts.

"What else can you do?" I ask.

Archan shakes his head. "I've not even had a kiss, and you want all my secrets. Anyway, next rule. No more lies."

My eyes widen. "I've never lied to you."

He continues to analyze me with that stare. "Fair enough. Don't manipulate the truth or omit facts, then." I raise my hand to interrupt; without pausing, he puts his hand on top of mine and gently pushes it to the table. "And you will share all facts regarding Khalkaroth." I frown. "The shadow man," he clarifies.

"Oh, okay… Well, the same goes for you. No lies or holding back information we need to catch Khalkaroth."

"Done."

"No harm is to come to my team."

"I can't promise no harm will come to them. I can promise none of my men will harm them, and they will protect them." My mouth falls open—he's promising protection for my team? I have to admit, I didn't expect that. He continues in a tone that dares me to argue. "Jed will work with you."

"Like a liaison?"

"No, more like a bodyguard."

I bristle. "I'm more than capable of handling myself."

"So I've seen. But Jed is for my peace of mind."

"More like a spy," I mutter.

He ignores me and continues, "You will *not* look for the Jar."

"Wrong. Khalkaroth wants the Jar, I want Khalkaroth—plus it seems like you need all the help you can get. If it affects humanity, then we have a responsibility to help. Also, I have your final locations from your files, remember? But so long as I get to look over it first if we find it, I'll give it to you." It's my turn to be immovable; I need eyes on that Jar to figure out what is going on and understand his motives. He watches me, gauging if he can dissuade me. Whatever he sees, he decides not to argue. I break the tension. "Is that it?"

"No. Dinner," he says.

I glance at the empty plates. "I hope you enjoyed it."

"You will have dinner with me tomorrow night. And I will be calling you Natia."

I grin. "To the name, yes. To the dinner, no. This is business, not pleasure."

He leans back in his seat and crosses his arms. "Dinner, tomorrow night."

"No."

"Then the deal is off. Good luck finding Khalkaroth. My team will work against yours and put obstacles in your way at every possible opportunity."

Zee growls.

I blink. "You're blackmailing me into having dinner with you?"

"I play dirty, Natia. I get what I want by whatever methods I can."

I stuff more french fries in my mouth and chew, giving myself time to think my way around the problem. My conclusion? I'm screwed.

"Okay."

A masculine, satisfied grin graces his lips just as a spark of inspiration hits me.

I give him a sultry smile. "It doesn't mean I have to be nice."

Duncan chuckles. "Good luck, Reinheart. A date with nasty Natia isn't something to be trifled with."

Archan's grin falters ever so slightly. I'll take that as a small win.

I change the topic. "What was in the parcels given to the shadow man?" So much easier to say that than Khalkaroth. Why do these demons have to have such stupid names? Why not Bob, Margaret, or Steve?

"Guess."

I lean back in my seat and cross my arms, mimicking him. "I thought we were past games?" When he doesn't say anything further, I share my two best theories and watch his aura. "I think it's either money or a fake Jar." The blue flames on his aura flare. So, it's one of them. He remains silent. I go with my best guess. "I think they're fake Jars keeping the shadow man busy, while you look for the real thing."

"Very good, Natia… We might have use for you yet." Condescending, egotistic pig.

He touches my face, and a look of fury glows in his eyes. "Who did this to you?"

I blink and push his hand away. "I'm not sure why you care, but I believe it was Khalkaroth. He was outside of the bar last night and thought I was your new toy. I corrected his assumption, and this was his response." I point at my bruised eye.

"I'll kill him," he grinds out as his aura flares a blinding red. Leaning back in my seat, I cross my arms and study his features. Nothing but genuine fury emanates off him, which inadvertently warms my heart. Why would he care? Because he wants me? Because he doesn't want me damaged? I'm not sure I could work this man out if I had a lifetime to do it.

"He gave me a message for you," I say.

He blinks. "What?"

Crooking my finger toward him, I lean in to whisper, "The game is lost. Chaos is against you, so sit back and enjoy the fireworks."

Pushing away, I escape his exotic, dizzying scent. Archan's brow wrinkles as I stand and pull my jacket on. I don't ask him to explain the cryptic message.

"I'll pick you up at seven tomorrow evening. Dress warm." He gives my body a slow perusal, his eyes tracking each dip and curve. "I

161

like this look on you more than the business suits." Heat prickles my face again.

"Hear, hear!" shouts a voice from the far left. Archan shoots Jed a look. I'm glad he's not looking at me that way. Jed smirks at him—weird dynamic there.

I walk toward the exit and notice Jed rising out of his seat. He pushes his blond-tipped hair out of his boyish face and focuses his hazel eyes on me.

Freezing, I point at him. "You stay. I'll call when we go on some dangerous mission." When he doesn't sit back down, I slide my gaze to Archan. "Smoothie is not coming with us."

Jed creases his forehead. "Who's Smoothie?" Archan stays silent. Sensing I'm not going to win this one, I shake my head.

"Smoothies lie," I explain, "they're advertised as being good for you, but in reality, they're filled with sugar. Some don't even have any real fruit in them."

Jed puts his hand on his heart. "When did I lie?"

"When you said you'd killed the demons without my help. I guess I could call you 'Goony' instead?"

"Why do you have to call me anything?"

"You're right. I'll ignore you completely."

Turning back to Archan, I make a circling motion with my finger, encompassing Zee, Aaden, and Duncan. "I have my fair share of six-foot-plus men. I don't have room for him. My apartment is full."

"I don't intend for him to live with you, Natia. He will watch the apartment from outside in shifts with my other men. You will call him when you go out on *any* mission, no matter how big or small. You will involve him in any plans you make to look for the Jar or Khalkaroth."

Huffing, I strut out of the diner with Zee, Aaden, Duncan, and now Jed following me. "Anyone would think I have a harem," I mumble.

Zee throws his arm around my shoulders. "Can I be your favorite?" Ugh, he's impossible.

Jed is behind us. "I'm the newbie. I need breaking in. It'll take time—submitting doesn't come easy to me." I utter some silent curses at the sky. I can't deal with the two of them driving me insane; Zee was already more than enough. We get in our respective cars, and I glance back at the diner to see Archan's gold eyes tracking me.

I swallow. This case needs solving before I make any stupid decisions.

Chapter Eighteen

Natia

A Taurus is both a lover and a fighter.

I swing my feet up on the dashboard. "So, Archan is protecting five of the missing people. Kelly Peterson is dead, although there's no body. Mary was laid out in plain sight; as if the shadow man, or Khalkaroth, wanted her found by Archan… or us."

Duncan scowls and chips in. "The symbols tattooed onto Mary's wrist are old, almost a lost language."

"When did you work that out?" I demand.

"At the diner. I've seen the circle with the line drawn through it extending to a smaller circle before."

Aaden looks at him. "Do you know what it means?"

"I think it's a warning."

I rub my temples. "We need to find this Jar before Archan. I wish I knew what it looked like—it might help us understand the bigger picture."

"Where are we going to search first?" Aaden enquires as he snaps his laptop open. "There are three left on their list: North Sentinel Island, the Iron Mountain, and somewhere in Poland."

"Well, Poland is an entire country, and the Iron Mountain is a massive underground storage system. I think North Sentinel Island is the easiest place to start with, but it's almost a day's journey to get there."

Duncan drums his fingers on the steering wheel. "I can get us there quicker." I swivel to face him, and he grins at me. "I can teleport us."

"I knew it! Why did you keep it from me?" I glance in the back at Zee and Aaden, who are both staring at Duncan with shocked expressions.

Duncan shrugs. "Apart from it being fun to keep you guessing, it's not something I advertise—Charlie knows, but nobody else at the SIP does." He turns to look at Aaden and Zee. "And that's the way it needs to stay."

Aaden and Zee nod their agreement. I get it, I really do. The SIP would be all over Duncan's teleporting ability, trying to figure out if it's something they can teach people to do. As if Zee has dug in my head, he asks, "Is that something you're born with, or something you learn to do?"

Duncan's jaw tightens. "Something you're born with. I'll study the layout of the island and compare it with the notes in Archan's files. We'll go tomorrow afternoon."

"Why not in the morning?" I wonder.

"Time difference. Do you really want to go to an island with a secret tribe that kills outsiders on sight at night?"

I shiver. "Wasn't aware of the resident killer tribe. Night would give us some cover, but no, daylight is preferred."

I point at Zee. "That means we can go see the coroner in the morning." He groans; he's even more squeamish than me around dead bodies. Some badass warriors we are.

I turn back to Duncan. "Any clue about what Archan being an 'ancient' means?"

He shakes his head. "No, but it's not likely to be something we can Google. I have some texts that might help."

"I can research this Jar and Pan," Aaden declares, his fingers already tapping on his keyboard. He frowns. "Although, 'Jar' isn't much of a description, and 'Pan' is a weird name that tends to deliver results related to cookware."

I snort at poor Aaden's frustrated features. "All the more reason to find the Jar first and get pictures of it before we hand it over to Archan."

Aaden hums. "I'll see what I can find out about Khalkaroth—that may lead us to more info about the Jar and Pan."

Zee's phone chimes from the back seat, and he pulls it out of his pocket. "Charlie."

"We need to tell him something," Aaden says. I nod as Zee swipes his thumb on the screen.

"Zee, update?" Charlie barks.

"I'll let Natia update you, boss. She's the one who brokered the deal with the devil."

I shoot him a glare. "Deal with the devil?" Charlie snaps.

I sigh. "We've had some developments with Archan and his team."

"You know what he is?"

"No. But they've agreed to work with us to find Mary's killer."

"Work together?"

I roll my eyes. "They aren't responsible for the disappearances. Wait... well, *technically* they are, but they're protecting them from the demon who wants them dead. I know you might not approve, but it's a way of getting closer."

Silence… until Duncan whispers at me, "Tell him about your powers."

I shake my head. "What was that about powers?" Uncle Charlie asks sharply.

Glaring at Duncan, I grind out, "I have an elemental power—air. It's only occurred once."

"When?" Uncle Charlie demands. I picture the shades of red he's about to turn.

"Last night."

"And why are you only informing me now?"

"You know why."

A long sigh echoes from the phone. "I won't tell anyone, Natia, so long as you let Duncan help you control it."

I frown. I'd expected more resistance, shock, questions. "Okay." I glance at Duncan, who's also frowning at the phone.

"Keep me updated." The screen blinks off. Aaden is already tapping away on his laptop, his tongue peeking out between his lips, no doubt diving into his research.

"I'll grab my books," Duncan mutters, deep in thought.

Zee points at me. "We're going to train."

I huff. Zee's training involves him kicking my ass, followed by me needing a muscle soak.

Changed into black yoga pants and a pink sports bra—I need to get my girly on somewhere—we enter the small training room in the basement of the apartment building. The room is basic, with some training mats laid out on the floor. We warm up with a set of stretches, squats, sit-ups, and push-ups. Zee teaches a mixture of martial arts, and he's taught me how to fight hand-to-hand—but my strength lies with my sword work.

Stepping barefoot onto the cool mat, I position my body, keeping on the balls of my feet with my arms raised, ready to defend or attack.

Zee clucks his tongue. "Your posture's sloppy… I shouldn't be pointing this out after four years of training." I tighten my abdomen and straighten my back. Without warning, Zee jabs my left shoulder then launches into a head kick. Instinctively, I duck, but he follows up with a low roundhouse kick, putting me on my ass.

He circles me. "Get up. You're defending, not attacking." We go again; this time, he pins me underneath him. "You're not going to hurt me. Stop holding back."

I nod, panting. He stands, offering me his hand to pull me up, and I take it. He strips off his light gray T-shirt, leaving him in his black sweats. His body glistens with a light sheen of sweat, highlighting the almost imperceptible, small, silver scars on his body.

He grins and flexes his muscles. "Like what you see?"

I fan myself with a hand dramatically. "Hmm, oh yes… Sure, you're good to look at. Too bad it's spoiled when you speak, with that narcissistic personality of yours showing its face. Plus, I couldn't be with a man who thinks he's prettier than me."

He gives me a half shrug. "You don't know what you're missing." I laugh and nod toward the duffle bag.

"Come on, big boy. Your time for groping me is over—let's play with swords." I grab my modified Sai swords. Instead of the dull prong in the center, mine has a sharp, double-edged blade. My grandfather commissioned them from his weapons department. Zee and I are equally matched in sword fighting, but I've been practicing moves I developed myself while training alone. The sound of clattering metal echoes through the expanse of the room, like the beginnings of a battle song, as we dance backward and forward.

Zee breathes heavily as he praises me. "You've been practicing. I'm impressed. Your technique is fluid and economical. We might need to find you someone else to train with who'll challenge you." We play first to three—I win.

He bats his long eyelashes. "First to five?"

"Nice try." I grin. "I won fair and square."

He rolls his eyes and sighs.

As I guzzle my water, slow clapping ricochets against the walls. I glance up and find Jed and Archan leaning over the viewing balcony. Archan's eyes swirl light gold. Typical—he's turned on watching a woman fight. My traitorous body responds with heat spreading throughout my limbs, causing tingling in my fingers and toes. It's different from Archan's seductive heat. This is my own reaction.

I put my hands on my hips. "What are you doing here?"

A wicked grin curves Archan's lips. "I could help with your training." Struggling to think of anything else but biting those soft lips, I use "Sympathy for the Devil" as my mental block. Archan lets out a full belly laugh, confirming he can hear me.

I growl. "I'm pleased I amuse you." Zee looks confused. I point to my temple, and Zee shoots him a harsh look.

"We are here to coordinate our work so we can cover more ground," Archan explains. His logic is sound, but I doubt his intentions, and I don't want him knowing all of ours. Then again, the more we speak to him, the more we can learn.

"Give me fifteen minutes. Wait in the lobby, and one of us will come and get you."

Without acknowledging the invitation, Jed and Archan disappear from the balcony. I pick up my towel, wiping the sweat from the back of my neck. Zee opens his mouth to speak, but I shake my head, still sensing Archan close by. We make our way back to the apartment, talking about fighting techniques and analyzing my performance.

Chapter Nineteen

Natia

Taurus—needs to be drunk to talk about personal shit.

"**W**e need to act fast. Archan and Jed will be here in fifteen minutes." Aaden and Duncan blink. "Don't ask. You need to hide any research about Archan, the Jar, and Pan." They don't move.

I clap my hands to snap them out of their stupor. As one, they shuffle to hide any papers they'd printed, and Aaden closes down his laptop. Organizing the crime scene photos in a file, I place it on the coffee table. Exactly fifteen minutes later, there's a knock on the door. Approaching it, I frown and peer through the spy hole. *Of course he couldn't wait for us in the lobby.*

"Password?"

Archan's deep voice sounds amused. "Enter the lion's den at your own risk." I glance at Zee, who smirks. Composing myself, I open the door. Archan's dark jeans hug his lean hips perfectly, and the midnight blue T-shirt strains against his muscled arms. It's deliberate. Meant to entice, to fantasize, to… I shake my head to dispel the thoughts.

He raises a sardonic eyebrow. "Can we come into the lion's den?"

I focus on Jed's impressive six-foot-five frame instead of Archan—he's safer. "Yes, of course." Stepping back, I indicate the two curved sofas. Archan stalks in as if he owns the place, and they sit opposite each other.

"Would you like a drink?" I offer, being the incredible host that I am.

Jed looks hopeful. "You have beer?"

"Sure. Archan?"

"Same."

I roll my eyes. "Didn't your mother teach you any manners?" I mumble. Grabbing five bottles of beer from the refrigerator, I pour myself a glass of rosé wine. After handing the guys their beer, I settle on the sofa next to Jed, opposite Archan, who's being flanked by Duncan and Aaden.

Archan's gaze flicks to Zee as he sits next to me. "Do you have any further information about Mary?" he starts.

"We don't have a cause of death, but I'll inform you as soon as we do. I bet you can get the post mortem report anyway," I point out.

Archan crosses one foot over his knee. "But I can't get your conversations with the coroner and detective, which won't be on the official reports."

I keep my tone mild. "I'll share all information, as per our agreement. I never break my promises. This isn't going to work unless we trust each other."

Look at me being the grown up. I feel like I've aged five years in five minutes.

Pulling out the crime scene photos, I spread them across the table and pick the one with the clear image of the symbols. Archan stiffens, and the flames around his aura flare. Awareness prickles along my skin, and a primal instinct tells me to run—the power and anger spilling from him are stifling.

"Do you know what they mean?" I ask, as if I haven't almost suffocated.

"It's a warning." He points to the circle. Duncan looks smug.

"What does the rest of it mean?" I ask.

He drops the photo back onto the coffee table. "If I asked you to stop investigating, would you?"

I shake my head. "We've been through this."

He thins his lips. "It's a warning for you, Natia. To stop."

My heart skips a few beats. "What have I got to do with this?" My voice sounds croaky; I down my entire glass of wine. Jed looks through the rest of the crime scene photos as I repeat my question. "What the fuck do I have to do with this?"

Archan studies me, like he's searching for something. "What are you?"

Duncan rises and stands behind me. "Again with the ridiculous questions. Why am I being warned?"

He ignores me. I stand and start pacing in front of the fire, all eyes watching my movements. "Are you human?"

Halting, I stare at him. "You've asked me something like this twice. I have human parents, George and Harriet Waterford. I grew up in Seattle where I graduated school with a 4.5 grade point average. I studied contemporary dance and work for a security firm, where I've learned how to fight supernatural beings. I don't turn into a banshee at night, grow horns when I'm angry, or feast on the souls of the damned." Aaden and Zee look amused.

I point at the symbols. "Now, tell me precisely what that says."

Silence follows my outburst, and Archan finally meets my gaze. "Death will follow the female warrior."

My legs shake, forcing me to sit. "How do you know I'm 'the female?'"

"Do you know of any other weapon-trained female involved in this?" I look over my shoulder at Duncan. He just rubs the base of my neck, staring off in silence. Turning back, I find Archan's stare narrowed on Duncan.

There is a knock at the door. The men turn their heads in unison—it's kind of creepy.

"Chill out, guys. I ordered Chinese, remember?"

Jed perks up and turns toward me in silent question. I pat his knee. "You can stay, Smoothie." I glance at Archan. "You, too, I suppose."

Zee collects the food and piles it on the dining table. Archan procures a seat next to me. The circular table, made to accommodate six normal-sized people, is surrounded by five tall men and me. Inevitably, his knee keeps brushing mine. I grit my teeth at the tingles.

Duncan shakes his empty beer bottle. "Anyone need another drink?"

They all have another beer. I request the bottle of wine and fill my glass to the top. I'm a lightweight, so I'm already on my way to being tipsy.

"What's the plan tomorrow?" I enquire.

"Are you searching for the Jar?" Jed asks in between slurping noodles into his mouth.

"Yes, we're going to North Sentinel Island."

Archan stiffens next to me. "No, Natia. I forbid it—you'll be killed. I can get you access to the Iron Mountain; you can help search there."

I pat his shoulder. "It's okay, darling, I'll be back in time for our date."

174

He slams his fist on the table. I jump, along with the noodles in the carton. "Fuck! You are the most stubborn woman I have ever met." Everyone but Jed stares at him in shock. I've never heard him curse… He really doesn't like being disobeyed—if he's planning on working with me, he needs to get used to it.

"Jed will go with you," he states, gritting his teeth.

"Duncan will be coming, too."

He nods, pacified. "Just be careful."

Glancing at my bare abdomen, he traces a finger along a star-shaped scar on my lower left side; he pushes me forward and glances down my back.

"It didn't go through," I whisper, shivering against the rough texture of fingertips.

"Who shot you?" His tone is so casual, he could be enquiring what type of coffee I prefer; but his raging aura tells a different story.

I straighten my spine. "It doesn't matter he's d… dealt with." I can see him studying me in my peripheral vision. Duncan's concerned expression catches my eye, and I shake my head. Lawrence being alive is something we need to deal with, but not today.

Something occurs to me. "You never asked how I'm going to get to the island and back in a day."

He swallows a mouthful of kung pao chicken. "I assume Duncan will be teleporting you."

My mouth drops open as I swing my head to Duncan, who doesn't look surprised. "Duncan is a powerful warlock—it's not a stretch that he can teleport. I assumed that was the plan when you said you would be back for our date," Archan continues.

"Oh," is my intelligent response. "Zee and I are going to the coroner's office in the morning. I'll update Jed as soon as we've finished," I change the topic.

Archan shakes his head. "Jed will come with you."

"No."

"No?" he repeats, apparently not used to the sound of the word being directed at him.

"No. The coroner is a friend, and we work closely with the detective in charge of the case. Seeing Jed will put them on edge; they won't discuss the case with me if he's around."

Some might think it's sad that I count the coroner as a friend, but Emi's incredible. I don't have to lie about what I do for a living, and she doesn't shy away from the various kinds of demon guts that often end up stuck all over me. Once she helped me shampoo a stubborn, sticky, unknown substance out of my hair—a step up from holding your hair back while being sick.

Standing, I turn on the sound system. "I promise I'll update Jed."

Whitney's classic "I Wanna Dance With Somebody" pumps through the speakers. Zee, Aaden, and Duncan groan.

"Pick something else, Locks."

Shooting Duncan a look, I take my seat back at the table. "And what, oh mighty DJ, would you have me play?"

"Anything else," he mutters.

"Anything?" I purr, hoping he falls for my trap. Archan picks up my phone from the table and scrolls through my playlists. I try to grab it, but I can't reach his extended hand. *Why do I surround myself with these Neanderthals?* Unless I want to give him a lap dance, there's no way I can reach my phone.

I shrug. "It doesn't matter. It's all my music anyway."

He smirks. "But the names you give your playlists are most entertaining. For example, 'Natia's happy songs,' or 'I've had a fucked-up day,'" his lips twitch, "'Natia's sexy songs.'"

Crimson creeps up my cheeks.

Zee catches my reaction and grins. "Play that one."

Snapping my gaze to him, I mouth, "Traitor." Unrepentant, he eggs Archan on. Awesome, they're bonding over embarrassing me. Before I can intervene, the opening chords of "Closer" by the Nine Inch Nails drifts through the apartment, talking about having mindless sex to escape reality—that's my personal interpretation. Don't judge.

I put my head in my hands to escape the five pairs of wide, surprised eyes.

Aaden clears his throat and starts undoing some of the cartons. "What else did you order?" Lifting my head, I smile at him and hope that's the end of the discussion. *Yeah, right.*

Zee prods me further. "Jesus, Natia, if I'd known kink was your thing, I could've arranged something."

Leaning forward with my elbows on the table, I glare at Zee. "You'll all be sorry when I figure out how to breathe fire." He sniggers.

Archan's warm hand covers my thigh. Is the man trying to kill me? I turn, ready to offer to remove his dick and feed it to the dog that lives in the apartment next door… but his regretful expression makes me blink.

Looking down at his hand, I whisper, "Not helping." He slides it away and returns my phone. I change the playlist to 'Natia's happy songs.' No one argues. I relax, trying to forget the brief look they've all had into Natia's dark side.

"Have you searched the island previously?" I ask Archan.

He nods. "It's been difficult; the natives aren't exactly welcoming. We've been on the island but have been blocked from searching all the locations we want to."

"Like where?" Duncan asks.

"There are several caves that are of interest. We've managed to search two, but the final one remains heavily guarded. Short of slaughtering the locals, we haven't been able to negotiate access."

Hmm, so he's against killing an entire tribe for their purposes? Brownie points in his favor. "So, the aim of tomorrow is to sneak past the locals and search the cave?"

"Jed can show you the cave we are speaking of," Archan says. "If it is the correct location, the natives will likely know what we're after, so let Jed take the lead."

I nod my head noncommittally. The person to take the lead will most likely have first access to the Jar—if it's there. I bite the end off a spring roll then spoon the filling into my mouth. Jed and Archan look at me incredulously.

Aaden laughs. "The spring roll's amusing."

"It's ingenious, and you know it," I retort, without looking up from my delicate task. One wrong move, and I could crack the pastry casing.

Zee studies the table. "Five bucks on chicken and cashew nuts." He takes out a bill from the back pocket of his sweats and slams it on the table.

Aaden rises out of his seat and inspects the contents of the cartons. "Hmm, I'll raise you ten bucks on the sweet and sour pork." They look at Duncan.

Instead of the food, he studies me. "I think she's in a double carb mood. I'll meet your bet, chow mein."

Jed and Archan have stopped eating and watch the exchange with curiosity. I grab the sweet and sour pork and spoon it into the empty spring roll. Aaden fist pumps the air and holds his hand out to Zee and Duncan. I roll my eyes.

Jed leans over to me. "Babe, that's brilliant. You've personalized your spring roll."

I smile. "You're growing on me, Smoothie."

He winks.

By my third glass of wine, I'm officially drunk.

Wobbling to the freezer, I declare, "Dessert," to nobody in particular.

It's my turn to fist pump the air when I find my favorite ice cream.

"Come to me, rocky road… you know I love you." Placing it on the breakfast bar and getting out a spoon, I eat directly from the carton—it's all mine anyway. I close my eyes and moan at the amazing taste of frozen chocolate and marshmallows. Now *that* chef deserves top money.

Someone clears their throat. I blink and find amused faces staring at me.

"What? I have no sex life. I need a serotonin substitute." I hug the carton to me and point to each of my guys. "It's not like any of you have a sex life—you need a release, too. How you get yours is your business, but me? I have frozen, chocolatey goodness."

Zee doubles over laughing, and Jed follows, slapping his hand on his knee as he completely loses his shit.

Aaden chuckles. "Did I mention she's a hilarious drunk?"

Ignoring him, I point my spoon at Archan. "And you. You're responsible for all of this." I suck another spoonful of ice cream into my mouth then wave my spoon around in the air.

Archan rests his arm over the back of his chair. "I'm responsible for what, Natia?"

Strolling over, I slide my ass on the table with my feet on the chair so I can look down at him—it makes me feel better. "The ice cream."

He flicks his eyes at the ice cream and grins. "In that case, can I have a taste?"

I shake my head. "I'm not sure you deserve it."

Aaden rolls his eyes as Duncan mutters, "She also becomes an incurable flirt." Ignoring Duncan, I have a few more spoonfuls of ice cream. My calf cramps painfully, making me scrunch up my face, and I rub it reflexively. The workout with Zee is catching up to me.

Placing the ice cream in front of Archan, I present him with the spoon. "Here… he's a good listener. I've just remembered I have a hot date with someone who will make me sweat and work out all of my tension."

His eyes widen as he watches me slide off the table and sing along to Wham's "Wake Me Up Before You Go-Go." I head to the balcony doors, slide them open, and stand for a moment, adjusting to the cool air.

I give the hot tub the eye. "Hey, you… as promised, here I am." Stripping off my yoga pants and sports bra, I dump them on the slate floor.

Duncan shouts, "Shit!" Then multiple chairs scrape across the wooden floor as I step into the hot tub. I hiss as my feet sting then moan as I sink deeper into the warmth already coaxing my cramping muscles loose. Wiggling around, trying to get comfortable, I realize the issue; I lift my ass off the seat, slip off my panties, and throw them over my shoulder. A masculine grunt follows the sound of a wet slap of fabric. I twist to look over my shoulder, just in time to see Archan peeling them off his head.

Have you ever had one of those laughs where the more you laugh, the more you can't stop? That was me, hysterically laughing, naked, in a hot tub.

"Is there room for one more?" Jed begs, wiggling his eyebrows.

"Do I look like a hussy?" I glare at him and lean to the other side of the tub to adjust the settings to massage and turn up the heat. The staff never set it hot enough. Zee groans.

Placing my hands on my hips, I turn to face them. "What?" Aaden and Duncan usher Zee inside, and Jed is looking at the sky like it's the most fascinating thing he's ever seen. Archan lowers his hungry gaze, and I do the same. Oh, shit… I have two options. Dive down, embarrassed, or own it. I decide to own it.

Continuing to stand, I stare Archan down. "Haven't you ever seen a naked woman before?" His eyes drift to my breasts, where my nipples have hardened. It takes everything I have not to put my arms over them.

"I have never seen *your* naked body, Natia."

Shrugging, I give him my back and ass. He hisses.

I push my spine against a strong jet. "I'm sure it's no better than the hundreds of women you've seen before."

He closes the space behind me, scoops my wet hair off one shoulder, then trails kisses from the sensitive skin under my ear to my collarbone. Instinctively, I turn my head to the side, giving him better access.

"I have never seen a body as perfect as yours. It makes me ache to touch you," he whispers, placing another kiss further down my chest, "and to fuck you until you're mindless."

I blink, his words clearing some of my brain fog. I glide to sit on the opposite side of the tub.

"You're the reason I need ice cream. Your date is tomorrow. Tonight, I'm all his." I skim my arms over the top of the water and smile. His face is priceless. "People don't say 'no' to you often, do they?" I quip.

He shakes his head. "Not until you." His gaze turns predatory.

I narrow my eyes. "Stop looking at me like that. I'm not a challenge; you can't control me. So don't even try."

A slow, wicked grin spreads across his face. Shit, I've made it worse. Deciding words aren't going to get rid of him, I scoop up some water and throw it at him, aiming for his face. But he's a giant, so it hits his chest instead—good enough.

Jed bursts out laughing as Archan wipes some of the water from his shirt. Vaguely, I hear a little voice warning me I'll regret this in the morning.

Suddenly, Zee steps outside, with Duncan on his heels, presenting me with a fluffy bathrobe. Archan tries to grab the robe, but Zee holds it tight. "Everyone inside."

Duncan glares at Archan. "Agreed… this has gone far enough."

I arch an eyebrow at Zee. "*You're* going to help me?"

"I've already seen you naked in the shower."

Archan growls, and I roll my eyes—alpha males.

Duncan steps up to him and whispers fiercely, "So this is the level you play at? Taking advantage of an intoxicated woman? Natia deserves more than some asshole that relies on his powers for seduction and manipulation. She needs someone to give as much as she does."

"And what's that?" Archan snaps.

"Everything. When Natia falls, she gives her entire heart and soul; she'll drown you in her love, and if you can't return that, then you're not good enough for her. The last person she fell for not only didn't catch her—he almost destroyed her. I'll be damned if I let that happen to my best friend again."

Archan fists his hands at his sides. "I don't want her to fall for me."

Duncan shakes his head. "Then you know nothing about Natia, because she doesn't do purely physical relationships."

The group goes silent; for once, Archan is completely speechless. Duncan steps away and turns his attention back to me.

I blink back the sudden tears and turn to Zee. "Open the robe so I can step into it, and look away." I'm surprised when he does as he's told.

Archan doesn't move until I head back into the apartment, decency restored. I reach for the wine, but Duncan swipes it. "Sorry, Locks, I'm cutting you off."

I pout and bat my lids.

Tense moment over, Archan chuckles and gives me a thin smile. "I'm seeing such a different side of you, Natia."

"Why does he call you 'Locks?'" Jed enquires.

Smirking at Jed, I crook my finger at him. He approaches me with a wide grin, anticipating a good explanation—it is, but not one I'm willing to give. "I could tell you, Smoothie, but then I'd have to kill you." It's Duncan's play on Goldilocks, my unusual aura locked up behind shields made impenetrable by his training.

He gives a derisive snort and sifts his hand through my damp caramel hair. "It's obviously something to do with Goldilocks."

I return his cynical response with an arched eyebrow. "I'm anything but predictable. Think less fairy tale and more paranormal." He scrunches his face at my cryptic response.

"Who wants to dance?" I shout. Yeah, I give people whiplash with my change of topic when I'm drunk.

Duncan puts his hands on my shoulders, nudging me toward the stairs. "As entertaining as you are, you need to go to bed."

Wriggling out of his grip, while yawning so wide I could swallow a baby elephant, I manage a garbled, "I—I'm going to b—bed." Pointing at Archan, I say, "And you're not invited." Zee laughs, and I point at him, too. "You neither."

Waltzing off upstairs, I drop the robe on the bedroom floor, climb between the luxurious, soft sheets, and drift into a dreamless sleep.

Chapter Twenty

Natia

A Taurus's biggest strength is common fucking sense.

Never. Drinking. Again.

The phrase should be printed on a bumper sticker and slapped on my ass. To summarize my embarrassment: My guys, Jed, and Archan had a glimpse of my darker side, I announced my nonexistent sex life, then I stripped naked, got into a hot tub, and told Archan there was no way in hell he was having me.

The door opens, and the smell of coffee drifts through the room. I put my head under the pillow. I don't suffer with hangovers, but I'm too embarrassed to look at anybody.

The bed dips. "Morning, sunshine." I grab the pillow above my head, securing it there.

"Go away, Aaden… If I stay under here, it didn't happen."

He chuckles. "Come on, you've got work to do." He lifts the sheets in an effort to get me out of bed. Cool air hits my naked body.

"Shit," he grumbles. I groan and throw the pillow at him as he drops the sheet back over me.

Pulling the sheet with me, I prop myself up against the headboard and grab the coffee from Aaden. "I may as well become a naturalist and walk around naked."

Aaden chuckles. "Emi called—the autopsy's done. She's expecting you in an hour. Detective Patton will be there." I down my delicious coffee while Aaden continues to sit on my bed.

"Could you leave, please? I need a shower, and as you're aware, I'm naked."

After grabbing a quick shower, I pull my hair into a high ponytail and dress in a set of leathers and a soft, sky blue tank top before leaving the apartment.

Zee and I park next to the coroner's office; a gentle breeze blows the saplings surrounding the freshly-painted, ivory, concrete building. We enter through the rotating glass doors to find Detective Patton sitting on a bench in reception, eyeing the strange water feature of Eros spouting water (from his mouth, thank goodness) onto a nude Aphrodite. I've always been confused about the choice of décor in the coroner's building. He takes in my attire and arches an eyebrow.

"Expecting trouble?"

I shake my head. "Maybe later."

"Did you figure out what the tattoo means?" he probes as we walk toward the autopsy rooms. I consider how much I should tell him. He's never let me down with sensitive information before, but this is specific to me.

"How much do you want to know?"

"Will it help catch the killer?"

"No, it was a warning to stop looking for him."

"I see. You'll let me know if it's important?"

I nod. "Of course."

We spot Emi's perfectly bobbed, satin black hair through the glass windows of the examination room and enter the cool chamber. The ventilation pulls the air out of the room, but the distinct smell of decomposing bodies lingers. Plucking a fabric mask from the box near the door, I go to stand near Emi. Zee and John exert their masculine tendencies and forego the masks to stand stoically near the body.

"Hi, Emi, it's been ages. Which I guess is a good thing, considering we only meet over dead bodies," I say.

Emi smiles, her Egyptian features and bronzed skin combining to make a classic image of Cleopatra. "We could fix that with a night out?"

"Great idea. We'll arrange it soon." I turn my attention to the body of Mary Conway and sigh. "So… down to business. What have you found?"

"The first notable thing is the tattoo on her wrist." She turns to John. "I saw you wrote that in your report. Did you find out what it means?"

"It's a warning," I explain.

She arches an eyebrow, waits a beat and sighs before pointing to Mary's ribs, where a dark bruise has formed on her left side. "There's bruising across the ribs; I think it's associated with the cause of death."

"Which is?"

"She died from a myocardial infarction."

"Great," Zee mutters, "she had a heart attack, and you don't know why."

Emi bristles. "It happens… particularly with the cases you bring in."

Shooting Zee a look, I intervene. "He didn't mean it like that, Emi. He's frustrated it doesn't help our case."

She gives me a sly smile. "If he'd let me finish speaking, there's more." As one, we perk up. She collects a tray containing Mary's heart and brings it to the table at the foot of the body. Collectively, we step closer, intrigued. She grabs a magnifying glass, angles it, and points to the right side of the heart.

"There are symbols branded into the tissue." We take turns looking through the magnifying glass. Zee slowly looks up to stare at me—the symbols are similar to the warning on her wrist.

I take a step back and fold my arms. "There aren't any wounds that would have given access to her heart, yet it was *branded*?"

Emi nods. "I've never seen anything like it. Have you?" John and Zee shake their heads.

I take out my phone. "Can I take pictures?"

"Sure, I'd be interested to know what they mean."

"I'll tell you what I can," I say, as Emi covers Mary's body with a white cotton sheet and rolls the cart to place her in a vault.

"So, what about this drink?" she asks, sealing the metal door shut and walking to her desk to jot down something.

"This case is taking all of my time… Let's get together afterwards."

"Where's the nerdy one?"

"Aaden?"

She looks up and nods, her eyes sparkling.

"He's working the case. Would you like his number?" I wiggle my eyebrows, and she blushes. The badass coroner and the badass analyst—what a combination. They could make quite the power couple. I wonder if Aaden will have the balls to make a move… I'll just have to give him a little encouragement.

She fishes through a drawer, writes on a business card, and hands it to me. "He can have mine. If he's interested, get him to call me."

I take the card and flip it over. She's written in loopy handwriting. *'Call me, E'.* I shove it in my jacket pocket. "He's shy, Emi. You might need to make the first move."

She shrugs. "I've given him my card. Ball's in his court. A girl needs to feel wanted, too."

She envelops me in a hug. "How about your love life?"

Zee clears his throat, stifling a laugh. I send a glare his way. "Nonexistent."

She sighs and flips my ponytail over my shoulder. "I find it hard to believe no one is interested, Natia. It's more likely you are chasing them off before they've even begun."

"She's not been very successful with the latest one," Zee mutters as John's caterpillar eyebrows shoot up.

Shaking my head, I huff. "He'll get the message, even if I have to stab him in the heart to make my point."

"Man problems?" John asks, shoving his hands in his coat pockets. "Anything I need to intervene with?"

"Not unless you call being an arrogant ass a crime."

He laughs. "If it was, I would have very few colleagues."

"Shame, I think I would like to see him hauled away in handcuffs."

Zee laughs. "I'm starting to see a theme, along with your choice in bedroom music."

Emi and John's eyes pop open wide. "I'll be sure to pass on your number," I mumble to Emi.

Chapter Twenty-One

Archan

Unknown origin.

Jed waves his flashing phone in my face and grins. "She called me instead of you."

I lean back in my leather chair and steeple my hands. "Put it on speaker."

"Hi, Smoothie, time for an update." Natia sounds nervous—probably because of her inebriated antics from last night. She doesn't strike me as the kind of girl to get drunk often, too much of a control freak—like me.

"Hey, sexy, wearing any clothes today?" Jed chirps, winking at me. Unaware of last night, Zac frowns as I punch Jed in the arm.

"What have you learned?" I demand, glaring at Jed, whose permanent grin gets wider.

A long pause. "Mary died from a myocardial infarction—"

"That's it? An unexplained heart attack?"

"Must be a male thing to interrupt," she mutters. A male sniggers.

"Who is with you?"

"Zee."

"Did you find anything else out?" Zac barks, glaring daggers at the phone like he can send his stare through the screen.

"Wonderful, now it's a party," she grinds out before sighing. "Yes, but let me finish speaking, if you don't mind." The phone goes silent.

"She had a heart attack, and there was bruising on the left side of her abdomen. Despite there being no wounds, the heart itself has been branded with symbols. We think it's the same language as the ones on her wrist." After several beats of silence, she chuckles, a warm sound that makes me want to smile—I resist. "Okay, you can speak now."

"Did you get pictures of the brands?" I enquire.

"Sending them now." Jed's phone signals a message being delivered. He opens the image, and we lean over the phone, wearing identical frowns of concern.

I initiate the mental link with Jed and Zac. *"Khalkaroth."*

"He's playing games with us," Zac says.

"Which he's dragged her in the middle of," Jed inserts, his smile now faded.

I rub my temple. *"Get these to Nathan for proper translation and watch Natia carefully. If Khalkaroth makes contact, I want to know immediately."*

A huge, impatient sigh echoes down the phone before she speaks. "Do you know what it means?"

Jed answers, his normal playfulness absent, "It's a further warning. We need time to fully decipher it."

There is a beat of silence, followed by a slightly higher-pitched Natia. "You could instantly decipher the symbols on the wrist. Why not this one?"

"It is more complicated," I explain truthfully. "There is more than one meaning."

"Need I remind you of our agreement to share all information?" she snaps.

I stiffen as ice coats my voice. "No. I am a man of my word."

A slight tapping indicates she's drumming her fingers, whilst the low *whoosh* suggests she's in a car. "Do you know who killed Mary?"

191

"Khalkaroth."

"How can you be sure?"

"The brands on her heart are the work of a powerful shadow demon. I only know of three that could do this. One is in Lucifer's bad books and so is currently on lockdown in hell, the other is too old to care, and the last is Khalkaroth."

"You seem to have in depth knowledge of the occupants of hell."

I chuckle. "It's my business to know the whereabouts of powerful beings."

"Neighbors from hell? Literally?" she jokes. Jed snorts. "Smoothie, we'll be leaving for the island at two o'clock."

His wide grin returns as he rubs his hands together. "Great, I'm ready for a bit of action."

The room falls silent; I glance at the phone to see if she's still on the line—she is. Jed shrugs whilst Zac crosses his arms.

Finally, she speaks. "Archan, about tonight—"

I sigh. Another human who breaks promises. "You agreed, Natia, and you said you keep your promises."

She huffs. "Stop interrupting and guessing what I'm going to say. About tonight—I don't want to discuss last night at all. If you have anything to say, do it now."

My features blank—I misjudged her. She's not trying to back out despite knowing how much danger she'll be in being alone with me; not her life, but most assuredly her virtue. Duncan's accusation of my lazy seduction sits like a lead balloon in my stomach. He's unquestionably correct; she deserves someone who will make an effort. "I said everything I needed to last night," I reply.

Jed gets in the last word. "Can I have a copy of your playlists, please?"

The phone goes dead in reply as Zac studies me carefully. Whatever he sees makes him frown. "The purpose of this date is to break her, correct?"

I nod. "Indeed."

Jed folds his arms. "What about Duncan's warning?"

"What warning?" Zac grinds out, his face turning to granite.

I run my hands through my hair. "He warned me when Natia falls for someone, she does it hard, and if I wasn't prepared for that, then I should leave her alone."

Zac smirks. "This is perfect."

Jed's smile slips. "You want her broken?"

"It will make it easier," Zac says, shrugging.

Jed shakes his head. "You're wrong," he tips his head toward me, "he's got to prove he's worthy of her heart. She won't just fall for the physical attraction. Natia's the whole package—she needs her heart and mind wooed."

My knuckles turn white. "And you think I'm incapable of that?"

He drops his arms and picks up his phone. "No, but Natia has high walls and an accurate reading for bullshit. The only chance you have with her is if you're honest with what you are and what you are not offering. If you can't give her your heart, then don't promise it."

"I won't lie to her."

"Good, just make sure you're not lying to yourself." He smirks. "I think this girl has the potential to surprise you."

I think back on her defiance, strength, accurate assessment of situations, and the stark honesty when she has bared her soul. She's the very definition of someone who wears her heart on her sleeve.

Jed's wrong. She already has surprised me.

Chapter Twenty-Two

Natia

Tauruses hardly ever lose hope; they have faith that everything happens for a reason.

My head snaps up as the air currents shift suddenly, and Jed appears out of thin air in the kitchen. His blond-tipped hair is pulled back in a ponytail, and he's wearing an all-black combat outfit with military style boots. Spinning around, he opens the fridge and grabs some milk and ingredients to make a sandwich. Wearing a cheeky grin, he quirks an eyebrow. "Want one?"

Recovering from his sudden arrival—that's going to take some getting used to; can they all teleport?—I blink at the pile of food. "Why are you eating my food? Doesn't *his majesty* feed you?"

He pulls a face. "Yeah, healthy shit… You have better food." He pours a glass of milk, sniffs it, then frowns at the carton. "Almond milk?"

"Yeah, she drinks nut juice!" Zee shouts from his lounging pose on the sofa. Jed chuckles.

Shaking my head, I slide my twin swords into the sheaths on my back. Jed pauses his epic sandwich making and gazes at me, while I eye the sandwich layers with interest and glance at my watch. I don't have the time a sandwich like that deserves—maybe I could get him to make me one later?

"What?" I snap, when he continues to stare at me.

"You look sexy as hell in your full leathers and weapons. He's got to see this."

Realizing his intent, I dive to grab him, touching his arm milliseconds before he teleports. He flashes me a mischievous grin and takes me with him. Shocked, I don't register the experience before we're standing in Archan's office. Archan sits at his desk with Zac looking over his shoulder at a computer screen.

Archan's mouth tilts up in a wicked grin as he peruses me. I smack Jed over the head, and he flinches, rubbing it reflexively.

I point between me and Jed. "You and me, we're done."

He pouts, making me chuckle.

"Questions, comments, fashion advice?" I quip, jutting my hip out in a catwalk-worthy pose. Archan's eyes begin to lighten.

I groan. "I don't have time for this. I'm working. Take me back, Smoothie."

Archan leans back in his leather chair. "That's warm enough for our date."

I roll my eyes as Jed grabs my arm. We appear in the middle of the living room, startling Zee so much he spills his coffee.

"Fucking hell! We need a warning system if people are going to literally start popping in and out of thin air," Zee grumbles.

I smack Jed over the head again, and Zee breaks into a slow grin. "What did you do?"

"I took her to see Archan for fashion advice," he snickers, as they both crack up laughing.

"Dude," Zee says, fist bumping Jed. *They're going to drive me insane.* Duncan suddenly appears in the kitchen, making me and Zee jump.

"What the hell!" Zee and I shout in unison. Duncan frowns, confused.

"Let's just go," I sigh. We do need a system—cow bells, maybe?

Duncan unravels an old map on the dining table, placing cups on the corners to stop it rolling back.

Jed points to a red arrow. "This is the cave we need to search."

Duncan runs his finger over a small clearing. "And this is where we're going to arrive."

"Wouldn't it be easier to just go to the cave directly?" I ask.

"It's warded from people teleporting inside, and it's likely the indigenous tribe will have sentries around the cave. We need to do some reconnaissance first," Jed says.

I nudge Duncan's shoulder. "Who's taking me?"

Duncan wraps his arms around my waist. "Me."

"Oh, wait." I dig around in my pockets for Emi's card and hand it to Aaden. "Emi's number. Her exact words were, 'If you're interested, give me a call.'" Aaden flushes, and I shoot him a wink.

Duncan tightens his hold and teleports. I'm sucked into a dark vortex and immediately thrown down what feels like a long vacuum, twisting and turning as wind roars in my ears.

Disorientation hits me, and my stomach churns. Just as I'm sure I'm going to vomit, my feet hit the ground, hard; I bend my knees to absorb the unexpected impact.

Duncan grins. "It takes a little getting used to."

Jed appears and immediately scans the area. The small clearing is enclosed by thick trees and shrubs. I reach out with my senses, sorting through all the background noise. Nothing but the flutter of birds' wings, their tweeting, and the crunch of small animal feet on the ground. No murderous natives—yet. Duncan points in the direction we need to go.

It takes several minutes of hacking the greenery with my swords to exit the clearing onto a worn dirt path. We have two options: follow it and risk running into the tribe, or veer off in the hopes of staying hidden. Duncan touches my arm.

I tilt my head at the path. Jed seems content to follow our lead.

Treading lightly, we walk for five minutes before the path widens and forks to the left. One path has recent footprints, while the other is dusty, unused.

Jed steps closer, and I catch his eye. I point at the recently-used path and put my hands together on the side of my cheek, indicating this is where I think they live and sleep. Then I nod to the other path and form a triangle with my hands—I'm almost positive the cave is this way. I swirl my finger in the air and point to the right path.

Jed screws up his face and looks between us incredulously, while Duncan simply stalks off into the forest.

Grasping Jed's hand, I stride into the trees but don't go as deep as Duncan. Thirty meters in, the air currents shift in front of us.

I put a hand on Jed's muscular chest and crouch down; he copies me.

I quickly close my eyes and concentrate. Large enough to be human—could be an animal, but they aren't making any sounds... so an animal would be unlikely.

Flicking my eyes open, I glance over my shoulder, sensing more movement.

Placing my finger on Jed's lips, I point in front of us, put one finger up, then point behind us. He nods. I point to my back then his.

He tilts his head to the side and raises an eyebrow, making me roll my eyes and crawl around him, placing my back against his.

Even I know, patience is a virtue in these situations. Jed, however, missed the memo. His warmth leaves my back as he rushes toward the unknown predator.

A whoosh of air sails toward us. Launching myself on top of Jed, I push him to the ground. He grunts. We glance up at the white feather tipped arrow lodged in a tree above our heads.

Jed teleports us about a hundred meters away, and I waste no time. Pushing up, I dart off, with Jed keeping pace at my side.

Two arrows glide past my face as I lean to the right, then the left.

Still running, I point at a tree ahead.

Jed frowns—it's times like this that it would be helpful to have telepathy.

Launching myself up the side of the tree, I grasp its lowest branch to haul myself up; the sharp bark scrapes my palms, causing me to lose my grip and slip. A strong hand hooks under my arm and drags me back up. Jed grins.

I sprint along the strong branch and somersault to the next tree. When I turn around, Jed's eyes are wide. I smirk at him. He follows, landing next to me with grace.

"Me, Tarzan; you, Jane," he whispers in my ear. I suppress an inappropriate giggle. It doesn't seem to fit with this life-threatening situation.

Another arrow whizzes past us.

We get moving through the trees and are so focused on avoiding being skewered that we don't anticipate the clearing ahead. I stop halfway up the final tree, and Jed slams into me, knocking me to the ground. I roll to my feet and dust off my pants.

"Nice entrance, Locks," Duncan mutters behind me. I swivel and find swaths of dirty rope binding him to the tree I fell from. Jed jumps down next to me. At least twenty men and women dressed in scraps of fabric point arrows and crude knives at us.

Behind them is the gaping mouth of the cave, dark and ominous. Three men lift their bows and pull back, placing tension on the strings. I panic—an urgent swell of power inside me releases, making me gasp.

Trees groan in protest, and every single one of the tribe fly onto their backs, including the ones that have crept up behind us. Five men immediately spring back to their feet—impressive. Knives in hand, they rush toward us, wearing murderous expressions. I pull my other sword from my back and widen my stance, ready for the attack.

But it doesn't come.

They hit an invisible barrier, which flexes like a trampoline and throws them back once again. Two of the men stand and begin to communicate in indecipherable, clipped tones, followed by several women, who add arm gestures to their speech, jabbing their index fingers toward me, their features tense and bodies stiff. The conversation abruptly ends and they turn me with wide eyes. As one, they get on their knees and bow, placing their hands on the ground. I glance at Duncan, who's now free from the tree and pushing his hand through the air as if touching something.

"Whoa, Locks, that's new—but useful. Good timing," he says.

More of the tribe arrive and fall to their knees.

I spin in a slow circle. "Well… this is unexpected."

"They seem to like you." Jed chuckles while scratching his head and frowning at me, like he's unsure of who I am.

"What now?" I mutter.

Duncan pushes me toward the edge of the barrier. "Time for first contact."

I put my swords away. How can I communicate with humans who, as far as I know, haven't had any contact with the outside world?

A short, plump woman with a beaded necklace steps forward. No, not beads—bones. I cringe. *Please let them be animal.*

Keeping her head lowered, she offers her hand. I look at Duncan and Jed, and they shrug, staring at the woman. Following my instincts, I step toward the barrier and notice it isn't totally invisible, as it distorts the air slightly. I run my fingertips along the surface, watching it ripple, the sensation sending little electric tingles up my arm. It's mine, I did this—therefore, logically, it shouldn't hurt me. Right? Taking a deep breath, I reach through the barrier, the sensation like pushing through water, and it disappears with an audible pop.

I take the woman's offered hand. She jerks my arm toward the cave, causing me to trip. This is going better than expected—unless they change their minds and roast us for dinner. Duncan and Jed stay close behind me. The old woman turns and barks out a harsh word, pointing back to the group; several of the tribe surround Duncan and Jed.

"I don't think you're welcome," I mutter to them, while keeping my focus on the woman's chocolate brown eyes.

"No way. We all go, or we don't go at all," Jed insists.

"If I get in trouble, you can just teleport yourselves in."

"It's warded, remember?" Jed grinds through his teeth.

I give him a determined stare. "How long have you guys been trying to access this cave?"

Silence.

"That's what I thought. Stay here—I'll be fine. I'm more worried about you," I say, glancing at the tribe, whose numbers keep increasing. All stay knelt on the ground. A firm tug on my arm reminds me I need to be on the move with the old woman. I take a read of her aura—purple with a smattering of blue. Hmm... spiritual, intuitive, and calm. Not the reading of someone leading me to certain death. Maybe they're a sexist community and don't value men? The women certainly seem to have the last say, and I think this older woman is their leader.

I follow her into the cave. The shining onyx walls glitter until we round a corner and are plunged into complete darkness. People talk about not being able to see their hands in front of them—this was literal right now. I stumble, and only the old woman's strong grip keeps me upright. She clucks her tongue. Ha, I'm being admonished. She whispers a few indecipherable words, and flames leap to life along the wall.

"You could have done that in the first place," I mutter.

She laughs.

"Wait, you understand me?" I squeak. "What's your name?"

No response.

"Wendy?" Silence.

"Katherine?" More silence.

"Betty?" She smiles. "Well, Betty it is, then," I declare.

She drops my hand as we enter a large cavern. I gawk at the ceiling, which is twice the height of a normal house. Walking around the edge of the circular room, I run my hands over the symbols and drawings that cover every inch of the walls. My brain tugs at a memory. Straining to remember, my jaw drops open.

They're the same symbols we found on Mary Conway.

201

Duncan needs to see this. Taking out my phone, I move in a circle to take panoramic photos of the walls. It's impossible to get everything, as the symbols go up to the roof. I glance at Betty; she seems unconcerned with me taking photos.

She drags me to the center of the room, in between where she's placed four candles in a square. She draws symbols in the dirt in front of each candle; a flash of an image from my studies at the SIP makes me realize the wavy lines represent water. I follow her other drawings—fire, earth, and wind. She fusses in the folds of her scrappy skirt and pulls out an object, which she hands to me. It resembles a star with a set of smaller stars on the edge of each point. It's the width of a small teacup, and I turn it over in my hands; it feels cool, like some sort of metal. I stare at it for a long time before meeting Betty's gaze.

"Um… thank you. What is it?"

She simply watches me with a bemused expression.

"Fine… not much of a talker, are you?" She pats my jacket. Looking at the object once more, I follow her silent instructions and slip it into my pocket.

Suddenly, Betty grasps both of my hands and begins chanting. The hairs on the back of my neck prickle with the presence of magic. Not sure what to do, I stand still and concentrate on her words. A pulse of power almost brings me to my knees, as a fireball spins around the room before igniting one of the candles.

Without pause, the earth beneath my feet begins to move, as if we're in the midst of an earthquake. A lump of dirt falls from the ceiling, hitting my shoulder. My breathing picks up as I fear it may collapse, burying us alive. As I've already explained, this is definitely not the epic death I have planned. The next candle ignites. Betty opens her eyes and stares at me.

"What do you want me to do?"

She rolls her eyes.

"Ha, you *do* understand me!"

She clucks her tongue, like a mother telling off her child. Placing a hand over my heart, she takes a deep breath, grabs my hand, and places it against her chest. Her heartbeat vibrates strong and steady against my palm. Several moments later, mine slows to mimic hers, and a strange power begins to swirl inside me. Betty nods at me in approval and thumps my chest once. I cough, and a sudden gust of wind whips around the edge of the walls. Another candle ignites.

I blink. "I did that? Cool—I think…?" I lean to step away, but she holds me tight and looks pointedly at the final unlit candle, making me draw my eyebrows together. I've shown no affinity for water. She takes a deep breath, as before. I indulge her and do the same; closing my eyes, I focus on her heartbeat and try to imagine something water related. A raging storm on the ocean crashes in my mind, and salt tingles my lips, making me lick them. I gasp as ice cold water pelts my face. My eyes snap open to the darkest storm cloud I've ever seen hovering above us. Instinctively, I duck.

Betty slaps me across the head, making me lose concentration on the cloud, and the rain disappears. *Okay, then. I'm confused… was that me or her?*

All four candles are now lit. Betty begins chanting again, and the flames rise higher; all we need now is blood, and we're ripe for an episode of one of Duncan's favorite shows. God, I hope there's no blood. I'm still trying to process the power in the room, from both me and her, when she slams my hands against the floor, forcing me to my knees. I yelp and try to pull away. She holds them firm to the ground, continuing to chant.

I tense my body. Old she may be, but *damn* she's strong. Extending and scooping my leg out, I prepare to knock her on her back, but the room becomes shrouded in darkness, and a gentle caress along my arm has me shrieking.

"Who's there?" I demand the darkness. Betty is nowhere to be seen.

Light seeps into the void as the dark curtain is lifted. Standing, I walk through the opening, seeking a reprieve from the consuming darkness. My feet lift off the floor. I'm floating. Comfort wraps around me like a soft blanket. Worries, fears, battles—old and new— disappear, and my entire body sighs, releasing a weariness I wasn't aware I was carrying. The weight of the world lifts, and a sense of peace overcomes me. If I had to guess, I would say this is what heaven feels like. "Am I dead?" I whisper. A spike of fear fleetingly jolts my nerves.

A rumble of laughter echoes from the swirling lights and colors surrounding me.

"No, Natia, you are very much alive. Relax. You are safe here," a deep, masculine voice reassures me. I believe him.

"Who are you? Where am I?" I ask him.

"Both questions take more time to answer than we have. Pick one."

"Who are you?"

"Your guardian. You are being tested to ensure you are worthy of the power within you. You are brave, strong, and pure of heart. You will not fail. The choice of how you use that power is yours. Choose wisely. Each path requires sacrifices and will achieve very different results. Beware of false prophecies. In all things, follow your heart, Natia."

I reach toward the entity that appears beside me. Ancient eyes stare into my own, their multicolored depths holding knowledge beyond our current world.

"That was a good deflection," I mutter.

Beautiful chiseled features come into view as he chuckles, the sound like haunting music. "Did you give me this power?" I wonder aloud.

"Originally, yes, Natia. Accept it, learn it, don't fight it—if you do, it will consume you."

"It's too much," I whisper, my fear of hurting those I love seeping into my thoughts.

He sighs. "Sometimes I worry I've given you too much, but for what you must protect, you will need it. You have good people around you—accept their offers of help. You can't do this alone." He kisses my forehead. "Stay safe, child. Next time, the better question would be for you to ask who *you* are."

"Wait…"

As I blink rapidly, Betty's smiling face comes into focus. She's still holding my palms firm to the dirt floor. My body is heavy, confused, and resentful of gravity. Betty steps back, releasing my hands. Pushing to my feet, I rise to stand next to her and follow her gaze to the floor at the center. With a deafening *crack*, the earth shifts, splitting open. A white marble pillar twists up from the ground, stopping when it reaches my height. A small object rests on top—the Jar.

When I say small, I mean jam jar size. I admit, I'm a little disappointed. Betty places it in my hands, pats my pocket where I put the star-shaped object, and taps the base of the Jar. I turn it over, finding an indent the exact shape of the star. Studying the rest of the Jar, my pinky fingers barely fitting through the twin curved handles, I squint at the tiny markings surrounding the rim. I'm not positive, but they look similar to everything we've seen so far—Mary's body, her heart, and these cave walls.

Betty shoves me back to the entrance of the cave. Outside, Jed shifts restlessly from foot to foot, his eyes pleading with desperate hope. I wiggle the Jar in front of me, but leave the star key in my pocket. I promised I'd hand over the Jar—nothing else. The tribe has shifted position to face the cave, but they're still kneeling.

I look over my shoulder at Betty. She smiles, with a secret that seems meant for me. "Thank you."

She tilts her head. "For this," I jiggle the Jar, "and for this." I squeeze the end of my hair and deposit some salty water on the ground. She grins. I wonder if she'd be up for magical training? I glance at her necklace and suppress a shiver. Maybe not.

Duncan looks me up and down as he wraps an arm around my waist. "Why are you soaking wet?"

"Later," I mutter.

Chapter Twenty-Three

Natia

A Taurus will care for you more than any other sign, but you have to earn it.

My ass hits the floor of the apartment. I glare at Duncan. "Sorry, Locks."

Jed holds his hand out for the Jar as I flip to my feet. Duncan gazes at it with longing.

"Wait. I agreed we'd hand it over after we had a look. Duncan, will pictures be okay?"

"If we *must* hand it over, then yes," Duncan grumbles.

Aaden takes some close-ups of the Jar, muttering about it needing cleaned and the quality of the photos. Finished, he hands it to an anxious Jed.

He rolls it over in his hands, looking directly at me. "Was there anything else in there?"

I inwardly cringe and try deflection, praying he isn't as astute as Zac. "Apart from Betty? What are you going to do with that?" I ask, pointing at the Jar.

Jed frowns. "Who's Betty?"

I flop onto the sofa. "The old woman."

Jed snorts. "You made friends with the leader of a savage tribe known for cannibalism?"

Zee trots down the stairs, laughing. "She has a habit of befriending the nasties of the world."

I shudder, remembering the bone neckless. "Nobody told me they were cannibals."

Jed gives us a little wave. "Laters, babe."

I roll over on the sofa. "We need an update on Mary's heart symbols."

"I'll get Archan to call you," he replies, before popping out of existence.

Zee sits next to me and tugs my hair. I slap his hand away, causing several leaves stuck in my hair to flutter around my face.

"Consider that your souvenir," I quip. "I need a quick shower, then we can discuss what else I found in the cave." I throw my phone at Duncan. "Check out the photos on there."

Duncan catches it, his face lighting up.

Clean and de-leaved, I sit next to the fire as we examine the photos. Some match those found on Mary's body. Charlie joins us on a video call, courtesy of Aaden's laptop.

"Duncan has updated me on how you reached the cave. Talk me through the rest of it, Natia. Leave nothing out," Uncle Charlie says, giving me his stern boss look that makes grown men cower.

"We were about to be attacked by the natives, and I managed to throw up some sort of shield around us, then—"

"Shield? What do you mean? You don't carry a shield," Uncle Charlie interrupts.

I bite the inside of my cheek; this is going to be a difficult conversation. "Yeah… so I used my elemental magic to form some sort of barrier."

"It was pretty cool," Duncan adds with an encouraging smile.

Uncle Charlie's eyebrows scrunch up as he waves his hand, indicating I should continue.

"So, after what seemed like some kind of argument, the tribe got on their knees and sort of bowed down." Uncle Charlie's eyebrows shoot up as I continue. "Their leader, an older woman, took me into the cave, which was covered in symbols—they seem to be written in the same language as the warnings on Mary Conway's body. I took pictures so Duncan can study them."

"Why wasn't Duncan with you?"

I glance at Duncan and tug on the end of my braid. Uncle Charlie is going to flip. "She would only allow me inside. Duncan and Jed waited outside."

"You went in alone?" he grinds out, as the infamous eyebrow starts jumping around.

I nod and note the pink shade of Charlie's face—stage one of his anger. "After a short tunnel, we entered the main chamber. Betty—"

"Who's Betty?" Uncle Charlie snaps.

Zee snorts as I answer. "The old woman. Anyway, she used some sort of ritual involving the four elements and candles to unlock a spell, which then revealed the Jar." I'm leaving a hell of a lot out of that explanation, which my ever-perceptive uncle recognizes.

His features soften. "The line is secure, Natia. It's my personal one."

I glance at Aaden, who nods. I'll be damned if the SIP learns about my powers before they're stable. Taking a deep breath, I launch into the details. "We called the four elements. Betty called fire and earth. I called air and water."

Duncan grins. "That's why you were wet. Your second affinity is water? That works well with air—I can teach you some good fighting techniques with those elements."

Uncle Charlie's face turns a deeper shade, hitting crimson—stage two. Instinctively, I leave out my meeting with the strange being and the gift of the key. "As discussed, you're not surprised she has a second affinity?" Uncle Charlie asks Duncan.

Wait, they'd been talking about me? Typical.

Duncan nods. "In hindsight, I believe her instinctual fighting skills have always been linked to an affinity with air. She's strong—normally, that leads to another element."

"Makes sense," Uncle Charlie says, his face lighting back to stage one.

"Right here," I mutter, holding my hand up. They need to be reminded they aren't in one of their private conversations about me.

Uncle Charlie sighs. "So what you're saying is a previously impenetrable tribe bowed down to you and gave you access to their protected treasure? Then you used your newly-found magic and controlled another element?"

I bite my lip. "That about sums it up."

He pinches the end of his nose and screws his eyes shut. "It strikes me as personal, Natia. You seem deeply involved, and are also working with Archan and his team. Have you figured out what he is yet?"

I shake my head. "No, and I'm not entirely sure of his motivations. But at least this way we have access to what they're doing."

"Which also means they have access to what *you* are doing, and knowledge of whatever is happening to you."

"Better than them working against us."

Uncle Charlie's stare hits mine, as he seems to delve around in my head. His left eye twitches a frantic rhythm. He knows I'm holding something back, but he doesn't push.

"Find out what that Jar is for, what Archan is up to, and who this Pan guy is." We all nod—it's a tall order, and Uncle Charlie knows it. "Contact me on my private line only, and if you need any further SIP resources or info, call me first." He's protecting me.

"Thanks, Uncle Charlie." He gives me a tight smile, and the screen goes blank.

Duncan turns to me. "Why didn't you tell Jed?"

I shrug. "He came for the Jar. The rest is private. Betty was showing me the cave, not anyone else."

Zee rubs his head and scowls. "Why do you think she only let you in?"

"Maybe because I'm female; they seemed like a matriarchal society."

Duncan tilts his head. "I hadn't considered that."

I shrug and glance around at the worried faces of my colleagues. Scrap that, I'm looking at my friends, people who worry and care about me, which makes my next decision easier. "I have something else to tell you."

"Oh my god, you're not pregnant, are you?" Zee snorts.

Rolling my eyes, I curl up on the sofa. "Before receiving the Jar, I had some kind of encounter… with something."

Zee laughs. "Descriptive."

"After we completed the ritual, I was in some sort of weird room—it felt like another world, actually. Anyway, he basically said I was being tested to receive my powers, I had some important decisions ahead, and sacrifices would be made no matter what."

"Sounds like an ominous fortune cookie message," Zee laughs, his nervousness bleeding through his sarcasm. In that moment, I realize we're more alike than we care to admit.

"Also… he said he's responsible for my powers."

Duncan's eyebrows shoot up, but he says nothing. I'll grill him about that later when whatever thought process he's having is complete—I'll get nothing out of him until then.

"That confirms it, then… You're linked to this—the Jar, Pan, mankind's imminent destruction," Aaden mumbles, nonplussed.

My head falls in my hands. "I guess."

"Do you think he's a guardian angel?" Zee asks.

My head shoots up, and my eyes widen. "Do those exist?"

We stare at Duncan, who raises his hands. "I have no idea." He pauses. "Contact Archan and see if he's willing to share what the symbols on Mary's heart mean."

Grabbing my phone from the dining table, I return to sit next to Zee and put it on speaker phone.

"Yes?" is his greeting. I roll my eyes.

I opt for an equally irritating response. "It's me."

"Thank you for finding the Jar; you have no idea the help you have given us."

"That's what I'm afraid of."

"It is not a bad reason—it's the exact opposite, actually."

"Then you'll be happy to share."

There's a pause. "No."

"Ah, so I'm taking your word that what you think is a good thing is also a good thing in my book?"

"You're going to have to trust me," he says, sounding irritated.

"Have you deciphered the symbols found on Mary's heart?"

A few beats of silence. I'm about to remind him of his promise again, when he speaks.

"Roughly translated, it means, 'All hope is lost' or, 'Mankind will lose all hope.'"

I tuck my legs under myself. "The first is present tense, while the other is a prediction. Which one is it?"

"I believe it is the future—a warning."

"Is it literal?" I ask. It sounds like a doomsday prophecy.

"It needs to be interpreted with other information."

"Information you have?" I probe.

He evades the question. "In part."

"Are you willing to share that information?"

"No."

"Figures," I mumble.

"It doesn't pertain to catching Khalkaroth, which is our agreement. If I find anything that does, you will be the first to know."

I hate that saying. You're not the first to know because the person telling you is the first to know. "Fine."

"See you at seven." As if I need the reminder. I disconnect the call.

"Me, Aaden, and Indiana Jones here will research while you're out," Zee says, nodding toward Duncan.

"Do you honestly think this isn't related to Khalkaroth?" Duncan asks.

"Archan's clever at answering questions. He said it wouldn't help us catch Khalkaroth—not that it isn't related."

Two loud raps sound on the door. Aaden jumps up.

"Password?" he asks.

"Nine Inch Nails," Jeanette's feminine voice responds.

I punch Zee in the ribs as Aaden opens the door and takes something from her.

Aaden places a single iris flower on the coffee table and hands me a note. The blood drains from my face. My hands begin to shake as I read it. Zee wraps an arm around me, as my hand drops to my lap. Duncan plucks the note from my fingers and doesn't look surprised after he scans it.

"What's wrong?" Zee asks.

I glower at Duncan. "Yes, Duncan, what's wrong?"

Aaden frowns as he leans over Duncan's shoulder and reads out the note. "See you soon, little Iris, L x."

"Who's L?" Zee presses, looking from my face to Duncan's.

"Hmm… let me think. Who might L be, Duncan?" Duncan's normally calm blue aura darkens.

Duncan reaches to touch my face. "Locks, I—"

I jerk to the side. "Don't. You knew. How long? The whole time, or just since he placed a bounty on my head?"

A muscle tics in his jaw. "And how the fuck would you know that?"

I flinch. "Archan."

Duncan runs a hand through his hair. "And how does he know?"

"At the bar… I had flashbacks. He caught images of Lawrence and knew about the bounty."

Three sets of eyes land on me. "He broke your shields?" Duncan blinks.

"No. He caught the flashbacks. I wasn't prepared for them."

214

"Can someone tell me what's going on?" Aaden jumps in.

I uncurl myself from the sofa and stand in front of Duncan. "Lawrence is the demon who killed my best friend in New York before I joined the SIP. He hunted me for my aura, and it seems he never stopped. Except Duncan let me think he was dead."

Aaden's eyes flick to my abdomen. "That's who shot you?"

"Yes, and now he's found me. How long, Duncan?"

Duncan looks past me. "You were traumatized. You needed to concentrate on your training. I've been hunting him for the last five years."

I curl my fists. "Look at me."

Duncan's warm brown eyes flash with fear. At the look on his face, the fight immediately leaves me. I step closer and wrap my arms around him.

"We'll deal with him like every other bad guy that needs putting down," I mutter.

The hair on top of my head lifts as he chuckles.

Chapter Twenty-Four

Natia

Don't let the calm Taurus fool you into thinking they are harmless.
When provoked, they are like an atomic bomb.

The definition of procrastination is the action of delaying or postponing something, and given that the outfits in my wardrobe have been mocking me for over twenty minutes, it appears it's a new personality trait of mine.

On the subject of Archan Reinheart, my heart, head, and body are in conflict. Self-preservation screams I should stay far, far away, my heart scrambles to keep its walls firm, while my body has simply gone rogue, constantly demanding attention. I grab a mid-length, pale gray skirt, a soft, pink cashmere sweater, and gray, knee-high, swede boots, leaving my hair down.

"You don't have to do this," Duncan shouts from outside my closet door as I dress.

I sigh. "We've been through this. I don't go, and he not only stops working with us—he works against us." Pulling open my door, I'm met with a wall of folded arms and pissed faces. Even Aaden is demonstrating he's no wallflower.

Zee drops his arms then runs a hand over the back of his neck. "I don't like it."

I scoff. "Nobody likes it. But mind games are Archan's MO."

"I don't think he's playing mind games, Natia. I think he wants you, plain and simple."

Sighing, I grab my bag and check my phone is fully charged. Aaden plucks it from my fingers and begins tapping on it. "It will be okay, guys. It's one date."

"Until he tricks you into another," Zee mutters.

"Not happening."

Aaden hands me my phone back. "I've activated a tracking app on your phone. We'll be able to find you anywhere."

Duncan wraps me in a big hug. "You call us if you're in trouble or want to come home early." Then they launch into a set of rules and a pep talk that causes my eyes to roll several times. I almost expect them to give me the birds and the bees conversation—Zee's version would be interesting. At ten past seven, we squeeze into the elevator. It seems they've decided to come intimidate my date.

Zee studies me. "Did you wear that entire outfit?"

Groaning, I smack him over the head. "Stop thinking about my underwear."

He huffs. "It's not me I'm worried about..." He slips his hand through the crook of my arm, pulling me close as we step into the lobby. "When a woman wears matching underwear to a date, it's because they've already decided to show it."

I swat him over the head again. "It can't be because it makes me feel sexy? Now *shhh*, I need to get my head around the next few hours, and you talking about my underwear isn't helping."

I let go of Zee and take several slow breaths. Remember, he blackmailed you, and you're pissed at him. Also, he's an arrogant asshole who looks down on you. Pep talk given, I feel better until I look at him. Wearing dark blue jeans and a gray cashmere sweater, he looks like he stepped out of *GQ Magazine*. His blond hair hangs in loose waves around his relaxed shoulders. His eyes trace every curve of my body, and despite my lack of exposed skin, I feel stripped naked by his gaze.

I give a slow twirl. "Do I meet with your satisfaction, Mr. Reinheart?" I aim for contrite, but it comes off a bit flirty. I'm going to have a sore hand from many mental slaps tonight.

He grins. "You are perfect, Miss Waterford."

I forget I have three surly men at my back until Duncan's arm brushes mine. He crosses his arms in a cliché big brother warning. "Hurt her, and I will hunt you down and kill you." Okay, then—no room for misunderstandings.

Archan tips his head in acknowledgement. "I have no intention of hurting her."

Zee jumps in with his big brother boots, aiming for maximum embarrassment. "You will not lay one hand on her, sexual or otherwise." I clench my fists and pivot on my heel to face Zee.

"Did you make sure to put condoms in my purse, just in case?" I snap. He huffs and puffs out his chest.

I wave my hand and mutter, "Good night, guys."

Aaden shouts one last instruction, "Have her home by midnight, Reinheart!"

He chuckles. "I wasn't aware you are Cinderella."

I grin. "Does that make you Prince Charming?"

Eyes hooded, he gives me a sinful look. "No, Natia, I am anything but a fairy tale. I do seduction, sin, and sex well… but I am not a nice man."

My skin heats in contrast to the calm, chilly evening. The lack of limo makes me search the street. He strides toward a black Audi R8 and opens the passenger door. I inspect the car. Fast, sleek, with a lot of attitude and unmistakable quality. He arches an eyebrow in challenge—he must think I'm contemplating running.

"I was deciding if the car suits you." I settle myself into the seat and turn on the radio; Rhianna's "S&M" blasts through the car. I crack up laughing as he climbs into his seat to what will now become his tagline—"'Cause I may be bad, but I'm perfectly good at it." He slides a glance my way, and I wave my hand at him, indicating he should drive. Shaking his head, he pulls out into traffic, revving the engine.

My grin widens. "What are you, seventeen?"

One side of his mouth quirks. "I assure you, I'm not seventeen in any way—my driving, my actions… or my intentions."

I study his profile in the city lights flashing by through the windows. "And your intentions are what, exactly?"

He glances at me. "To break two of your surrogate brothers' warnings," he pauses, "and I won't be hurting you." I blush, praying the angels are in my corner tonight as I beg for the strength to not make stupid decisions.

"You're planning on making me late? A little presumptuous—my phone's on a timer to play a fake call, which will require my immediate attention at home."

He laughs out loud. "I never know what you're going to say."

I shrink in my seat a little—I know I'm a bit quirky, some might say weird. But to have it pointed out to you on a date? His hand touches mine on my lap, snapping me out of my pity party monologue.

He glances at me without slowing the car. He frowns as his thumb runs across my knuckles. "It was meant as a compliment. Predictable,

219

superficial, and fake are now the norm. You are honest, you surprise me, and you make me laugh. I have not done that in a long time. You have already given me a gift no one else can." He pulls his attention back to the road and his hand back on the steering wheel. A muscle jumps in his jaw as I stare at him, at a loss for words. *What am I supposed to do with that?*

We head east, to an unfamiliar area of the city.

"Where are we going for dinner?" I ask, suspicious.

"It is a surprise, but we are going somewhere else first."

My head snaps to face him. "I only agreed to dinner."

He shakes his head. "Relax... you will enjoy it. Anyway, it's a date."

My thoughts filter through the conversation at the diner. "No, I only agreed to dinner."

He chuckles. "Last night, you told me you would be back for our date. I assumed you meant it."

I blush and fold my arms over my chest. "I cannot be held accountable for my actions last night."

He slows down to take a small road to the right. We wind down a few streets, and finally, he turns onto a dirt track; the street lights disappear, and I only catch glimpses of trees where the car headlights shine like a torch. He pulls into a makeshift parking lot, lit by lanterns hanging from the trees that create a path to a small building. Jumping out, he rounds the car, opens the door, and offers me his hand, which I take.

Thick trees surround us in every direction. "This isn't where we play hide and seek in the dark and one of us dies, right? It's inventive, but I'd rather not have to chase you first. Kicking your ass would be so much easier if you'd take it like a man and stand still."

220

He glances at my boots. "Hmm, I think I'll pass. Your heels look a little dangerous for ass-kicking." I laugh, relaxing a little.

A petite Asian woman greets us in the small building. "Good evening, Mr. Reinheart, Miss Waterford." She hands Archan a key and ushers us to the other side of the building, looking a little flustered. *You and me both, sister.* "I hope you have a pleasant evening." She leaves us, hurrying to the parking lot.

Exiting the building, my heels wobble a little on the pebbled path. Archan takes my hand, his warmth a pleasant contrast to the chilly air. My breath catches as I glimpse the unexpected magical wonderland spreading out before us. Trees decorated with hundreds of small orb-shaped lanterns surround a large pond, and pale yellow light dances over the various statues positioned around the water. Fairy lights hanging from the trees ignite as I pass them. The scene is reflected in the pond, and lilies in various shades, from white to pink, float on the water, creating a delicate perfume that surrounds us. I glance at Archan, who is silently studying me.

"Why are they open at night?"

He follows my gaze. "There are two types of lilies—night bloomers and day bloomers." He tugs me toward the bridge. Like a child at Disneyland, I'm trying to look everywhere at once. He pauses on the bridge. Letting go of his hand, I lean over the wooden rail and spy a school of foot-long orange and yellow fish, visible in the lighting under the bridge. Watching the rhythmic sway of their bodies, a constant dance, I sigh. Warmth engulfs my back, and two strong hands grip the handrail, trapping me. We aren't touching, but every nerve starts buzzing around my body, making me restless. He peers over my shoulder.

"Why the sigh?" he whispers, as if a hundred people surround us when, in fact, we're alone. I gaze at the fish, letting their hypnotic dance soothe me.

"They look peaceful, relaxed… lazy, even. Their bodies move next to each other, never restless, enjoying the calm created by their closeness. While part of our world, they truly thrive in a world of their own." I place my chin on my hands, and he groans, as it pushes my ass into his body. Blushing, I straighten up, adding another mental slap for the evening. He chuckles but doesn't move.

"Do you think they are happy?" he asks.

"Why wouldn't they be? Here in this paradise, they have no predators. They have a family with no complications, no worries about being hurt."

"Is that what you do? Protect yourself by living in your own world?" he muses.

I spin to face him and tilt my head. "Yes."

His golden eyes search mine. "Don't you feel lonely living in your own world?"

"Don't you feel powerless living in other people's?" I whisper.

He pushes a stray strand of hair from my face. It's a gentle, caring gesture, so unexpected. I move toward his heat, shivering as his body connects with mine. His hands remain on the bridge as he angles his face down. His fierce, golden, glowing gaze studies me. I bite my bottom lip.

I'm procrastinating—again.

His gaze falls to my lips, and my heart skips a few beats. He enfolds me in his arms, pulls me flush against him, and runs his thumb over my bottom lip, dragging it free from my teeth.

"Stop biting your lip, Natia. Or I'll bite it for you—hard," he rasps.

I don't comprehend his words until it's too late. "I'll take that as an invitation to take the kiss you owe me," he mumbles, grasping my chin between his fingers and claiming my lips in a gentle but firm kiss. He runs his velvety tongue over my bottom lip, coaxing me to open for him. Catching his lower lip between my teeth, I nibble it. In response, a low, needy sound rumbles from his throat. Wrapping my hands around his neck, I tug his head closer.

Fingers skim over the naked skin between my sweater and skirt, making me gasp. He uses my surprise to push his tongue past my lips and glide it against mine. A small moan escapes me as he caresses my spine. The kiss turns fierce, possessive. My back arches, pushing my breasts against him. He bites my lip, pulling it between his teeth, then gently swipes his tongue against the sting.

Powerful arms grasp my thighs. He perches me on the handrail of the bridge, pushes to stand between my legs, and lets go of my back.

"Archan," I gasp, wrapping my arms and legs around him. A guttural growl vibrates against my chest as my core presses against him. He pulls his face away a little at a time, making me chase his lips to maintain the kiss. Squeezing my thighs, I trap him and grasp his hair to drag his head back to me. I devour him, demanding everything. His touch skims my ribs before he tests the weight of my breasts in his palms and rolls my nipples through the lace of my bra. He swallows my moan as sparks ignite inside of me; an explosion of adrenaline and excitement makes me feel lightheaded and giddy. A pleasurable sting erupts on my scalp as he tangles his hand in my hair and nips at my quickening pulse, diverting blood to the sensitive spot.

"That hot, deep throbbing between your legs that I put there? It needs release. I can give it to you…" he rasps, pushing himself against me, giving me glorious friction.

223

I'm so lost in sensations that I jolt when the water splashes next to us. Breaking the kiss, I lean back to see two fish throwing themselves above the water.

A nervous bubble of laughter leaves my lips. "Guess they're not always peaceful." Spell broken, I let go of his neck and hold onto his forearms for balance. He slides me against his body to the ground. Daring to look at him, I find his eyes full of need, desire, and disbelief. His usual wicked façade is absent—he looks real, vulnerable. I blink. That's a little heavy for the quick and dirty fuck he's looking for.

His eyelids fall, the fan of long eyelashes splaying across his smooth skin. He takes my hand, kissing each fingertip before nipping the final one, making me squeal. "Come, you need to see the last part."

Curiosity is a weakness of mine, but not being a cat, I consider myself not in danger, so I follow him. I unconsciously touch my sensitive, swollen lips; he smirks at me, making me yank my hand away.

There's the Archan I know.

Walking in silence, I roam my gaze over every aspect of the scenery, studying the trees and statues that look like mini pagodas. He slows, indulging me as I wander from the path to skim my hand over the various bushes. I pause to stroke a flower open to admire its yellow center and deep pink petals.

The sound of rushing water beckons me down a small path. Moisture tickles my lips as I walk through tall bushes and enter a small oasis. A backlit waterfall sparkles like an iridescent curtain. Finding a path leading behind the waterfall, I almost squeal in delight. The mist encircles me, dampening my skin. Archan follows, and we sit on a bench in a small cave, gazing through the cascading water. The hypnotizing sound calms my mind from the kiss.

This date is dangerous. Being alone with him is dangerous. Going to the restaurant with people, sooner rather than later, is safest.

I stand. "Okay, I'm hungry. Lead the way."

He gives me a forced smile. "Your wish is my command."

I let him take my hand. In my excitement, I'd hopped, skipped, and jumped across slippery wet stones in stiletto boots. We take a different route back, but it's no less beautiful.

Settled in the car, I turn to him. "Thank you... That was wonderful."

His lips quirk in a small, genuine smile. "Which part did you like the most?"

Smug asshole.

We head back toward the city. "What restaurant are we going to?"

"An exclusive one."

I roll my eyes.

Ten minutes later, we pull into a parking lot surrounded by gourmet supermarkets. "Are we stopping to do your shopping?" I ask incredulously. He's already out of the car and opening my door.

As I take his offered hand, he answers, "We are shopping for our meal."

"You're cooking? Isn't it easier to go to a restaurant?"

"We are cooking, and easier, yes—but not as fun."

In the supermarket, he picks up a basket and walks down the aisle. He looks so domesticated, such a contrast to his power image. I stop and stare at his back, taking the opportunity to admire his ass. Don't judge—I'm a red-blooded woman. He turns to face me and arches an eyebrow. I hurry to catch up.

"What are you cooking?" I ask.

"*We* are cooking sushi."

I shake my head. "I burn water, and I'm a terrible cook. Now *eating* sushi? I'm pretty much an expert."

He drops Arborio rice into the basket and several other ingredients, ignoring my complaints. He'll realize within five minutes of cooking that I'm better off out of the kitchen. He asks what kind of sushi I prefer and collects the ingredients, as well as some rocky road ice cream. Back inside the car, I make one last attempt at saving us both the embarrassment of my cooking.

"There's a little sushi bar a few blocks away. We could save time and go there instead?" I suggest.

He shakes his head. "You can learn."

Nope, still wasn't getting the point. "You need to show me where the emergency exits and fire extinguishers are, then."

He chuckles and squeezes my thigh. "Trust me." I try to hold back my shiver, but fail.

We drive toward Elliott Bay, the opposite direction of his private penthouse suite at Reinheart and Hunter's headquarters.

"Where are we going?"

He grins. "It's a surprise."

After a ten-minute drive, we arrive at a harbor, where several yachts are moored. I jump out of the car, not waiting for him. One of the yachts is lit with hundreds of fairy lights. I'm speechless—I love boats. The yacht is so large, it would need a crew.

I gasp. "Is this yours?"

"No, I stole it," he deadpans. I whip my head around to him. His eyes sparkle with amusement.

"You joke?" I return his deadpan face before scaling the ladder to the deck, not caring about the view he's getting of my ass. Inside the yacht is a kitchen, large living area, and three ensuite bedrooms, with an enormous bed in the master suite. I scurry back to the kitchen, not wanting to be caught alone with Archan in the bedroom. His lips twitch at my fast pace and flushed face. He's unpacked the shopping, arranged the ingredients, and laid two cutting boards next to each other on the countertop.

"Come here," he commands. I almost fight him but decide against it; otherwise, we'll bicker the entire evening. I stand next to him and point to the saucepan containing rice and cold water.

"Shouldn't that be hot water?"

"It needs to soak first. We are going to prepare the fillings. You seem adept with a blade."

I arch an eyebrow. "You're giving me a blade?"

He hands me a knife. "I trust you."

I laugh, and he simply studies me. "Oh, you're serious?"

He hands me an avocado. "On this occasion, I don't believe you mean me any harm. But don't worry—I'll reassess on a regular basis. Cut this into thin strips."

He prepares the shrimp. My stomach grumbles, and a few seconds later, an antipasto platter appears in front of the chopping boards. My mouth waters.

Archan picks up a prosciutto-wrapped asparagus. "Open your mouth, Natia." I obey, and he places it in my mouth, allowing his fingers to brush my lips. I chew with obvious pleasure then reach to get another one. He bats my hand away, rips a piece of flat bread, scoops up some pesto, and brings it to my mouth. This time, I'm careful not to catch his fingers.

"I can feed myself," I mutter.

He gives me a wicked smile. "But would it be as much fun?"

I slice my avocado, cursing the slippery texture. "This is like trying to slice a Brolog's penis."

He barks out a laugh. "Are you speaking from personal experience?"

I shrug. "Brologs' penises are on their faces; removing it is the easiest way to kill them. But they're sticky and slimy…" I mock shiver, "not my finest moment."

He lays out a baking sheet, and we line it with seaweed. Then he pours us each a glass of wine—it's cold, crisp, and clean. The rice is placed on the heat, and we retreat to the sofa to share the rest of the platter.

As I unwind the ham off the asparagus, he asks, "Tell me about your childhood. How did it come to pass that your grandparents raised you?"

I don't react. It's something I get asked a lot. "My parents left to live in Florida when I was two. They weren't prepared for parenthood, so my grandparents offered to look after me. I barely remember my actual parents; they stopped visiting when I was ten. My grandparents gave me a wonderful childhood. I love them immensely."

He turns toward me and props one ankle on his opposite knee. "And your grandmother passed away?"

My shoulders tense. "Yes."

"Do you miss her?"

"Every. Single. Day," I whisper, glancing away and cursing the telltale sting in the corners of my eyes.

He puts his wine glass down on the table and runs a hand through my hair before cupping my nape and studying my face. He opens his mouth but is cut off by the alarm dinging. He places a chaste kiss on my forehead, gets up, stops the alarm, then glances over his shoulder.

"Come, we haven't finished cooking."

Sipping my wine, I ignore his demand. The next few minutes pass in silence, making me believe I've escaped the madness of the kitchen.

"If you don't come here, I will come and get you, and you may not like it," he pauses, his voice deepening, "then again, maybe you would."

I hurry to the kitchen, not wanting to test his theory. I'm following his instructions to place the avocado on the bed of rice, when I feel his hands at my hips, pulling me back into his body. My eyes widen, as my body reacts to his hand gliding across my stomach. He pulls open the drawer that my body was blocking and retrieves cutlery. I look over my shoulder and glower.

"You could've asked me to move."

He chuckles, the sound low and sensual against my ear. "Yes, I suppose I could have."

I'm not sure I'm going to survive the rest of this date.

Releasing me, he startles me with his next question. "You have only had one sexual partner. Why?" My blood starts to boil, and Carrie Underwood's "Before He Cheats" bounces around my mind, reinforcing my shields.

Answering my choice of song, Archan mumbles softly, "He betrayed you."

I focus on my avocado and stay silent, afraid I may prove him wrong and use the knife in front of me after all.

"It's been five years, Natia. But you've had no more lovers. You're a stunning, intelligent, and passionate young woman. Why?"

"I'm overqualified," I mutter, finishing the avocado layer. I wipe my fingers on a dishcloth, fold my arms, and turn to face him; he's wearing his serious face, so I provide the complex answer he's seeking. "I spent too much time loving the wrong person, or what I thought was love. I've not met anybody I'm willing to give that power to again. I want someone who will love me with a madness that scares us both sometimes, but not to where we fear it. I need someone to trust to unmask my every desire." *Someone who awakens me, like you*, my stupid brain inserts. *Don't fall for it*, I warn myself. "I don't see the point in one- night stands or half-hearted relationships. I don't judge those who have them—it's just not me. I can't even kiss half-hearted. I'll wait an eternity for that one person, even if it means being alone."

He's staring at me with a mix of wonder and confusion. I sigh. "I don't need a psychological assessment, Archan. I'm happy as I am. What's next?"

It's his turn to be unbalanced; his eyebrows pull together. "Excuse me?"

I point at the food. "What's next?"

We finish the sushi and slice it into bite-sized pieces. I get my phone and take a photo; he raises an eyebrow.

"If I don't take a photo, the guys won't believe me."

He adds a side salad to our plates and carries them outside. Following him with our wine glasses, I mumble about the cold, but when we reach the deck, it's being warmed by heaters and is toasty. A table has been set in the center. "Witchcraft" by Frank Sinatra drifts from speakers set in the floor, and the twinkling fairy lights finish off the romantic atmosphere. I take the chair he's offering.

230

Last hurdle, Natia, then home.

"Jed mentioned your command of elemental power on the island," he says.

"Of course he did," I mutter, shoving a bite of sushi into my mouth.

"You didn't tell me you were a witch at the diner."

I spin my fork in the air. "It's new—I'm figuring it out."

His eyebrows creep up. Excellent, I forgot twenty-five-year-olds don't typically get new powers. If he wasn't curious before, he definitely is now. Congrats, Natia—you complete idiot. I give myself a mental golf clap.

"Jed said it was a strong shield—not something new witches are capable of."

I shrug. "I'm an overachiever."

He tilts his head and studies my face. "How new is this power?"

I grit my teeth. "This week. Seems meeting you has brought out the magic in me." Ha, I continue to applaud my stupid mouth.

His lip twitches. "You think it has something to do with me?"

I shake my head. "No, I'm just having an exciting week."

He sighs, and we fall into companionable silence, eating our food. The night is clear as I look up at the full moon. My gaze flicks to my food, around the yacht, then back to him. I point my fork at him in accusation.

"How did you get in my bedroom?" He has the audacity to look confused. Before he can evade the question, I cut him off. "That wasn't for you to read. It's private, and a breach of my trust."

He shrugs, dropping the pretense of innocence. "In all fairness, it was before we struck a deal, but after you had been in my personal apartments and abused *my* trust."

231

My mouth does an excellent goldfish impression. I stab a piece of sushi, pop it in my mouth, and chew. My heart trips over its rhythm as I realize what he must have read—about him. Opening my mouth to explain, I pause. Light gold eyes stare at me with lust and desire. Heat flares in my body as I remember our kiss.

"Stop looking at me like that," I demand.

A wicked smile breaks out across his face. "You said that last night."

"I'm reinforcing my point," I quip, with as much dignity as I can manage. "You're confused about the purpose of this little façade you have going on here. You can try to seduce me with words, food, actions—but at the end of the day, you want something quick and dirty, the exact opposite of what I'm looking for."

"Who says it will be quick?" I notice he leaves the dirty part out and huff out a breath. His grin fades. "You think I want one night? You're wrong. It wouldn't be enough. I'm beginning to think I should keep you."

I tip my head back and study the twinkling stars. "You can't keep someone. I'm a person, not a thing."

"Semantics. You would be mine."

"For how long? Until you're bored? See someone else that catches your eye?"

"No one has caught my eye quite like you, Natia. That should tell you I'm looking for more than sex." My head snaps forward to examine his features. The sincerity there is almost my undoing… My heart picks up speed. Is he asking for more? A relationship? The intense attraction is almost too much to handle, but not enough to take a risk on; however, if he's offering a chance at his heart…

His eyes flash with an emotion I can't pinpoint—fear? Then he speaks, snapping that thread of hope. "I warn you, Natia, my thoughts are dangerous and impure. The fact that I haven't stripped you naked and reduced you to a beautiful mess is a testament to my self-control. When that snaps, you should be scared.

"I will give you pain with pleasure and unravel your darkest desires. As I control your body, you will shatter and surrender as you come apart in my arms. You will scream my name. I will ruin you for any other man, and you will crave the oblivion only I can give you."

A violent anger courses within me. Apparently, he needs this spelled out.

Chapter Twenty-Five

Archan

Unknown origin.

Natia clenches her jaw as she struggles with my words. A flash of fear crosses her beautiful face—yes, she should be scared. I have promised to take away her control—smash her inhibitions, free her desire. She wants to surrender, but her walls are so high she can't see past them to know she's disconnected from the world.

She's a beautiful contradiction, loving those around her so fiercely, she would die for them. Yet, she has built a cage around her heart, not accepting their love back. She offers kindness and acceptance, but denies any offers of help and expects rejection. She is surrounded by people who care about and love her, and yet, I sense a deep loneliness.

A wild fire burns in her eyes, so fierce she could light up the pits of hell. I relive that devastating kiss from earlier. She is right—she doesn't kiss half-heartedly. She gave me everything in that kiss. Raw emotions flooded my consciousness, as I tasted what it would be like to have her. It had floored me with its intensity and honesty. It undid me—*she* undid me.

Rising, she stalks toward me, her stunning face flushed pink from the night air. She pushes between my legs and places her hands on the arms of my chair, caging me. My hands twitch with the urge to pull her onto my lap and push my growing erection against her core. I'm already addicted to the sweet little moans she made earlier. A strong, icy wind in the otherwise calm night lifts her hair. She brings her face close enough that our breath mixes, and I watch her eyes turn azure with desire. A strong pulse of power from her ripples across my skin, and my eyes widen in surprise.

She smiles and keeps her husky voice low. "I told you, I'm everything you can't control. You underestimate me, Archan. Don't try to get inside my head—it's darker than you can handle. When I finally give myself to someone, they'll look at me and accept my demons; they won't try to master them. And I don't scream for anyone. I will walk through the fires of hell and emerge from the ashes before I bow down to any man." She grabs my hair and yanks my head back, pinning me with her fiery gaze.

"Instead, I will bring every man I meet to his fucking knees. I wasn't born to be quiet and submissive. I was born to shatter the world with my fingertips and go to war for those I love. Continue to underestimate me, and I'll show you what it'll cost you."

Small leaves encircle us, whipping faster, wrapping us in a mini twister. Grasping the nape of her neck, I close the distance and give her a brutal, bruising kiss. Instead of pulling away, she rivals my passion with an uncompromising wildness and hunger. My hands glide down the curves of her body. I grip her hips, ready to pull her onto me, when she breaks the kiss and gives me a triumphant smile.

"To his fucking knees," her sultry voice whispers against my lips. I have to have this woman, possess her, make her mine. But now I'm afraid that once I have her, I might never let her go. She would be mine for eternity. Am I selfish to tear her away from her life, rip her chances of being loved in return away? Definitely, but I would worship her like no man can.

She draws herself up. Unearthly sapphire eyes hold mine as I stare up at her in awe.

Her gaze flicks over my shoulder, and she suddenly hisses in pain. My eyes scan her body as she reaches into her boot and pulls out a dagger. I freeze.

"Show yourself, you coward!" she calls over my head. I rise to my feet and stand in front of her, but she growls and steps to my side. Three shadows creep in the darkness on the dock. As she heads toward the steps, I put my hand on her arm and shake my head.

"Let them come to us. They will find it difficult to hide in the shadows on the boat."

She nods, and we move to the entrance of the living quarters. Her breathing is calm, her heartbeat slow and regular. She would indeed go to war for those she loves. We cock our heads in the same direction at the same time, listening to the soft footsteps. I'm amazed she can hear the quiet noise. Most humans can't drown out background noise to discern the subtleties of specific sounds. Two sets of footsteps approach us, one from the left and the other from the right. She points to the right and thumbs to the left. I stiffen with indecision; I don't want to leave her to face an unknown threat. As if reading my thoughts, she rolls her eyes at me before slipping out to the right.

I step out as my attacker tries to ambush me from the side. The force of my kick has him sprawling backward.

I put my foot on his chest, lean down, and snap his neck with my hands.

A feminine grunt of pain from the other side of the boat has me moving fast. Natia straddles a demon as she slices through his neck, and he bleeds out in seconds. Her sweater is covered in blood. She pushes against his chest to stand and appraises me for injuries. I almost laugh—like anything could hurt me.

She's strolling toward me when I sense a swell of power behind me. I continue to face her, not alerting my attacker to my knowledge of his presence. He lifts his weapon, aiming for my back. As he releases whatever is in his hands, I duck and swivel on my heel, ready to catch the weapon. But Natia leaps over my crouched form. Her dagger leaves her hand and sails over my head toward our foe. An explosion of power knocks me to my ass as she snaps a shield into place around us. I wrap my hands around her waist to pull her down just as she screams in agony. She thrashes for a brief moment then goes limp in my arms.

"Fuck," I breathe. Khalkaroth disappears with her dagger in his hand and a smirk on his face. Cradling Natia, I teleport us both to my apartments, lay her on my bed, and mentally shout for Zac and Nathan. They appear within seconds, their faces etched with worry as they catch sight of my shirt soaked in blood.

I point at Natia. "It's not mine, it's hers." They swing their gaze to Natia's unconscious form, only noticing her now.

Zac lets loose a breath and runs a hand over his head. "Well… this could be a solution to one of our problems."

His head bangs against the wall as my hand wraps around his throat. He pales.

"No harm will come to her. Do you understand?"

He nods, and I let him go. Materializing a blade, I cut her sweater, being careful around the knife lodged near her heart. Tiny black lines

237

are spreading around the wound. I place my hand below the dagger and begin using my power to draw the poison away from her heart, and into me. Her sweat-soaked skin is burning hot, and the fever convulses her body as she writhes under my touch. She coughs, and blood trails out the corner of her mouth, down her neck. I pull harder at the poison, and she convulses again, violently. Nathan pulls my hand away, his gray eyes softening.

"It's making her worse. Stop, while we think this through," he urges. I tear my fingers through my hair.

"Who was it?" Zac asks.

"Khalkaroth."

Nathan goes to touch her, and I grab his arm. "Touch her, and you will lose your hands."

He freezes, his eyes widening. "I need to examine her to see if I can determine what she's poisoned with." Slowly, I release his arm and nod.

"Can you undress her?" Nathan asks. I slice through her skirt, and Zac removes her boots, leaving her almost naked. Her normally bronzed skin has turned pale and sallow. There is a tiny barb sticking out of her thigh with similar black tendrils spiraling from the wound.

Nathan points to it. "See what you can do with that." I yank out the spike and put my hand over the cut to pull the poison into me; it comes easier, and her body relaxes. I remove my hand—her thigh is clear of the poison. I groan as a lancing pain tears through my body, and my heart misses a few beats before I expel the poison on a breath of charcoal-coated air.

"No," I whisper, coughing.

Zac whips his head around to look at me. "What is it?"

"Eitr." They stiffen and look at Natia with pity. The pain must be excruciating. Eitr is the Poison of the Gods—a rare paradoxical substance, containing both death and life. But I've never known anyone to survive it. The death is slow, as the poison corrupts the soul.

I place my hands on her wound again, but Zac grabs my wrist. "You can't take that much into yourself. It could kill you. She won't survive… It's already taken root in her soul."

Clenching my jaw, I grasp her hand. Her body is on fire, but her hand is ice cold, a sign her organs are shutting down. Roaring my rage at the world, the windows shatter; the shards pause like glittering diamonds before being swept away into the night. The howling, icy wind rushes inside, swirling around each of us and stealing our breath. My emotions trigger my squad to appear, one by one. I wrap Natia in a blanket as they gather around the bed.

"Find him!" I snap, not caring who does it. Zac shouts various commands, and Barney replaces the glass in the windows. Jed can't seem to tear his eyes away from the sight of Natia, visibly shaken to the core as he watches the life leech from her.

I slide my body next to hers and push the damp hair from her face, wanting nothing more than for her to open her eyes. Time passes slowly, as I mentally beg her not to die.

"You are a warrior—now walk through those fires of hell and emerge victorious like you promised. You have truly brought me to my knees, Natia. Now return and fucking keep me there."

A breeze washes over me, the promise of a storm in the air. I cast a glance at the windows to check Barney has mended them all.

"Nice to know… Now be quiet, I'm busy trying to live here."

I stare at her unmoving body, not sure if I imagined her voice in my head. It's impossible. She squeezes my hand, almost imperceptibly.

"You think too loud. Go to sleep or something. But no groping—it's not an attractive quality when you can only get a woman who's unconscious and on the brink of death."

I almost laugh, placing my forehead against hers. *"Fight this, Natia."*

The breeze is gone, but the scent of the storm lingers. She lies still, making me question if I have hallucinated.

Sometime later, Nathan comes with a tray food and water for me. When he sees me next to Natia, he pauses and blinks. I've never offered comfort like this to anybody. I dare him with my eyes to say something.

He holds his hands up. "It's not that. Do you know how long it's been?"

Glancing at the clock, I see it's eight. "About seven hours… your point?"

He shakes his head. "It's eight o'clock at *night*. It's been over twenty hours." I glance out the window, noticing for the first time the inky black sky.

"She's survived longer than she should," he remarks, in shock. "Can I look at her wound again?" I pull back the blanket to expose the top half of her body. We both stare at the wound. The tendrils of black have receded, so only a small spider web surrounds it.

"She's fighting it," I whisper, in awe of her strength.

Nathan cocks his head. "I think we should remove the blade."

"No. Apart from the poison, we don't know what kind of damage the knife has done. I can heal it, but it will take even more out of her body. She is only human. We should wait."

Natia's seductive voice slinks through my mind; she sounds stronger.

"Stop being a pussy and take the knife out, and do something about my leg— it itches, and I can't move my arms to scratch it. Also, this human *saved your life, so suck it up, oh mysterious one."*

Nathan frowns and glances around. Finally, he stares down at her. "Did she just...?"

"You heard her?" I can't believe this. He nods, speechless.

"Am I not speaking clearly enough for you two? Take out the knife and scratch my leg!" Natia snarls, clearly irritated.

We both chuckle. I can almost hear her mental eye roll.

Nathan retrieves several towels from the bathroom. We wrap one around the wound, ready to stanch the flow of blood. Nathan grips the hilt and tugs on the blade. The second it's out, I lay my hands across her heart and start to heal her. A brief pain shoots through me as I remove the last of the poison.

Nathan and I stare at her expectantly. She lifts her hands to my head, pulls me closer, and presses her lips to mine in a soft kiss, before nipping my bottom lip, hard. I jolt as she opens her eyes, a small smile playing on her lips.

A halo of gold lightning surrounds her turquoise iris. I stare, transfixed, as her eyes flash and sparkle, the vivid electricity weaving throughout the blue. I suck in a breath. Impossible—she has the eyes of the gods. Something I've not witnessed in millennia, something no human has ever owned.

"That's for not thanking me," she whispers. She blinks, and the gold disappears, making me wonder if I'd imagined it.

Chapter Twenty-Six

Natia

Taurus—one of the strongest signs of the Zodiac. Meaning your chances of winning against one is probably not worth the risk.

"Can I have my sheet back, please?" I tug it out from where Archan is perched on the bed. He kneels on the floor and covers me with more blankets. I glance at him, amused. He raises an eyebrow, and I point at him. "You being down there—it's a good start."

Nathan clears his throat, looking embarrassed.

I can't resist toying with him. "Aw, Nathan, you can be my bridesmaid. You don't need to ask." Archan puts his head on the bed, his body quaking with silent laughter.

Zac barges into the room with three other men. I only know Barney. They stare at me in disbelief. I look down to double check the blankets haven't fallen, giving them a show. No, all good here.

"How? What? When?" Zac stumbles over his words.

I lean forward, smiling. "Sweetie, I'm gonna need you to round up those few remaining brain cells together and work with me, okay?"

Barney cuts off any further intelligent conversation from Zac, who glares at me, his eyes burning. "Her team is downstairs; we're holding them in the containment area. The warlock has repeatedly tried to teleport in." Archan's head snaps up.

"You're holding my team hostage?" I hiss. "Why? Have you hurt them? I swear, for every single hair harmed, I'll ram your balls one inch further up your backside."

The two unknown men shuffle their feet, their hands drifting over their crotches. I swing my legs over the edge of the bed, just as Jed appears out of thin air with Aaden and Duncan. I launch myself at them, and they encircle their arms around me. Inhaling Duncan's scent, my body relaxes. They hold me even tighter when I begin to pull away.

I pat them on their backs. "It's okay, guys. I'm okay, promise."

Jed begins laughing as cotton fabric tickles my shoulders then shifts against my ass—my mostly naked ass. Another mental slap. I'm on a roll.

Archan turns me around to begin buttoning up a shirt; his shirt, I realize, as I inhale his sensuous, masculine smell. I swat away his hands when he gets to the third button, and he gives me a wicked grin. Suddenly remembering our last conversation on the boat, I decide to test out this new communication I've discovered.

"You may have made me delirious with your touches and kisses, and you may have inadvertently seen me half naked—twice. But your 'I'm so dark and mysterious' act, followed up with the 'Let me control and dominate you, Natia, and I'll let your inner freak out' speech is not *happening. So take a step back, and remember my reply back on the boat."*

Jed is the first to keel over laughing, slapping his knee. Nathan joins him. I groan—no way. My face is too sore from all the mental slaps.

"Can I take that back?" I mumble.

Archan grins at me. "Yes. But that would mean it *is* happening."

I throw my hands up and groan. "Never mind."

Barney and Zac cross their arms over their chests with equal looks of suspicion. Archan goes back to buttoning my half-open shirt, and Jed is still wiping tears away when Barney speaks, "I'm not sure what I'm more shocked at—that she can communicate telepathically, or that she's rejected him."

Jed laughs again while holding his sides.

A thought pops into my head. "Wait, is that why you're all always tilting your heads?"

Barney snorts, his brown eyes crinkling. "We don't do that."

"You do! It's infinitesimal, but still there. I noticed it the first time we had breakfast." I point at Archan. His brow furrows—apparently, Mr. Perfect isn't impressed at having a flaw pointed out.

Nathan presses a glass of pink liquid in my hands, and I eye it with suspicion. He sighs. "It will help heal you. If Eitr poison isn't going to kill you, nothing I give you will." I take a sip and find it sweet and tangy.

Shirt now fully buttoned, I glance at the blood-covered sheets, pale, and look at Archan. "Is all that mine?" I ask calmly, as if I'm not staring at a scene from a horror movie.

"Yes. You were badly hurt," Archan answers in an equally neutral voice.

I try something else telepathically, concentrating on Archan.

"Can I project my thoughts to one person?"

"Yes, you are doing it now," he replies.

"Good. Can you speak to me telepathically without me making contact first?"

"Yes, but you would have to be open to it. It's like a tugging sensation. Your mental shields are strong. I doubt anyone could contact you telepathically without your permission."

"Then thank you."

245

"For what?"

"For saving me in return." He frowns, a look of confusion and fear flashing through his eyes.

"Who was it?" I ask aloud, my gaze flitting to the bloody sheets.

"Khalkaroth," he replies, watching my reaction carefully.

I blank my expression in an attempt to control my emotions. "Where's Zee?" It's unlikely he's chosen to sit at home, waiting for our return.

"We have him in containment. He was a little… volatile," Jed pipes up. "I'll return him to your apartment the second you're home."

"Locks," Duncan speaks up. I turn to him. He makes a small gesture at his temple—right, shields. I don't even think, picking "Toxic" by Britney—appropriate on so many levels. They all laugh, every single one of them.

I huff. "Don't you all have something better to do than eavesdrop in my head?"

"But it's so entertaining," chokes out Jed.

Ignoring him, I turn to Duncan and Aaden. "I need to go home." Duncan frowns.

"What is it?" I ask.

"I don't want to be out on the streets. I'd rather teleport you."

I wave my hand. "Okay, beam me up, Scotty."

Aaden snorts. "He can only take one of us at a time."

I nod. "Take Aaden first, it's no problem."

Duncan eyes Archan over my shoulder. "I'd prefer to not leave you alone."

I shrug. "Then take me first."

"I don't want to leave you alone in the apartment either."

I roll my eyes. Archan wraps his arm around me, pulling me firmly against his chest. "I'll meet you there," he says. I feel the pull of moving through space, except it's different this time. Ribbons of color caress my body in a welcoming embrace, and time seems to slow down. Warmth and serenity envelop me—it feels like coming home. Before I can talk to Archan about it, we come to a smooth stop, and the familiar surroundings of my bedroom come into view.

"That was…" I search for the best description.

"Much like being teleported by Duncan, but smoother, I imagine. I have had more practice."

I frown and lift a finger to debate the differences, but a sexy smirk tugs at his lips, stopping me. His eyes begin to lighten. I put a hand on his chest and take a step back. "No."

"No?" he parrots, frowning.

"Archan… come on. Our philosophies on relationships don't match."

He stalks toward me. "Have you stopped to ask me what my philosophy is, Natia? Or have you assumed I only want your body? Do you think I value the rest of what you offer so little?"

"When all your talk is saturated in sexual tension, it's fairly obvious."

My back bumps into the wall as he pursues me. "I won't lie and tell you I don't want you. I do." Bracing his hands against the wall, he traps me and runs his nose along my neck. "But you missed the part of me being interested in your life, your desires, your wishes, your fears." He leans his forehead against mine. "I want to know every part of you, inside and out."

A nervous tremor goes through my body. "You are doing this to break my shields," I whisper.

247

He leans back and locks his eyes with mine, boring straight through to my soul. "At first, yes, that was my intention."

"And now?"

"Do you mean me harm?"

I shake my head. "No."

"Do you have malevolent motives for pursuing Khalkaroth, the Jar, or Pan?"

Sighing, I shake my head again. "No."

"Then my reasons have changed. Keep your shields, Natia. But don't deny yourself simple pleasure because you're afraid."

Pushing on his solid chest, I slip under his arm. "I'm not afraid, and you obviously didn't hear me on the boat."

He snorts, turns around, and leans against the wall. "You're terrified, and I heard you loud and clear. You're terrified that I might satisfy so much of what you want that you would be lost to me. There's nobody more qualified to handle your darkness and demons, Natia. I don't want you at my feet, I don't want your submission—your fire is what attracted me in the first place. Only a fool would douse that. But what you think you need and what you actually need are two different things. You need someone to show you what it's like to lose control, to trust someone to hold you together when you fall apart—that's the part that terrifies you. That I would shatter you and leave the pieces."

"That trust has to be earned."

Stepping forward, he tucks a piece of hair behind my ear and smiles down at me. "Then I shall earn it."

"What about love?"

He cups my cheek. "You're a romantic, Natia. I can worship you, protect you, and give you everything you will ever need. But I can't promise you love."

"Then we are still worlds apart."

He stiffens. "You will be mine. Deny it all you wish. It makes no difference in the end. I did want to tear down those walls—now I want you to let them down for me, begging for me. I've made my motives clear, including having you under me, screaming my name."

I shiver at the mental image and stride toward the bathroom, before I leap on him and prove him right. "Not going to happen."

"You should be dead."

My step falters. "Is that a threat?"

"No. You survived the Poison of the Gods. No one survives it. Once Khalkaroth figures out you are alive, he will stop at nothing to get you. He will most likely drag you to the bowels of hell as a present to Lucifer himself."

Reaching the bathroom, I slam the door and slide my ass down to the cool, tiled floor. The weight of his power leaves the room.

Chapter Twenty-Seven

Natia

A Taurus is often so bubbly and confident in front of friends that no one notices the raging bull charging inside.

Lying on the sofa with my feet stretched over Jed, I hum in pleasure as he rubs them. Snacks cover the coffee table, and several empty pizza boxes litter the floor. Zee, who returned a few minutes after Archan left, is on his fifth cycle of channel flicking, as Duncan offers the use of his Netflix account.

I grin at Duncan. "Zee, check out the recently watched list."

Various sounds of amusement fill the room as we peruse Duncan's recently watched shows, which include episodes of *Buffy* (knew it), *Supernatural*, *Ghost Whisperer*, and *Once Upon a Time*. It feels good to laugh with people I love. Even Jed seems to be worming his way in. He returned with a message that he's helping protect me and that Archan expects Khalkaroth to make a move to kill or kidnap me—awesome.

"Interesting choice of viewing for a demon hunter," Jed muses.

Aaden puts his laptop on the floor. "Are we going to talk about—"

"No," Duncan, Jed, and I chorus.

"You don't even know what I was going to say," Aaden blurts out, crossing his arms.

I groan. "If it's anything to do with the Jar, Pan, my near-death experience, god poisons, powers, or Archan, then the answer is no."

Aaden huffs—but he knows there's no arguing.

Zee, who's sitting next to Jed, taps my leg. "Your choice, Natia. Being almost killed by a mythical substance gives you control. Only for tonight, though. Don't milk it." He winks. I lean over Jed to take the remote and flick through the movies. I debate whether to torture them with a rom com, but it would torture me, too, so I put on *The X-Files* movie. Duncan groans.

Grabbing the popcorn bowl, I place it on my lap. "It's a classic! Suck it up and get educated."

"You've seen this a hundred times, Locks," Duncan mutters.

"The existence of aliens is still a mystery. One I intend to solve."

Jed's eyes gleam with amusement. "You fancy yourself a Scully type, don't you?"

I sniff haughtily. "We share certain qualities. I have a spooky sidekick." I tip my head at Duncan. "I have a job investigating the weird and mysterious. But I'm supremely more badass than her. Then again, she has the whole doctor-intelligent-sexy thing going for her."

Jed waves his hands up and down my pajama-clad body. "You have the whole sexy-intelligent-leather-wearing-warrior thing going for you. Wait, don't Mulder and Scully almost get it on in this film?" Jed asks, eyeing me and Duncan. Duncan and I sport equal looks of horror, as I begin childishly mock retching.

"Natia is like my little sister," Duncan tells Jed, explaining my bizarre behavior.

Zee grins. "I should be Mulder."

I throw a handful of popcorn at him. Zee plucks the pieces off his shirt and tosses them into his mouth. "I think we're more like the Scooby gang," he declares.

"Only if I can be Scooby Doo," I say. All four of them look at me in confusion.

"What? You expect me to be Daphne? How stereotypical. I suppose Aaden is Velma, because he's nerdy. Zee is Fred, because he's vain and full of himself. Duncan must be Scooby Doo, because, well… he's a talking dog, and that's magic. Leaving Jed to be none other than Shaggy himself."

Jed holds a finger up. "I'll be Shaggy on one condition. I get to drive the Mystery Machine."

"Hey, I do the driving," Duncan complains.

I snort. "How can you drive? You're a dog."

Duncan starts tapping on his phone. "Scooby Doo drives, it's his van. I'll prove it."

We wait for him to complete his search. His face falls. "Oh, you're right… It's Fred."

Zee fist pumps the air then turns to me. "You do know Daphne is in love with Fred, right?" I stick my tongue out at him.

Aaden's cell buzzes on the table; he grabs it, and his cheeks tinge pink. Given he's surrounded by a group of very observant government agents (plus whatever Jed is), he should expect what comes next.

"Who's that?" Zee asks.

"Nobody," Aaden mumbles, stuffing his phone in his back pocket. Our cells declare an incoming message. I frown and twist to scoop mine up off the floor. Zee starts laughing.

"Oh, buddy. I need to school you in the art of sexting if you're wondering why she would be bringing the 'girls' to a date. She means—"

My eyebrows creep up as I lean forward and smack Zee upside the head, but I can't help but grin at Aaden, while Duncan shows him his phone. Aaden's face is bright red as he rubs his hands down it. "I must have accidentally sent it to the group text."

"Is this to Emi?" I ask. Keeping his head in his hands, he nods. "I think it's sweet you're texting! Are you going on a date?"

He shrugs and continues to hide like an awkward teenager. "Don't you have anything better to do than discuss my love life?" he mumbles.

"Yeah, we can always discuss Natia and Archan," Jed helpfully supplies.

I smack Jed this time, causing him and Zee to fall about laughing and squash my legs. "You're just trying to live vicariously through those who actually have a love life."

"Because you have such an endless stream of dates," Zee deadpans.

I shrug. "I'm picky—sue me."

"You're not picky—you just give off an 'ask me out and I'll eat your intestines for breakfast' vibe."

"I give off no such vibe." I glance around. Everyone, including Duncan, suddenly finds the walls, ceiling, or floor fascinating. I fling my hands in the air. "Fine—I have a vibe. Pity Archan seems to be unaffected by it."

"Or he's a masochist," Zee states.

I roll my eyes and go to redirect the conversation back to Aaden's imminent date, but I see him peeking out at me from between his fingers with a pleading look. I take pity on him and allow Zee and Jed to continue to tease me. Eventually, they give up and focus on the mind-boggling alien knowledge as provided by Mulder and Scully.

Two hours later, I wrap up in a dressing gown and go outside to lie on a lounger. Instead of being relaxed, I'm restless, with an electric energy buzzing through my body that has been building since I woke in Archan's bed.

Zee follows me outside. "I've come to make sure you don't give the ferry boaters a free strip show."

I hold a finger up. "That was one time, and I was drunk."

"Alcohol is no excuse for bad behavior," he admonishes. He sits on the edge of my lounger near my chest, and I shuffle to make more room. "I was worried about you tonight," he confesses.

"I'm okay. Apparently, not even the gods can kill me." I change topics. "Fancy a training session?"

"I don't know, you were practically dead less than twelve hours ago."

"You know the old saying, 'What doesn't kill me…'" I retort.

"Too soon," he mutters.

The glass door slides open, and Duncan joins us, plopping down next to my feet. They all seem to be gravitating toward me, reassuring themselves I'm still alive.

"I thought we might have a training session," he mentions hesitantly.

I shoot Zee a look. "See, he isn't worried."

"Worried about what?" Duncan asks.

"About training me."

"I'm a little worried. But you need it now more than ever. The sooner we begin, the quicker you can protect yourself. How do you feel?" The itchy feeling intensifies. "Restless," I confess.

"Do we know the effects of this poison?" Zee enquires.

Duncan shakes his head. "I've heard of it, but in all honesty, I thought it was a myth. Natia's survival is going to gain some attention, from both Archan and Khalkaroth."

"I don't think I'm in any danger from Archan."

They both glare at me. "Don't fall for him, Natia. He's only after one thing," Zee says, making me snort. What a fatherly comment.

"So, training… physical or magical?" I ask.

"Both," they chorus.

"Hone the skills you have, practice the new ones," Duncan explains. "Plus, if you're restless, some physical exertion might help."

Piling into the training room, Zee and I spar in an effort to calm my erratic nerves and clear and center my mind. Then Duncan spends some time discussing my affinity with air, since that's the magic that first appeared.

"Close your eyes and concentrate. The magic is around you. Try to pull it into you," Duncan instructs for the tenth time. In an hour, I've progressed from paper ruffling to making my water bottle topple over. Duncan runs his hands through his hair.

"I'm sorry. I'll keep practicing."

He rubs his hands together. "When you've pulled it into you before, how did you feel?" My eyes flick briefly to Zee, who's sitting against the wall.

"Angry. But I wasn't pulling anything. It was like I was pushing it out."

He frowns. "That's... interesting. Can you replicate it?"

"Maybe, if someone pisses me off."

We glance at Zee. He throws his hands in the air and stands. "Fine, but don't put me on my ass if you can help it."

I nod, wiggling my fingers at him. "Okay, say something to piss me off."

"Hmm..." He pauses. "I've checked out the extra lingerie in your drawers and the interesting things they've left for you to sleep in. Much better than the shorts and T-shirt you normally wear. Although seeing your sexy legs is always a sight that makes me think about all the things I wanna—"

I crouch, as my body heaves with laughter. "Did you really go in my wardrobe looking at my underwear?"

He studies the wall. "Yeah."

"You creep! I should get a freaking restraining order against you. Oh my god, you didn't try them on, did you? Tell me which ones so I can have them washed," I joke.

Zee goes red.

My jaw drops open. "Which ones?"

"I haven't worn your underwear."

His normally burnt orange aura flares red. "But you've worn someone's?"

"It was a one-time thing, and she got off on it!"

"Aren't there help groups you should be attending?"

He levels a glare at me then Duncan. "Tell anybody, and you'll need a food taster for a year." I cross my fingers over my heart, trying to stifle the laughter that keeps bubbling up my throat.

Duncan interrupts, "Kids, this isn't working. Why don't you try accessing the memory and the emotion attached to it and use that to focus?"

Closing my eyes, I center my thoughts on the anger and frustration I felt when Zee and I argued. Nothing, nada—there's no magic in this girl. Maybe it was a fluke? Although meetings with mystical beings suggest otherwise. I refocus and mutter, "Okay, magic, time to make you my bitch." I fling my hand toward the water bottles—the middle one wobbles, while the other two stay as still as stoic guards. I puff out a breath and glare at Zee, who starts laughing at my pathetic attempt.

Duncan steps behind me and squeezes my shoulder. "I'll do some research into the different techniques used to train witches."

Glancing over my shoulder, I frown. "You haven't trained a witch before?"

He shakes his head and runs a hand through his hair. "No, most witches have family who train them from an early age. I avoid getting involved."

"But even you were trained once," Zee comments.

"Sure, a long time ago. I hate to say it, but maybe Jed or Archan can help?"

Zee glares at Duncan as he asks, "What about the SIP trainers?"

I shake my head. "No, we keep this away from the SIP. I don't want to disappear for months while they decide if I'm stable enough to be let loose in society."

"Let me do a bit of research first. I think once you figure out how to access your power, the rest should come fairly easily."

Zee grabs his towel and water. "Right, well with that pitiful workout, I'm off to the gym." He pats me on the head as he strolls out. "Don't worry, Natia. You'll figure this out."

Duncan and I head back to the apartment. But the buzz of energy surging through me has hardly dissipated, and it's making me jumpy. I head to my room, grab some flip-flops, and throw a bathrobe over my bikini.

Jed glances up from another epic sandwich. "Hot tub again? Naked?" My nakedness is becoming an issue—won't they just let it lie?

I eye the sandwich. "No, I'm going for a swim. Zee is in the gym, so I won't be alone. Save one of those for me?"

Jed jumps out of his seat. "There's one in the fridge already made. I'm coming anyway." He gives me his best hard stare. "If you refuse, I'll tie you to the bed." I glare back. "*And* call Archan," he adds with a wink.

"Fine," I snap, opening the apartment door.

Jed grabs the belt on my robe, pulls me back inside, and shuts the door. "You can travel first class now, baby—no need to slum it." Then we're being pulled through space. The experience is similar to the one with Archan, but quicker. We land next to the empty pool, and I cling to Jed.

"You okay?" he enquires, rubbing my arms.

"A little dizzy… but it's passed. Nothing to worry about." Someone pounds on the window overlooking the pool. Zee's holding a large weight in one hand, mid curl, and looks at us with a questioning expression.

I point to the glass. "You go work out with Zee, if that's your thing. You can both protect me from there."

"Okay. How much trouble can you get into in an empty swimming pool with two of us watching over you, anyway? One of them incredibly handsome and irresistible."

I chuckle. "Don't tell Zee that's what I think of him; I'll never live it down."

Jed pulls an imaginary knife from his heart. "You wound me, fair maiden."

"Smoothie, if I'm a maiden, then Lucifer has been welcomed back into heaven."

He chuckles before disappearing and reappearing next to Zee before I can blink. Zee jumps and mutters—presumably—a curse at his sudden arrival.

Dumping my bathrobe on a chair, I double check all my bits are covered in the white bikini. I snap my head up in response to another bang on the window, revealing Zee and Jed appraising me. I roll my eyes and dive into the water. I didn't plan on swimming for too long, assuming exhaustion would set in soon. Thirty laps later, the pent-up energy hasn't gone anywhere. If anything, it's worse.

Twisting onto my back and staring at the ceiling tiles, my mind drifts to thoughts of Archan, the poison, and my powers. My life has changed so much in a matter of days—it's no wonder I'm agitated. Who the hell is the mysterious being in the cave? I've contemplated returning to have a discussion with the self-professed bestower of my powers to see if he can't give me a handbook of how to use them, as well as an explanation of everything that's going on and what it has to do with me.

I'm trying to take it all in my stride, deal with it in typical sarcastic Natia fashion, which generally staves off the panic that might consume me. However, I think I might be reaching my heavy shit quota for the week. I've barely accepted that we've stumbled into some kind of biblical prophecy when the universe chucks magic into my personal mix, with a side helping of sexy alpha male who makes me question everything I believe is important. What is love? Affection, the need to be with someone, to protect them, never cause them harm or humiliation, a chemical reaction in our brains? I'm not sure who can define love. Poets, authors, and musicians offer their interpretations—maybe it's different for everybody?

A shadow scuttles across the ceiling, moving unnaturally. I tense, blink my eyes clear of water, and right myself. Scanning the room, I spot the shadow in a corner, and a putrid smell licks up my nostrils.

"Khalkaroth," I whisper.

He crouches at the edge of the pool, out of view from the window. "You know who I am. Good, but do you know *what* I am?"

I grit my teeth. "You're the ball sack who knifed me in the heart with poison."

He laughs and raises his hands. "Yet, here you are… one of the few in eons to have survived the Eitr poison. Only gods have beaten it, and they always come out stronger. Do you feel stronger, Natia? Is the power growing inside of you? I know who you are. But I think, my dear, you have no clue."

My entire body trembles as his twisted face melts like candle wax, before settling back into humanoid features. He continues his speech, unaware of the pitching water beneath my feet. "If you come with me, I can teach you how to access and harness that power. I can tell you who you are and what your destiny is."

"And why would you do that?"

He grins, displaying a set of sharp yellow teeth. "You're powerful. More than you know. Your very will can level this world."

"Why on Earth would I be interested in doing that?" I spit at him.

"Look around," he jeers. "This twisted paradise you call Earth… it's falling apart, Natia. Spinning out of control. It's on the brink of destruction."

"And you want to save it?" I scoff.

He shakes his head. "Hell, no—I want to control its destruction. Done my way, we can slaughter the part of humanity that is rushing the human race toward its end."

The pool's entire body of water rises above me in a twirling cyclone, leaving me standing in the middle of an empty pool. Khalkaroth looks up in shock, just before the water crashes and throws him against the wall. Blood drips down the tiles where he lays, and scarlet water streaks toward the pool. Arms grab me from behind, but air expels from me in a sharp burst, casting the stranger away. I feel the power swell inside me, pressing against my skin, my bones, my entire being.

I scream from the sudden pressure in my skull and collapse into warm arms as darkness claims me.

Chapter Twenty-Eight

Natia

Tauruses aren't overly emotional, but they are easily hurt.

Pain threatens to shatter my skull into a thousand-piece jigsaw. I try to run, but it grips me, rendering me paralyzed. The voices make it worse. I can't tell if they're just in my head or all around me, screaming at me. Using everything I have, I push them away, the agony demanding all my energy. Darkness pulls me under again, and I welcome it with open arms.

Awareness comes back as cold water drips into my mouth. The pain has mercifully lessened, but I keep my eyes firmly closed.

"Natia?" Archan's mental voice pushes against my shields. I let him in, finding I have no energy to fight.

"You need to come back to me. Fight the darkness… I know it's seductive, but it's trying to control you. Find the light and follow it," he encourages softly. I inhale his scent, the richness enticing but also comforting. The more I concentrate, the more light I can see. It's coming closer, but the darkness clings tight, and invisible hands slide over my body.

"Hold me," I mumble.

I feel Archan's strong arms cradling me and nestle into his warmth. Chasing his scent with my nose until I come in contact with his skin, I breathe him in deeply. The light comes closer and closer, until the darkness is no more. The pain recedes, and I squint my eyes open to find I'm in my bedroom.

Archan's chest rumbles as he tells someone to turn off the lights. People start talking at the same time, and I put my hands over my ears and push into Archan's chest.

"Everyone out," he rumbles. Feet shuffle across the carpet before the door clicks shut.

"Why are you in my bed?" I ask, my voice quiet.

He laughs low. "Saving you. Again."

I push away from him. "Saving me from what?" My eyes focus, revealing his perfect features, and for the first time, his naked chest. I glance down, double checking that's the only part of him naked. I'm kind of disappointed to find he has sweats on.

"From yourself," he says, watching me carefully.

"Myself?"

He pulls me back to his chest. "What do you remember?"

I don't have the inclination, or energy, to fight him. "Swimming, then Khalkaroth appearing... He said some crap about the poison and surviving it. He wanted me to go with him," I chuckle, "like that's going to happen."

"Anything after that?"

I try to piece together the flashes of images in my mind.

Water in the sky... Air around my body... Blood running along the tiles...

"Did I do something with the water? And wind? I was trying to protect myself. I think I hurt him." I look up into Archan's golden eyes. "Did I hurt him? Is he dead?"

"Not dead, but you did hurt him. He escaped into the shadows before I could reach him."

I ball my hands into fists to keep them from trembling. "If you find him before me, I want in. Promise me."

He hesitates, and I elbow his side, earning me a soft growl. "I promise."

"What about the water?"

At this, he struggles for the right words for a moment. "You raised an entire pool... then threw it at him. The air you felt was a mini tornado, with you in the calm center."

"Wait. There was a second attacker, they tried grabbing me. Did you catch them?"

"That was me."

I cringe. "Oh."

"It will teach me not to grab you from behind. It was instinctive. You were protecting yourself in a dangerous situation."

"What about the pain?" I ask in barely a whisper, as if speaking too loud will invite it back.

"I believe you experienced an overload. How were you feeling before your swim?"

"Like I was going to explode with energy... Power was buzzing across my skin. I thought wearing myself out swimming might get rid of it."

He goes silent. I push back up from his chest, and he schools his features carefully.

"What's wrong?" I ask, panicking.

"Your powers are coming too fast for your body to handle. Has Duncan talked to you about being an elemental witch?"

"Yes, he said most witches have an affinity for two elements at most. So I have air and water."

He nods. "Is this the first time your affinity for water has shown itself?" I stiffen. "Natia, don't lie to me. This is important. You were infected with a substance we know very little about. I want to know if the extent of your power is linked to that."

Scratching my eyebrow, I try to find the right words. "Hmm... in the cave on the island, there was a ritual to retrieve the Jar requiring the four elements."

"Makes sense," he mutters.

"How does it make sense?"

"Never mind, continue."

I huff. As usual, he wants to take information but not give it. "I summoned air and water—that was the first time for water. I was practicing earlier in the evening but could hardly manage anything. I don't understand how to control it."

He squeezes his arms around me. "I can help you manage them until you have full control."

"Okay."

He blinks. "Okay? No fight? No 'I can do this without you?'"

"No fight. I need to get control before I really hurt someone."

My fingers trace the intricate patterns of the tattoos covering part of his chest and shoulder. He saved me once again, protected me while I was vulnerable, and dragged me back from a darkness I don't understand. I glance up at him, his gold eyes swirling with a barely restrained desire. Unable to stop myself, I follow my fingers with my lips and place soft kisses on his chest, which rumbles as a low growl

265

escapes him. Feeling empowered, I straddle him and run my hands over each toned muscle, as he flexes under my touch. I continue to kiss his collarbone, nipping lightly. He doesn't move, keeping his hands on the bed. Ending my exploration at his jaw, I draw back, as his molten gaze studies my face.

"What are you doing?" he murmurs.

His jaw tics as I place feather-soft kisses on his eyelids and cheeks.

"Keeping you on your knees," I say in a husky voice. He groans as I caress his mouth with my tongue, licking along his bottom lip. He parts his lips, and I use my tongue to seductively stroke his. His hands twitch, making me wonder how far I can push him before he snaps. Leaning back, I peel my bikini top off my body and let it fall to the floor. His hungry gaze drops to my naked breasts.

My hands caress my own breasts and draw my nipples into tight peaks. Moaning softly, I close my eyes as the sensation tightens my core, and heat pools between my legs. Hot breath dances over my nipples, making me snap my eyes open to find Archan blowing on them. The rules of the game are clear; he won't touch me—unless I give him permission.

Taking the plunge over a cliff I might not survive, I arch my back, pushing my breasts forward. The second my flesh touches his mouth, he flips me onto my back and presses his weight against me. I moan at the contact. He kisses me brutally, stealing my breath. I wrap my legs around his waist and start to wiggle his sweats down with my feet.

Fabric rips, and his fingers slip through my slick folds to rub slow circles around my clit. His mouth catches my moan, as I lift my hips, wanting more. He slides two thick fingers inside my wetness and curls them, and my breath hitches as he hits a gloriously sensitive spot.

"Gods, you're so hot and wet for me," he mutters against my mouth. When he doesn't move, I lift my hips and work myself on him. The friction builds, winding me tighter. He leaves my mouth and trails a hot path down my stomach. Wrapping a hand around my thigh, he clamps down, halting my movements.

I growl at him. "Don't you dare stop." He laughs against my thigh, which he's now nipping and kissing. He moves but keeps the pace slow. "You need to go faster," I whisper, as my breathing comes quicker and my pulse trips over itself in anticipation. He doesn't speed up, keeping me on the edge. I clench around his fingers, my orgasm just out of reach. Leaning down, he licks his way up to my clit, before sucking it. Pulling a pillow over my face to muffle the scream, I explode.

What could be seconds, minutes, or hours later, he pulls the pillow back from my face and looms over me with a smug grin. "Like I said—I will make you scream." I hit him over the head with the pillow clutched in my hand. He catches it and kisses me.

I resume pushing his sweats down with my feet, but he grabs hold of my calves, stopping me.

"Not like this," he groans, his voice rough.

I frown, confused. "Like what?"

He lays next to me, his head resting on his palm. "Earlier this evening, you didn't want me anywhere near you. You've been through a lot in the last twenty-four hours, and I need you at your full strength to do what I want to do to you."

"I changed my mind. With the shit the universe keeps throwing at me, I fear my lifespan may be shorter than expected. So screw that." I roll, push him onto his back, and kiss his chest, working lower.

"Natia, stop." He hooks his hands under my arms and pulls me up gently. "You're making this hard."

I raise an eyebrow and stare at his erection under his sweats. "I know," I tease. He chuckles but holds me tight.

"Really, not like this. Ask me at your full strength, when you haven't nearly died in my arms just hours before. I don't want you to regret it."

I stare at him. "You're joking? You're saying no, and I have to ask you for it?"

He glares at the ceiling. "Yes."

"Get out," I snap. His eyes flick to me in surprise. "I'm not good enough for you? Fine. You're obviously someone who enjoys the chase, and now I've said yes, you've lost interest. I'll never beg you, so please do hold your breath while you wait."

I push off the bed, pulling a blanket with me to cover my body. He makes no move to leave. "Go. Now," I command, the new feeling of my power winding tight within me. I'm struggling to contain it when he speaks.

"Natia, that's not what I meant. I want—"

I point at him. "You had your chance. You had me in your arms while I came apart for you—you promised to pick up the pieces. You lied." Power pulses from me, making the bed slide across the room and crash into the wall. Floorboards creak under the strain.

"Bloody hell," he mutters, examining the floor. "Shut it down, now," he warns, as if he has the right to tell me to do anything. I scream in frustration, and the crystals on the chandelier shatter. The apartment groans under the pressure, as a slight shift of the ground warns me to pull the power back.

"Leave, and don't come back." My voice is a broken whisper. The embarrassment of giving this man any power over me threatens to break me. I'd almost given him my body...

He disappears as multiple people crash into the room.

Chapter Twenty-Nine

Archan

Unknown origin.

Fuck. I just ruined any chance of having her.

I saw in her eyes the resolution. She will not forgive me. She thinks I want her to beg, missing the fucking point. I could have taken advantage of her. She was vulnerable, whether she knew it or not. I don't want her to beg—I want her to come to me strong, of her own free will. She believes she isn't good enough? She's the most worthy woman I've ever met. Letting her hands and mouth trail over my body whilst not touching her was agony… And I don't give up control—ever. Definitely not in the bedroom. Yet, I'd given it to her.

The small sounds and moans she made as I was touching her drove me insane. I wanted to bury myself in her heat. The way she arched her back, wrapped her leg around my head whilst she came apart… I don't think she was even conscious she'd done it. She held a pillow over her head to muffle the scream she couldn't hold back, and I smiled in satisfaction. I felt humbled I was the first person she had trusted in five years to touch her. She doesn't realize I'd grasped that trust with both hands, which is why I denied her. Her world is falling apart, and she's seeking out something she can control.

Jed appears, his face twisted with rage. "What the fuck did you do?"

"You forget yourself," I snap, steadying my voice. In my current state, I might kill him.

He ignores my warning. "She shook the very foundation of the building!"

"I know."

"Did she reject you? Did you get into an argument? It's no excuse. She's been clear—she doesn't want you."

"And I suppose she wants you?" I hiss, as a strange emotion twists my stomach.

"Don't be ridiculous. Stay away from her. She's unstable, and you make it worse with your outlandish power games. With a third element, we know where this is heading—she'll be a full elemental, maybe the strongest magical human we've seen in a long time."

Without waiting for a response, he leaves to go back to her.

Standing at the window looking over the city, I try to understand her. An elemental witch, with air, water, and now earth in her control. She's so strong, she's dangerous. People don't begin their powers by controlling large bodies of water and creating earthquakes. When we met, she could sense the changes in air currents, meaning she already had an affinity for air.

Her survival of the Eitr poison had proven the myth it was life as well as death. Some gods had survived the Eitr poison—but most didn't. How had she done it, and at what cost? Nobody but me had glimpsed her eyes. Those gorgeous eyes lined with cosmic power... Is that where this magic is coming from? I could do with speaking to Kay, but he's been missing for decades. Not unusual; he often disappears to tend to his other duties. He'll appear at the crucial moment, whenever that may be.

271

Michael hands me a glass of scotch, his power declaring his arrival better than any greeting. He is almost strong enough to rival me.

"Penny for your thoughts?" he asks. He enjoys learning this era's strange sayings. Some of them I don't understand like, "There's no use crying over spilt milk." But this one I'm familiar with.

When I don't respond, he laughs. "Oh, brother, don't tell me it's a girl?"

I grumble incoherently. Apart from Zac and Jed, Michael is the only one I share anything personal with that may be used against me.

"The Waterford girl?" he probes.

I turn and stare at him. I need to have a chat with Zac about discretion. "She's confusing, an enigma."

He puts a hand on my shoulder. "You always were a sucker for puzzles."

"Logically, I should stay away. But I seem incapable. Following her survival of the Eitr, Khalkaroth has upgraded her status from kill to capture."

Michael sighs. "Zac told me about the Eitr. Do you think she has anything to do with the threat?"

I furrow my brows. "My instinct is yes, but logically, other than her investigation of Mary's murder, I can't understand how."

"Follow your instincts. Keep her close. It will become clear. Zac wants you to break her shields."

I shake my head. "That won't be happening. If she lets me in, it will be because she wants to—not because I coerced or forced it."

"Hmm..." He swirls his remaining whiskey in the crystal tumbler.

"What?"

He shakes his head. "A little birdie told me you have found the Jar." Again with the inane sayings.

Retrieving the Jar from my safe, I mentally summon Zac, Nathan, and Barney, purposefully leaving Jed out. We sit around the dining table with the Jar in the center.

Michael reaches for it tentatively. "It's smaller than I imagined."

I nod in agreement. "How close are you to finding Pan?"

Placing the Jar back down, Michael sighs. "That's why I'm here—I felt Pan's power here in Seattle earlier today, probably following the Jar." He pauses, looking like he's sorting through options. "We could set a trap with the Jar, keep it simple. Or we could keep it safely locked up and wait for Pan to make a move."

"It's risky to set a trap. If Khalkaroth comes instead, he could escape with the Jar before we kill Pan. Then it's game over, and we've lost," Zac says, gazing at the Jar as if it holds the answers to how we should proceed.

"Even if he comes, Pan won't be far behind. If we distract him long enough, it will draw Pan out. What about the inscription on the Jar?" I ask.

Nathan nods at me. "It confirms what the scrolls say about the five protectors."

"And that's us," I conclude.

"It would seem so." Barney suddenly looks around, narrowing his eyes. "Where's Jed?"

I grind my jaw. "Protecting Natia." Where I should be.

"The Jar also says Pan holds the key to the destruction and will tip the balance," Nathan adds.

Michael looks around at all of us. "So… trap or wait?"

"Trap. I need this over with. Set it up," I mutter, not admitting my decision is in part to get away from Natia. Jed's right, I make her unstable; she needs space to deal with everything that's happened to

273

her, and I need to focus on my mission. Then I remember the binding promise I made her. I sigh. "We need to include Natia on the plans to lure Khalkaroth." Apart from Michael, they stare at me in disbelief.

"I don't think that's—" Zac starts.

I interrupt him, "I made a binding promise to let her in on any plans to capture or kill Khalkaroth. But I won't mention Pan. If Pan comes, I will deal with Natia and her team."

"Was she aware of what she was doing when she bound you?" Michael asks. My squad shifts their eyes to me.

"No. Unlike most of her kind, she's direct and doesn't like leaving loopholes."

Zac shakes his head. "On the subject of Natia... she's getting more complicated by the day. She hides her mind behind the strongest mental shields I've ever seen. She works for a secret organization that kills supernaturals. She's a skilled fighter, with unusual strength and senses. She's a late-developing, but strong, elemental witch. She survived the Eitr poison, and to top it off, she suddenly develops the ability to communicate telepathically. Who the fuck is she?"

"Let's not forget she argues with—and refuses—Archan. Even though it sounds like you pulled out the big guns last night— romantic walk *and* a dinner? Now that's quite a power," Barney quips.

"Otherwise known as a date," Nathan mumbles.

"When have you known him to date? Normally, it's 'Hello, pretty,' and they're putty in his hands." Barney laughs.

"You forget the part where we were attacked and she almost died."

He shrugs. "Eh, semantics… She won't forget it in a hurry. Something to tell the kids when you tell how you met."

Michael chokes on his scotch. "You've known the girl days. Is it that serious?"

"No—" I start, just as Barney interrupts with, "You'll see for yourself when you see them together."

Zac thrums his fingers on the window. "Maybe taking her isn't such a bad idea. Khalkaroth wants her."

I resist the urge to punch him. "You want to use her as bait?"

Michael puts a hand on my shoulder. "We have the Jar as bait. Natia is an incentive, and she's coming anyway, given the promise you made. We'll keep her safe."

She will not be coming if I can help it, but given Natia's proclivity for doing the exact opposite of what I want and her stubbornness, I doubt she'll listen to my advice to stay home.

Chapter Thirty

Natia

Taurus—I'm not stubborn; I'm just right.

Zee, Duncan, and Aaden move to the dining table to begin deciphering the pictures of the symbols on the walls and the Jar. I consider Jed, as he sits next to me on the sofa. He's not aware of the extra symbols or the ritual I undertook to retrieve the Jar. My instinct is to trust him, despite him working for a man whose intentions aren't clear—well, other than to destroy me emotionally. Beg… The man wants me to beg. It'll be a cold day in hell before that happens.

I go for a direct approach with Jed, hoping to read his indigo and silver aura for any sign of deception. Holding his eyes, I give him the choice. "Smoothie, there are some things we need to discuss. You aren't aware of all the information, so I have to decide whether to let you stay and help, with the understanding that anything you see or learn will stay within these four walls. Or you leave."

He doesn't hesitate and stares right in my eyes. "Stay and help."

"I need a promise," I tell him.

He grins and grasps my hands. "I promise nothing I learn here will leave these four walls."

"Truth. He stays," I inform the guys.

Jed jumps up and strides to the dining table. "I can help with the deciphering. I know some of the symbols."

Duncan's eyes gleam. Typical—excited at the prospect of picking a fellow nerd's brain. We spread the photos of the symbols across the table.

Jed freezes and blinks. "Where the hell did you find these symbols?" he asks, picking up each one in turn.

"In the cave," I explain.

His eyes widen. "You never said anything."

I squeeze his arm. "Don't take it personally, Smoothie; my agreement with Archan was to give him the Jar, not disclose everything I found."

Inhaling a long breath, he nods. We work on the symbols using the previously deciphered messages, the internet, and some ancient books of Duncan's. Jed proves useful, pointing out symbols he knows. After a while, pale orange streaks paint the sky, signaling the rising dawn as we stop for a coffee break.

Duncan summarizes what we've found so far. "There's the owner of the Jar, who 'sits on it.' There are five protectors, each sworn to protect either the owner or the Jar. This owner is the key to the Jar. The symbols on the Jar say mankind's destruction lies in their hands. They're a powerful ancient who will be awakened when the balance needs to be tipped—"

"Wait," I start, "Archan said he was an ancient."

I swing my gaze to Jed, who puts his hands up. "I'm here to help, but I can't answer certain questions."

The corner of my mouth tips up. "Fair enough. Your reluctance to answer tells me all I need to know."

He sighs. "Sometimes you're too perceptive for your own good."

"Is the 'owner' Pan?" I ask nobody in particular.

Jed grunts. My grin gets wider. An affirmative, then.

"Is Pan good or evil? Is he trying to save or destroy mankind?" I press, frustrated at the double meanings.

Duncan leans over the table and grabs a close-up photo of the Jar. "The symbols on the Jar and the ones in the cave don't match up. We'll have to keep working on it."

Jed makes a frustrated sound.

I pat his thigh. "Use your words, Smoothie."

He leans his head back and stares at the ceiling. "You need to release me from my promise."

I frown. "Why?"

"This needs to be shared... before events unfold that can't be undone," he declares cryptically.

I shake my head. "No."

"Fucking stubborn woman," he grinds out. My eyes widen, and I freeze, shocked.

He stalks around the living area, muttering about stubborn women who don't know when to trust. He's so flustered, certain that something we've found is important enough to tell Archan, that I almost give in. But I don't fully trust Archan, so I stand my ground.

My phone starts buzzing in my pocket, and I pull it out— "Unknown Number." I frown and adopt my passive, yet professional voice. "Natia Waterford."

"It's me," a deep baritone rumbles, sliding over my skin like silk.

I hang up.

Something strange tugs on my mind. I frown. It happens again, stronger this time. Cautiously, I let it in, still protecting my shields.

Archan's smooth voice rings through my mind. *"Was that really necessary?"*

"What do you want?"

"We are going to try and lure out Khalkaroth. It will be dangerous—stay at home."

I stifle a growl and take a deep breath, locking down my emotions. I can almost hear his eye roll that I'm pretty sure he's learned from me.

"Stop growling at me."

"You heard that?" I ask, panicking—can he read every thought?

"You directed it at me. I can't read every thought, but I can catch snippets of your emotions—your anger and hurt. Let's talk about this later."

"Let's not. What's the plan?"

"He wants the Jar. We're going to place it somewhere easy to find."

"Are you sure you can catch him?" I press.

"Yes," he practically spits out.

"Where and when?"

"Stay home."

"No, you promised to share your plans. I want in."

"Fine. But if you're coming, you need to train first. One hour, my office."

Duncan snaps his fingers in front of my face. I blink. "What?"

"Where did you go?"

"Archan wants to help train me before we help him capture Khalkaroth."

Duncan looks around the room. "He's contacting you telepathically now?"

Jed halts his pacing. "Do it, Natia. You'll not find a better person to help you with this. Put aside your differences and focus on the bigger issue."

279

I tilt my head back and puff out a breath. He's right, and on reflection, I know our fight was more about the clash of Archan's poor choice of words and my temper. I answer the presence hovering in my mind. *"Fine, a truce. One hour."*

Chapter Thirty-One

Archan

Unknown origin.

$\mathcal{D}$angerous. That is the one word I would use to describe the woman currently stretching her leg against the concrete wall. She's the perfect, yet perilous, blend of strength, innocence, sin, honesty, and natural beauty that would bring any man to heel. She arches her back and pummels the air with her foot several times—a warm-up routine, I realize. Her balance is incredible, an overhang from her dance studies. She whips her T-shirt and yoga pants off, revealing a bright pink sports bra and barely-there black spandex shorts. Jed wolf whistles, causing her to roll her eyes.

"So, how you wanna do this?" she asks, placing her hands on her curvy hips and arching an eyebrow. I glance at our audience: Zac, Zee, Jed, Duncan, and Aaden.

"Leave us," I instruct.

Zac and Zee fold their arms across their chests. With their identical hard expressions, they could be brothers. "Not a chance," Zee says, as Zac raises an eyebrow in agreement.

"She needs to focus, without an audience. You can wait outside."

She waves her hand at the door. "It's fine. We aren't going to start rolling around naked."

Jed shifts from against the wall. "Thanks for the imagery, but it wasn't what I was thinking. The last time you two were alone," he points at Natia, "you caused a mini earthquake."

She rubs her forehead. "Agreed, but we've called a truce. Plus, didn't you mention this room was warded?"

She's right. We brought her to my training rooms below Reinheart and Hunter, where my squad can let loose without fear of hurting anybody—other than themselves.

Duncan tugs on Zee's arm. "We'll be right outside. Holler if you need us." He hardens his gaze and turns it on me. "Training. That's what you're here for." I nod as they leave the room, with Zac throwing a final calculating glance over his shoulder before shutting the door.

I cut straight to the point. "First, an explanation of last night."

"No."

"No?"

She sighs. "I get it. You thought you would be taking advantage of me—but you wouldn't have been. I'm stronger than that. But it's fine. You underestimated me, I overestimated you. Let's just train."

I suppose I should be thankful she understands what happened. But she's still pushing me away. I crook a finger at her. "Let's see what you've got physically."

She frowns. "I thought we were training my magic, not my body." I grin as she waggles her finger. "Don't, just don't." A blush creeps up her neck.

"Too easy," I mutter.

Her mouth drops open. "I didn't mean it like that."

I stalk toward her, and unlike most, she holds her ground. Grabbing her hand, I flatten it on my bare chest. The spark of attraction bounces between us as I tap her hand against my thudding heart until she picks up the beat. Her eyes flash with amusement as her lips tug up.

"If you start singing 'Hungry Eyes,' I'm going to ask Zac for help instead." I frown. "*Dirty Dancing*? The legend that is Patrick Swayze?" I tilt my head, and she rolls her eyes. "Ugh, never mind."

"With each heartbeat, try to pull the power from inside then manipulate it into what you want. Concentrate on air. Your magic comes from the outside world, but it is intricately woven within your body; it's an extension of who you are. You already know how to use your body as weapon—the trick is to weave the magic with your existing skills so it becomes natural."

"Not sure it will ever feel natural… One minute I can't find it at all, and the next I'm throwing around an entire pool."

I sigh and push a loose tendril of her caramel hair behind her ear. Goosebumps break out along her neck as her pulse flutters. "Have you always had strong mental shields?"

She thins her lips. "Not as strong as this, no."

"Was it easy learning how to strengthen them to this extent?"

She shakes her head. "No."

"Was it easy keeping them up relentlessly?"

She bites her lip, and I struggle to focus. "No."

"But now they're as easy as breathing?"

She nods once. "Yes."

"Your will is strong, Natia. I have no doubt that, with practice, using and controlling these new powers will become equally as easy. They will become another tool in your arsenal that, given the amount of danger you run headlong into, will be vital in keeping you alive."

"So, why am I fighting physically at the same time as learning my powers?"

"When are you most likely to need them?"

She sighs. "In a fight."

I nod. "Exactly, and we don't have the luxury to teach you baby steps. Tell me, in the times your power has shown itself, what were you feeling?" A look of pure frustration contorts her features. "What's wrong?"

"I already tried this tactic with Duncan. He wanted me to pull the power to me and conjure up the pissed off feeling I had when I threw Zee across the room. It didn't work."

I grin. "Why did you throw Zee across the room?"

She blushes, igniting my curiosity. "He said some rude things."

"About?"

Her eyes flash. It's about me. Did she defend me, or was she annoyed at her own reaction to me?

"So, the second time, I was also pissed when I faced Khalkaroth."

I nod, deep in thought. "Should I call Zac?"

Natia rolls her eyes. "Pretty sure it's me that infuriates him. He just amuses me," she mutters. "Then again, I could do with comedic entertainment. Zac!"

He appears in the center of the room with his arms folded. "What?" he grinds out.

"Hey, Zacy... how's it hanging?" She bats her eyelashes.

He turns to me, barely contained fury tensing his muscles. I chuckle. "She's making a point."

"What the fuck is wrong with you?" he mutters at Natia, who starts shaking with laughter. Then he disappears.

"See, only amusement on my behalf." She crosses her arms and pouts. "Poor Zacy."

I shake my head and step away from her. If only she knew who she was baiting. "Let's do this a different way. Forget the magic. I want you to fight me first."

Startling me, she sprints toward me. Her muscles tense before she launches herself, and I move my arms, ready to grab her around her waist. But her jump is too high, and she manages to wrap her thighs around my face before thrusting her weight down so I collapse backwards. She rolls off me and springs to her feet, leaving me blinking at the fluorescent lights. "I might have enjoyed that under different circumstances," I pant.

She snorts and, taking advantage of my stunned state, grabs my arm and twists it back around, forcing me to roll. I allow it but grab her wrist and pull her underneath me. I grin down at her. "I see you're not below kicking someone when they're down."

She pats my cheek, a brilliant grin lighting her face. "Absolutely. The fights I have aren't in the safety of a ring. Typically, it's to the death, and kicking someone when they're down isn't playing dirty—it's essential for my survival."

"It wasn't a criticism. Take every advantage you have."

Her long, bare legs wrap around my waist, caressing the naked skin of my back. Arching her back, she pushes her breasts against my chest. "You're playing with fire," I mutter against her neck, nipping her accelerated pulse. In a split second, she has me spun around and is straddling my chest. Her elbow slams into my throat, cutting off my air. "What are you doing?" I rasp.

A slow grin spreads across her face, her eyes bleeding to that alluring azure. "Taking every advantage I have."

Wrapping my hands under her ass, I stand with her clinging to me. She releases my throat and, with a pout, drops to the floor. I laugh. "You're playing with the big boys now, Natia."

She rolls her eyes as she strolls to the center of the room. "I'm not sure how to even respond to that."

"Do you have any routines you practice alone?" I ask.

She nods. "Sure, Zee taught me a few."

Leaning against the wall, I wave my hand. "Let's see them."

She moves with a grace and fluidity most will never accomplish. Lost in the moves, I can tell some are her own, improvised to complement her strength and ability. My eyes track the long lines she creates with her limbs, the obvious strength and tone of her body flexing with each move. "You fight like you dance," I comment as she stops, slightly breathless.

She cocks an eyebrow. "Strong and dirty?"

I smile—I've found myself smiling more with her in the last few days than what I can remember doing in decades. Stalking toward her, my eyes track the bead of sweat trickling down her throat. "You've already experienced a dangerous overload and burn out with your magic. You need to use it in controlled bursts and look out for the signs that you're using too much."

"Can it kill me?" she asks, nibbling her lip.

"Yes." Releasing her lip, she thins them instead—far less sexy, but infinitely less distracting. "With power comes responsibility."

She bends over and laughs out loud. "Come on! You're killing me! You're near enough stealing Spiderman quotes without even knowing it?"

I sigh and run my hand through my hair. Her laughter dies out, and she stands up straight, her body tense. One look at me, and she falls to the ground laughing again. I wait for her to collect herself, and as she stands, she waves her hand at me. "Okay, okay, I'm done. I've got this." Her lips twitch a few times as she meets my eyes, but thankfully, she holds herself together.

I move on. "When you fight, you need to know the right time to use your magic. It's not all the time; otherwise, you'll burn out quickly, and either the thing trying to kill you will get lucky, or you'll kill yourself. So think of it as a complement to your existing skills. Now we just have to get you to access it."

"So, no taking advice from Mickey and commanding the broomsticks to tidy the house?" she asks.

I frown. "Mickey?"

She throws her hands up. "This is ridiculous; my humor is wasted on you. I miss Duncan."

"And if Duncan had been successful in your training, we wouldn't be here."

She scowls. "You're an ass."

"And you have a stubborn streak a mile long with a sarcastic mind and a sassy mouth you hide behind when you're scared." I snap my fingers as the emotion driving her power becomes clear. "Zac!" I call. This time, he thunders through the door, slamming it behind him.

"You have your phone?" I ask Natia. She nods, grinning at Zac. "I need a speaker for her phone," I tell Zac.

He disappears and reappears twenty seconds later with a large Bluetooth speaker that resembles a boombox from the nineties. "Thanks for playing fetch, Zacy." Natia smirks as he bends and places the speaker at the side of the room.

He stands, swivels, and stalks toward her. "Don't call me that."

"Zacy? It's cute... a nickname for a friend."

"Zac! Leave!" I shout. He mutters some curses before disappearing. "Tell me what you've understood so far."

She folds her arms and glances to the side. "That magic is an extension of myself. I need to use it as a compliment to my fighting and be careful of how much I use. That I should time it to my heartbeat and try to pull it into myself."

I nod to the speaker and head toward the door. "Good enough. Pick something to train to."

Grabbing her phone, she picks the music, and the beginnings of "Natural" by Imagine Dragons echoes in the room. Flicking the light switch, I plunge the room into darkness. "You weren't just pissed the times you managed to call your power, Natia—you were scared."

Her breathing picks up as I come to stand behind her. "Focus on your heartbeat, on your connection to the power, the adrenaline pumping through your veins. Now, let's see what you've got." Cranking up the music, the bass drowns out any other sound. Her only choice is to focus on her magic; without her other senses, it's her only defense. Breezing past her, I slip her braid over her shoulder, before moving to the other side of the room. Her foot snaps out in the air, missing me by inches.

I initiate our mental connection. *Too slow. You're not utilizing everything you have.* Rushing forward, my foot loops her ankle, and her back hits the floor. *You'd be dead right now. Stop letting your fear rule you. Fight me, Natia.*

She anticipates my next move, rolls, jumps to her feet, and ducks, avoiding my fist.

Better. Now, let's see some of that power.

My magic runs a hot length up her spine. She flinches but doesn't strike—at least she knows I'm nowhere near. She needs a push. I risk her wrath and tease underneath her breasts, pooling an almost unbearable heat there. The air crackles, and the scent of a breaking storm floods the room. A flash of sapphire eyes gives away her location, and I teleport to the other side of the room. Her magic tracks me, and the air slams me against the wall. I stay in place but use my shadow to pull her feet from under her. She spins as she tumbles and douses the invisible darkness with water. *"What the hell was that?"*

"Do you always know the capabilities of your enemy?"

"Apparently not."

I pin her to the floor with velvet tendrils of midnight. Her panic coats the room, the tang of ozone my only warning before lightning strikes around her, slicing the strands and freeing her. *"You're defending. Attack—"* I grunt as my lungs expel the air shoved out of me; my hands grip my chest from the force of the invisible punch. *"Better."*

Wrapping my magic around her body, I constrict her movements and let a ribbon wind around her throat. *"You think Lawrence will wait around while you figure this out?"* I taunt. A crack in her shields appears, and sunshine briefly drowns the shadows before she slams it shut and follows the lyrics to the music. I blink, not sure what I've just witnessed.

She grunts as the earth rumbles around us, cracks appearing on the wooden floor. A storm rages, and forks of lightning ignite the room as I tighten the noose and get close. My fingers skim her jaw. *"You can't hurt me. Let go."* The floor breaks into a thousand pieces, and wood shavings scatter the floor as the pieces sharpen into stakes. They swivel in the air as the brightest emerald eyes I've ever seen catch mine, before they turn and point in my direction. She's not only strong; she's controlling multiple elements at the same time.

"Let me go, Archan."

Allowing a teasing smirk to appear, I give her the final push by brushing my lips over hers. Deafening thunder drowns out the music as the stakes stream toward me. Grabbing her body, I drop my magic from her flesh and form an impregnable bubble before delivering a kiss that steals her breath. The stakes splinter as the raging storm continues outside our sphere of safety. She wraps herself around me like I'm her lifeline. *"Do you feel the connection, Natia?"*

She draws back, sliding her hands to cup my face. *"Do you?"* Frowning, I pull back.

The door slams open as the men pile in, each jaw dropping in turn as they take in the chaos. *"Is this part of her training?"* Zac asks, as Jed grins at us.

"It was necessary."

She glances at the ceiling, watching the elements collide in the world she's created. *"I did that?"*

I nod. *"You've accessed it; now, it's time to control it. I don't want you to just let it go—close your eyes."* Uncharacteristically, she follows my command. *"Now grab hold of it and tame it. Let it run through you like water over rocks."* Grasping her hand, I press it to her heart. *"With each heartbeat, allow the power to become quiet. Recognize its difference and allow it to become part of you."*

The room quietens, allowing the bass of the newest tune to carry through the room. I drop the shield and step away from her. She blinks her eyes open and takes in the destruction—the charred walls, wet ceiling, and torn floor. Someone cuts the music.

She pulls her bottom lip between her teeth. "Sorry, I'll pay for that."

Chuckling, I shake my head. "No need—it will be back to new in an hour. It's seen worse. The main thing is the result. Do you understand the emotion you need to access your magic?"

Her eyes flash before she hangs her head and tugs on my mind. *"Fear. Will I always need it?"*

"No, Natia. Tell me, could you access it now?"

Glancing up, she levels her gaze at the floor and points her index finger at some of the broken wood. It whips around in a mini tornado. She grins.

Laughter bubbles out of me as I press her hand down. "You don't need to actually point to make it happen."

She shrugs. "I know, but it looks good for dramatic effect."

Everyone but Zac snorts.

Now, time to discuss us. We keep going around in stubborn circles. I want her, she wants me. This should be simple. Of course, it's Natia, so simple is against her very nature.

"We need to talk about last night."

She takes a step away, nibbles her lip, and glances at our audience. "Not now. Where and when for Khalkaroth?"

"Five p.m., the old warehouse district. We'll fill you in on the plans then," Barney says.

I sigh. I've lost her to the mission for now. She wants to distract herself with danger; it's apparently easier than dealing with her whiplash feelings toward me. "It's a capture, not kill mission," I warn her.

She nods. "I'll see you at the warehouse later." Then, she turns on her heel and stalks out the door. Everyone but Zac follows.

He glances around the room as the floor starts to repair itself, the wood slotting back together. "She's strong."

I huff out a breath at his understatement. I know this is only the beginning... There's something special about Natia, and I don't only mean her magic. I intend to peel back her many layers, unlock her secrets, and make her mine. The desire is unbearable now. I'll show her the love she craves is overestimated—what I can offer is so much more. Will she try to run when she finds out who I am, what I am? Probably. But there isn't a rock in this universe she can hide under.

Chapter Thirty-Two

Natia

Taurus. I am Earth. Air cannot move me. Water cannot drown me. Fire cannot scorch me.

𝕯 ark clouds form an oppressive barrier over the sun, and the scent of ozone is strong, promising a storm, as we sit in the car waiting for Archan. I massage my temples. Grrr, Archan—what the hell am I doing? The guy has me twisted in knots I can't even begin to undo. He's proven he would protect me from anything… anything but himself, that is. I think I know his fear, even if he doesn't. He claims he can't offer love. Perhaps it's because he thinks he's incapable, or maybe—like me—he fears the power it gives someone. I can't begin to fathom the lifetimes he's lived and the potential heartbreak that comes with that length of time. Giving in to Archan would be like jumping into a tsunami and clinging to the hope that I could ride the waves when, in reality, the devastating undertow would pull me so far down—I'd never again see the sky. However, he might be my weakness, but he also makes me strong. I've never felt so sure about my own strength; in the span of a few short hours, he linked me to a world where I can protect those I love with a power to rival the most evil foe.

Jed nudges me in the ribs as he squirms to get more comfortable. He stayed with us; it's as if he's decided to join our gang. I shift around in the back seat, stuck between Jed and Zee; the now-familiar buzzing sensation dances across my skin, making me twitchy and irritable.

I push Jed. "I need out—I feel like I'm suffocating." He jumps out and offers his hand, and I grasp it. My breathing is too quick, making me dizzy. The second I'm outside, I feel better and reach under the passenger seat to retrieve my swords.

Zee scoots across the back seat and jumps down next to me. "I didn't realize you were claustrophobic."

"I'm not."

Gravel crunches as a car roars toward us. I roll my eyes—a black SUV.

Jed puts a hand on my arm. "It's just Archan."

"I know. I'm just disappointed at his lack of imagination."

Zee starts laughing. "She has a thing against black SUVs—she thinks they're cliché."

Jed nods and tilts his head, chuckling. "You know, I've never thought about it before... but you're right."

I kiss his cheek just as the car comes to a stop, and Archan steps out, followed by Nathan, Barney, and a new guy in his late thirties with short hair the color of straw, bronzed skin, and sky-blue eyes. "I may just love you, Smoothie. You understand me more than most."

A low growl comes from Archan. Here we go—alpha male time.

Jed smirks at him. Ha, didn't expect that; I'm still baffled at the dynamic between the two of them.

I peruse Archan as he approaches, analyzing him from head to toe. He's wearing a black roll-neck sweater and combat trousers, with boots laced up to his ankles. His hair is tied back, showing his sharp cheekbones and strong jawline. The whole look suits him. But then what wouldn't?

"Is this your typical fighting attire?" Archan asks. His eyes lighten as he takes in my protective leathers and the swords strapped to my back.

No, nope, not happening. Not here anyway. "Yes. You've seen it before, or are you having an 'ancient' memory problem?"

A wicked grin curves his lips, as Mr. Arrogant makes a reappearance. "And you have freedom of movement?"

"Yep. Now we've appraised my wardrobe can we discuss the plan?"

The newcomer snorts a laugh, flashing me pearly white teeth. "I like her."

He offers me his hand. I eye it with indecision, but eventually, the etiquette from my upbringing wins over, and I grasp it firmly. A buzz of power licks up my arm and lifts the hairs on my neck. "I'm Natia."

"Michael." Ah, the elusive Michael Hunter, Archan's business partner. An amazing sunshine aura threaded with hints of gold surrounds him.

"Excellent. Now we have enough players for baseball. How's your pitch, Michael?"

He grins, his eyes crinkling in the corners. "I have a wicked curveball."

"Archan's already covered third base, but I think he's hoping for a home run," Jed helpfully adds.

I roll my eyes and beat down any embarrassment. "He should count himself lucky if he even gets to play on the team," I mutter.

Aaden scratches his ear. "I'm so confused... What are we talking about right now?"

Archan shakes his head as if to dispel my presence. Thunder rumbles above us, and the sky steadily turns a deep gray, the promise of rain now a certainty. He glances at the sky then at me with accusing eyes. I smirk. Your fault, buddy. You taught me too well, and I'm a fast learner. I can control the weather.

Zac appears out of thin air and rolls out a map on the hood of the car. "Aw, Zacy. We've already sorted out teams. You'll have to sit on the bench." I run my eyes over him. Something is different, and the second I realize it, I smirk. "Being the awesome friend that I am, I'm gonna do you a solid and let you know you *aren't* in the minority of men that can rock a man bun."

Michael barks out a laugh as Zac's stormy eyes harden. He frowns and glances around the stoic faces of the gang. I could hug them for playing along. He huffs and turns back to the map. "We're going to set up in this warehouse, putting our people here," he points to a back corner, "and here," his finger lands on the left wall.

Duncan peers over my shoulder. "Good choice."

Zac's eyebrows creep up, and I quickly explain it's the warehouse Duncan and I often use to trap demons, like Eric. It has two doors, front and back, and no windows; in other words, it's extremely easy to corner someone in there.

Barney leans on the car and stares at me. "We've turned on the power so we can use the lights—he'll have fewer shadows to hide in." I scan the nine of us. If we work together, we can get this asshole.

"Don't underestimate him, Natia. He's not your average demon. He's higher level and very dangerous," Archan cautions.

"Thank you for the warning. I can handle myself."

"I know you think you can, but—"

I cut him off, sick of the overbearing male routine. "We've had this conversation—you underestimate *me*, piss me off, then—"

He cuts me off this time. "Then I save you." My hands twitch to reach for my swords; his eyes flick to the movement, and he smirks. Letting the anger flow through me, I fight to control the emotion and power.

"You will wait outside, in case he escapes," he continues calmly. A surge of power strikes from my head to my toes, making me wobble as a bolt of lightning blasts the ground no more than ten meters behind Archan. I'm connected to it, it belongs to me... and I can make it strike anywhere.

He raises an eyebrow. "A tantrum at this point is unhelpful. Like I said, we will talk about us later." I stare him down, unblinking. *Maybe I've finally mastered the death stare?*

Jed intervenes before I do something I'll regret (maybe). "Archan, stop antagonizing the powerful but unstable witch you piss off every time you open your mouth. Natia, stop taking the bait—you're better than that."

Zac suddenly gasps.

I glance around. "What now?"

He waves his fingers around his face. "Your eyes... they've changed." I glance at Zee and Duncan for confirmation.

Zee edges closer. "Cool, you have white lightning in them."

Everyone leans in. "Like Thor?"

"No, more like forks of lightning crackling around your irises," Zee mutters, grasping my chin and moving my head side to side.

"They were emerald earlier, when you were training," Jed comments.

"They change with the elemental power she is commanding," Archan says, tracking Zee's hand on my chin.

"Okay then." I shrug, pushing Zee's hand away. Silently, I try not to panic—one problem at a time. And in the grand scheme of things, my eye color isn't even in the top ten. I'll add it to the ever-expanding memo for the mysterious being in the cave. "We aren't waiting outside. I've proven I can be of use." Little sparks of static electricity jump between my fingertips as I point behind me. Another lightning bolt strikes the ground. "And you know I can fight. If you need someone outside, use someone else."

Everyone stares over my shoulder, watching the random sparks of lightning dance on the ground. Zac blinks and recovers first. "Fine." He gives me a distrustful look and points to the door. "You and your men flank the entrance."

"Stay close, and remember, it's a capture, not kill mission. I need him alive," Archan says, tilting his head the tiniest bit. He's communicating with his team again. I narrow my eyes as he grins at me.

We move to our respective posts in the warehouse, and Archan stands twelve meters to the right of me. Nathan appears in the middle of the damp warehouse and places the Jar on the dusty floor, like a prize. I think it's unlikely Khalkaroth will walk into such an obvious trap, but Archan and his men seem sure. So we hunker down and wait.

After two hours, I inwardly groan. My legs are cramping from my position on the floor. A familiar tug pulls on my mind; I'm tempted to ignore it, but it may be important.

"What?"

"Sore?" he asks, amused.

"Fuck off," I snap.

He sighs mentally—how, I have no idea, but it's there. *"You've already acknowledged I didn't reject you. I want you. When you come to my bed, you will have no regrets, no excuses for why you made that decision other than wanting me."*

"You might be waiting for some time."

"What are you afraid of?"

Falling and never finding my way out. Loving you and not having it returned. Being made to feel like a possession, a prize, rather than a person. *"Zombies."* His chuckle caresses my mind like silk, just as a sharp cramp in my calf has me gritting my teeth.

"The last time you had sore legs, you stripped and got into a hot tub. I could help after this is over." My growl permeates the mental link. *"Temper, temper, Natia."*

"I don't have a temper—I just have a quick reaction to bullshit."

"Your smart mouth is going to get you in trouble."

"It's when I'm silent you should worry." I decide to play him at his own game. *"You're right, I am sore. Jed can help. He's an excellent masseur... and the tub is big enough so he can get in with me, naked of course. He needs to be in the spirit of the occasion. Maybe I can retire the ice cream?"*

He growls audibly.

"Temper, temper, Archan."

He drops the link.

Twenty minutes later, minuscule changes in the air currents ripple over my skin. I experiment with my telepathic abilities and reach out mentally to the team.

"He's here, left side of the front door. He's stopped moving, but you can't see him."

"Are you sure?" Zac asks. I groan, trying to contain the sarcasm that begs to escape me.

299

"She's having a sargasm," Jed helpfully supplies to explain my mental grunt.

"A sargasm?" Michael asks.

"She's so overwhelmed by the urge to respond sarcastically, she can only roll her eyes and grunt."

"I love it," Michael muses.

I roll my eyes, confirming Jed's analysis. *"Yes, I'm sure."*

"How can you tell?" Barney asks, returning us to the moment.

"Air currents."

A tendril of power curls around my neck, and I struggle to breathe as it tightens like a boa constrictor. Just as I'm going to pass out, it releases me, and laughter echoes around the warehouse. Light floods the space, and everyone springs into action. Aaden, Zee, Duncan, and I form a line blocking the exit then stalk forward to force him to the back wall. I take three steps before an invisible force sweeps us off our feet and dumps us on our asses outside. The doors bang shut.

I jump up and put my hands on my hips. "Shit, Archan just pushed us out!" I glare at Duncan. "Can you get us back inside?"

He studies the door. "Not that way."

Grabbing my arm, he teleports us to the roof of the warehouse then returns for Zee and Aaden. I crouch and stare through a skylight in the center of the roof, watching Archan's men pop in and out of existence, trying to catch Khalkaroth. I study his movements carefully, observing his technique of evading Archan's men; he's using the shadows created by the various leftover boxes in the warehouse. We should have cleared it completely.

I turn to Duncan, mulling a plan over. "Can you remove the glass without any sound?"

He nods. "Yes, what are you thinking?" I describe my plan, but Zee isn't on board.

"Zee, you need to remember who I am and what I can do. You saw what I did outside earlier. We need to use these powers to our advantage." I look around at all three of them. "Stop letting your emotions rule you. This mission has brought us all closer, and I'm so grateful to call you my friends. But we still have a job to do," I finish, kissing Zee's cheek. "Anyway, I have an awesome bodyguard." That earns me a smile.

I nod at Duncan, who makes the glass disappear, take one last look at the fight, then silently countdown my entrance.

Unwinding the whip from my belt, I coil it around my arm and walk toward Zee. He reaches out to clip the tether to my waist, and seconds later, I run toward the opening and flip in the air at the last minute. Time seems to slow down as I descend into the center of the room, landing directly over the Jar. I expel the power I've allowed to build inside of me and, with a gust of air containing the strength of a hurricane, knock every single person off their feet, including Khalkaroth. The building groans against the pressure.

Snapping the whip to wrap around Khalkaroth's foot, I jerk my arm, sliding him toward me.

Leaping over Barney, I loom over Khalkaroth, drop the whip, and with a metallic whistling, pull my swords from their sheaths.

He shrieks as I plunge one into his left shoulder, pinning him to the floor. *Capture not kill, capture not kill*, I repeat.

I raise my other, ready to administer an incapacitating blow just below his heart.

As I thrust down, he grabs the sword, and the sharp blade slices through his palm like butter. His hand hits the butt of the sword between the two protective prongs as something thick, warm, and spiky wraps around my throat.

I glance behind me, seeing a tail protruding from his torn trousers. The darkened, forked end grazes my cheek. He grins up at me, revealing those gross, sharp, yellow teeth. "Thought you would never arrive, darling. Now we can go." He reaches for the Jar.

Archan's boot slams on his hand, crushing his long fingers.

Khalkaroth rips the sword out of his shoulder, grabs me, teleports to a corner of the warehouse, and slinks into the shadows; his tail unwinds from my throat and is replaced by his uninjured hand. "Give me the Jar, or she dies."

Archan narrows his eyes and slides his hands into his pockets. "Go ahead—she doesn't matter."

Khalkaroth clucks his tongue. "I don't think so. I've watched you with her. You like her, my old friend, more than any other. She intrigues you... Quite the enigma, isn't she?"

"Your information is out of date. She is nothing special. Women with twice her beauty and half the trouble fall at my feet every day. Take her—she's a toy, a used and broken one I have lost interest in."

My heart stutters as that tsunami wave threatens.

Khalkaroth whispers in my ear loud enough for Archan to hear. "Is that true? Are you such a disappointment, or are you too dark even for him? Don't worry, I can handle you." He licks my ear, thick saliva sticking to the shell. I cringe at the sloppy, wet sound.

Archan's words confirm he's lost interest, and now he's giving me away like a possession he owns. Blood pounds in my ears, as embarrassment turns to anger. My skin prickles with power. I thought I was all out of juice after my entrance. It's different now—hot, wild, and dangerous.

An image pops into my mind, one I haven't seen before—but I somehow know I need it. Closing my eyes, I concentrate and push my power out. The air around me heats, and Khalkaroth cries out. I open my eyes to find myself inside a circle of blue fire, with symbols drawn on the floor—identical to the image that flashed before my eyes.

Khalkaroth is sprawled on the ground, as Archan stares at me with a mixture of fear and awe. "Get out of the circle now," he commands.

Duncan sports an equal look of fear. Guess being in here is bad. I move to step through the flames and jerk as Khalkaroth's tail winds around my calf, the spikes digging into my muscle. My chin hits the concrete before I can get my hands out to stop myself, and I nip the end of my tongue between my teeth.

"Fuck," I groan, spitting blood onto the floor. Grabbing the dagger from my waist, I lean down and flick it through his tail; he shrieks—a high-pitched sound that makes me wince. The severed end falls off my leg and flops uselessly to the floor, while the foot-length stub twitches as it leaks blood. Dragging myself to my feet, I step through the flames unharmed, and everyone, apart from Archan, takes a step back.

I pause. "What's wrong?" I look at Duncan.

"You need to finish the job and put out the flames."

"What job?" I ask, confused.

Archan steps toward me, slow and careful, as if scaring me will cause something bad to happen. It will if he gets any closer.

I put my hand out, watching the blue flames dance down my arm and around my naked hand. Looking down, I find my entire body is on fire and let out a little scream. I'm not burning, but it's the natural response to being on fire, and my badass image should *not* take a knock because of it. Archan takes another step toward me.

I glare at him. "Of all the people in this room, you're the last person who needs to come near me." I point at Khalkaroth. "Even he's further down my shit list than you."

He stops and, for once, keeps quiet; thank the Lord for small mercies. Jed steps forward, hazel eyes studying me like a frightened animal. I nod. "Tell me what I need to do."

Archan's jaw tics.

"You bitch, you can't hide forever!" Khalkaroth shouts from the circle. I ignore him, concentrating on Jed and now Duncan, who's found his balls and decided to approach me.

"He's in a banishment circle... which you've somehow created. You finish it by saying a few words. Done correctly, he won't be getting out of hell for a long time," Jed instructs.

Cries of pain echo in the warehouse as Khalkaroth tries to use the shadows to escape, but the fire holds him down every time. Duncan and Jed agree on the correct words for me to chant.

"Let me out! Pan must die!" Khalkaroth screams at Archan.

Archan frowns. "I don't know what you mean. Don't worry, we'll make sure Pan meets a swift end."

I run through the words in my head several times—the slightest wrong inflection might cause the warehouse to go up in flames. I close my eyes and begin to chant.

Khalkaroth laughs maniacally. "You fools! You have no idea, do you?"

On my final word, the flames leap so high you can't see inside the circle; just as fast, they drop to reveal an empty space.

"Now you need to put out the flames," Duncan commands. I concentrate, grasping the tendrils of wild power snapping around like a crazy octopus, and yank them back inside me. The fire drops, revealing scorched earth. It takes more effort to pull the power back enough to extinguish the flames on my body, and by the time I'm done, I feel like I've run a marathon—not that I've ever run a marathon, but this is how I imagine it must feel.

My legs wobble. Jed and Duncan each grab an arm, and I lean on them, not caring that I look weak. I've just done what they couldn't.

Archan approaches me—when will this man get the point? "How many times do I need to tell you to leave me alone? Haven't you humiliated me enough in the last twenty-four hours? You've rejected me and described my unimportance and apparent failure to impress in the bedroom to everyone here. You just offered to pass me on like a possession. You've made it clear there are women less complicated and more beautiful than me at your disposal—so why bother with me at all? I knew it..." My voice catches in my throat, and I try to swallow past the huge lump that's appeared there. I remind myself to breathe as I ride the final crashing wave that takes me to shore. "I knew you were like this. I knew you couldn't be trusted. But you just had to have me, didn't you? Archan and his little game..." Tears fill my eyes, and I struggle to blink them back. "Well, there are two things you need to know. One, you never had me, so don't presume to know me. Two, you will never have me. The deal is complete. Stay away from me."

Archan flinches, a look of pain briefly crossing his features. I assume it's his ego taking some damage.

I let go of Jed's arm and kiss his cheek. "Sorry, Smoothie, I'm going somewhere you can't follow. I'll see you soon. You have my number—use it."

"Natia, you know full well I didn't mean it," Archan implores.

Ignoring him, I wrap myself around Duncan, taking comfort in his strength and familiar scent. "Take me back. I need to be alone."

The odd sensation of twisting assaults me, making me dizzy as we land in the garage at HQ. I continue to lean on Duncan for a long time. Eventually, I look up at him, and he gives me a squeeze. "You did good today. You're a full elemental witch, and your control is improving."

"How many full elemental witches do you know?"

He shuffles his feet. "None."

"None, as you don't *personally* know any?"

"As in, I don't know of any in existence." I blink several times; it's too much. He kisses the top of my head. "We'll figure it out."

I quirk an eyebrow. "No wonder everyone was staring at me like I was Lucifer himself."

He chuckles. "Your eyes were shining with cobalt flames. They may have thought you were."

My eyes go wide. "No way."

"Yes way. Don't take it personally; they were just shocked. Conjuring a banishment circle for a high-level demon was pretty impressive for your first outing with fire—most just light a candle."

We both snort. "They could have thanked me for it, though."

He looks at me seriously. "They're grateful, Locks. Although they did want him detained, not banished." He pulls on the end of my braid. "You know Archan said those things to save your life. He wanted to make it seem like you weren't important to him. If you paid attention, you would have seen the tension in his body and felt the waves of anger pouring off him. The man was barely restrained."

"He was angry that I was about to banish his precious demon, and the things he said were too personal after rejecting me. So deep down... maybe. But right now, he confuses me. It's best he stays away." A lump forms in my throat at the thought of never seeing him again. I remind myself that I'm planted firmly on the ground rather than being bounced around in the violent storm that is Archan.

"I've got to go back to Aaden and Zee, and you need to rest. I'll update Charlie and come and find you later. You okay to get back to your room?"

"Yeah, I feel stronger, thank you."

I blink as he disappears—nope, still not used to it.

Chapter Thirty-Three

Natia

Taurus—under the anger, there's hurt. Under the hurt, there's pain. Under the pain, there's love.

Jack eyes me over the breakfast bar for the sixth time as I sip the coffee he made me and relax into the familiar surroundings. His aura floats between a dull brown and an angry red. He's all over the place.

I sigh, the steam billowing across the space between us. He slides me a plate with some cookies. Grabbing one, I stuff it into my mouth, accepting the peace offering. "Thanks," I mumble, concluding there's no time like the present to figure out his issues. "Everything okay?"

He grabs a cookie and leans back. "Sure, why wouldn't it be? How's the case?"

I sigh and roll my neck. How do you sum up the events of the last few days? We teamed up with the enemy, who may or may not be the enemy—but is definitely powerful. Then we got tossed into the middle of a biblical prophecy foretold to destroy mankind. We found a magic Jar but handed it over to our enemy/non-enemy, and we're searching for someone named Pan, who may or may not be here to end the world. I just banished a powerful demon. Did I mention I'm a full elemental witch with the power to make small earthquakes and lightning? "Umm… complicated."

He shoves his stool back, and the metal screeching against the floor makes me wince. "Right. I get it. I'm not part of the team."

I grab his arm. "Jack, wait—" He shakes me off and storms down the corridor toward his room. I should go after him, but exhaustion tugs like lead on my limbs, so I make my way to my room, pull on old pajamas, and climb into bed, leaving my door open so Zee, Duncan, and Aaden will wake me when they return. I collect my Kindle from the floor and catch up on some much-needed time with my favorite books, relishing reading battle scenes I'm not involved in. My eyelids grow heavy, my head foggy. My hand goes lax before I finish one chapter, and I drift to sleep, dreaming of gold eyes and heated hands caressing my body, setting it alight with blue fire. Slowly, my dream shifts, becoming malevolent, as cold steel presses against my throat. I try to scream, but it won't leave my mouth. A solid weight presses against my body, making it difficult to breathe.

"Stupid bitch, thinking you're special waltzing in like a princess. No interview, no testing, no pain of not knowing if you're good enough. It's time you hurt a little to understand what the rest of us had to go through," a rough voice hisses.

Realization hits—I'm not dreaming. I fight my way back to consciousness, dragging open my eyes to reveal Jack's angry stare boring into me, his pupils narrowed to pinpricks. I try to speak, but a cloth chokes the back of my throat. My head lolls to the side; my Kindle is lying on the floor, while my reinforced steel door is closed and locked. Help isn't coming.

I clench my fist and swing to punch him, but something constricts around my wrist. I glance up. My hands are secured tightly to the top of the bed. I try to lift my legs to kick him, but they've been bound to each side of the bed, too.

The air shimmers next to me, revealing the outline of a humanoid figure. I squint, trying to make sense of the shape, when Jack roughly squeezes one breast; I groan at the wicked pain. "You're not meant to be so awake, but it's okay… If you relax, you might enjoy it," he hisses, winking. The humanoid figure becomes more solid, and a shiver racks over my body. Jack cups me, hard, making me twist my head back to him. "I doubt you'll relax, frigid bitch. I'm going to enjoy knocking you off that pedestal."

The knife leaves my throat. Fabric tears, then cool air breezes across my bare skin as he forces his fingers inside. A soundless scream vibrates through me, and I tense as pain lances through my gut. He smiles, a violent lust clouding his eyes.

I squeeze my eyes shut, and a tear slides down my temple.

He punches me in the face, and I inhale through my nose sharply as the crunch of my cheekbone follows a blinding pain. "You need to be reminded you aren't that pretty," he grunts, as he strikes me again, making me see stars, and begins thrusting his fingers. Warmth spreads between my legs as agony spears my abdomen. He removes his fingers, unbuckles his jeans, and pushes my knees further apart.

"Seems I've already wrecked your pussy," he laughs coldly. I feel pressure at my ass, and I tighten reflexively, struggling against bonds that I should be able to break. Frustrated he can't progress his assault, he pummels my stomach, over and over.

The shimmering figure finally appears—Lawrence's terrifying true form comes into focus as he whispers into Jack's ear and grins at me.

My mind has broken, it must have. The living quarters are warded against demons. I'm sure I must be placing the trauma of four years ago with now and trying to make sense of Jack's violence.

Jack's eyes narrow on my face, and the pressure shifts forward to my opening. Jack pushes his fists against my pelvis, pinning me in place. The pain from my face becomes background noise as whatever is wrong with my stomach flails against his weight, and I scream so loud into the gag that my voice breaks. Jack tenses his muscles, on the brink of doing something that will change the both of us for the worse. But before he can, something snaps, and a familiar swell of power rushes through me. Closing my eyes, I release it in a sharp thrust—my muscles jerk. The weight from my body disappears, and a whack against the concrete accompanies the snap of bones.

Tears run into my ears as sleep tries to pull me under. Adrenaline should be shooting through my veins—my coffee must have been drugged.

Lying limp on the bed, my power is once again absent, burnt out, I cling to the pain to keep me conscious—my insides burn like I've been skewered with a hot poker. Panic nearly overwhelms me as I tremble, fearing the damage might be irreparable. My body cramps, trying to force me to curl into a tight ball. Instead, I'll have to wait until I'm found. I swallow the burning bile that rises in my throat. Think, Natia! How can you break free?

My inspection of the room reveals no inspiration. I'll need to wait until the drugs wear off, by which point the guys will know something is wrong. I only ever close my door, but never lock it. I could be found by anyone—or worse, everyone.

Best possible scenario—I control who finds me.

The mental link.

Fighting to focus my mind, I prepare to reach Duncan, and then pause. Could I bear for him to see me like this? But if anyone is going to see me, it should be my best friend. Forcing my mind to focus past the pain and onto Duncan, I imagine invisible threads connecting my mind to his. I feel a slight tug.

"Duncan?" No answer. The thread goes slack. I try again, but still, nothing.

I contemplate Zee and Aaden, but I can't bring myself to do it. There's only one other choice… I consider waiting it out. But it could be Uncle Charlie who finds me. My internal muscles constrict, wrecking my body and making me strain against the bonds. My wrists drip with blood.

"Archan," I whisper. The thread is strong and snaps into place immediately.

"What's wrong?"

My tears flow freely as relief washes over me. *"I'm—"* I cry out as lightning slices my hips.

"You're hurt. Where are you?"

"At the compound."

"Where the fuck is that?"

That's right, he doesn't know. Telling him compromises the SIP. *"Get Duncan. Tell him I need help,"* I moan, whimpering at the burning radiating down my legs.

"Fuck that. Tell me now."

I stare at the ceiling through bleary eyes. *"Promise me you won't disclose the location to anyone else."*

"I promise. Tell me where you are."

"Two levels beneath Crown Security, Inc., in an underground bunker."

I feel like I've just betrayed everyone I love.

312

Minutes pass before a crash of power fills the room, and I groan as it pushes against me. Archan stands frozen at the side of the bed, sweeping his gaze over my mostly naked, swelling body. Raging flames surround his aura, like a multicolored sun. He removes my gag just as pain wraps around my abdomen so fierce it almost takes my consciousness. Bile rises in my throat again, and this time, I can't stop it. I twist my head to the side and vomit over my pillow.

"Archan," I plead, as a wave of shame washes over me. He meets my eyes with pity and anger.

"Don't you dare..." I mutter, my voice trembling, "don't you *dare* look at me like that."

He breaks my bonds with no effort, the ropes stinging as they slide from my wrists and ankles. Grasping my stomach, I roll to my side and catch a glimpse of the blood-covered sheets. Archan crouches in front of Jack, checking his pulse.

"Is he alive?" I ask hoarsely.

Instead of answering, he picks me up, cradling me in his arms. I arch my back and scream in agony at the change of position. A fresh rush of wetness coats my thighs, and I fight to stay awake as black dots dance in my vision.

"Hold on, I've got you," he whispers softly, as space bends and colors flash by. This time, I barely notice them.

I'm back on Archan's bed, where Nathan and Jed wait.

"Nobody but you," I beg Archan, gripping his shirt.

He shakes his head. "I'm sorry, Natia, I need them to help heal you."

He rolls me onto my back, trying to avoid touching swollen areas. I fight against him, not wanting to be exposed. A cool breeze drifts over my skin as someone lays a sheet over me, and I stop resisting.

313

Archan throws his suit jacket on the floor, dumps his watch on top of it, and rolls up his shirt sleeves. I concentrate on his every move, trying to ignore the pain. He sits next to me and holds my gaze. "Nobody else will ever know." The bed dips on the opposite side, and someone takes hold of my hand. I glance over—it's Jed. I panic as my body begins to go numb.

"I can't feel anything," I whisper.

Jed squeezes my hand. "It's me. I'm numbing the pain."

Archan holds my face, his hands gentle. "Natia, focus on me. I need to heal your injuries. You're bleeding. I need to touch you, but not inside. Do you understand?" I nod, my cheeks heating. I close my eyes and stay quiet, keeping my breathing under control. A healing warmth suffuses my lower body. When I open my eyes, Archan is studying my face, not with pity, but with respect and compassion.

"She needs blood, now," Nathan declares. He sounds far away. Strewn across the floor are multiple towels saturated with blood.

"What blood type are you?" Archan asks.

"O negative."

"Fuck," Nathan grinds out. It's rare, so I don't blame him.

Archan doesn't take his eyes from me. "Get it from the blood bank."

Nathan disappears. Archan pulls down the sheet to lay his hand across my swollen body. He checks each injury, making sure I'm fully healed before he moves on. He growls when he reaches the bruises on my aching left breast.

"Where is he?" I ask, anger lacing my voice.

"Dead."

My eyes widen. "What? You killed him?"

He takes a deep breath. "It wasn't me." I pale at the implication.

"It was me?"

"Yes."

I force my mind to go blank to hold back my maelstrom of emotions. All it serves to do is concentrate them into a tiny ball. Archan grasps my face. "Control it, Natia. We are in a fucking skyscraper."

"Concentrate, Natia. Don't let it control you. Try letting it wash through you rather than holding onto it," Jed urges, trying to calm me. I let the ball of power unfurl, but keep it contained inside me—it works.

Nathan appears and quickly begins the blood transfusion, and Jed lets go of my hand; the numbness recedes.

"Does anything hurt?" Archan asks, scanning my body.

Just my dignity, pride, and strength. "My ankles."

Shame washes over me again, as I remember being tied down, helpless. His hands stroke my sore ankles, and the sting disappears. He tucks a strand of damp hair behind my ear.

"Sleep... You're safe," he says, getting up from the bed. I catch hold of his hand, and he pauses. "What do you need?"

I swallow the lump in my throat. "Clothes," I answer, swallowing harder, "a shower... and to not be alone."

The last shreds of my clothes hit the bathroom floor, and Archan guides me to sit on a bench inside the shower as he adjusts the heat and angle of the spray. For some inexplicable reason, I don't feel embarrassed sitting naked in his shower. I look around, trying to distract myself. He has an abnormally large shower, and I find it timely to investigate why people have such big showers.

"Why do you have a shower big enough for more than two people? I get the two, even three, at a push. But more—sounds complicated."

He smirks down at me. I need that look—the one without the knowledge of my attack. "I'll bear in mind your interest in three people, but you might be disappointed. I'm not convinced I could share you."

"Great, another male in my life who dodges answering simple questions," I mumble. He chuckles. I shiver as jets of water hit my skin—hot, but not hot enough. He disappears into the bedroom then returns wearing nothing but long shorts. He watches me carefully, and I smile. Satisfied I'm not going to freak out, he moves to stand behind me.

"Can you turn up the temperature?" I ask.

He turns one of the dials clockwise, and the heat turns my skin pink. He massages shampoo firmly into my scalp then pours more into his hands and rubs it into the length of my hair.

I hum in appreciation. "You're good at this."

"Lean your head back," he instructs. Doing as I'm told, I keep my eyes open. He has a look of intense concentration. I get the feeling he applies this level of intensity into everything he does. Giving me the full treatment, he runs conditioner through my hair, using his fingers to tease out the tangles without tugging on it.

"If you lose your millions, you can always become a hairdresser's assistant," I mumble.

"Hmm, I would be the whole package—styling, too."

I laugh. "I wouldn't let you near my hair with scissors for a million dollars."

Stopping his ministrations of my hair, he stares into my eyes. "Are you sure?"

I tilt my head, contemplating it. "I'm sure."

"Why?"

"Money isn't everything—happiness is. And I'm happy with my hair."

He shakes his head in disbelief. "You mean it, too."

"Why wouldn't I?"

"Do you know how many people would turn down a million dollars to have their hair cut? You constantly surprise me." He laughs under his breath and fixes me with one of those stares. "Never change, Natia. You have a heart that's pure." He grins. "Hopefully with some wicked thoughts, though, in particular about me."

I reach up and place my hand on his cheek. "Thank you," I whisper.

His eyes widen. "For what?"

"For caring for me, for understanding what I need, and for not treating me like a frightened animal."

He stops washing my hair and places a hand over mine. "Your strength astounds me every day. This will not change that. You will grieve, you will deal, and then you will fight."

I quickly look away. My strength just killed a man. I'm not judge, juror, and executioner.

Shower complete, he gives me one of his T-shirts and a pair of sweats.

"Maybe I should keep a change of clothes here if I'm going to keep ending up in your bed," I quip. I have no energy for the mental slap I deserve.

His lips twitch. "Are you going to keep a toothbrush here, too?" I smack his arm.

He cocoons me in several blankets then lies next to me, knowing all I need is his presence. I shuffle close to feel his warmth and breathe in his heady scent. Finally, staring into his gold eyes, I'm able to give in to the sleep that has been trying to claim me for the last few hours. My final thought is the realization that Archan wouldn't crush me in a storm—he would ride it out with me.

Chapter Thirty-Four

Archan

Unknown origin.

Her features contort with a pain I can't fix. This is a pain she will need to come through alone. Nausea rolls through me as the image of her vulnerable body tied down and swelling with the force of the attack flashes in my mind. I can still hear her screams of agony as blood spilled between her legs. Her chemically tainted blood would have most people unconscious for hours—not my little badass fighter, though. She had pulled against her bonds so hard, she tore skin. Even helpless, she fought.

The boy crumpled against the wall had almost every bone in his body shattered. Remorse had flashed across her features when she realized she had killed him.

He deserved none.

If he wasn't already dead, he would have been soon. The only difference being she made it quick.

I've never met anyone as strong-willed and determined. She's a storm that can break anything in her path. Every time she's knocked down, she fights harder. This will be no different.

I touch my cheek, remembering her hand. This woman has humbled me again with her trust in me when she was so vulnerable, despite hurting her earlier. I didn't deserve it, but I did relish it.

I sense Jed behind me. He comes around the bed to see her face, his hair disheveled. "How is she?"

"Physically, fine. Emotionally… she will get through it."

He regards her with awe. "She's strong."

Deeply asleep, her face twists with emotions, as her mind struggles to process all she's been through. Not just the attack, but her powers, surviving the Eitr poison—and, it seems, me. "You're stronger than anyone I've ever known," I mutter to her.

"Duncan teleported into her room when he couldn't rouse her. He saw the blood, the ropes, and the body. He turned up in reception twenty minutes ago, and he's refusing to leave until he sees her."

I stiffen. "Does he think I hurt her?"

He shakes his head. "No. But somehow he knows she's here and is obviously concerned. What do you want to do?"

I roll off the bed and stand. She whimpers and scoots into the spot where I had just been. I run my hands over my face, conflicted. "We promised her."

"I know. I don't have a good solution."

"Is it only Duncan?"

"Yes."

"Bring him." I'm resolved, even though I could be making a decision she may never forgive me for.

A minute later, Jed appears with Duncan. Nathan joins us.

Duncan takes in her small body wrapped in countless blankets.

"What happened?" he asks, forcing his voice to remain neutral. He is trying to hold in his emotion. Good luck with that.

"The people in this room are the only ones who know what happened. I haven't asked her the details. She will tell someone if she wants to. She made me, Jed, and Nathan promise no one else would find out." He goes to interrupt me, but I continue, "Let me finish, Duncan. You're smart enough to put the scene together. But you'll need to wait for her to tell you."

He sits on the bed. She softly murmurs a prayer for mercy, and he reaches for her, his eyes turning glassy.

I place my hand on his arm. "You can't stop the nightmares. All you can do is be there for her."

He drops his head in his hands. "How bad was it?"

I swallow. "Bad." I can't bear to tell him any more—at least he can be spared the details I wish I could forget.

"Anything permanent?"

"No, she's fully healed."

"That's something," he mumbles.

She shifts closer to him. An irrational jealousy floods my veins. I know he's her friend, but it doesn't stop me from wanting to throw them all out of the room and protect her.

Her nose crinkles. "Duncan," she whispers softly.

"I'm here." His voice breaks as a tear escapes down his cheek. He's not embarrassed to show his love and compassion for her. I envy him this. I haven't felt that in so long, I'm struggling to process the emotions Natia stirs in me.

Her eyes flutter open. Her features relax until she takes in the scene of the four men in front of her. I watch as the memory of the attack crashes into her.

She locks her pained eyes with mine. "You promised."

Duncan speaks before I can answer. "Look at me." Her eyes move to his. "I put it together when I got in your room. He told me nothing. I figured you were here. Don't blame him, Locks. I would have torn the world apart looking for you."

She glances down, as pink floods her cheeks. "Who else knows?"

"I haven't told anyone, but they'll have forced their way into your room by now. I took care of Jack's body... but not the room." She flinches.

He takes hold of her chin gently. "No, Locks. You will *not* feel guilty. You were defending yourself. Don't spare him one thought. Plenty of monsters play at being human. Evil comes in many forms, and he was more evil than half the demons we kill."

Well put.

She looks away again. The guilt will haunt her for a long time—it's part of who she is.

"Find out who knows," she whispers, trying to gain control.

He frowns. "Now?"

"Yes, minimize it. Stop Uncle Charlie from finding out. Tell anyone who knows I don't want to talk about it," she shifts her gaze to me, "ever."

Jed teleports with Duncan as Natia sits up and leaves the heat of the blankets. She stares around the room for a full two minutes as Nathan and I stay frozen, waiting for the breakdown. She cocks her head at me. "We should get a dog," she says, confusing the hell out of me. She gives me that beautiful, deranged smile. "A Labrador maybe?" She looks me up and down. "Um, you seem more like a small dog person, one you could tuck in your suit pocket like a Chihuahua. We could name him 'Bruiser.'"

"What?"

"Okay, not a Chihuahua then. We could go the other way and get a Great Dane. He could follow us around like a guard. We can train him to growl at Zac." She giggles.

I shake my head as she continues. "Where do you live? My house is in a good school district, but probably not as big as yours. Maybe we can do weekends at mine? What do you think, Nathan—will the in-laws like me? Are they, like, really old? They gotta be, right? I mean, he describes himself as 'ancient.' Do you think our age difference will be noticeable? Do you even know what a post, tweet, or poke is?" She arches an eyebrow.

"What are you talking about?" I'm starting to debate if I need to get Nathan to check her mind to see if it's broken.

"What about YOLO? But then again, it's redundant if you're immortal. Are you?"

I blink. "Am I what?"

"Immortal?"

"Define immortal."

"You can't die."

"Then no, I'm not immortal."

"Huh, sucks to be you—guess YOLO applies after all."

"You low?"

She snorts and points at me. "You should see your face." Nathan chuckles.

I stare at the pair of them, dumbfounded. "I don't understand."

Interrupting our insane exchange, Jed and Duncan reappear, looking worse than they did before they left. Duncan's sympathetic look has her laughter drying up immediately. She stands on the bed; my sweats look ridiculous on her.

"No!" she shouts, pointing at him.

He swallows and raises his arms. "I'm sorry, Locks. He already knew."

She lets out an ear-piercing, agonized scream as she clutches at her chest. I cringe at the pain lancing through every decibel. Her hair lifts around her. When nobody reacts, I stalk toward her. "Lock it down! Now, Natia. You will destroy this building and the hundreds of people in it!" Her anger dissipates, and she slumps onto the bed.

"Who else?" she asks Duncan, her voice monotone, defeated.

"Zee and Aaden."

"The whole gang. Maybe we should have a group meeting?" she snaps.

"I'm so sorry." The grief on his face seeps into his tone.

"Stop apologizing. It's not your fault." She wraps herself back up in the blankets and hunkers down in my bed.

Duncan looks confused. "Don't you want me to take you home?"

"I'm not ready to face them yet. Give me time, Duncan."

He looks at me. I shake my head and return to lay beside her. Her pulse beats rapidly in her neck, whilst her jaw is locked tight. Her eyes bore straight into my soul, her pain cutting it out slice by slice. She glances at my lips and looks away. I debate grabbing the bastard from the depths of hell and tearing him into strips over many years, but I don't move. She needs me more than she needs my wrath unleashed in her honor.

Chapter Thirty-Five

Natia

Taurus—your will is stronger than a thousand armies, and it takes a lot for someone to break you mentally.

Pale blue sheets pulled over my face dim the sunlight dancing through the trees outside my bedroom window. The sun has no right to be shining, like it's been doing for the last four days, mocking me with its cheeriness. Combined, it makes up the one week of sunshine Seattle has gotten this December. It's as if the heavens themselves are laughing at me.

I groan as my bladder demands my attention and throw back the sheets. I blink at the full force of the sun and head to the bathroom, catching my reflection in the dressing table mirror—I'm a mess. My hair has formed an impressive nest on top of my head, my eyes are dark, my complexion is pale, and my teeth need brushing. Sighing, I deal with the last one; it's the easiest to rectify, I suppose.

Teeth relieved of their bacterial fur, my stomach groans in protest at the lack of food I've eaten in the last four days. I shuffle to the kitchen. Two heads appear over the top of my sofa.

"Nice to see you up," Duncan greets me, giving me a tight smile. I ignore him. There are at least two of them invading my house at any given time, standing guard against an enemy already dead.

I yawn loudly. "Go home, guys… I'm fine." Despite spending all my time in bed, sleep evades me. When I do sleep, I wake screaming, feeling phantom steel at my neck. I locked my door after the first time the guys piled into the room and found me clutching my blankets, trembling and gasping.

"Can I make you something to eat?" Zee asks.

"Not hungry," I mumble, glancing at him. I wish I hadn't. I can't stand the look of pity and worry etched on his face.

The side door swings open, and Uncle Charlie strides inside, a look of shock on his face as he takes in my appearance. "You look terrible, Natia. It's time to get up and let us help," he says, trying his authoritative tone on me. Pouring a glass of orange juice, I ignore him and shuffle back to my bedroom, locking the door behind me.

Sleep comes and goes. The sunlight, which makes the silvery blue swirls on my wallpaper sparkle, turns dull. I couldn't face going back to HQ. The places where I haven't been attacked are shrinking. I'm lying on my back, counting the small cracks in the ceiling for the third time, when my nose crinkles. The scent of dark chocolate, sandalwood, and vanilla swirls around my nostrils—Archan.

Rolling into a fetal position, I bury my head under the sheets. Each evening, when the sun falls and the darkness rules, he returns to lie next to me in a silent vigil—my pulsing star amongst the shadows of my mind. He doesn't push, doesn't try to placate me with words of comfort that would only fall on deaf ears. No, somewhere in his long life, he's learned to create solace with his presence alone—or maybe he just doesn't know what to say. Archan's a man of action, reprisal, a warrior that demands vengeance. He's an avenger without a foe, so instead, he attempts to slay the demons crawling in my mind without speaking a word or lifting a finger.

Tonight is different, though. A cool breeze tickles my skin as he lifts the sheets. I clutch them, expecting him to drag them off.

326

Instead, he climbs under. Warm hands pull me into his body as he wraps around me. His hot breath fans my neck as he strokes my hair; the calming motion lulls me to sleep. He holds me as I scream at the monsters hiding in the shadows and cry out at the phantom pain. Sometime in the night, I wrap myself around him, but when the sun rises, he's gone. Instantly, I miss his warmth and safety, but feel stronger.

Drawing in a massive breath, I fling off the sheets and stalk to the bathroom, showering and dressing for the first time in five days. Hair still damp, I head to the kitchen and find the whole gang in the living room. Uncle Charlie, Jed, Zee, Aaden, and Duncan stop talking and stare at me. I pop bread in the toaster and start brewing some coffee.

"Anyone want anything?" I ask nonchalantly. Nobody moves, so I raise an eyebrow.

Jed recovers first, running a hand through his blond-tipped locks and walking over with an empty mug extended. "Coffee, please."

"Milk and sugar?" I ask, as I retrieve the butter and milk from the refrigerator.

"Just milk."

Aaden opens his mouth. I can tell by his expression he's about to ask about my feelings and so forth. I raise my hand and stop him. "If you want me here—stable, talking, and out of bed—don't ask me how I'm feeling, how I'm sleeping, or if there is anything you can do." The toast jumps up, and I grab it and start smearing it with butter. "I'm okay, I have nightmares, and the best thing you can do for me is treat me normally."

Jed studies the contents of the refrigerator as I pour some coffee and milk into his mug. "Whose turn is it to do the shopping? All we have is cold pizza," he mutters.

"I'll have that," Zee calls, still watching me. Uncle Charlie stands and heads toward me. I stiffen, expecting him to hug me, but he pauses, noticing my body language.

"Love you, Natia." His voice is soft.

I force a smile. "You, too."

"I'll do some shopping. You want anything special?" he asks me.

"Something with layers, key lime pie, a cheesecake, and some rocky road ice cream."

"Anything not dessert related?" he presses, sounding amused.

"Nope! I'm on a dessert-only diet for the next month," I declare, contradicting myself by chomping on my toast.

I sit in the armchair he's vacated and look at Jed.

"As much as I love your company and appreciate your concern, you need to go back." He looks hurt, so I reach over and pat his knee. "Don't worry, Smoothie, I still love you. You can come and see us later; I just need to debrief with my team."

He nods and disappears. I blink—someone disappearing while standing is weird enough, but someone sitting with one leg crossed? I don't think I'll ever get used to it.

I eat my toast slowly as waves of nausea roll through my stomach. "I'm assuming Archan still has the Jar and we haven't found Pan, fully deciphered the symbols, or established who these mysterious five are. And let's not forget—we need to figure out why I suddenly have these powers."

Duncan nods. "That just about summarizes it."

"What's the priority?" I ask.

Aaden grabs his laptop from the floor. "You are."

I shake my head. "The elusive Pan should come first."

Duncan perches on the arm of my chair. "Cracking the meaning of the symbols and their relationship with you may lead us to the significance of the Jar and Pan. Also, we need to keep working on controlling your powers."

My throat goes dry, my toast suddenly tasting like cardboard. "Makes sense. But we should be trying to understand what the Jar is and does. Archan has gone to great lengths to get it."

"How about a compromise? You three look into the symbols and your powers; Duncan will need to help control them anyway. I'll research the Jar and Pan," Aaden proposes.

"We'll work out of here," Zee decides.

I go to argue, when Duncan stops me, his warm eyes pleading for me to understand. "It's your home where you feel the most comfortable. Your grandfather's house is a two-minute walk away; you can escape us if you need to. We can sleep in your guest rooms, if you don't mind?"

I look around my living room at the empty mugs and plates scattered across the hearth and tables, and I nearly cry at the state of the five-hundred-dollar rug I treated myself to last month. My pillows have been thrown on the floor, and blankets are strewn across the sofas haphazardly. The window seat is covered in various food wrappers. I'm not a neat freak—I don't have the time—but I *am* tidy.

"If you're staying, you need to tidy this shit up. Then *keep* it tidy," I grumble, pointing in the general direction of the mess.

Zee salutes me. "Yes, ma'am."

I try to smile before I jump up and head toward the door. "I'm going out for a few hours. I have my phone."

Zee narrows his eyes. "You shouldn't be alone."

"Why? The threat to my life has been dealt with. You're treating me differently—and you need to stop. I've dealt with it. Move on—I have." I pull open the front door.

They all look around at one another, not making eye contact with me. I take that as my opportunity to shut the door behind me. None of them follow.

Free of my self-professed protectors—I don't point out I can probably kick their asses with my newfound powers—I walk up the hill to my grandfather's house and enter through the rear garden doors, my usual entrance. Various staff greet me as I search for my grandfather, finally finding him in the kitchen.

He looks up from a table of food and beams at me. "Thank god you're here—come and taste these hors d'oeuvres."

Picking something resembling a sausage and apple concoction, I give him my verdict. "That one's nice."

"I'm useless at this kind of thing," he says sadly. My grandmother used to do all the preparation for the parties and balls they've always held.

"I'm glad you're here," he says, reaching for my hand, "I was hoping you would come to the Christmas ball. I miss you being there."

I look out the window at the garden, now kept solely by a gardener rather than my grandmother. A memory of her in a sunhat and a long, flowing, lemon dress pruning roses and picking some for the vase she kept full in the kitchen tugs at my heart. I swing my gaze to where the vase should be. It's there, but empty. "I'm not sure, Gramps. It's difficult to do things I used to do with her."

Sadness and grief color his aura, and I realize how selfish I'm being. He's done this alone for five years. I came back to mend my

330

relationship with him, and while I'm less distant, I'm still repeating my mistakes.

I suck in a deep breath. "I'll go. But don't abandon me with the Parkers. They'll start planning my wedding to their eldest son… Neil, is it? They'll also advise me about the best schools to send our children."

He laughs, his eyes sparkling. "Deal! No abandoning."

"I'm going out. Can I borrow the car?"

"It's your car, Natia, you don't need to ask. The keys are in the drawer next to the sink." I grab them. "Would you like me to come with you?" he asks, the easy smile sliding from his face.

"How'd you know where I was going?"

He leans on his elbows and levels me with his special Gramps stare—it's a Waterford trait I need to learn. "You haven't driven your own car in four years, you do nothing for yourself, your every thought and action consumed with work… I don't need to be some secret government agent to figure out where you're going on this particular day of the year."

A maid wanders through the door clasping a large tray of champagne flutes. "Not so secret if you keep blurting it out like that," I mutter.

He chuckles. "Do you want company, sweetheart?"

I shake my head. "I need some time alone. Maybe you could follow in an hour or so?" I try to control the tremor in my voice.

"Sure, I'll be there soon."

Before leaving the house, I pluck a yellow rose from an arrangement in the entrance hall.

331

Sitting in the Lake View Cemetery parking lot, I procrastinate—a new personality trait of mine. I haven't been back since the day we buried my grandmother exactly five years ago. I stare at the rose on the passenger seat.

Stop being a coward, Natia. Get out and face your fears.

It takes me ten minutes to find the right gravestone. I lay the rose on top and sit against it, not caring about the cold, damp ground. Confession is good for the soul, right? I'm not sure this is what they meant, but it's not like I can blurt out my life to a priest and hope he doesn't call the police or the mental hospital—so I opt for the dead.

"Hi, Gran... it's me, Natia. Ha, like you don't know. If you're a heavenly being, you'll know it's me," I ramble. "I'm sorry I haven't visited. There's no excuse—so I won't give you one. Look... I just miss you, okay? I'd hoped to make you proud, but I've let you down. I miss the 'me' I was when you were here."

I swallow the lump in my throat. Grief changes us. Some people cling to each other for comfort; others hide. I hid, and the girl that loved without fear disappeared. I used to be softer, free, more hopeful, less cynical, and gloriously naive to the true evils that walked the Earth. "I've tried to sort things out with Gramps. He's forgiven me, but I don't deserve it. Uncle Charlie's the same. I'm humbled by their forgiveness."

An invisible bird chirps a cheerful song from the fir tree overlooking Gran's grave, unaware or uncaring of the grief-ridden environment it's chosen to sing in. Or maybe it is aware, and that's why it's here.

"I'm so tired. I've been broken for so long; I've forgotten how to let people in. I'm lonely." Even though heartbreak for my grandmother is crashing over me, Archan's golden gaze swims before

332

my eyes; that man is always interrupting me. "If you've been watching, Gran, then you've seen him." I roll my eyes and chuckle, sniffling a little. "Honestly, I'm not sure what you'd think of him. Didn't you used to say something like 'never trust a man who takes longer to get ready than you?' He must take longer, Gran—even in battle he looks like an avenging angel. Then again, you also said that 'trust has to be earned.' He's done so much to deserve that trust, and I want to, but I don't know how to open my heart, and I'm not sure he would want me if I did. You would think him being old would make him a romantic, when really, he's more of a pragmatist. Or maybe he's just jaded. I'm self-aware enough to know that I'm falling for him—but can you be happy with someone who doesn't fall for you in return? I want what you and Gramps had."

I put my head between my knees as the tears flow, and I begin to fall apart. "Do you know what's happening to me? I wish I could talk to you. I'm so lost in the darkness growing inside me. I took someone's life—damning my soul. I'm not a good person, I know it... I'm so sorry. Gran, I always thought I would see you again..."

Sensing someone watching me, I lift my head—it's Archan. How does he always find me? I look away, embarrassed by my tears—more weakness. "Please leave me alone," I whisper, my voice hoarse. I scarcely remember to shield, using Sarah McLachlan's "Full of Grace" at the last second.

Ignoring me, he sits down so we're shoulder to shoulder and plays with a strand of my hair. "Go away," I mumble. He rubs the base of my neck, staying silent. I give in and lean on him, placing my head on his chest, his warmth a comforting contrast on my cold cheek. The tears fall freely as my heart breaks. He wraps a strong arm around me and kisses the top of my head, making me feel safe and protected. Closing my eyes, I drift in and out of sleep.

A hand on my shoulder shakes me awake. Gramps stares down at me, a small frown marring his forehead. "Are you okay, sweetheart?"

I look around for Archan, but he's gone. "I'm fine, Gramps," I mumble, feeling a little disoriented as I stand. My ass is stone cold, and my legs are cramping from sitting in the same position for too long. A white rose rests next to my yellow one on top of the headstone.

Uncle Charlie wanders up the path toward us, holding a wreath. He stops when he sees me, looking shocked.

I greet him, my voice soft. "Hi."

"Hi," he replies, coming to stand next to me. We all look at Gran's grave. My uncle finally breaks the silence. "You need to forgive yourself. She would." He tilts his head toward the grave. "We all deal with grief differently. But you're stuck being angry. You need to let go and accept it."

I stay silent, knowing he's right. Uncle Charlie lays his wreath next to Gramps's bouquet of yellow roses. Then Uncle Charlie and I head back to the parking lot, leaving Gramps alone.

I shove my hands in my jeans pockets. "We're looking into the symbols to figure out how all the different parts fit together." He nods, deep in thought. "We can't just keep stumbling around in the dark, hoping the answers will fall into our laps."

He leans against his car, parked next to mine. "What do you need?"

"Zee, Aaden, and Duncan, for now. Apart from you, they're the only ones who know about my powers, the Jar, and Pan. Until we figure out what is happening, it needs to stay that way. If the government catches wind of my abilities, they'll confine and test me."

He folds his arms across his chest. "Agreed. Use the mission to look into Archan, as your cover. Where's your base?"

"My house."

"You have the penthouse if you need to go to the city," he reminds me.

I bob my head. "Aaden is researching the Jar and Pan. Zee, Duncan, and I will be looking into the symbols. Archan can decipher them, but I'd rather he didn't know about our continued investigation. I don't know how he'll react."

"Do you think he would hurt you after spending so much time saving you?" As soon as the words leave his mouth, his face falls. "He, uh… he was the one who rescued you last week?" It's almost as if he can't bear to meet my eyes. I put my hand in his.

"No, I don't. But whatever this is, it's big, and honestly, I'm not convinced he's on the right side. The lines are blurred."

"Don't ask him for help unless it's urgent and desperate. Do you understand?" he orders, arching an eyebrow when I don't answer immediately.

"I understand."

Entering my house, I find Duncan hunched over the photos of the symbols spread on the dining table. Zee has leaned a whiteboard against the wall and listed 'the five' and, in a separate section, my abilities. Aaden is lying on the sofa, a picture of the Jar on his laptop screen.

I make myself useful by preparing lunch. The cupboards and refrigerator are fully stocked with the shopping Uncle Charlie must have left.

"Hey, guys, what do you want to eat?" I shout.

Zee is the first to answer. "A sandwich would be good."

"What kind?"

"Surprise me!"

"Duncan? Aaden?" I enquire.

"Same," they reply in unison. Now I can't cook, but I make a mean sandwich—it's a food done in layers, after all. Deciding on a double ham and cheese piled with lettuce, I brew a pot of coffee and hand the sandwiches out before moving Aaden's legs on the sofa so I can sit next to him. I manage half my sandwich before my stomach clenches, as it continues to recover from my hunger strike.

I tap on the screen. "Is that the Jar I gave to Jed?"

Aaden uses his sleeve to rub the barely visible finger mark I left behind. "No, it's a replica of a jar from ancient Rome."

"What happened to the original?"

"It was lost in the Ancient Roman Era."

"So the original is the one I gave to Jed?"

"I think so."

"Where is the replica now?"

"On display in the Vatican. Duncan is keen to get a look, as the pictures we took of the symbols aren't clear."

"I don't suppose they would loan it to us?"

Aaden misses my sarcastic tone, shaking his head. "Unlikely. We may have to sneak in and hope we can avoid security."

I cheer up instantly. "Oh, goody! I get to use my badass moves avoiding laser beams and such." Aaden rolls his eyes, and Zee chuckles. "What? I like it—it's like an obstacle course."

"One where you might die—again," grumbles Duncan, without looking up from his book.

After returning my dishes to the kitchen and collecting empty plates along the way, I slink up to Duncan, bat my eyelids, and use my sweetest voice. "Can we go tonight? Pretty please?"

He focuses on me. "Okay." *Well, that was easy.*

"Do you want to call Jed?" Aaden asks.

Running my hand through my hair, I sigh. "My gut says yes. But we're looking into an artifact his boss is planning to use. We don't know what it does... so no."

Zee taps me on the shoulder, and when I turn around, he's holding my swords. I cradle them to my chest. "My babies," I croon. I must have left them at the warehouse. "Thank you."

"How grateful are you? Like kiss on the lips? Open mouthed, of course," Zee asks with a cheeky smile and a wink. I give him a peck on the cheek, and he grumbles something about rewards not being in keeping with the prize.

Chapter Thirty-Six

Natia

Tauruses have the willpower and determination to get whatever they want, and they aren't too bothered by rules, either.

Squashed in a van with Duncan, Aaden, and Zee outside the Vatican, I scratch my scalp that's irritated from the wig I wore earlier when Zee and I took a tour to scope out the security. The exhibition's in the most secure part of the building, with multiple security measures and four guards walking on a constant rotation, leaving a two-minute gap when the replica Jar isn't being guarded.

Zee peers at his watch. "1 a.m. It's time."

Aaden feeds the security cameras a false loop, while Duncan teleports Zee into the office next to the exhibition. Zee checks the communication devices.

"Hey, baby, get your leather-clad ass in here so I have something pretty to look at. This place is boring, and Duncan's not my type."

"Communication's working, then," mumbles Aaden, his steel gray eyes hardening. He gets pissed when we don't take his tech seriously.

"See you soon." I nod at Aaden. "If anything happens, abort and go home. If Duncan can't get to you, there are plane tickets. I've sent the details to your email."

He narrows his eyes. "Follow the plan. I'll see you later." Duncan reappears and wraps his arm around my waist. My body gets sucked into the familiar twisting sensation. I've almost gotten used to teleporting—almost. Landing, I stumble and lose my balance, tumbling into Zee's arms.

"I knew you were head over heels for me." I put my finger over Zee's lips and smack him over the head, and he gives me a wicked grin.

"Timing?" I ask Aaden.

"You're a go in thirty seconds."

Counting down, I blow out a breath, causing the stray hairs from my ponytail to lift off my face. On zero, I step silently into the gleaming marble hallway, which leads to the open archway of the exhibition. I click the timer on my watch—two minutes before the security guard does another sweep. The Jar is located at the back of the room, encased in glass.

"Lights off?" I check with Aaden.

"Affirmative. One minute forty-five."

"I wish you wouldn't do that... It puts me under unnecessary pressure."

"One minute forty."

Zee climbs the opulent white and gold wall using special grips. I cringe, hoping he doesn't leave any dirty marks. Snipping wires, he disables the pepper spray meant to flood the room if the pressure sensors on the floor are triggered. It's a separate security measure from the main alarm, and should I trigger it, we don't want our getaway hampered by blinding gas.

Flinging two tethers at the domed ceiling, I jump through the arch and keep the tension tight, avoiding the floor as I'm suspended above the Jar.

"One minute," Aaden helpfully informs us.

I nod to Duncan to remove the glass. He flicks his wrist, and it disappears. Ha, cool. Maybe if we were less altruistic, we could become international thieves.

"Natia, focus," Zee grinds through his teeth.

Humming the *Mission: Impossible* theme, I tilt my head toward the Jar and wink, indicating I'm about to lift it and potentially trigger the silent alarms.

"The guard is power walking, he'll be on you in ten seconds," Aaden urges.

Duncan grabs Zee and disappears.

I swing to the side. One of the tethers loosens, sending me into a spin. My limbs flail. Upside down, I splay my legs against the intricately-carved center of the domed ceiling, and my hands and feet scramble to find purchase on the curved surface.

I feel like Spiderman, or Spiderwoman. Maybe he needs a feminine sidekick? I'd need my own superhero name…

The shadows should conceal me, but if he uses a flashlight, two things could get me in trouble. One, the glass has disappeared from around the Jar. Two, and probably more noticeable, there's a woman dangling upside down from the ceiling.

Footsteps stop in the archway, and a flashlight swings through the room like a lighthouse signal. He doesn't change the angle and misses me completely. He updates his superior in Italian—finally, the moment when my many hours of language tuition pays off other than ordering nice food.

"Sector two, clear. It must have been the breeze again that caused the change in pressure." I almost sigh in relief, until he follows up with, "Yes, sir. I'll stay a few minutes to make sure."

I stifle a groan as the light swings through the room again, still missing me. For the next two minutes, the guard's relaxed breathing becomes a ticking clock, as sweat forms on my face and my hands become slick.

"All clear, sir. Moving on," the deep voice reports. He keeps talking, but it soon becomes distant. Duncan and Zee appear. It takes a few seconds for them to spot me. Zee tilts his head, looking at my ridiculous position, and smirks. He mouths, "One, nil." I roll my eyes and peel myself from the ceiling.

Using only one tether requires balance and coordination. Luckily, I have both.

Lowering myself to the Jar, I take the disc weight from my pocket that we hope will keep the same pressure on the mat's sensor. Lifting the Jar, I replace it with the weight almost simultaneously and wait a few seconds.

"Triggered. Plan B. You have company in thirty seconds," Aaden utters. Releasing the tether, I drop to the floor and follow Zee and Duncan, who are already running toward the panic room Duncan opened earlier. Piling in, we shut the door. The last place they would look is the Pope's panic room.

"Can you teleport us out?" I ask Duncan.

"No. As expected, the wards went up the moment you triggered the sensor."

"Who wants top bunk?" Zee asks, wiggling his eyebrows at me as he leans on the bunkbeds.

"You take it," I offer.

"Hmm, I suppose I've always wanted you underneath me," he jokes. A look of unease crosses his features seconds later.

I walk over and hug him. "Stay as you are, Zee. I need normal. I need the teasing and the games." I stare up at him as his arms wrap around me.

"So, you want to sleep in the top bunk, too? It'll be a snug fit, but I'm okay with spooning."

Planting a kiss on his cheek, he rewards me with a grumble about him not kidding.

I retrieve the Jar from the table and twist it around, staring at the tiny symbols. "It certainly looks the same." I pass it to Duncan. "Can you decipher them?"

Duncan pulls a pair of glasses out of his inside pocket and perches them on his nose. I blink, as Zee cracks up. Hopefully, this room is soundproof. "Since when do you wear glasses?" I ask, dumbfounded.

"Since I need to read symbols written in size three font," he mutters, turning the Jar around.

"Hogwarts called, you got the job," Zee sniggers.

Duncan ignores us, engrossed in his symbols. After a few minutes, he releases a heavy sigh. "They aren't the same as the original. I need my books."

"Harry wouldn't need his books—you have Ron and Hermione, you should be able to figure this out," Zee chuckles, trying and failing to keep his face straight.

Duncan frowns and glances up at him. "What are you talking about?"

"Harry Potter," I explain.

"How can you not know about Harry Potter—you're a certified wizard who watches every supernatural series, both new and old!" Zee scoffs.

He rolls his eyes. "Harry Potter is a kid thing, isn't it?" Oh, poor Duncan... He's missed out on an epic part of literature history because he thinks he's too old. "And I'm a warlock, not a wizard."

"What's the difference?" Zee asks, furrowing his eyebrows.

"Caliber."

Zee snorts. "Oh, so it's magical snobbery?"

Duncan sighs, runs a hand through his hair, and changes the subject. "I guess we have time to go over our findings so far."

"Did you get any further yesterday?" I ask.

Zee nods. "The symbols from the cave indicate that the five protectors are protecting the owner, which is Pan, rather than the Jar."

"Wow, that changes things."

Duncan takes over. "Indeed. They have different roles: a protector, a warrior, an illuminator, a father, and a harmonizer. There are two possibilities. Archan and his men, or it could be us."

"Gut feeling?" I ask.

"Us," they say in unison.

I sit at the small table. "Why us?"

Zee answers, "Mainly because of you. The demon warned the warrior to stay away. You've come into your powers as if something was dormant and has awoken, ready to protect."

I think back to the message left on Mary Conway's wrist. "It wasn't really a warning." I stare at the Jar. "The symbols said, 'Death will follow the female warrior.' It's more of a message than a warning. What if we misinterpreted it?"

"Nothing new there," Zee mutters.

"What if it means that death will follow if I fail?"

Duncan leans on his elbows, looking tired. "Like a book, you can't read a paragraph in the middle and expect to understand the story or the context. Without having it all, it's a best guess situation."

"So, if I'm the warrior… who are you?" I ask.

"We think Zee is the protector, I'm the harmonizer, Aaden is the illuminator, and Charlie is the father," Duncan lists.

"We need to find Pan," I point out, drumming my fingers on the table. I can't shake the feeling something doesn't fit.

Zee drops into the chair next to me as I turn the Jar around in my hands, as if doing so will compel it to reveal its secrets. "Back at the diner, Archan said the Jar would help locate Pan, so what's the hold up? Or has Pan already been found?" Zee proposes.

"Didn't you find it odd that Archan and his men found it 'difficult' to apprehend Khalkaroth in the warehouse?" Duncan asks.

I frown, thinking of his instruction to capture, not kill. "He was waiting for Pan," I conclude.

"Makes more sense than them struggling with one demon," Zee says.

I turn the Jar upside down to find the star-shaped indentation, identical to the original. The one my star most likely fits into… Something stops me from telling Duncan and Zee. Keeping back something this important feels strange, but for some reason, I just can't bring myself to say anything.

Duncan spots me examining the bottom and steps behind me for a better look. "Looks like something should fit into the mark, like a key. I wonder if that's how it's opened. Not that it should ever be opened, if the symbols from the cave are to be believed."

"What do you mean?" I probe.

"They describe an evil like no other—the last evil to be unleashed," Duncan mentions absently, as if he isn't discussing the end of the world in nondescript, scary terms.

"The Renevate demon said something about 'the last evil...'" I remember.

"I know. Everything points to the Jar containing something nasty." Zee shivers.

I scratch the back of my neck. "Doesn't explain why Archan wants Pan dead."

I put the Jar down, ignoring Duncan's musings over the key and the threat it poses. "I've been meaning to ask—when teleporting, how do you know where to land? You never land on a person or a table... or *in* a table. I bet that would hurt."

"It's one of the mysteries of the universe," Duncan answers.

My mouth drops open. "Oh, no you don't! It's a mystery you can solve right now, so spill your secrets." He grins as he stares down at me. "Zee, hold him."

Zee wraps his arms around Duncan from behind, and I raise my hands so they're just above his hips. "I won't go easy. Tell me now, and this can stop before it even starts."

Duncan smirks. "Do your worst, Locks."

I dig my fingers into his ribs and tickle him; he tries to bend over, but Zee's stronger. I stop after a minute to let him catch his breath. "Surrender now! Resistance is futile."

He shakes his head. I go back in for another tickle.

"Stop, stop, I give in!" he gasps.

"Spill it, Dumbledore!" Zee shouts, in an apparent random Harry Potter obsession.

Duncan rolls his eyes, catching his breath. "When you feel the twist, it's searching for a clear spot, making sure there are no objects—including people—in the way before we land."

Zee releases him. "I guess that makes sense… A bit anticlimactic," I grumble. "Why does your teleporting feel different from Jed and Archan's?"

Duncan's forehead creases. "In what way?"

"It's more like flying through ribbons of color. Smoother, too. I get a sense of peace, rather than going on a fast fairground ride."

Duncan's eyes widen. "It sounds more like moving through dimensions."

"Is that something you can do?"

He shakes his head. "No, Locks, it's not. I've never met anybody who can. It's theorized only gods and higher beings can do that."

I snort. "No wonder Archan's ego is bigger than the entire Avengers' put together. We knew they were different, and now you know someone who has traveled through different dimensions."

"I'm being serious. And if they have bad intentions, I'm not sure what we can do," Duncan mutters grimly.

"He has the Jar, but not Pan. So we find this person first and figure out his intentions—if he's here to unleash the last evil or protect us from it," Zee says.

I make some coffee with supplies I found in the panic room while we mull over the possibility of facing higher beings. In a truly terrifying way, it makes sense. Khalkaroth tried to stab Archan with the Poison of the Gods. The power cloaking Archan is intense and great, and he's able to leash it. The only time I felt it leak was back at HQ, in my bedroom. Other times, it was done intentionally, as warnings. Archan's team all have power, too—not as strong, but stronger than anything I've felt before.

If he found out I was a protector of Pan, would he kill me?

I'm lying on the top bunk with my eyes closed, turning over the possibilities of whom, or what, Archan is, when a hot breath tickles my ear. I slap my hand blindly to the side. "Knock it off, Zee."

"Not Zee, sweet Iris," a seductive, deep voice rumbles.

I shoot up, knocking my head against the ceiling. Duncan and Zee sit at the table with their legs bound to their chairs and arms secured in front of them. Both are gagged. Lawrence, in his handsome human form, sits between them; he points at the only empty seat across from him.

"Come join us, Natia. We need to talk."

I blink. Tensing my muscles, I ready myself for an attack. Lawrence reaches inside his suit jacket pocket and whips out a knife, pressing it against Zee's throat. Anger rolls through me.

"I just want to talk," Lawrence drawls reasonably.

I jump down and slide into the empty seat. I glance at Duncan, wondering how the hell I hadn't noticed them being tied up; he doesn't speak but dramatically rolls his eyes in the back of his head. I screw up my face in confusion. Ah… shields. As I start the opening lyrics of Iron Maiden's "The Number of the Beast," Lawrence laughs.

"I'm flattered, but I'm not quite that high up."

Can everyone read my mind? I shrug. "I thought you were royalty."

He narrows his eyes. "I'm more interested in you."

I put my hand over my mouth and yawn. "Let me guess—you still want to know what I am? Four years, and you still have the same inane question?"

He crosses his ankle over his knee. "No, I know what, and who, you are. I'm here to offer you a deal."

"No, wait, I think I've got it—come and join your evil minions, and I can have everything my heart desires?"

He chuckles. "Not quite. My offer is this—join me, and I will teach you how to use the power you have bubbling away like the apocalypse inside you. I will tell you who you are, your legacy, and your destiny."

"And if I don't?"

His eyes flick between Zee and Duncan. "I'll be merciful and only kill one... your pick. How is Jack, by the way? You survived, but did he? I didn't realize his hostility would erupt in such a... *delicious* way."

Icy fingers prickle my spine, and my shoulders flatten as flashes of Jack's livid face skip across my mind. I keep silent and blank my features.

Lawrence throws his head back and laughs. "He's dead? Oh dear, sweet Iris, killing someone not in their right mind will have consequences for a soul such as your own. He was easy to manipulate—a gentle push here, a harsh word whispered there, and I created the perfect monster."

I blink. "I thought... but the wards."

"You thought what? I wasn't real? Naive girl, your wards won't keep me out." My stomach rolls as the knowledge that Jack wasn't himself when he tried to... I shake my head.

"But he hated me." I glance between Zee and Duncan, who have nothing but understanding in their eyes for the murderer in their midst. I should have known, should have waited for help…

"Don't feel too bad. Jack's need for violence was bubbling below the surface; he just needed a little help enacting it." I've told no one of Lawrence's involvement with my assault. I was certain I had imagined it in some twisted PTSD episode.

Lawrence glances at his watch. "Tick tock, Natia. I don't have all night."

I scan Duncan's face. He shakes his head furiously. "Can I think about it?"

"Of course. It will just cost you one of their lives. But I'm a generous man, so I'll give you a *tiny* bit of information. You are *not* one of the five, Natia."

Without warning, Lawrence slices Zee's throat and disappears.

"You have one week," his disembodied voice echoes.

I clamp my hand over the blood pouring from Zee's throat.

"No, no, no… Don't you dare die on me!" I shout.

Duncan starts making incoherent noises against his gag. Right, he can heal Zee. Letting go of Zee's neck, I grab a kitchen knife and slice through the ropes on Duncan's arms. He grasps the knife and frees his own legs. Spinning back to Zee and slipping in his blood, I shove my hand against his throat and let out a string of curses as Zee's eyes flutter closed.

"Zee, stay the fuck with me!"

Duncan pulls my shaking hand away. The force of Duncan's magic causes me to stumble and grab onto the table for support. I stare at Zee, willing him to wake up. Duncan lifts his hand away, and I see that Zee's neck is knitted together—new, bright red tissue replaces the gushing wound.

"He needs blood," Duncan presses.

"The wards?" I ask.

"Still up, probably will be for a few hours yet."

Zee's pale face shines with a fine layer of sweat. "Can he wait?"

Duncan shakes his head.

"I'm a universal donor." I stand and begin hunting for what I need. Duncan opens kitchen cupboards, banging them shut in frustration.

"Natia." He turns to me with a large first aid kit. We both stare, stunned, at the comprehensive medical kit. Duncan grabs the transfusion tubes and needles.

"Is it weird that the Pope has transfusion gear in his first aid kit?" I ask, sitting next to an increasingly pale Zee. I pull my black, long-sleeve top off and hold my arm out. Duncan swabs the crook of my arm with an ice-cold antiseptic wipe, making me shiver. I turn away as the needle pricks my skin, and he begins the transfusion.

He sets his watch timer for five minutes. "We don't know how fast you're donating, so we need to keep it to the minimum he needs." He places a chocolate bar in front of me and sets about making a cup of sugary coffee. "Eat."

My stomach turns at the thought. I've still not fully recovered my appetite, and the encounter with Lawrence has ruined it completely. I pick at the chocolate, making myself swallow one square at a time. The coffee is far too sweet, but I gulp it down. The last thing we need is for me to pass out. Duncan's watch beeps.

"How are you feeling?" he asks.

I look at Zee—his color is improving. "I'm okay. Keep going."

Duncan takes Zee's pulse from his wrist. "A few more minutes."

I bite my lip. "He's going to be okay?"

Duncan nods. "He'll be fine."

Chapter Thirty-Seven

Natia

Taurus—the most stubborn sign of the zodiac. Congrats.

Several tense hours later, the Vatican opens to the public, and the wards lift. Duncan finds Aaden at the airport and teleports us back. Sitting around my living room, we fill Aaden in on everything that happened.

"Wait, so we get rid of Khalkaroth, and Lawrence turns up?" Aaden clarifies.

"At least they're taking turns," I snort.

Duncan glances up from the book he's reading. "Lawrence is a whole other league. He teleported into a heavily warded building and overpowered me and Zee in seconds. We need a plan."

I look at Zee. "I'm so sorry I—"

Zee grabs my face, his spring green eyes boring into mine. "Don't you dare blame yourself, and don't even think about sacrificing yourself. I'm alive. In fact, I feel good." The rapidly healing, pale pink scar on his neck shines in the sunlight streaming in through the window.

"Lawrence was there when Jack attacked you," Duncan states softly, staring at me with a compassion I don't deserve and definitely can't handle.

Fighting the sob that gets stuck in my chest, I clutch at my heart, as if it's gotten stuck, too. "I thought I'd imagined it. But he was influencing Jack to assault me. It wasn't his fault... Duncan, I killed an innocent man."

"It doesn't exonerate him," Duncan snaps.

"No, but it doesn't exonerate me either."

"You did what you had to."

"I murdered someone. I'm not sure the self-defense excuse flies in heaven."

"You think you're going to hell for that?"

I shrug my shoulders in defeat and change the direction of the conversation. "What about Lawrence declaring I wasn't one of the five?"

Duncan frowns, refusing to tear his eyes away from me. "This conversation isn't finished, Locks. But as for what he said, consider that he could be playing you."

"You have no idea what I've got to do with this?"

Duncan drums his fingers on the book's edge.

I glare at him. "What do you know?"

"It's a work in progress."

I stand and hover over him. "Tell me."

Duncan shakes his head. "Not now. Soon. I'm more than likely wrong. I hope so, anyway," he mutters the last part.

I throw my hands in the air as Duncan sticks his head back in the book.

353

It's amazing how quickly people find their own little spot in a room. After two days, Aaden's butt has made a permanent dent in the sofa, Zee's heels have made imprints on my dining chair, and Duncan's shoes have worn a short path along the carpet from the dining table to the window. Between bouts of training with Duncan and Zee, I make sandwiches, order pizza, and judging by the sounds Duncan makes when I speak, add unhelpful comments about our lack of progress.

Zee's exciting board has gained little insight since we stole from the Vatican. Duncan is going crazy with the conflicting messages the replica Jar is sending compared to the actual Jar and thinks he's translating it wrong. On the third day, Duncan throws his glasses on the table and puts his head in his hands. "I'm struggling with the translation. We need Jed."

I put my arm around him. "My gut says to trust him. Plus, you're right—we do need him." I look at Zee and Aaden. "Do we agree?"

They bob their heads.

I call Jed and put him on speaker phone. "Hey, Smoothie, how'd you like to join our book club?"

"Book club?" He sounds puzzled.

"Exclusive, members only. Snacks provided."

He sighs. "Your house?"

"Yep."

"What time?"

"Started ten minutes ago, you missed pledges."

Two seconds later, he appears in the kitchen and begins rummaging in my fridge. I roll my eyes as he gets every ingredient he can find to make a sandwich.

"What? I need refreshments if I'm joining."

"Same rules as last time—the promise still holds," I remind him.

He exhales dramatically, in a move sure to put any self-respecting teen to shame. "Okay."

Sandwich made, he joins us at the dining table and almost chokes when he sees the Jar. "How?"

I pat his hand and grin wolfishly. "We haven't stolen from you. This is a replica we stole from the Vatican."

He raises his eyebrows. "I'm not sure that's any better," he mumbles, picking up the Jar. "It's an excellent replica... but the symbols are slightly different. Not much, but it'll change the meaning."

I bat my eyelids. "We know. But we still want to know what it says, so we need help to interpret it."

"Is there something in particular I'm looking for? It helps if it's in context," he adds, slurping a smoothie—huh, ironic.

"So, we've figured out there are five protectors." Jed nods. "You already knew that?" He shrugs and stuffs part of his sandwich in his mouth. "We've figured out from the cave symbols that they are protecting Pan, not the Jar." The silver in his aura flares. Ah, finally—something he doesn't know.

"Where does it say that?"

Duncan shoves the relevant photos at him. He spins them around and goes silent. I grab the photo with the bright pink asterisk on it—it coordinates with Zee's board. I wonder if he was one of those kids with thousands of different highlighters and colored pens at school... I tap the photo. "We believe this warns of the last evil residing in the Jar and of mankind's destruction should it be released."

He grabs the photo and blindly puts his sandwich down, missing the plate and leaving a mess on my dining table. His mouth hangs open. "The problem is your Jar—the original—says the opposite and encourages us to open the Jar. But we think the cave and the replica disagree."

Jed nods and scoops up his abandoned sandwich. "What do you want from me?"

Duncan shoves the Jar back at him. "I want to know if what I've interpreted from the replica is correct, and we need help figuring out what is true with three sources of information—two of which suggest opening that Jar will be a disaster, while the Jar itself says go for it."

"You're forgetting the manuscripts. They clearly point to Pan being a problem and the Jar being a good thing," Jed adds.

Duncan huffs and unfolds some large books. "I've not forgotten—I just can't make sense of it. The Dead Sea Scrolls and Codex Sinaiticus don't talk about any prophecies like this, and the symbols on the Jar and the wall aren't in the same language." Jed grabs one of the books, and his eyebrows shoot up. "Copies—accurate ones," Duncan explains.

Jed skims through the largest one, landing on a page near the center. "These aren't in the same language because they weren't written at the same time, and your historians haven't quite learned to decipher the hidden text in these documents. I'll show you how to look for the prophecy and how it matches what we believe."

"What language is in the cave, then?" I ask.

Jed sighs. "It's a lost language, an ancient one. But like most languages, it shares traits with others—enough that it can be deciphered."

"So you'll help us understand what the replica Jar says and how it links?"

Jed nods. "How are you dealing with your powers?"

"Better—I'm not setting random things on fire now. But I still manage to drench Zee every time I reach for water."

"Are you sure that's by accident?" he chuckles, a smile tugging at his lips.

"I'm not," Zee mutters.

Staring at Zee, Jed points at his own neck. "What happened?"

"Walked into a clothes line." Zee covers the scar with his hand.

Jed raises his eyebrows. "In December?"

Zee makes a noncommittal noise and grabs my hand. "Come on, let's get practicing."

"Air today!" Duncan shouts as we step outside.

Zee groans. "Are you joking? I've been knocked on my ass enough this week, plus you know that scary thing she does with the trees…"

"Give her a physical workout, too," Duncan adds, amused.

Zee grins slowly at me. "Payback, baby."

Four hours later, we drag ourselves into the house. Zee's drenched and sports several scorch marks on his combat trousers and long-sleeve top. I'm limping and holding my ribs.

Duncan, Jed, and Aaden stare at us. "Don't ask," I mutter on the way to the shower. Zee grunts something similar behind me and goes to the bathroom.

Showered and redressed in jeans and a pale blue V-neck sweater, I sit on Jed's knee dissecting a piece of raspberry cheesecake, as there aren't enough chairs—much to Zee's disappointment.

Jed's notes are strewn in front of me. I point to where he's written "Pan" and a few symbols. "What does this mean?"

He peers over my shoulder and taps his fingers on the table. "It refers to the owner as an ancient, which you already knew."

I put my hand over his to stop him. "You do that when you're hiding something."

He shakes his head. "I'm confused."

I stare into his hazel eyes. "Explain."

He leans back in his chair, putting distance between us.

"This says that—that Pan is the *hope* for mankind and protects the Jar. It's definitely not the same inscription on the real Jar. I'd like Nathan to have a look."

"No," Duncan and I say.

Jed brings his arms around me and searches my face. "Release me from the promise, Natia."

"What's with the 'release' thing? Most people would just break it if they felt that strongly."

"You have bound me. I literally can't talk about anything said here."

"Oh, I didn't realize... is that because of my powers?" He shakes his head, as Duncan makes a noncommittal noise of frustration. I snap my head toward him. "What?"

Duncan and Jed have a silent stare off, where I wonder if they're telepathically communicating. Duncan's eyes widen slightly as he looks away. "Nothing," he mumbles.

Frowning at Duncan, I put my hands on Jed's face and twist him back to me. "Look, tell me what's so important you need to tell Archan, and I'll consider it."

Jed shakes his head and pulls away, releasing a long breath. "I can't."

My lips tilt down in frustration. "Sorry, Smoothie, it's not that I don't trust you."

He nods, giving me a squeeze.

"So according to this, Pan is benevolent and is protecting mankind. Did you find anything else?" I ask.

"This inscription says Pan is an ancient, but instead of mankind's destruction lying in their hands, this says mankind's *salvation* lies in it. It describes how they're awakened when mankind is in crisis, and they're here to restore the balance, rather than tip it," Jed explains, burying his head in my shoulder.

I rub his arms, trying to soothe whatever internal struggle he's going through. "We already knew about Pan being an ancient, and the last part lines up with the symbols from the cave. As for salvation lying in his hands, we did debate the double meaning. This suggests he's mankind's hope."

Jed tightens his arms around me and mumbles into my hair, "Fuck, you need to let me out of this promise. This needs to be discussed with Archan. Now."

"So you can kill Pan?" I ask quietly.

He lifts his head, gives me a gentle shove, and stands. I almost flop to the floor, but Duncan catches me. Jed looks at me with hurt, disappointment, and resolve before he disappears.

I blink. "What the hell?"

Zee shrugs. "I think you hurt his feelings."

"Maybe… but he looked determined," I mutter. Something occurs to me.

"Hide the research and the Jar—now!" I urge. "I think we're about to have visitors."

Just as Duncan returns from my bedroom, where he's hidden the Jar in my safe, Archan, Barney, Nathan, and Jed appear. With Zee, Duncan, and Aaden, the testosterone is palpable, and there's about four square feet left in the room. Jed scans the table, looking for the research. His eyes harden. *That's right, nothing to see here.*

As I wind my way through them, I whisper into Jed's ear, "You're out of the book club." He stiffens.

I put the coffee pot on. "You should've called ahead, I could've made lunch. I can offer you coffee and snacks." Grabbing some chips, I pour them into a large glass bowl. Archan prowls toward me, and I open our mental link. Let's see if I can coax him into my storm. He'll either splay his emotions raw, like mine, or he'll retreat to what he knows and hide behind a seductive aura built to break others and shield himself.

"I appreciate everything you've done for me, and I'll never be able to repay your kindness. But I know you. I know you still consider me something to conquer and own. And you told me love is something you can't—or won't—offer. Nothing has changed between us."

He examines my face closely, no doubt taking note of the dark circles under my eyes. *"Everything has changed. We need to talk about this."*

"Do we? For my sanity, stay away from me. I'm trying to be pleasant. Don't ruin it."

He takes a seat at the breakfast bar. I drop the mental link before he can answer and block the pull as he tries back. I've delivered my warning. The rest is up to him.

Chapter Thirty-Eight

Archan

Unknown origin.

"I'm not making you an omelet," she spits, ever defiant. Several of the men turn and raise their eyebrows.

I drag the large bowl of chips toward me. "I have been told you're good at sandwiches."

Zee snorts, and she shoots him a hard look. It will take very little to make her pissed enough to challenge me. Jed says she has gained good control over her power, even when provoked. I doubt that will apply to me. I think of the ruined practice room and meet her furious gaze—after seeing what she's capable of, she's proven control isn't one of her strengths.

She grins at me, all teeth. "I am."

I send a caress of warmth over the back of her neck. She leans into it then scowls at me. "You knock that shit off right now."

"Our understanding is over; that includes all terms." I take a chip from the bowl.

She leans over the counter toward me. "Don't push me, Reinheart... You won't like what happens."

She's stunning, particularly when she's angry. Her turquoise eyes glimmer with a certain wildness. I lean toward her, imitating her actions, so her soft lips are inches from mine. She needs to release the anger and hurt—toward me, the others, and herself. Then maybe we can move on. Talking isn't going to cut it. So I provoke her. "Is that so?"

She retrieves the milk and sugar and places them next to the coffee. Maybe I played this wrong? "Excuse me, gentlemen. I have something that needs putting in its place. Please help yourself to the milk and sugar." She points at me. "You. Outside. Now." No, the woman definitely has some issues to work through.

She stalks out the door. I teleport outside, standing in front of her, and she almost walks into me.

She balls her hands up. "Move."

My hands twitch with the need to fist her hair and pull her head back to kiss her so deeply, she knows she's mine. She's clinging to anger in hope it will save her from me. She was mine the moment she chose to trust me with her vulnerability, the second she put her hand on my face and let me see inside her soul, the minute she held me tight to help her through her nightmares. Instead, I step aside and glance up—ah, we have an audience. The men have come outside, each holding a mug of coffee; they begin to pass the bowl of chips around.

Natia stalks through the waist-high fence out of her garden and onto the lawns of her grandfather's mansion, passing several scorch marks. This should be interesting.

Putting a fair distance between us, she turns and glares at me. "Last chance, Reinheart. Knock the seduction off."

She doesn't realize it, but this is foreplay. Instead of answering, I run heat along the inside of her thighs. Without warning, a gust of air I would estimate at a hundred miles per hour knocks me off my feet and pins me to the ground. Ice cold water materializes in a bubble and is unceremoniously dumped on me.

362

Jumping to my feet, I wipe the water out of my eyes and laugh. "You have been practicing." The ground rumbles open and drops me into a ten-foot-deep hole. She creates a cyclone around me, pinning my hands to my sides, or at least, that's what she thinks. The heat caresses under her breasts. Furious aquamarine eyes flash as she adds water to the cyclone, freezing it around me and locking me in a block of ice. I'm mesmerized by those eyes. Each element has taken on its own identity.

"You *don't* get to touch me. You tried handing me off to a fucking demon in front of people I love. I'm not a toy to be passed around, someone to manipulate to your advantage. You're a selfish bully with a clear agenda to own me, and your ego has probably convinced you that you already do. Well, be damn sure I was never yours, and I never will be. Find someone else, someone who's willing to bow down to the great and mighty Archan Reinheart."

I almost laugh. She was mine the second she stepped on that roof and challenged me. She just needs a tiny push to get to the bottom of this anger she keeps falsely directing at me. Cracking the ice, I teleport out of the hole and dust a piece of invisible lint from my dark jeans. I arch an eyebrow. "Is that the best you've got, baby?"

She growls. The branches of the ancient oak tree behind her twist around, making it groan loudly. She releases the tree, and large branches splinter and launch themselves at me as it spins back into place. I sidestep each one. Her eyes flash silver as a bolt of lightning strikes about five meters from me, then another, then another. Two mini tornados touch down and whip the air around us.

"Shit, that's one powerful, pissed off witch!" Barney shouts over the howling winds.

Nathan laughs. "This is better than any reality show."

"Pass the chips!" Jed yells.

I cross my arms and watch her cheeks flush with fury. They are right—she is far more powerful than I realized.

"You know the truth, Natia. The things I said in the warehouse were to save you. I was scared." I drop my arms then run a hand through my hair before exposing how I feel. "For the first time in a long time, Natia, I was scared of losing someone. I was scared of losing you."

She blinks, and her hands pause midair in whatever destruction she was about to unleash. "You can't lose what you never had. But say I accept that—not more than twenty-four hours before, you rejected me. The second I gave into your relentless pursuit, you were no longer interested. I let you in, and you destroyed any trust I had in you."

"Again, you know the truth. I might be ruthless—but I will not take advantage of a frightened woman. And you were frightened, Natia. I want you more than I've ever wanted someone, but your world was and is spinning off its axis. Every day challenges your beliefs and morals. The universe isn't as black and white as you want it to be—good people do bad things, and for good reasons. It wasn't your fault, Natia. Let it go."

She screams, as the sky flashes white and a powerful roll of thunder shakes the ground. Gold lightning streaks her irises—the same eyes I saw when she fought the Eitr poison. She lifts her hands, power rolling off her, and I brace myself, not sure where this is going. She whispers something under her breath. It sounds like the ancient language; apart from the symbols on the Jar, she shouldn't even know it exists, never mind speak it. An eight-foot coil of blue fire surrounds me. Symbols appear in the air above me and on the ground beneath my feet. I try teleporting, but she's trapped me. I study the symbols carefully; she's trying to banish me, but it won't work. However, the results will be far from pleasant. "Natia, stop. You're powerful, a tempest ready to destroy the world, but you have to breathe—don't go down with your own storm."

She doesn't hear me. Nathan and Barney surround the circle, trying to see a way through, while Jed and Duncan attempt to talk Natia down. Duncan places a hand on her shoulder, only to be thrown a hundred feet back by an electric shock.

I pull on the thread to her mind, and mercifully, she lets me in.

"Listen to me. Everything I have done is for you, to protect, to heal, and to save you."

"You hurt me. I trusted you, and you hurt me."

The pain in her voice is raw; she's holding me up to an unfair standard, putting me on a pedestal so she can easily knock me off and away from her heart. She has been let down by people she loves in ways she doesn't understand. She thinks she abandoned those she loved in grief, when they abandoned her just as much. She reasons the idiot boy was within his rights to betray her because she was following her dream. She's convinced herself her attacker deserved mercy and she's damned her soul. She cripples herself with guilt, and I'm the first person she's held responsible for her pain to protect herself. Not one of these people has asked for her forgiveness, admitted their part in her pain.

I catch her eyes. *"I know. Forgive me."*

A sob erupts from her throat as the flames drop, scorching the ground, and the symbols disappear. Jed puts his hand on her arm, but she shrugs him off and storms into her house, leaving the door open.

Barney looks frantic. "Fuck, she was going to try—"

I interrupt him, "It's fine, Barney. It served its purpose."

Nathan runs a hand through his hair. "Did you see her eyes? I know they change, but what the hell was the gold about? Is it the Eitr?"

"I suspect so. I need to go to her."

They look at me like I've gone insane. I teleport to her bedroom, where she's standing with her hands on her hips. Without warning, she pins me against the wall, flattening her body against mine, and wraps her hand in my hair, tugging my head down. Dangerous turquoise and gold eyes challenge me, cosmic power brimming just below the surface.

"If it was truly lies, you're sorry, and you're willing to change… prove it," she whispers.

I lift her up, and she wraps her legs around me as I reverse our positions. I brush my lips against hers. She keeps still, not reacting. I run my tongue along her bottom lip before pulling at the delicate flesh with my teeth. As she parts her lips, I tease her tongue with my own.

Still, she doesn't move.

Pressing my body against hers, I pin her in place and fist her hair, pulling her head back. Nuzzling her exposed neck, I place kisses along her soft skin and nip lightly. She jolts as her heart beats faster against my chest, and I feel her gathering heat against my cock. She's so responsive, yet her eyes remain open in challenge. Those eyes— fuck, they are captivating.

I dominate her mouth until she gives in. Small hands glide under my T-shirt, the fabric abrasive in contrast to the softness of her fingertips. It lands on the floor with a light thump. My muscles tense and flex under her exploration. Leaning forward, she grazes her tongue over my nipple, biting it lightly. I groan at the delicious jolt of pain.

I grip her throat and kiss her. "My turn." I push up her sweater, exposing her gorgeous breasts encased in deep red silk. I pause just above her head and wrap the sweater around her arms, locking them in place. I take in her beautiful body, each curve perfect. Pushing down the cups of her bra with my free hand, I take a nipple between my teeth, applying pressure until she gasps then moans as I pull back, grazing it. I bathe the tender flesh with my tongue then repeat with the other breast, until she begins squirming and arches her back off the wall.

"Forgiven me yet?" I whisper against her ear.

She shivers. "Nope."

I chuckle and pull back. "What do you want?"

Lust-filled azure eyes blink at me in confusion, as if nobody has ever asked her.

"You," she finally answers.

"How?" Silence. "Do you want me fast and hard against this wall? Do you want me soft and slow on the bed? Do you want to be pinned under me, or riding my cock?" She blushes a beautiful shade of pink.

Dropping her legs and unbuttoning her jeans with my free hand, I cup her pussy, finding her hot and drenched. I groan. "You're on fire for me."

She struggles against the hold I have on her arms. I let go and throw her sweater across the floor. In a swift move, she pulls my hand from her jeans and grabs my other hand, placing them behind my back.

A wicked smile curves her lips as she walks me backward to the bed. "Don't move," she mutters. Curious, I leave my hands behind my back as she pushes me down.

She makes short work of my shoes and jeans then straddles my lap, growling a warning when I try to cup her ass. She presses her slight weight against me, encouraging me to lay flat. Her lips trace the tattoos on my chest, nipping to give that slight bite of pain she's figured out I like. Running her fingers over my head, she scratches my scalp then grasps my hair, holding me in place as teasing, tiny kisses rain down on my lips. When I try deepening the kiss, she moves away, holding my hair and preventing me from chasing her.

"I'll only entertain this for so long."

"Patience is a virtue, Archan."

She gives me a devastatingly sexy smile before continuing to drive me wild with her mouth on my skin—neck, chest, then lower on my stomach. A brief glide of her hand on my cock over the fabric of my underwear has me groaning. She cups my balls and applies a small amount of pressure. I grab her wrists and drag her up to kiss her.

She pulls back, her eyes full of lust and satisfaction.

"We need to stop," she breathes.

"What?" I ask, confused.

"You've had a harrowing experience. A newbie witch nearly banished you. I wouldn't want to take advantage of you in your vulnerable state. *Ask me* when you're feeling better," she utters, placing a chaste kiss on my forehead.

Climbing off me, she redresses. She's scrambling for control, a way to take the reins, and revenge, which is punishing the both of us. I rub my hands over my face then reach out and grab her arms. "You've made your point. Take your clothes off."

"No, honey, you need time." She pats my arm.

I sit up and drag her between my legs. "I'm not claiming to be a nice man. I'm not. But I will protect you and I do want you. I want to do wicked and sinful things to you. I will give your fantasies life, and give life to fantasies you never knew you wanted. If you trust me with your desires, I will make you forget your name, but scream mine. Every inch of your body will crave my touch. You will come on my cock more times than you can take, and when you're lying on my bed, a beautiful, quivering mess, I will make you take more. I can be that darkness you crave and the oblivion you need. I won't hurt you, Natia. You just need to surrender to everything I can give you."

She freezes and stares at me with an unreadable expression. I'm almost holding my breath waiting for her answer. When she doesn't speak, I add one more thing, which I immediately realize is a mistake. "You only need ask, Natia."

She narrows her eyes and pushes back from me, fastening her jeans and banishing any chance of me having her here tonight. "Is there anything else you came for?"

I want to kick my own balls. Defeated, I dress and allow her change in conversation. Because there is something we came here for, except I don't know what—Jed's garbled instructions led us here for a reason. "Jed suggested I visit you and we should make it a group reunion. I'm assuming by his strange request you have bound him to a promise he is trying to get around."

"We've both bound him. He's struggling with some sort of dilemma. Since he won't share your intentions, I assume you have locked him in a similar deal."

Tying my shoes, I bristle. "My men are not bound—they're loyal."

She hands me a hairbrush. "So are mine, but Jed works for you. Let him tell me what's bothering him so much."

I look at myself in the mirror, smiling at my mussed hair. I toss the brush on the bed without using it. "No, you release him."

"Not a chance." She grins at me. "Guess we're at an impasse."

"I guess we are… with the information, anyway. Whether you realize it or not, you have brought me to my knees."

She pulls back and avoids my gaze. Staring at the floor, she redoes her braid.

"I don't have time for this now," she whispers.

"Avoiding your feelings, Natia?" She stumbles as I pull her back and kiss her. Surprising me, she wraps her hands around my nape and deepens the kiss, pouring every emotion she feels into me: passion, hurt, excitement, loss, lust, devastation, grief, and hope. It's like riding a storm on the rolling sea: breathtaking, uplifting, devastating. It doesn't just chase the lingering numbness of time, it decimates it. Panting, she breaks the kiss, leaving me bereft and starving for the light she just forced into my soul. I squeeze her waist and rest my forehead against hers.

"What was that?" I mutter, locking eyes with her hypnotic gaze.

She blinks up at me and runs a thumb over my jaw. "That is what you're missing out on. That is what you refuse to acknowledge as magnificent. That is just a taste of what having my love feels like." She swivels and stalks out of the bedroom, then tosses over her shoulder, "Avoiding your feelings, Archan?"

Chapter Thirty-Nine

Natia

You win a Taurus's trust through actions, not words.

Six hulking male specimens perch in various spots around my compact living space. "I hope you were suitably entertained," I drawl, fisting my shaking hands at my sides. I just revealed how I felt to the unknown creature lurking in my bedroom. It's either a colossal mistake or an ingenious move; only time will tell.

Barney jumps to his feet and heads toward Archan, who's followed me from the bedroom, fully dressed, thank god. But he's left his hair uncombed, announcing to the world what we'd been doing, or what we'd been about to do. I'm human, not a saint—it took every bit of my willpower to back away from him.

"They have more information on the symbols," Barney informs him.

Archan raises an eyebrow. "I see. And when were you going to share this information?"

I lean back against the kitchen counter. "I wasn't."

"We agreed you would share any information—"

I cut him off. "As you recently pointed out, the deal's over. I'm no longer obligated to share everything with you."

His eyes harden. "You don't realize the seriousness of the situation."

I study my nails, scraping dirt from underneath one. "Actually, I've finally realized the seriousness of it for the first time since we met."

"Then you know we need this information."

"I've figured out you *want* this information, and something I've found must be important. We agree to share, or you can go home."

He pauses with a slight tilt of his head. Barney and Nathan do the same thing. I smirk.

"What's the consensus with your team?" He frowns, and I point to my head in answer. "I told you—you tilt your head."

He glowers at me. "Are you going to share everything you know?"

Staring at Archan, I keep my head perfectly still and initiate my mental link with Duncan.

"What do you think?" I enquire.

"Jed's so determined, it would be prudent to share some information. I don't sense any malice from Archan or his team."

I glance at Barney, Nathan, and Jed, paying attention to their auras. While weirdly beautiful and hypnotic with their various metallic shades, none of them radiate anything negative. *"We stick with our theory of me being the warrior... if they ask. Let them do most of the talking. It helps that Zac isn't here."*

"Agreed."

"We'll share whatever has Jed in such a state then take it from there. Let's sit." I wave my arm toward the living area. I head to the window seat, but Jed wraps his arms around me and drags me onto his lap on the sofa.

"Thank you for trusting me," he whispers.

Archan growls, and large muscular hands lift me out of Jed's arms. I smack at Archan's chest. "Don't manhandle me! I don't want to sit on anybody while we have this conversation." He sets me down on

372

the chair vacated by Barney and perches on the side, wrapping his arm around the back. It's the best I can hope for.

I nod at Jed. "Okay, start."

"You need to release me," Jed begins.

I frown. "Okay, I release you from the promise. You may tell Archan anything you've learned while you've been with us."

Jed sighs, as if a great weight has been lifted. "We need the other Jar."

I blink. "Why?"

Archan looks between us. "What other Jar?"

I nudge my elbow into his side. "This is going to be a long night if you don't let us speak."

"It needs to be fully deciphered, and Nathan needs to view it, to see if he agrees with my interpretation so far."

I jerk my chin at Zee. His green eyes darken, obviously unhappy, but he gets up and heads to my bedroom. Jed opens his mouth to explain, but Barney cuts him off. "Wait, Zac will be here in three, two…" Zac appears in the kitchen and looks around the room.

"Wonderful, my day is now complete," I mutter, glancing at Duncan. Our chances of hiding any information just diminished. He strides over to the side door and leans his back against it, placing a foot on the bottom.

I cock my head; as if he could stop me from leaving. He stares back at me with a stony expression. Zee appears with the Jar, rolls his eyes when he sees Zac, and hands it to me, reseating himself next to Jed on the sofa.

Archan, Barney, Nathan, and Zac gawk at the Jar. "We didn't steal it from you. It's a replica."

Nathan holds his hand out. "May I?" Reluctantly, I hand it to him.

"Where the hell did you get a replica from?" Zac demands.

I glance at the floor. "We stole it from the Vatican."

Barney chokes on a laugh. "You're kidding? So you *did* steal it."

I flick my hand. "Technicalities."

"It's not the same," Nathan mumbles, turning the Jar in his palm.

"I know, but we thought it prudent to decipher it anyway."

"Hmm… it's only certain symbols, but the meaning will change significantly. I don't see the point of deciphering it if it's not the same," Nathan finishes, placing the Jar in Archan's outstretched hand.

I twist my hands in my lap. "We need to go back to the beginning. On the island, there were symbols on the walls of the cave written in the same language as the Jar." The room falls completely silent. I take a deep breath. "We found information from those symbols that Jed thinks is important. Then when he saw the Jar, he became more insistent we tell you. So here we are."

All eyes swing to Jed. "The symbols in the cave talk about the five protectors," he slants a look at Archan, "which we already knew, but Duncan and Zee identified the different roles: a protector, a warrior, an illuminator, a father, and a harmonizer. They haven't said as much, but I believe they think they're the protectors."

I glare at Jed. "I didn't say anything about making conclusions, and given you have the real Jar, we assumed you think *you're* the protectors."

Jed shrugs. "Anyway, the symbols in the cave and on the replica Jar indicate the protectors are for Pan, as opposed to the Jar itself."

Zac groans. "I fucking hate double meanings."

I laugh. "Pity we don't have an 'ancient' to help decipher these symbols more thoroughly. Oh wait, we do." I glare at Archan.

Jed sighs. "Hey, you two, let me finish before you start the fireworks. My big concern is the symbols on the wall and on the replica Jar both say Pan holds mankind's salvation in their hands, that they're awakened when mankind is in crisis and are here to restore the balance."

Archan's eyes are glued to me. I quirk an eyebrow. "What?"

He glances at the Jar in his hands. "Are you drawn to the Jars, Natia?"

I frown. "No, I'm driven to figure out what's going on, and I'm trusting you're on the right side of this."

Zac comes to stand next to Archan, smirking at me. "Is that everything?" Zac asks. I feel a solid push at my shields. I glare at him while quickly reciting "Suspicious Minds."

"Stay the fuck out of my head. I trust you, and you pay me back by trying to break my shields? Oh, and you still have shared nothing."

Archan glares at Zac and asks me, "What do you want to know?"

Putting distance between us, I move to the window seat. "Apart from what you make of everything we've told you, I want to know why you want to kill Pan."

Archan runs a hand through his loose hair. "To stop a prophecy. One where mankind is destroyed."

I glance out the window; the scorch marks from my power are still smoking. "And you still believe that after everything Jed has told you?"

Archan glances at the Jar. "I need to see the symbols from the cave. This replica is different from the original. I take it you feel I shouldn't kill Pan?"

"No, definitely not. Something tells me killing him would have terrible repercussions—did it not concern you that Khalkaroth wanted him dead also?"

Archan and his team do the tiny head tilt. "We believe he was trying to mislead us into doing his bidding. A final attempt to control the fate of the world before you banished him."

I sigh, conceding the possibility. "Also, there's the problem of what's in that little Jar you have. The symbols on the wall and the replica Jar indicate it's the 'last evil.'"

Archan looks at Jed, who nods in agreement. Turning back to me, Archan explains, "There's a prophecy hidden within the Dead Sea Scrolls and the Codex Sinaiticus, where Pan stops mankind from receiving the salvation held in the Jar. If we kill Pan, we can restore balance to the world by opening the Jar."

"What do you believe is in it?"

"Hope."

My jaw drops open as my mind connects the dots. "We're talking about Pandora's box?"

Aaden spits some coffee back into his cup. "As in, 'Pan' is Pandora? We are looking for *Pandora*?"

Zee frowns. "But it's a jar, not a box."

I shake my head. "Common misconception. In the myth, Pandora was the first human woman. Zeus created her to punish man for receiving the stolen gift of fire from Prometheus. He made sure she was irresistible by getting the gods to gift her with beauty and so forth. Then he sent her to Prometheus's brother, who married her. Zeus gave her a jar as a wedding gift but warned her never to open it. However, Pandora had been gifted with curiosity, meaning she couldn't resist; she released the evil it contained upon the world. If I remember rightly, she managed to close the Jar before she released hope—the common interpretation is that she saved hope for mankind. It was a sixteenth century scholar who misinterpreted the text and turned 'jar' into 'box.'"

Zac glowers at me. "You seem very knowledgeable."

I shrug. "I took classical studies."

"Why now?" Aaden queries. All eyes snap to him in confusion, and he flushes under the attention. "I mean, what has caused you to search for Pan now? And why right now, at this point in time, are you seeking to open the Jar?"

Nathan taps a finger on his chin, clearly thinking through his answer. "Pan's power leaves a trace. It's been absent for many years, and until recently, we could barely follow it."

"Also, the prophecies are clear about the timing. It will happen before the end of the year."

I blink. "That gives us a little over a week."

Archan strides over to the window and blocks me in. "This is confusing at best, but in light of this information... I will refrain from killing Pan. For now. But I do still need to find her. Do you know where she is?"

"No. If you believe opening the Jar will save mankind, why don't you just open it?"

"We need Pan, or the key."

My stomach flips as I picture the star-shaped object tucked away in the bottom of my wardrobe. I could end this now—give them what is clearly the key to an object meant to either save or destroy us. I blank my features and recite Taylor Swift's classic advice, "Shake It Off."

Archan narrows his eyes and grips my chin. "What aren't you telling me?"

I pull out of his grasp and scramble for an excuse. "Lawrence found me."

Duncan's eyes go wide, and Archan curses.

I point at Zee. "He tried to kill Zee." Zee tips his head back, showing the faint pink scar.

"He wants me to go with him. He knows about my powers."

Zac narrows his eyes. "He wanted you before your powers. Why?"

I shrug and play dumb. "If you're talking about my kidnapping, he wanted to eat me. I think?"

Zac continues to give me that x-ray stare before rolling his eyes. "I don't buy it," he snarls.

"It's the only answer you're getting. He's given me a week to join him, which was three days ago, then he'll start killing people I love and care for."

Out of nowhere, Jed stands and punches the wall, part of the plaster crumbling underneath his fist. "Why didn't you tell me?!"

I blink at his outburst. "It wasn't important to what's going on here."

"You're right, but it's just as important."

I unfold myself from the window seat, push past Archan, and go to Jed. "You're joking, right? We're talking about mankind's destruction, and you think my life is important in comparison?"

He pauses, his eyes burning as he grasps my face. "I'm not going to say your life's not important, Natia, so if that's what you're wanting to hear, I'm sorry. The Jar and Pan are important, yes, but Lawrence seems to be the most pressing issue here. We can't have half your team dying when we're this close to ending this. And we can't lose you, Natia… ignoring this won't make it disappear." He blushes and turns away.

I throw my hands in the air. "I'm not ignoring the threat. Duncan is looking into banishment circles to see if we can find one strong enough for him."

Archan laughs. "You won't. I've already told you—he's a prince of hell."

I arch an eyebrow. "Really? And the banishment circle I placed you in earlier?"

"Wouldn't have worked."

"You looked worried enough."

He studies me. "You can't banish someone that doesn't belong in hell."

I blink then stare into his golden eyes, sensing his sincerity. "That's reassuring."

"Can I see the symbols from the cave?" Nathan requests, breaking the tension.

"Only if you promise to share anything you decipher."

Nathan nods.

"Sorry, Nathan, I'm a little wiser to this promise deal now. I need you to speak the words."

Nathan stands, stretches, and sighs. "I promise to share anything I decipher from the symbols you give me. Okay?"

I point to the folder on the dining table Zee must have retrieved when he got the Jar. Nathan opens it. He sucks in a breath.

"What?" I enquire.

"When you said *some* symbols, I didn't realize you meant the entire cave."

Archan looks over Nathan's shoulder.

I grab Archan's arm and turn him toward me. "My gut says opening that Jar and killing Pan are bad."

He nods. "I will hold off doing anything until we learn more. But remember, you have a replica, and it could have been planted to confuse us."

I fold my arms across my chest. "I hadn't thought of that."

Archan folds his arms in a mirror pose. "I will hunt down Lawrence and encourage him to leave you alone."

I open my mouth to tell him to keep out of it, but Duncan places his hand on my shoulder. "He's offering to help. Accept it—we need it."

"Thank you," I mutter to Archan.

Grasping my folded arms, he tugs me to him and devastates my mouth with a toe-curling kiss, only pulling away when Barney clears his throat in the universal sign that the PDA is getting more than PG. Archan brushes his lips across my ear. "We aren't finished."

I don't deny it. "I know."

Archan, Jed, Nathan, Barney, and Zac disappear. I take a deep breath. The room instantly feels twice as big, except I'm left with my three friends, whose looks range between concern and skepticism.

"What?" I ask, picking up some dirty cups from the floor.

Duncan shakes his head. "What are you going to do about Archan?"

My eyebrows scrunch together. "I don't know."

"Do you want him?"

Aaden finds his seat on the sofa. "A little direct," he mutters.

"Yes? No? I don't know."

"What did he say to get you to calm down outside?" Zee quizzes.

"Sorry."

Duncan chuckles. "Never underestimate the power of a sincere apology."

"He confuses me."

"He scares you," Duncan mutters.

I rub my temples as Zee collects some more dishes and joins me in the kitchen. "What? Do you have a little 'dissect Natia's emotions' group going on with him?"

Zee chuckles and bumps my arm. "You're not that hard to read. Whatever you want, though, we'll be here for you."

Duncan begins walking around the house, erecting wards to keep prying ears and eyes out. He shares his thoughts in between muttering words I don't understand. "Anyway. The sharing of information went well, I think."

I study his movements, wondering if I can cast wards. "At least they've agreed to hold off acting on the Jar and Pan."

Aaden glances up from his laptop. "Do you trust them?"

Drumming my fingers on the kitchen countertop, I nod. "Yes, their intentions are good, but Archan's right—the replica Jar is different and might be there to confuse and mislead."

In a moment of pure domestication, Zee reorganizes the dishwasher to fit every last dish in and offers it a smug smile like he's achieved something worthy of a Mensa Prize. "You honestly think a set of potential gods has it wrong?"

Aaden looks baffled. "Gods?"

"Duncan believes they're some kind of all-powerful beings, maybe gods, because of the way they teleport. It's a long story... Duncan will fill you in."

I put my head in my hands. "I'm back to being confused. One, are we really dealing with gods? Two, who the hell am I, if I'm not one of the protectors? Three, Pandora—really? Argh! This hurts my tiny brain."

Zee rubs the top of my head. "Your brain isn't tiny. But you refuse to go out with me, so I guess I do have to question your intelligence."

I glare at him. "Are you suddenly interested in testicular reconstructive surgery?"

He barks out a laugh just as a light and airy familiar voice floats just outside the house. A gentle knock echoes around the room—all the guys freeze and stare at the door like hellhounds have come for our souls, and not my stylist here to prep me for tomorrow.

"Come in!" I yell.

A short, plump lady in her sixties appears, carrying a number of garment bags. "Hey, Nat! I'm here with your dress choices to make you gorgeous…" She stops when she sees the guys, her eyes growing wide.

"She's already gorgeous," Zee mutters.

"Hi, Mary. This is Duncan, Zee, and Aaden, my colleagues."

She composes herself. "Oh, I see. Should I pop these in your bedroom?"

"Sure, I'll be along in a few minutes."

I sigh and stare up at the ceiling. Damn! I completely forgot the Christmas ball is tomorrow night. Duncan clears his throat, gathering my attention. All of the guys are staring at me with their mouths slightly open. "Umm, are we missing something here, Natia?"

I groan. "I promised my grandfather I would attend the Christmas ball," I explain.

Zee snickers. "Would you like me to stay around and help? I could make sure you have the correct underwear on? It can be tricky making sure it doesn't show." I smack him over the head. "You have a dirty mouth."

He grins at me. "Indeed, but I've been assured it tastes divine."

I sigh. "If you guys want to stay here and continue to work on the inscription, I can catch up after the ball. We need to focus on finding Pan. I'm sure she can shed some light on this mystery. However, tonight I need to pick my dress and check the florists and staff have prepped the house accordingly. Then tomorrow I've promised to help organize the chaos that precedes the ball and attend said ball."

Aaden grimaces. "You don't look too happy."

"I'm not, for a lot of reasons."

Mary reappears. "Ready for you!"

Chapter Forty

Natia

A Taurus doesn't get mad or even. You just become irrelevant when you screw them over.

Supposedly, people only remember twenty percent of a conversation. So why do I remember every single word of the one I had twenty-four hours ago? *I will protect you... I want you... I can be that darkness you crave... You just need to surrender... I won't hurt you... We aren't finished.*

I shake my head—maybe because he's burrowed his way deep in my soul, and my stupid heart hangs on to his every word? I've come to a number of conclusions over the course of the day, while ensuring the champagne glasses are in the correct place and the napkins match the tablecloths. One, Archan is like the Borg—resistance truly is futile. The only thing I can do is control the descent. Two, I need to come clean about the key—at least to my guys. Secrets can only hurt us and set us on a disastrous path. Plus, it's the literal key to Pandora's Box or, in reality, the Jar, and if I tell the guys, maybe I won't feel the need to carry it around with me. Even now, it sits in my clutch. Three, heels are torture devices masquerading as fashion—all balls should make sneakers compulsory at black tie events.

Sighing, I slip on the deep purple satin heels and stare at my reflection in the silver-gilded floor-to-ceiling mirror. My hair is in an elaborate updo, and my makeup is dramatic, with smoky eyeshadow that makes my turquoise eyes pop. My black dress has a fitted, plain, black bodice with two thin straps that streak diagonally over one shoulder. My back is bare, apart from the intricate gold roses painted on one side. The full tulle skirt reaches my calves at the front then dips at the back to trail on the floor. A vintage half masquerade mask decorated with tiny crystals and a lace design that shields one eye finishes the look.

There's a knock on the door. "Natia, are you ready?" my grandfather asks.

I open the door and hand him the mask. "Put this on for me?"

He grins. "I don't know, sweetheart, I don't think it will suit me."

"Ha ha, Gramps."

I face the mirror and hold the mask in position. He ties the silk ribbon and peers over my shoulder at my reflection. "You look beautiful, Natia... Your grandmother would be so proud of the captivating, smart, young woman you have become." His words tear at the part of me that's been so tender these last couple of weeks. A sudden sob gets caught in my throat, and I turn to put my head on his shoulder. *I will not cry, I will not cry, I will not cry.*

He holds me close and pats my back. "Come on, sweetheart... our guests await."

"She's with us, you know, Gramps."

"I know. She still admonishes me for eating too much chocolate and not doing enough exercise." I laugh as we make our way to the top of the sweeping grand staircase, complete with a red carpet; it's like something out of a fairy tale. My grandma was a romantic and liked to make an entrance.

I hold tightly to Gramps's hand as we walk down the wide stairs. "Don't let me fall."

"Never, sweetheart. We can't have a repeat of the 2003 summer ball, can we?"

I nudge him gently with my elbow. "That's not fair! My dress was too long. I tripped over it."

He chuckles. "Natia, the dress didn't reach the floor. Your grandmother would have never allowed it. Find a better excuse, or stick with the truth."

"And what would that be?" I enquire innocently.

"That you had a crush on Adam Taylor, and you went stomping down the stairs in a temper when you saw him give Wendy Thomas a glass of punch."

He had me there. "He shouldn't have been giving anybody punch but me."

"Natia, she was seventy-three years old."

"That's beside the point."

We crack up laughing before catching ourselves to look like the classic stony-faced hosts we're meant to be. I sweep my gaze over the room; there must be over three hundred people here.

I lean over and whisper, "Did you invite every eligible bachelor in Seattle? This isn't a 'marry off Natia by Christmas' ball, is it?" I start panicking a little, a bit worried my theory may be true.

He laughs. "You're more than capable of finding your prince when you're ready, sweetheart."

"Remember that when you're trying to get me to dance with skinny George over there who's investigating the origin of his brains via his nose, or Ben, who's rearranging himself in front of three hundred people." Gramps follows my gaze, and we both chuckle.

I spend an hour with Gramps, being led from family to family, who all say how wonderful it is to see me back. I don't point out this is one ball, and if I could help it, it would be the last. Social duty complete, I head to the far-right corner to sit in the window—my little safe haven when the party gets to be too much.

On my way, I grab a glass of champagne and some unrecognizable canapés, one of which has three small layers: cream, pink, and brown. Not the most visually appealing combination of colors for food—but it's in layers, so I couldn't resist. Dropping my purse next to me on the floor, I swing my feet onto the window seat, pull my knees up, and slide my back against the wall, allowing me to hide behind the heavy drapes.

Selecting my first canapé, I carefully pick the top cream-colored layer off and pop it into my mouth. My brain sorts through the possible flavors—something cream cheese based, I think. Just as I start to peel back the pink layer, a familiar, deep, baritone voice rumbles, "I see you still have strange eating habits."

I don't react; having spotted him earlier, I knew he would talk to me at some point. Instead, I don't look away from the, as yet, unidentified pink layer, not wanting to drop it on my dress.

"Why would I ever stop, Dalton?" I chirp, popping the pink layer in my mouth and scrunching up my face. Salmon, yuck! Nothing good ever came of whipping fish into mousse. I take a sip of my champagne, the light fruity bubbles cleansing my mouth. I eye the final brown layer with suspicion and promise retribution should it let me down like its predecessor. Taking it between my lips carefully, I find it's crunchy—oh, cracker! I pop the rest in my mouth and frown. A salmon cheesecake? And Aaden thinks they pay chefs top money to put flavors together? Maybe I'll steal one and demand he taste it.

I look up and quirk an eyebrow at Dalton. "Oh, you're still here."

"I didn't want to interrupt you and your date." Dalton waves a hand toward the other canapés I've perched on a table next to the window.

"Thanks for your understanding. As you can see, we haven't finished making out yet."

I pick up the next one, a ball encased in pastry. I lift it to my lips with the intention of nibbling the pastry off first.

"Listen, Natia, we need to talk."

With a sigh, I put the pastry ball down, frustrated at the delay of finding out the mysterious filling. I wipe my hands on a napkin as he moves to sit on the seat at my feet. I push my legs out, blocking him. His jaw tics. Maybe he'll get the hint and go away?

He grits his teeth. "Natia." *Didn't think so.*

"Dalton."

"Me and Jessica, we're over."

"I'm aware."

His eyes widen. "Why haven't you come to see me?"

His ego knows no bounds. I look at him for the first time; his gray eyes are boring into mine. I used to find them attractive—now, they look cold and flat. I can't help but compare them to the complex depths of the golden eyes that haunt my dreams. He's dressed in the obligatory black tux; he's filled out, but kept his body fit. I have to admit, he still looks good—too bad for him, I'm no longer interested. Raising my gaze to his face, I find him wearing a smug smile, believing I've just checked him out. Channeling my inner Archan, I arch an eyebrow. Dalton narrows his eyes.

"I've been busy... washing my hair."

He pushes his hands in his pockets and grins. I realize with some satisfaction, he does nothing for me—literally, no sadness, no longing, no lust, no anger. Nothing. "But you came tonight knowing I would be here."

The eye roll I give him is like a strong reflex. "Are you confused? You came to my ball, not the other way around."

He chuckles. "Your smart mouth has gotten sassier. I like it."

I snort. "Nothing I've done or become is for your approval, Dalton. Find some brainless twit who will forgive the fact that you love yourself more than you love them."

His lips quirk up. "And you're wearing my favorite color because…?"

"Because the dress code is black. That must mean every woman here is dressed to get your attention—you're that much of a catch, way too good for me. Now take your cheating ass away from my corner and go and chat up someone interested." I raise my glass in the direction of the room and take a sip.

"Cheating? I didn't cheat—you left."

Spitting the champagne back in the glass to avoid choking, my eyes widen as he remains serious. I tilt my head, wondering if he's had his memory tampered with or if he's just this stupid. His eyes flash in satisfaction. Ah, he's goading me into an argument—apparently a shared technique among men to get women to speak to them. Except, for it to work, you must have some passion for the man demanding that attention in the first place. Dalton's mistake is I don't even feel hate for him—there's nothing, nada, zilch. It's freeing in a way I didn't understand, realizing that part of my heart has healed.

The smile that grows across my face matches the intensity of the scowl on his. "What's the problem, Natia? Have you forgotten what it's like to be fucked by someone who makes you scream out their name?"

"No, but I've finally found someone who can."

He clenches his fists and scoffs. "I see… Sure. And where, may I ask, is this man?" He surveys the room, challenging me.

"Right here," a deep, smooth voice purrs. My head snaps up to Archan, my mouth parting slightly.

Shit. I had no idea he was here.

He offers me his arm. "Care to dance?" I give him a huge smile as I initiate our mental link.

"Your timing is impeccable."

"Seems I'm saving you once again."

"Don't push it, Reinheart." His lips twitch.

I slide off the seat and take his arm. "That would be lovely."

Dalton extends a hand to Archan and deepens his voice. "I'm Dalton Miller."

Archan raises one perfect eyebrow. "I know." He ignores Dalton's hand and guides me toward the dance floor. His hair is down, framing his beautiful face, and his eyes glitter with amusement. His custom-tailored tux shows every flex of his muscles as he moves. He looks like a god among men—and perhaps he is. If I was a maiden in a different era, I would probably use a fan to cool my face and swoon right about now—maybe. After a moment, I realize he's actually leading me to the dance floor. I raise my eyebrows. "You dance?"

He squeezes my hand. "Of course."

Halting in front of the band, I pull his hand back and grin at him. "Pick a dance."

He looks at me, confused. "A dance?"

I give him a teasing smile. "Pick a dance, I'll pick the music."

He tilts his head. "We'll start you in easy... Let's foxtrot."

"Starting in easy, huh? A little presumptuous. Who says you'll get more than one dance? I have many suitors." I wave my hand, indicating the rest of the room.

He leans in closer, holding my eyes. "Is that so? And when you've picked your suitor for the evening, what then?" I lick my top lip and swallow, trying to wet my suddenly dry mouth. He moves his lips to my ear and whispers, "When you've had me wrapped around your body, you will want no other."

"Are we still talking about dancing?" I croak. He gives me a crooked grin, making me hitch in a breath—that look should be illegal. After giving the band my choice, Archan winds us to the center of dance floor. He clasps my hand in his and slides his other hand under my arm and around my back.

I grin. "I'm impressed. You know how to hold a lady."

"Were you ever in doubt?"

The band begins playing the sensual notes of "Fever" by Peggy Lee, and we start to glide across the dance floor. He looks down at me and gives me a wide, genuine smile. He leans down to my ear, his breath making the stray hairs on my neck tickle. I shiver. "An appropriate choice, Natia."

The only heat is his natural warmth, yet my skin sings with the pleasure of being near him; his smell is intoxicating, fogging my mind with thoughts of sin and delicious pleasure. He's proving it's me and him—no power games. And it's disarming.

"You look magnificent, Natia. An enchantress. Every man in this room is wishing they were me right now, holding your amazing body close, listening to you laugh, feeling your heartbeat next to theirs, and your breath caress their cheek." He lowers his hand to the small of my back, pulls me closer, and nips my ear. "But they can't… You're mine."

My breath catches in my throat. Mayday, mayday—controlled descent aborted. Does anyone have a manual for surviving this roller-coaster?

We dance to a few more songs; apparently, he's determined to prove he can dance. When we take a break, I go in search of champagne while Archan goes to the restroom. I spot a waiter and head in his direction.

Dalton steps in front of me with a sneer on his face. "Who's the boyfriend, Nat?" I straighten my spine. This man will not get a reaction out of me—he doesn't deserve one.

"None of your business."

"Oh, I think it is. You're back from your little fantasy of being a dancer—it's time you come back to me, where you belong, and stop acting like a cheap slut on the dance floor."

Everyone in the immediate area takes a step back, forming a small circle around us, and gawks. I keep my voice quiet. "I'm sorry. Was it not you I found in my bed with my friend after five years of being together? Was it not *you* who thought a good break-up strategy was to have sex with someone else?

"You have done nothing with your life since leaving college. You contribute to society in no useful way, and the air you breathe is being stolen from a billion other people who deserve it more than you. Instead, you spend your days in mommy and daddy's golf club, talking *'business'* with the boys. You're a sanctimonious pig. You have no passion, no desire to become something more than you are today, and have no craving to make this world a better place."

I turn to walk away, but he grabs my arm. I pluck a drink out of the hand of the woman next to me. "Take your hands off me before I break every one of your fingers," I hiss, just before I throw the drink in his face. He instinctively lets go, and I hand the glass back to the skinny, wide-eyed woman and stalk off, my dress rustling.

My emotions begin to boil, and power whirls inside me, begging to be released. I throw open the doors leading to the garden and step into the cool evening air. I inhale sharply, not realizing I've been holding my breath, and stalk toward the guest house—my house. My heel gets caught in the grass, and I tug off my shoes, feeling the crunch of the frozen ground beneath my feet; it cools my emotions. My anger and embarrassment seep into the dirt beneath me.

I make my way down a small hill toward my house and the tree swing Gramps put up so many years ago. Facing away from the main house, I sit on the wooden perch and lift my feet off the ground. The momentum of the swing moves me in slow circles. Holding the ropes, I lean my body back and let my head fall to look at the stars. My eyes trace the constellations, settling on Cassiopeia. Away from the city, you can see thousands of tiny bright lights peeking through the inky sky.

I feel him before I see him—a swell of warmth and power. His scent of dark chocolate, sandalwood, and vanilla wraps around me.

He stares down into my eyes, pulling me from my star gazing. "What do you see?" he asks.

My eyes drift back to the sky. "A plan for humanity born out of chaos. A map for our salvation, one that God gave us the instant he breathed life into mankind. A billion souls waiting to be born, looked over by a billion souls who have already lived, and a universe out of our reach, not because we don't have the technology, but because we don't have enough faith; yet, only the darkness reveals such magnificence."

He holds the ropes, steadying the swing, and follows my gaze. His breath mists in the cold, giving the illusion of clouds passing over the stars.

"Who are you, Natia?"

I blink. "You've just answered your own question."

"You see beauty where others have become numb and ignorant to it. You find pleasures in the small things other people miss altogether. How you see the world is unique… You don't think like anybody I've ever met." He reaches down and traces the curve of my jaw. "The storm that lives inside you consumes and dominates me, Natia."

I pull my body up straight, and he wraps his jacket over my shoulders; it smells like him, making me sink deeper into it. He steps in front of me.

"Take me home, Archan."

He glances over his shoulder toward the guest house. "Lead the way."

I shake my head. "Not mine—yours."

"Natia," he warns.

"Don't you dare tell me no. I want to make stupid decisions and lose control for once. I need the oblivion only you can create, to drown in the sensations only you can make me feel. I want the darkness only you can make me crave. Make me forget—just for tonight."

He hooks a hand under my knees and one behind my back, swinging me against his chest. "That, I can do."

Chapter Forty-One

Natia

A heartbroken Taurus will build a cage around their heart. You have to be special to reopen it.

"You can put me down," I squeak. He stares at my feet. Oh yeah, shoes. He carries me around the outside of the house to the front. Zac leans against a sleek gray Aston Martin Valkyrie, holding my purse. He throws the keys to Archan and opens the passenger door, as Archan places me in the warm, soft leather seat and drops my purse into my hands. He shuts the door and says a few quick words to Zac. Curious, I try to lip read, but to no avail. The door next to me thumps shut as Archan's body fills the car.

"Zac was your date?" I quip.

He laughs. "More like my wing man."

I lean my head back against the seat and let out a breath, which mists up the glass. I draw an angel. He glances at me then stares at the window with an unreadable expression. "Sorry, do you get annoyed at people who draw things on their windows?"

"It's fine. Why an angel?"

"It's Christmas, why not?" I retort, drawing a cartoon devil. "There, I've restored balance."

As we drive, he asks, "Do you want to talk about it?"

"What?"

His hands tighten on the steering wheel. "Dalton, the dick who dared to lay a hand on you."

"No, he isn't worth the air you and I breathe. He can't hurt me... I was just embarrassed."

We're speeding along the interstate, as Archan expertly weaves in between the cars. I peer at him. "In a rush?"

"Making sure you don't have enough time to change your mind."

"And if I did?" I tease.

Reaching over, he glides his hand up my dress to rest on my inner thigh. My heart skips a few beats then beats faster as my blood heats.

"I would... persuade you," he replies. He leaves his hand on my thigh, his thumb rubbing small possessive circles on my skin.

Thirty long minutes later, we approach a set of ornate metal gates. They start to open automatically. He pulls through them before they've opened fully, almost clipping the car.

I yelp. "Careful! You don't want to damage Charlotte."

"Who's Charlotte?"

"Your car."

"You named my car?"

"You haven't?" I run my hand along the subtle leather as the car rumbles along the gravel. "She's a thing of beauty—she deserves a name."

"Why Charlotte?"

"Sounds as snooty as you are, but still beautiful," I tease.

He cuts the engine, gets out of the car, and makes his way around to me, opening the door. "Come on, before you abandon me and go for a night out on the town with Charlotte."

"You'd let me take her out? I feel like Charlotte and I are old friends, two souls reunited."

He scoops up my shoes and purse then pulls me up and tosses me over his shoulder. I squeal.

"Not a chance," he says, amused as he jogs up several stone steps. He's like a cave man returning home with his conquest. I'm disappointed to have not paid enough attention to the exterior of the house as he puts me down in the entrance hall.

I turn around. "Wow." An enormous fire burns in a hearth twice my height. Fluffy taupe rugs cover an oak floor, and two sofas piled with scattered cushions sit in front of the fire. A rustic chandelier hangs from the ceiling, which is three stories high. A wide, sweeping, wrought iron staircase leads up to the first floor and several closed doors. My eyes fall back to find him staring at me.

"Do you like it?" he questions, genuinely interested.

"It's amazing; just not where I pictured you sleeping."

He guides me to the staircase with his hands on my arms, his expression smug. "You pictured me sleeping?" I dig my elbow backward, aiming for his ribs, but he anticipates it and grabs my arm, spinning me to face him. "If you aren't going to be nice, I will have to carry you up the stairs and restrain you for my safety." I blush. Laughing, he weaves his fingers through mine and pulls me up the stairs. We round the balcony overlooking the entrance hall and ascend another staircase. On the top floor, there are two doors at opposite ends of the landing.

"Pick one," he commands.

Butterflies flutter in my stomach. "Erm... is this like what's behind door number one, etcetera...? And the other one leads to certain death?"

He grins—he's being playful. The magnificent Archan Reinheart is teasing me. "Pick one, Natia." I glance between them and point to the door farthest away. He pushes it open and pulls me inside. The lock quietly clicks, making me jump. Another fire blazes in front of two chairs on the far side of the bedroom. A large ornate mirror is propped in one corner, and floor-to-ceiling windows are covered by heavy navy drapes. Candles are dotted around the room, creating a soft glow. Music plays in the background, and Halsey's "Not Afraid Anymore" surrounds me and punctuates the moment with my decision—it also suggests he took careful note of my playlist. But my eyes are drawn to the largest bed I've ever seen. Tall spiral oak posts protrude at each corner, and the headboard is full of intricately designed carvings. It's covered in crisp, white cotton sheets.

"Why so big?" I breathe.

"I like the space," he whispers into my ear.

My mouth falls open in a silent *oh*, and my feet are suddenly glued to the spot. I'm in the lair of a powerful, dangerous being, and I came here willingly. Before my brain can question my actions, he begins undoing my hair, taking care to remove each pin and tease my curls loose with his fingers.

He nibbles and kisses his way from my ear to the hollow of my collarbone. "This is a beautiful gown, but you are severely overdressed." He undoes the zipper slowly, giving me the chance to object. As soon as it's clear of my hips, I step forward and let the dress fall to the ground, using my foot to fling it into the corner with my shoes and purse. He hitches in a breath, giving me a feminine sense of pride. I start to pivot, but strong hands on my hips stop me. He kneels on the floor. I gaze down at him over my shoulder and give him a sultry smile.

"Finally, I have you on your knees at my feet, where you're meant to be."

He returns my grin. "Don't worry, Natia, your turn will come."

I blush. He places a hand on my foot and lets his fingers trail over my ankle and up my calf, placing a gentle kiss on the sensitive skin behind my knee. Tipping my head back, my eyes flutter closed as goosebumps break out over my body and heat swirls inside me. His fingers skim the outside of my thigh then glide over the curve of my ass. He hooks his fingers in the waistband of my black lace panties and pulls them down like he's unwrapping me.

Standing, he runs his hand through my hair; he fists it and pulls my head back, twisting it toward him and creating a slight sting of pain. I gasp. He pushes his sensuous lips against mine in a surprisingly soft kiss. He nibbles my bottom lip, pulling at it, demanding entrance. When I don't give it to him, he increases the pressure on my scalp, making my mouth part in surprise. Taking advantage, his tongue sweeps into my mouth and tangles with mine. We pull away panting, and he releases my hair. I turn to him, and this time, he lets me. Molten gold eyes swirling with desire lock on my face; he pulls me against his body, my nipples scraping on his shirt—it's too much, and not enough at the same time.

"There's no going back, Natia. If we do this—you're mine," he whispers, holding the back of my neck as he gives me another demanding kiss, which I try to take control of, but he won't let me, pulling back every time until I get the point and let him devour me. "Do you understand?" he says against my lips.

"Yes," I breathe.

"Say it."

"I'm yours."

Something wild flashes across his eyes as he walks me backward, and I jump as my thighs hit the mattress. He retrieves a wide, black silk ribbon from a drawer next to the bed. My breath comes faster.

"Close your eyes, Natia."

I stare at the ribbon and nibble my lip.

He grips my chin with his fingers and forces me to look at him. "Do you need oblivion?"

"Yes."

"Then close your eyes and trust me."

My eyes close as the silk presses over my skin; he knots it at the back of my head. I lift my hands to it, but he pulls them away and kisses my fingertips. "Trust me."

Picking me up, he tosses me onto the center of the bed, making me yelp in surprise. I become disoriented by the sound of fabric hitting the floor then footsteps, first to my left, then to my right. The bed dips at my feet, and he kisses, licks, and nibbles his way up my legs. "You've been reading my journal again," I mutter.

"I read it once—I have a good memory. And I promised to make your fantasies come true. We can take the elevator to my office tomorrow."

Hot breath plays across the inside of my thigh, making me shiver, my body sensitized to the slightest touch. I'm burning from the inside out, and the pulse in my center increases, crying for attention.

This slow torture is heaven and hell. I run my hands through his hair and tug, trying to pull him up my body. Grasping my hands in one of his, he holds them on my stomach. With the other, he pushes a finger into my wet pussy. I cry out at the sudden intrusion, lifting my ass off the bed, then I push down to force him deeper. He doesn't move. I growl, and he chuckles. Pinning one thigh open with his shoulder, he moves his finger in a deliberate, slow rhythm. His thumb rubs circles over my clit at the same lazy pace.

"Faster," I demand, surprised at my own confidence. Lips curl against my thigh, but he doesn't change speed. He kisses and nibbles the sensitive flesh on my inner thigh, hard enough to zap bliss straight to my center. My stomach clenches, and my free thigh wraps around his head.

"I'm close," I murmur, writhing on the bed. I wind tighter and tighter, feeling myself near the precipice, then he withdraws his finger. I'm about to curse him, when flips me onto my stomach and recaptures my hands at the bottom of my spine. I throw my head back as he plunges two fingers inside me. My wetness coats them, and I wiggle, trying to get him to move faster.

"Gods, Natia, be still. It is hard enough resisting being inside of you," he rasps.

"Then stop resisting!" I snap.

He straddles my calves and lets his weight push me down, his hard length lying against my ass. "No."

"Why the hell not?"

"You need to let go."

"I'm happy to let go, I just need you inside me."

"Someone recently told me patience is a virtue."

"That someone wasn't going to strangle you at the time!"

Keeping hold of my hands, he kisses up my spine. His fingers pick up speed as my slickness coats my thighs. He takes me to the edge again and stops. I bury my face into the soft sheets and scream.

Silk slides against my wrists, and I immediately stiffen.

Archan feels my body go still and rubs my back softly. "It's not tight enough to hold you," he reassures me. "I'll take care of you—I promise."

My breathing slows, and I pull at the silk, finding it loose enough that I could easily slip out of it. Trusting him, I nod in silent agreement.

He rolls me onto my back with my arms behind me, making my back arch, and takes my mouth in a bruising, brutal kiss, the promise of no mercy evident.

"Let me see you," I breathe.

"Not yet… You're not ready," he replies in a husky voice.

I roll my eyes, not that he can see.

"I'm ready for anything, just fuck me already."

He slaps the side of my ass playfully. "That was for rolling your eyes at me."

"How?" He slaps my ass again. "Ow."

"Ready for anything, are you?" he enquires, his tone serious. My mouth goes dry at the open invitation I've given him. Heat surrounds my nipple as he sucks it into his mouth, pulling hard and making me moan. He grazes it with his teeth. I go to put my hands in his hair to hold him there, forgetting they're still tied behind my back. He pays the same attention to my other breast, driving me mindless. My body trembles from the need to release.

"Archan, please," I moan, not sure what I'm begging for. He moves his mouth across my stomach and pushes my thighs open wide with his shoulders.

"Yes, Natia?"

"I need—" I gasp when he pushes another finger inside me, stretching me to my limits.

"What do you need?" He places his hand on my stomach, keeping me still, and stops moving his fingers. "Tell me what you need."

My mind goes blank. After waiting for a minute in silence, he pulls his fingers out of me, and I cry out at the loss. His lips claim mine in a sweet, soft, tender kiss. A small moan leaves my mouth. His chest vibrates as he rumbles in pleasure. He reaches behind me, and the silk slackens, allowing me to wrap my hands around his neck and draw him closer. A startled gasp escapes him as the force of my hold knocks him off his elbows, and some of his weight falls on me, pushing me into the bed. He tries to lift his body, but I wrap my legs around his ass and lock my ankles, keeping him pressed to me. He rubs himself against me teasingly.

"If you stop now, me and you are not going to be friends," I breathe.

He chuckles, kissing and sucking my neck while nudging at my entrance. "We are just friends?" He pushes an inch inside me and stops. He grazes his lips across mine and cradles my face in his hands. "Look at me."

I open my eyes, not realizing he's removed the blindfold. Blazing gold eyes reflect the candlelight, almost glowing.

"If your world crumbles, I will build you a new one. I will chase away every fear and protect you from your nightmares. If you go blind, I will be the light in your darkness. When you lose your faith, I will help restore it. Surrender to everything, the pain, the hurt, the anger, and if your mind shatters, I will find every piece and put you back together. I have you... Let go, Natia."

He pushes inside, making me wiggle my hips to try and accommodate him. He sits back and rests my calves on his shoulders, pushing deeper. I put my foot on his chest to push back, as the fullness is too much, but he locks his hands around my thighs, keeping me still.

"Natia."

"Yes?" I answer in a breathy voice.

"Oblivion, remember?"

He grips my hips and plunges the rest of the way inside me. I explode, crying out as my back lifts off the bed and the ecstasy pulls every muscle in my body taught; he moves slowly, drawing out my climax and letting me adjust to him. He rolls us, making us both groan as he sinks in deeper. Holding my hips, he lifts me, moving faster. The tension in my body builds as each thrust rubs against me, driving me higher.

"I've imagined you like this since the day I met you," he rumbles. I put my hands on his chest and begin countering his thrusts. Sitting up, he twists my arms behind my back and captures my wrists in one of his large hands. He fists my hair and pulls my head back, and my back arches as a startled cry escapes me. His mouth tortures my sensitive nipples, each tug sending a wave of pleasure to my center. When he releases my hair, I lean forward and bite his shoulder, as the sensations threaten to overwhelm me. He groans and nips my neck. "Look at me. I want to see your eyes when you come." Meeting his gaze, he gives me a crooked grin and places his forehead against mine. My breath is coming so fast, I'm dizzy.

Seconds before my orgasm crashes, he whispers, "Let go." I scream his name as my blood roars and white-hot pleasure shoots through my veins. I shatter into a million pieces, each one of them being pulled in every direction. My mind spins as beautiful galaxies wrapped in color, filled with billions of stars, rush past me. Something shifts inside of me as I come apart in his arms, a freedom I've never experienced before.

"Eyes, Natia," he growls. He grips my hips hard and thrusts once more, keeping his gaze locked with mine as he whispers my name, before throwing his head back and growling deep and low. Burying my head in his shoulder, I inhale his scent. He holds me to him as our hearts slow and our breathing becomes even.

"Gold," he murmurs against my neck.

"What?" I say, confused.

"Your aura—it's all the colors surrounded by gold."

I pull my head off his chest to find him staring at me in awe.

I smile and brush my lips against his. "It's pretty, but not the whole multicolored flame thing you have going on."

He stiffens. "You can see mine?"

I shrug. "Of course. Freaked me out the first time we met."

The bedroom door smashes against the wall, and in stalks Zac, holding the Jar. "Where is she?" he barks.

"Erm, right here," I mumble, color flooding my cheeks. He looks at me like I'm stupid, then his eyes widen.

"Your aura," he gasps.

Archan holds me tight to his chest in an attempt to protect my dignity, except my naked ass is on display—then again, who hasn't seen my naked ass by this point?

"Get out," Archan grinds through his teeth. Silently, Zac holds out the Jar toward us, which begins emitting a pure white light. I stare, wide-eyed.

Archan takes my face in his hands. "It's you?"

I frown. "What's me?" The hard look in his eyes makes me scramble off him, grabbing a sheet on my way to wrap around me. I back away toward the fire.

Archan runs his hands through his hair. "Your shields… I should have known."

Zac takes a step toward me; I hold out a hand, and he pauses. "Known what?" I press, my voice shaking. Archan lunges for me, and I panic, scramble away, then appear on the other side of the bed, minus the sheet, which is dangling in Archan's grasp. It's my turn to stare in disbelief.

"What did you do?" I whisper.

"I did nothing, you flashed!" he roars.

"You were the one who grabbed the sheet!"

"Don't be coy, Natia. The game's up. I've found you," he snarls, as various emotions play across his face: anger, hurt, and finally determination. The weight of his terrifying power crushes me to the floor.

Shocked tears slide down my cheeks. "I'm so confused," I manage to croak out.

A knife materializes in his hand, and I flinch, as understanding dawns.

"I'm not Pan!" I squeak.

He laughs, but it's empty and cold. "I almost believed you. Hiding in plain sight. Trying to convince all of us not to kill you—clever, but foolish. And the decoy Jar." He points the knife at me. "Don't move."

Zac empties my purse onto the bed, and Archan picks up the blue velvet pouch that tumbles out of it. Undoing the ribbons, he tips out the small star-shaped key I carry with me everywhere so it doesn't fall into the wrong hands. Seems like an idiotic thing to do now.

"Explain something. If you're not Pandora, why do you have the key and why is the Jar calling to *you*?" Archan spits, spinning the key around his palm in one hand and the knife in the other. Zac steps closer with the Jar.

I swallow at the obvious threat. "I was given the key. I have no idea about the Jar."

Archan swaps the knife for the Jar with Zac.

Turning it upside down, he studies the key and the base. "Stop your lies. It is time to end this."

I watch, horrified at his intent. "No, Archan... No, you're wrong!"

He raises a mocking eyebrow. "I'm wrong? You want to continue to let mankind suffer? You think you have the right to withhold hope from a race struggling to understand right from wrong? There is so much hurt, desperation, and helplessness. You think if you keep it from them, they will survive?"

"Of course not! But I'm *not* Pan, and I haven't lied to you," I cry, stunned.

Ignoring me, he inserts the key into the base and turns. Nothing happens. The three of us take turns staring at each other and the inanimate Jar.

I blow out a relieved breath. "What the hell? If that had worked, you would've released the last evil on the Earth."

Zac narrows his eyes. "*You're* the last evil on Earth."

"I know we don't see eye to eye, Zac, but that's quite the insult."

The Jar topples to the floor, and an inhuman, maniacal laugh erupts from Archan's lips.

Zac and I swing our gaze to him. Strange obsidian eyes stare at us from a familiar face. Archan crouches next to me and grasps my chin, turning my head to the side and examining me. His eyes trail down my exposed body.

He smirks. "I've wondered for eons what my captor looks like. It seems I've been blessed—torturing you will be fun."

"Archan?" I whisper, staring in shock at the thick black ring suffocating the flames around his aura.

"Get away from him, Natia," Zac hisses, the knife no longer pointed at me. I stand on shaky legs as Archan follows me.

My fingers brush across his cheek. "Don't do this. Come back to me."

The malevolent grin curving Archan's lips slips, and gold bleeds through his obsidian gaze. He kisses me fiercely. "Run, Natia," he whispers.

I blink as the gold recedes. His hand snaps around my throat, squeezing. I shut my eyes, bracing myself for death. The familiar sensation of folding space and time surrounds me, and when I open my eyes, I'm drifting through the colored ribbons, alone. A sense of peace and belonging fills me. Shutting my eyes, I give myself over to the feelings of home and safety. Seconds, minutes, or hours later, cool air blows along my body, and my mind mourns the loss of the other world. I crack open one eye.

"Locks, nice of you to drop by. But, even in your own house, the normal etiquette is to come with clothes," a familiar voice rumbles. I open my eyes fully and fling my naked self into Duncan's arms. I pull back and heave a shuddering breath, reaching for the words, but I can't seem to find them.

All I know is Archan is gone, and my true name is Pandora.

If you want to stalk me to curse me out, you can find me here –
Facebook reader's group – Adaline's Warriors (where you will find
a group of the most awesome, like-minded people who are currently
sharpening their knives).

Instagram - @adalinewinterswriter (my main hangout because of
all the amazing, supportive people there).

Email – adalinewinterswriter@gmail.com (all threatening emails
will be laughed at, then deleted).

Acknowledgments

Writing a book is grueling, isolating, emotional, and exhausting – but it's an adventure and accomplishment. But no author is without support and mine begins with my family. To my husband, thank you for unending support and for answering seemingly crazy random questions. I'm sorry for the mediocre cooking and glazed over looks as I fell into scenes. To my daughter, thank you for your unblemished look at the world and for asking simple questions us adults often forget to ask. To my sisters, Stella – the ultimate alpha reader and one man support group, and Dana – my social media queen! Bless you both for your unwavering positivity and brilliant creativity. Mum, for reading the first chapter so many times and telling me that you're proud – it means the world. Dad, for the best advice ever, "Stop changing your book for others, write to please yourself and then send it to a professional."

Thank you to the few precious friends I trusted to tell that I was setting out on this journey. Your every encouragement and positive words were heard and helped.

To my family over the pond - the team at Write My Wrongs. In particular Madison, the wonder editor, for your encouragement, dedication, support, and for understanding Natia and Archan – they truly grew up under your guidance. Chrissy – my fellow educator, cheerleader and life coach.

And finally, thanks to anybody who has taken their precious time to read my book. I hope you enjoyed it - and would appreciate an honest review, they are the life blood of an author.

Adaline x

Seducing Hope: The Playlist

Patience – Guns N' Roses
Gettin' Jiggy Wit It – Will Smith
Pour Some Sugar on Me – Def Leppard
Boombastic – Shaggy
Respect – Aretha Franklin
Highway to Hell – AC/DC
Strip That Down – Liam Payne
Stuck in the Middle with You – Stealers Wheel
U Can't Touch This – MC Hammer
Under Pressure – Queen
Shape of You – Ed Sheeran
Hit Me With Your Best Shot – Pat Benatar
Sympathy for the Devil – The Rolling Stones
I Wanna Dance With Somebody – Whitney Houston
Closer – Nine Inch Nails
Wake Me Up Before You Go-Go – Wham!
S&M – Rhianna
Before He Cheats – Carrie Underwood
Witchcraft – Frank Sinatra
Toxic – Britney Spears
Natural – Imagine Dragons
Full of Grace – Sarah McLachlan
Mission Impossible Theme
The Number of the Beast – Iron Maiden
Suspicious Minds – Elvis Presley
Shake It Off – Taylor Swift
Fever – Peggy Lee
Not Afraid Anymore – Halsey

Printed in Great Britain
by Amazon